SHERLOCK HOLMES

The FORTY THIEVES and other stories

SHERLOCK HOLMES

The FORTY THIEVES and other stories

DAVID MARCUM, EDITOR

JAICO PUBLISHING HOUSE

Ahmedabad Bangalore Chennai
Delhi Hyderabad Kolkata Mumbai

Published by Jaico Publishing House
A-2 Jash Chambers, 7-A Sir Phirozshah Mehta Road
Fort, Mumbai - 400 001
jaicopub@jaicobooks.com
www.jaicobooks.com

Published in arrangement with
MX Publishing Ltd
335 Princess Park Manor
London, N11 3GX

To be sold only in India, Bangladesh, Bhutan,
Pakistan, Nepal, Sri Lanka and the Maldives.

SHERLOCK HOLMES
THE FORTY THIEVES AND OTHER STORIES
ISBN 978-81-8495-884-3

First Jaico Impression: 2016

Page design and layout: Special Effects, Mumbai

Printed by
Repro India Limited, Mumbai

Contents

COPYRIGHT INFORMATION

PART I: 1881-1889

In 1874, while visiting the home of a University friend (see "The Gloria Scott"), Sherlock Holmes realized that his life's calling was to become a Consulting Detective. Moving to Montague Street in London, he commenced his career. A few years later, John H. Watson received his Doctor of Medicine degree and eventually joined the Army. After being wounded at the Battle of Maiwand, he returned to England, where he was introduced to Sherlock Holmes on New Year's Day, 1881. They agreed to take rooms at 221b Baker Street. Within months, Watson was assisting Holmes on his various investigations. In the mid-1880's, Watson married his first wife, about whom only limited facts are available. Although now wed, Watson often found time to assist in his friend's adventures. Following the death of his first wife in late 1887, Watson returned to 221b, where he lived until his second marriage to more well-known Mary Watson (née Morstan) in mid-1889. This volume covers this earlier period from soon after Holmes and Watson's first

*meeting through the early months of Watson's second marriage. During this time, Holmes was building his practice, and Watson did not publish any narratives of Holmes's cases until late 1887. Thus, Holmes was still somewhat unknown at this point. It was during this interval that the two first became friends, and then "brothers, not in blood, but in bond."**

**From the film Sherlock Holmes (2009)*

The Tale of the Forty Thieves

by C.H. Dye

In perusing the records of the many adventures I shared with my extraordinary friend Mr. Sherlock Holmes, I am reminded how often the problems came to us in waves. Holmes might go weeks without a case, and then have several appear hard on each other's heels. So it was in the spring of 1887, when it seemed for a time that my friend might never get a chance to rest. I attempted to procure him a few days respite in the country after the months he spent in France, untangling the threads of the Netherland-Sumatra Company scandal, but as I have written elsewhere, that visit was interrupted by murder. We were not even a day back from Reigate when he was petitioned by Stephen Grice-Patterson to unravel the apparent haunting and thefts on the island of Uffa, in the Firth of Clyde. It was as well that I accompanied him to Scotland, for it took the both of us to lay the "ghost" after three night watches and a mad chase across the heather. By the time we set sail for Glasgow, all my medical instincts were aroused once more on my friend's behalf, but he insisted on returning to London by the night train, rather than taking a hotel and embarking in the morning.

We arrived at Euston Station at an hour when the dairymaids were still portioning out their wares to sleepy scullions, and the great metropolis had just begun to stir itself. We had just emerged into the light of the early morning sun and were casting about in search of a hansom when we were hailed by a familiar voice. Inspector Gregson of Scotland Yard was waving to us from the door of a growler on the street. "Mr. Holmes!" he called again. "Doctor Watson! Cabbie, draw us alongside those two gentlemen." We waited until the cab had parked beside us to give the Inspector our good mornings, and he returned them with alacrity. "You have no idea how glad I am to find you back in London."

I cannot say that I returned the sentiment with enthusiasm. A new case held little appeal. I have never quite lost the knack of sleeping under uncomfortable circumstances, thanks to my time in the Army, but I had spent most of the last fifteen hours travelling in an overcrowded railway compartment. I wanted nothing more than a bath and my breakfast. And I was concerned about Holmes, whose normal pallor was underlain with grey and whose eyes lacked their usual spark. He had forestalled a black mood by taking cocaine whilst we were awaiting our train in Glasgow, but had paid for the respite with restlessness. While I had dozed, he had fidgeted and read, restocking his pile of newspapers whenever opportunity presented. Still, he greeted the policeman with a nod and gladly accepted Gregson's offer of a ride to Baker Street.

No sooner were we on our way than the Scotland Yard detective asked Holmes, "Did you read about the Cartier bracelet while you were out of London?"

"A chain of diamonds and sapphires, stolen from a courier in the Strand last Friday. The company has offered a reward for its return."

"Yes. The courier, Hammond, didn't even realize he'd been robbed of his goods right away. He'd been jostled once or twice in the crowd, but he swears each time he checked his pocket and felt nothing amiss. But when he came to his destination, the bracelet was gone from the case. As neat a job as I've ever known."

"An ordinary crime," I interjected, hoping to keep Holmes from taking interest.

"Ordinary enough," Gregson agreed. "Were it not that the Foreign Office has become involved. They won't say why the recovery of the bracelet is so important, and I shan't speculate, but every man in the Yard is looking. And now a possible clue to the matter has come up near Elephant and Castle in Southwark. Do you know the area?"

"Tolerably." Holmes said, his fingers tapping against the pocket where he kept his cigarette case. It was empty, I knew, and so was mine, victim of his long sleepless night. "It is the intersection of several roads and a railway line. Not the richest of London's districts nor the poorest, although the Walter's Almhouses are home to more families than they were built for. The Baptist Tabernacle is the landmark most think of, although the area derives its name from a coaching inn mentioned by Shakespeare. They are building an underground station there, I believe."

"They are indeed, and there are two rival gangs which have stepped up their efforts to keep or take control of the nearby streets. It's made for a good many fights, a few robberies, and an increase in all sorts of other crime, particularly shoplifting and pickpocketing." The inspector tapped his bandaged leg. "Two nights ago Lestrade was on Brook Drive investigating a robbery when he came across one of the fights. He managed to blow his whistle and summon the nearest constables, but he got his shinbone cracked by a heavy belt buckle."

"Were the miscreants apprehended?" I asked, for I did not like to think of our frequent visitor being injured.

"Three were. Five escaped," Gregson said. "It would have been six, but for three constables, Hopkins, Madison, and Gambit, who gave chase. They cornered the third man, Jack Porter, in a rathole off of Lamlash Street. But along the way there, Porter ran through a room full of women and children sitting down to their dinner, and the constable nearest his heels, a young fellow named Hopkins, noticed as he tried to follow that the woman nearest the fire took one look at his uniform and thrust a paper in her hand towards the flames. Then Porter overturned the table for a distraction, and went out the window. Hopkins lost his footing and fell amidst the beans, and it was left to Madison and Gambit to catch Porter and tuck him into a Black Maria. Hopkins, meanwhile, realized that he recognized the woman who was berating him for destroying her supper – a pickpocket well known to the force by the name of Nettie Hannigan. Do you know of her?"

Holmes tapped his steepled fingers against his chin and nodded. "She is sometimes called 'Red Nettie', is she not? Not because of her hair, which is brown when she has not been using henna, but because of the strawberry mark which shows on part of her left ear and down her neck."

"That's right. She was caught with the goods a time or two when she was younger, but she's grown more canny since. Pretty enough, in her way, and does piecework, apparently, for a manufacturer of ladies accoutrements. Hopkins reports a sewing machine in the corner of the room, among other things." Gregson reached into his pocket for a sheaf of handwritten papers.

"Is there a connection between Miss Hannigan and the Cartier theft?"

"Nettie was apprehended on suspicion of shoplifting three hours after the theft near Charing Cross, though the female searcher found nothing and she was released. But here, let me read you what Hopkins reported. 'The force of wind from the table overturning blew the burning paper out of the center of the fire before it could be entirely consumed, and it fell under my eye. I saw the word 'police' and the word 'reward', in the portion already blackened, and a moment later one of the women poured the firebucket over me and the paper. I saw that three small pieces were unburnt and was able to recover them by putting my hands on them as I got back to my feet. The wet paper stuck to my hands, and I was able to preserve it within my handkerchief as I pretended to clean myself off and made my apologies to the women. Once back at the station, I investigated the scraps. All three bore typewritten letters. The smallest one had ' H U F R M '. The second largest '*O W S L* – full stop – *X P Q*', and the largest, ' *C E L E T in the paradol chamber until it is safe to C O L* '. Now I ask you Mr. Holmes, what can that be other than an order to keep a bracelet in the paradol chamber until it is safe to collect the reward?"

"The paradol chamber?"

"Yes. '*P A R A D O L*'. Have you ever heard of it?"

"Are you certain that was what was written? Could it be that the *l* was rather an *x*?"

"It was typewritten. There was no mistaking one letter for another." "Ah." Holmes scowled, but I could see that he was intrigued by the puzzle. "I should like to speak to Constable Hopkins directly, if possible."

"He's due to testify on another matter this morning," Gregson said, "but I'll let his sergeant know. The sooner the better. Hammond's company plans to treble the amount of the reward tomorrow. They're pressed by the Foreign Office too, and are far less concerned with bringing the thief to justice than they are in recovering the lost gems. But if we can find this mysterious chamber before morning, we might not have every treasure hunter in the city getting in our way."

Holmes shook his head. "I know London as well as any man alive, and I have never heard of a Paradol Chamber."

"And what does 'paradol' mean?" I wondered, foreseeing a long morning consulting our dictionaries and other reference works. "It sounds like the name of a patent medicine to me."

"Or a chemical compound," Holmes said, thoughtfully. "The-*ol* suffix points to an organic substance or an extract of some kind. But I associate the word with music. I believe it may be a family name, if not here, then on the Continent."

"I was thinking more along the lines of a secret society," Gregson admitted. "And I hoped you'd have heard of it, Mr. Holmes."

"If it is a secret society, it has kept its secret well," Holmes said. "Were there no other marks upon the page? No other words Hopkins might have seen?"

"None that he mentioned in his report." The Inspector passed over the pages to Holmes to read as the cab pulled up outside of 221b Baker Street. He absorbed the material quickly and quietly as I retrieved our luggage and went to unlock the door, and then handed the report back to Gregson. "I see that Hopkins was careful to write the letters out in capitals, to avoid any confusion, but he doesn't say whether the typewritten letters were also capitals. Still, it does eliminate the possibility that the word was paradox."

"Then we'll have to keep looking." Gregson tipped his hat to us and got back into his cab. "I truly hoped you would have the answer at your fingertips, Mr. Holmes. But that's neither here nor there. Perhaps one of our informers has heard the name. I'll head in to Scotland Yard, and have Constable Hopkins sent round to Baker Street once he's done in the courts. Good day, gentlemen."

We made our way upstairs, after asking our excellent landlady Mrs. Hudson to provide us with coffee at her earliest convenience, and soon traded our outer layers for dressing gowns and slippers. Holmes lit a pipe, of course, and began to sift through the newspapers which the boy had collected for him during our absence. "Here is the first mention of the bracelet," he reported after a moment. "It was made for a Slavic princess, and was to be delivered to her embassy when it was stolen. That, no doubt, is the reason why the Foreign Office is involved."

"Do you think it was stolen deliberately then, as an affront to the lady?"

"Not if Red Nettie had anything to do with it," Holmes said. "She is an opportunistic thief, like most shoplifters and pickpockets. Which should be a comfort to the Foreign Office, since I doubt she has any notion of the value they place upon the bracelet."

"So we could leave the mystery to the police?" I asked, torn between my desire to see my friend take a proper rest and my uneasiness over the intervention of the Foreign Office.

"We could," Holmes said. "Except that the word 'paradol' has intrigued me. Take a look at our bookshelf, my dear fellow, and I'll see I can discover anything in the agony columns."

The coffee came, and then our breakfasts, but of the word "paradol" we could find no trace. Our reference works having failed us, Holmes decided to consult an expert, or several. "There is nothing which the researchers at the British Museum like better than to clutter their brain attics with irrelevancies. No one man can know everything," he said, as he dispatched the boy with a stack of telegram forms. "And it is as well to admit it." He sat down at the table and spooned some kedgeree from the salver onto his untouched plate.

My own plate had been filled and emptied again, but I poured myself another cup of coffee. "Especially not if he has the habit of sweeping away the facts he thinks of as clutter. Although given the reputed tidiness of your own 'brain attic', I cannot help but wonder what it was that made you ask if the word could be 'paradox'."

Holmes grimaced. "Even the best broom can't reach every cobweb. Were the word 'paradox' and not a 'paradol', I would have directed Gregson to Professor Martin Hoffmanstall, and his cabinet of curiosities near Hampstead. He had, as I recall, a gravity defying room in the garden of his former establishment at Brighton, and 'Can you solve the paradox?' was a prominent line in the banner above the door."

"I take it that you did," I said, for it was evident in my friend's manner that the memory was a personal one.

"Any child could, once aware of the basic principles of optical illusion. The room is set an angle, and all means of comparing it to the horizon obscured. In it, water appears to run uphill and persons to change size, depending on where they stand. I thought it well worth tuppence, even knowing how the trick was done, and the trick was easy enough to duplicate. I'm sure it wasn't the only one."

"It's a shame then, that we cannot substitute one letter for another," said I. "Such a chamber sounds more than adequate as a hiding place."

Holmes poked at his breakfast and then set down his fork. "We'd still have to find it, and even then we might be doing little more than chasing a wild goose. For all we know, the paper which Constable Hopkins collected has nothing to do with the missing bracelet."

"What other word ends in '*C E L E T*'?"

"Princelet?" Holmes suggested, and then leaned his elbow on the table and rested the bridge of his nose against his fingertips. "Not that a princelet held in any sort of chamber would be less urgent a matter."

"Eat something, Holmes," I said. "It will ease the headache."

"I haven't time."

"You do, you know. You'll have to wait here for Hopkins to arrive and for any responses to your telegrams. You will have time for your breakfast. You will have time for another pipe. You might even have time for a bath and a shave."

That earned me a smile, as Holmes rubbed thoughtfully at the growth upon his chin. "You know me too well, Doctor. Very well. I will take the rest you are urging upon me, since nothing can be done until we know more. And how will you fill the hours? A nap, perhaps?"

A nap sounded like an excellent idea. But I knew that

Holmes would be more likely to take the rest he needed if he knew that the case was proceeding. And there was at least one task that was well within my capabilities. "I thought I might go over to the Public Records Office and see if I can find the name 'Paradol' anywhere. It is quiet and cool in the reading rooms there, and whether I succeed or not, it will still narrow our search."

"Better yet, try the churches of Southwark," said Holmes. "Begin with the Baptists and go on to St. Mary's of Newington. Gregson can set a constable trolling through the records of the nation. Let us concentrate our energies where we might have the greatest success. Tell them you've come across the name in a family Bible. And don't forget to ask the vergers. They'll know their gravestones off by heart."

I nodded. "Will you place advertisements in the newspapers as well?" I asked, thinking of the many occasions when he had done so in the past. "There must be someone in London who knows the word."

"If Gregson's theory about a secret society is correct, that would instantly inspire the criminals to move the bracelet," Holmes said. "No, Watson. If we're to find the 'Paradol Chamber' while it still contains the bracelet, we must exercise some discretion and limit ourselves to reliable sources."

I took a hansom cab. It was unusually warm for May, and I remembered that the day was as long now as it would be in late July, and the sun as high. As the cab went along Piccadilly, I noticed Professor Robert Bentley approaching the headquarters of the Linnean Society. I realized this was an opportunity I should not forego. Bentley had also trained as a surgeon, and was a member at my club. I had seen him there on several occasions, his bald head rising from the wild disarray of his sidewhiskers like a mountain beset with an overgrowth of untamed shrubbery. I doubted he knew my name, but my face might be familiar. And a more reliable source of information about organic compounds than Bentley and the other fellows of the Society I could not imagine.

I had the cab driver stop and approached the great botanist with my question, and much to my surprise, he nodded when he heard the word 'paradol'. "It's a fairly obscure reference," he said, "But I believe it is the pungent principle of the spice derived from *Aframomum melegueta*."

I tugged my notebook from my pocket. "*Afromomum...*" I began to write, and Bentley interrupted me.

"You might know it as Guinea pepper, or 'grains of paradise'. It's the latter name, I believe, from which the word 'paradol' is derived."

"I couldn't find it in the dictionary," I admitted.

"I would be surprised if you did," Bentley said. "Come inside and see if our library can do you better."

My excitement waned when I discovered that the word 'paradol' had been coined just three years prior, when the substance was identified in a paper by a chemist called J.C. Thresh. Still, I had discovered something, and when I emerged from the Linnean Society, I went to the nearest post office to send the information to Holmes. The reply came within half-an-hour. "Paradol also a name in France. Lucinde Paradol sang in Paris Opera. Proceed to parishes, I will research importers of grains of paradise." So now, instead of a single thread, we had two. And at least we knew that the word could be a name. I set off for Southwark again, feeling hopeful.

By early afternoon, I was feeling much less hopeful. If anyone named Paradol had ever been born, married, or buried in Southwark, they had done so without the knowledge of the churches nearest Elephant and Castle. I had even gone as far afield as the nearest Catholic establishment, that being the most likely religion of an immigrant from France. I stopped to telegraph Holmes for further instructions, and was gratified by how quickly came the reply, telling me to meet him at Simpson's in the Strand at my earliest convenience.

Being much closer, I reached the restaurant well before Holmes, and decided to take my luncheon in the upper room, where I could observe the street below. But once seated, I allowed myself to close my eyes for a moment, and I was quite asleep when I was found by Holmes and PC Hopkins. A touch on my shoulder roused me.

"May we join you, Watson?" Holmes asked, although he was already taking the seat beside me and waving Hopkins into the chair opposite. "This is PC Hopkins. Constable Hopkins, my friend Dr. Watson."

"I'm pleased to meet you, sir," Hopkins said. He was a well-set up young fellow of about twenty-three, his bright blue eyes trying to take in the entire restaurant at once.

"And I you," I said absently, reaching for my now tepid cup of coffee. "I'm sorry I fell asleep, Holmes."

"It's hardly surprising after the past week. After we eat you can head back to Baker Street, and I will take the next shift of hunting," Holmes replied. He looked much better than he had in the morning, although there were still shadows beneath his eyes. "There's an importer in Rotherhithe who specializes in spices from Africa, and given your lack of success in the churchyards, it must be worth a try."

"I don't see how it could be, sir," Hopkins interjected deferentially. "I mean, I can't imagine anyone from the gangs at Elephant and Castle taking orders from the gangs at Rotherhithe. They're natural enemies."

"Improbable, I grant you, especially given that Red Nettie is an up-and-comer in the Forty Thieves. Nevertheless, we must eliminate the possibility," Holmes said.

"The Forty Thieves?" I asked.

"A gang of women who operate out of the Elephant and Castle district." Hopkins said, as if he were reciting from a manual. "A majority of them are widows and orphans at the moment, although some of the senior members are married. In plain view, they teach girls skills they might use for legitimate trades, like dressmaking. But they practice Faginy as well, teaching the younger girls the arts of picking pockets and shoplifting and other petty crimes."

"They're frequently out on the Strand," Holmes added, "which is why I wanted to meet you here."

I looked out the window, down onto the passing pedestrians. The sun was beating down and the awnings were out, and most of the women passing had put up sunshades to protect their complexions. "I don't know how we'll recognize them," I said. "I can't see past the umbrellas."

Holmes paused in the act of signalling the waiter to clap his hands together, his whole demeanor changing with the strength of a new thought. "Hopkins," he said urgently, "Show me again the evidence you brought with you."

"All right, sir," Hopkins said, bewildered, but he brought out an envelope with the three scraps of charred paper carefully preserved between cards. I looked at them as Holmes examined them, his fingers tapping on the table as if it were a piano keyboard. They were just as the report had described them, other than a broader gap than normal between the words "is" and "safe". Holmes clearly saw more than I, however, and he chuckled as he indicated that Hopkins could put away the envelope once more.

"Watson, I've changed my mind. When we finish eating, would you care to join me in a stroll along the Strand?"

"If I can be of assistance," I said, curiosity as always overcoming any hesitation. I knew the signs of Holmes on the right track, even if he seldom vouchsafed his reasoning beforehand.

"Constable Hopkins, I would ask you to join us, but I think your uniform would alarm our quarry, and she'd no doubt recognize your face. Go and send word to Inspector Gregson that we are very likely going to be able to retrieve the bracelet this afternoon. Then find the constables patrolling this beat and ask them to be certain that, if we do confront Red Nettie, none of her acquaintances take to their heels with any of her accoutrements."

"Yes, sir, of course, sir, excuse me, sir," Hopkins practically leapt to his feet and departed with a vigour I could only envy.

Holmes watched him go with an indulgent expression. "I have hopes that that young man will make a detective in time," he said. "He shows a distinct talent for observation."

"And he listens to you, the way the older detectives don't," I observed.

Holmes shrugged, but I could see that he was pleased. "It is always easier to work with someone when they have little reason to cling to preconceived notions. I can only hope to live up to his expectations. In the meantime, let me turn the tables upon you, Doctor. You need to eat," he said, and raised his hand once more to summon the waiter. "It will help to dispel your headache." Coffee and sandwiches refreshed me, and while I cannot say that I was at my best when Holmes and began our promenade along the Strand, I was alert enough to spot Nettie Hannigan before my friend had a chance to tug my sleeve. She wore a dress of light pink organdy, cut according to the most recent fashions, and her hair was swept up defiantly to reveal the mottled red mark on her neck, which explained the pugnacious expression that marred her otherwise attractive features. I would never have guessed her to be a thief, and would have placed her instead amongst the young wives and hopeful maiden daughters of shopkeepers or tradesmen, that class which was rising by an application of hard work. Her umbrella was exceptionally large, made of silver silk, with a heavy bamboo shaft and handle. It sheltered both her and the younger girl by her side, whose dress betrayed its self-made origins by an uneven hem and a crooked seam.

"Do you remember when I fell at the Cunningham's?" Holmes murmured, just loud enough for me to hear and nod in reply. I remembered his ruse very well indeed, for it had alarmed me greatly at the time to see him take such a nervous fit. "Do you think you can do that? And fall against the ladies as you pass?"

"I can try," I said, for there was little time to demur. Holmes bid me good afternoon and headed into the nearest shop, and I acknowledged him and kept walking forward. I did not think I could mimic his entire performance, but it was easy enough for me to place my cane badly and let my bad leg collapse. I fell, as I intended, against Nettie Hannigan, and to give her credit she did her best to catch me, though she had to let go of what she was carrying to do so. We tumbled down together, and once fallen I did not have to pretend to be in pain, for my knee struck a protruding cobblestone, and it was all that I could do not to disgrace myself with bad language.

Miss Hannigan's exclamations were not so discreet, though she kept her voice low. When she saw that my pain was genuine, she dispatched her companion to fetch a glass of water, and then helped me to the kerb where I could sit and massage my leg. She stayed by me, too, offering her handkerchief for the tears that had started from my eyes at the sudden blow. A moment later, Holmes appeared through the growing crowd, my cane in one hand and Miss Hannigan's umbrella and parcels in the other. "Watson?" he said, aping concern. He hadn't had time to change his attire, but he'd rearranged his hair so that it came down over his forehead, and his expression was that of a far more ingenuous man.

"I'm all right," I growled, even as I wondered what he was up to. I carefully extended my leg, checking to see what I'd done to myself. "I think it's just a bruise. Thanks to this lady, I didn't strike the ground with my full weight. I apologize, ma'am. I should have placed my cane more carefully."

She waved aside the consideration with an unexpected graciousness that made me feel ashamed of my pretense. "There's worse reasons for landing in the gutter," she averred, with a laugh. "Here's Lucy with some water for you, and good thing too. You're red as a parson's nose."

I mumbled something about the day being hot, and accepted the water. I was flushed from embarrassment, not heat, and I knew it, and the thrill of attempting the ruse was giving way to the realization that I had not the skill to maintain it. At that moment, Holmes stepped in, offering the parcel and umbrella to Red Nettie. "It was awfully good of you to help, Miss. but are you sure you're not hurt? You fell too," he said, in a voice much higher than his usual pitch and with a distinct Newcastle accent.

"I'm all right, but my dress isn't," she said, pointing out the large tear at which had parted the flounce from her hem. I flinched, remembering that my foot had come down on the edge of the fabric.

"I'm so sorry." This time my apology was more sincere, but I was still startled when Holmes pulled out a five pound note and pressed it into her hand.

"This should cover the damage, shouldn't it?" he asked, bouncing nervously on his toes. "I'm afraid I don't know what ladies dresses cost in London."

"This should be plenty," Miss Hannigan said, and coquetted her lashes at him. "Perhaps you and I can meet again, once it's mended?"

Holmes tittered, "Oh, I'd like that," he said, fluttering his hands nervously in a manner that had me ducking my head to keep from staring. "Shall I give you my card?" He dove a hand into his pocket and then frowned. "Oh, dear, I've left the case at the hotel. But you can call there, at least until Tuesday. At the Northumberland. Ask for Henry. Stephen Henry."

"Stephen Henry," she repeated, taking his hand for a moment.

"And now I should get my friend into a cab. Oh! There's one. Cabbie! Oh, cabbie!" Holmes dashed off to intercept a nearby growler.

I kept my head down, rubbing at my face with the hand

that wasn't pressed against my knee, and beginning to shake with both the reaction to the pain and the laughter I dare not indulge at Holmes's antics. I didn't know why he didn't just confront the lady, but I was grateful enough for the opportunity to cease making a spectacle. A small crowd had gathered, and several hands helped me up into the cab, but I managed to wave and say thank you again, to the air in the general direction of the two ladies I had discommoded.

As soon as the cab turned a corner and the Strand was out of view, Holmes gave a great shout of laughter and buffeted me on the shoulder. "Well done, Watson! I didn't know you had a career in the theater." He tapped the roof. "Driver, wait here a moment."

"I don't," I said, trying to turn up my trouser leg so I could examine the bruise that was forming over my patella. His exuberance would have been welcome were it not that I was feeling rather misused.

"What was all that in aid of, Holmes?"

"A moment, Watson." Holmes leaned out the window and whistled. Not a minute later, Constable Hopkins had joined us, and Holmes had told the driver to go on to Baker Street. "There," he said as he settled back against the seat. "Now we can be comfortable."

Hopkins, perched opposite, looked at my friend with a puzzled mien. "I thought we were going to arrest her," he said. "And now you've just let her go."

"With five pounds in her purse," I added.

Holmes shrugged. "It was the only note I had with me," he said. "And I had not intended that she would damage her attire. Very clumsy of you, my dear fellow."

I took the admonishment in the spirit in which it was being given and merely raised an eyebrow at my effervescent friend. "So what is the result of our encounter with Miss Hannigan, Holmes? I have a bruised patella, she has five pounds, and you...what do you have?

"This," Holmes said, passing his hands across each other

like a stage magician before pulling a glistening chain of gems out from his sleeve.

"The Cartier bracelet!" I exclaimed, the pain in my leg forgotten. Hopkins applauded like a schoolchild at a Punch and Judy show.

"Where was it?"

"In a hidden compartment in the bamboo handle of her sunshade," Holmes said. "In other words a..."

"*Parasol* chamber," I finished, groaning with the realization of how much of the day I had spent in chasing wild hares.

"Precisely." Holmes could not have been more pleased with himself.

"How did you know?" Hopkins asked, and I echoed the sentiment. "When Watson mentioned the umbrellas, just after you informed us that the older women of the gang were teaching 'dressmaking and the like', I considered how easily a dedicated seamstress could also make an umbrella. Then I remembered that amongst the respectable occupations open to unmarried females, typewriting is one of the most easily learned. I confirmed my supposition by comparing the letters on the scraps of evidence against the arrangement of keys designed by Mr. Sholes for the Remington typewriters most commonly available. The scraps were not code, as I originally thought, but finger exercises to train typewritists in using the machine without having to look at the keys. As the *s* and the *d* keys juxtapose, I assumed a simple keyboarding error. Inspector Gregson was wrong, it was indeed possible to substitute one letter for another."

I laughed. "Brilliant, Holmes. But why not have Miss Hannigan arrested?"

He put the bracelet into my hand. "I meant to. But she seemed kind enough to a gentleman who was injured on the street, and since I was able to retrieve the jewels without raising the alarm, I thought better of it. Miss Hannigan, should she be foolish enough to use her doctored sunshade to conceal ill-gotten goods again, will be caught and sentenced for some less perilous trinket. But in the meantime, we shall make back my small investment fivefold, and still have time for a nap."

The Strange Missive of Germaine Wilkes

by Mark Mower

London – Monday, 25th May 1891 – It will come as no surprise to many of you who have long followed the exploits of my dear friend and colleague, Sherlock Holmes, to learn that one of the most frequently asked questions I am now faced with is, "When did you first learn of Professor James Moriarty?" It is a query to which I have given much thought and some speculation in recent days, imagining that the name had first come to my attention only a month or so ago. But yesterday, while looking back over a sheaf of notes I had retained from the late summer of 1887, I was finally able to pinpoint with some uneasiness the moment when Holmes first alerted me to the existence of his arch-nemesis.

I had called in at Baker Street just before ten o'clock on a bright and sunny Saturday morning in August to find Holmes in an ebullient mood. Apart from looking somewhat tired and pallid, he appeared to be in reasonable health and was quick to jump up from his favourite armchair to greet me as I entered the upstairs room at Mrs. Hudson's direction.

"Watson, my dear fellow! What a pleasant surprise, and such perfect timing. I am currently awaiting the arrival of Inspector MacDonald, whose earlier telegram informs me that he has a conundrum that Scotland Yard cannot solve. I trust that will serve as a sufficient inducement to get you to linger a while and share a fresh pot of tea with me. I am sure that my wife will not begrudge you a couple of hours in my company – especially now that you have purchased the birthday present she has wanted for some time."

"Indeed Holmes, that sounds splendid," I replied, "but I am at a loss to know how you could possibly have ascertained the nature of my earlier errand."

I could see the glint in his eye as he realised that I was, as ever, confounded by his powers of deduction. "A simple case of pulling together the discernible clues into a workable hypothesis, my dear fellow. A couple of months ago you mentioned to me that my wife was keen to fill your newly-decorated parlour with a suitable piece of furniture. You joked about how much that was likely to cost and how much time you had already spent trying to find an ornate chair or couch that would suffice. When we were last together – less than two weeks ago – walking back to 221b, we passed Druce's Furniture Showroom on the corner of Baker Street. I noted that your eyes dwelt a little too long on the stylish chaise longue that Mr. Druce has positioned very cannily in his window display. And armed with the knowledge that my wife's birthday falls in early September, I had thought at the time that you were minded to buy the piece and had hesitated only because of the hefty price tag."

"You are not wrong there," I admitted, disappointed that my thoughts and thriftiness had been so transparent. "But how did you know that I went back today to purchase the couch?"

"A few tell-tale observations to add to what I already knew," he continued. "As you always do, you carry your cheque book in its leather case in your inside top pocket. The case is slightly too big for the pocket and has a habit of poking out occasionally. Realising that this is a Saturday, and your bank is therefore closed, I can only speculate that the cheque book has been used to make a significant purchase. And reflecting on the fact that Druce's Showroom lies less than two-hundred-and-twenty yards from here, it seems reasonable to assume that you have already purchased the chaise longue and thought you would call in to see me while you were so close to your old haunt. Furthermore, your obvious smile and upbeat humour this morning suggests that the transaction has not been too damaging, by which I mean that you successful haggled with dear old Druce to give you a discount on the item in question."

I could not hide my astonishment, but was happy to point out a minor blemish in his otherwise comprehensive account. "Holmes, you clearly do not know Druce well at all. A discount was out of the question. What I successfully negotiated was free delivery of the piece on my wife's birthday!"

We both laughed as Holmes poured the tea and then raised an eyebrow at a further knock on the front door, before exclaiming: "Excellent, MacDonald is as punctual as ever."

Having poured another cup and exchanged some pleasantries with the man from Scotland Yard, Holmes was keen to get on with the business at hand. The amiable detective was happy to oblige.

"Aye, it's a puzzle alright. For some time, we've been aware that a gang of bank thieves has been planning some raids in the city. They are led by a one-time banknote forger called Germaine Wilkes, an American by birth. Late last night, one of my men spotted Wilkes walking through Westminster and promptly arrested him. We now have him under lock and key at the Yard, but he is proving to be most uncooperative and saying very little. At some point we will have to release him."

I was the first to interject. "Surely, you have sufficient evidence to hold him. Was he carrying anything that could incriminate him or provide a link to his known accomplices?"

MacDonald looked crestfallen and explained that he had spent all night interrogating Wilkes without success. He then reached inside his tweed frockcoat and drew out a folded sheet of paper. "The only piece of information we managed to find on him was this," he added, handing the opened note to my colleague. "The difficulty we have Mr. Holmes, is that we can't make head nor tail of it. And knowing that you're a man who's accomplished at solving all manner of riddles, we thought it might be one for you."

Holmes had fallen silent as he gazed intently at the page before him. His eyes rapidly scanned the missive and then he broke off, looked across at me and held out the note. "What do you make of it, Watson?"

I held in my hands a single sheet of foolscap paper, on which was printed the following:

Right 2, Left 3, 1, Right 3, 3, Left 2 – NO HIDE BIRDIE ID

Eager to make some sense of the seemingly unintelligible message before me, I thought of Holmes's methods and began to apply the same degree of scrutiny. "It seems to me that we have two parts to this message," I ventured. "The first few words suggest an instruction of some kind; perhaps a marching sequence, a map direction or even the coding sequence required to open up a safe or bank vault. The second part, in capital letters, may well be the substance of the communiqué, the real point that the author wishes to convey."

Holmes was unusually enthusiastic in his response. "Bravo Watson! I concur with you completely. The message does indeed appear to have two distinct parts and it would seem logical that the first is some form of instruction or direction-marker for the reader. What else?"

Egged on, I then suggested that the form of the note seemed significant. "Why bother to have this typeset and printed when it could so easily have been handwritten?"

This time is was MacDonald who replied with some eagerness. "My thoughts exactly, Dr. Watson. And if you look at the back of the note you will see that the imprint of the type has gone through the page, which tells us that the message was hand-typed rather than printed."

"Indeed it was," concurred Holmes. "A fact that we can take to be highly significant, I suspect. So, do you know who sent the note, MacDonald?"

The Inspector looked bemused. "No, how could I possibly know? Wilkes has refused to say anything about the note and where it came from."

"My dear Inspector. I thought your intelligence on Wilkes and his cohort of bank thieves might have extended as far as the knowledge that, while they are believed to be operating as a discrete gang, they have much broader connections to a large criminal network operating across London, parts of Europe, and as far as North America. It should come as no surprise that Wilkes hails from the other side of the pond. My contacts tell me that he was chosen specifically for his role by the real puppet-master in the criminal fraternity."

MacDonald tried to hide his frustration, but realised that Holmes had the upper hand. "So, Mr. Holmes, who do *you* believe sent the note to Wilkes?"

Holmes looked at him directly, and addressed him without a hint of conceit: "I have no doubt whatsoever, that this message was sent by the very person who directs all of the major operations of the criminal network I have described. That person is none other than Professor James Moriarty. I have it on good authority that Wilkes had previously been Moriarty's favoured lieutenant in a counterfeiting ring that once operated out of Cincinnati."

"How can you be so sure Holmes? And who is this Professor – I've never heard you mention him before?"

Holmes turned his gaze towards me, and for a split second a look of fear passed across his face. "That is because I had hoped to spare you, indeed protect you, from the knowledge that we now have a criminal mastermind operating with relative impunity from a base in London – a man who is more than a match for any of crime agencies which exist in New York, Paris or London itself. He is cunning and formidable and exceedingly dangerous. By day, he masquerades as an academic, eminent in his field, mentoring the very brightest student minds. By night, he casts off the gown – operating under a different cloak – and directing the endeavours of a very different class of followers. Make no mistake, Watson, Moriarty is behind this, and the less you know of him, the better it will be for your sake and your wife's."

The casual reference to my beloved wife had the desired effect and I offered no further challenge. I could see also that MacDonald had been listening intently, taking in this new information and looking slightly awestruck at Holmes's assertions. In the silence that followed, it was he who spoke first.

"So, where does all that leave us with this note, Mr. Holmes? Are you able to tell me what it means and whether I should continue to hold Wilkes?"

"I am sure I can crack the meaning behind this communication and set you on the right path. But I will need some time and your indulgence for a short while yet, as I need to make a short excursion into town. It is now half past ten. Could I suggest that we reconvene back here in Baker Street in two hours' time? I will instruct Mrs. Hudson to have waiting for us a light luncheon of bread and cold ham."

MacDonald was visibly relieved. "That sounds wonderful! I am very grateful to you, Mr. Holmes, and will take my leave. I will be back promptly at 12.30, as you suggest."

When MacDonald had gone, I took the opportunity to try and get Holmes to talk more about the enigmatic Professor Moriarty, but all of my gentle questioning brought little by way of a response. "I can tell you nothing further at this stage Watson. I really do have to go into town. A short spell of shopping should do the trick. I should then be in a position to tell you the substance of the message from Moriarty."

Without further explanation he was off, heading down the stairs of 221b, through the front door, and out into the street before I could even think to ask if he wanted me to join him. I resolved to await his return and find out whether he really could make sense of the strange note to Germaine Wilkes.

In Holmes's absence, I read the headline features in *The Times*, keen to find out if there was anything in the press that might shed some light on Wilkes's activities or the shadowy network of crooks that were being directed by Moriarty. The big news of the day was that a major financial fraud had been uncovered in a provincial bank in the south of England. There was also news that a cruise ship had run aground off the coast of Cornwall, with the loss of ten lives. Equally disturbing was the announcement that the previous evening a British politician had been found dead, close to Westminster Bridge. The report said that Augustus Waldringfield, the Member of Parliament for Chippenham East, had been found stabbed to death. It speculated that his death may have been linked to his much publicised opposition to the Irish Home Rule bill which had been defeated in the Lords the previous year. The article went on to say that it was well known that Waldringfield had been a fierce critic of the Fenian Brotherhood, the group thought most likely to have carried out the attack.

A little over an hour after he had departed, Holmes was back in Baker Street, clutching a large box which I imagined was the result of his mysterious shopping expedition. I was quick to express my surprise at his behaviour.

"Holmes, in all the time that I have known you, I cannot recollect another occasion on which you have left an active case in order to spend time purchasing something for yourself. Please tell me that this is some curious aberration on your part!"

"Watson, your instincts have not deserted you. This was no routine purchase, my friend."

He began to unpack the box, revealing a black mechanical instrument, along the front of which were positioned numerous keys, marked by different letters of the alphabet and other recognisable symbols. With care, he set the instrument down on his writing desk, and stepped back to admire its appearance.

"I have here a marvel of the modern age. A Sholes and Glidden patent typewriting machine, manufactured by the American firm of E. Remington and Sons. It was first produced in 1875, and is becoming more popular on both sides of the Atlantic, replacing the need for costly typesetting, and enabling even the most humble of offices to produce their own printed stationery. The arrangement of the keys enables the typist to adopt a standard finger position in order to use the machine. With experience, practice and dexterity, I am told that a regular operative can type out at least 40 words a minute."

He had heartfelt enthusiasm for this mechanical contraption and proceeded to insert into it a single sheet of paper taken from the drawer of the desk. I felt I had to express my obvious confusion. "I'm sorry Holmes, but I don't see what this has got to do with the note we are trying to decipher?"

"Well, let us return indeed to that very note, before MacDonald reappears. We shall look at it afresh." He spread the note out before us to the right of the typewriter. "Let us consider first its form. The page has been typewritten and deliberately so. Moriarty is telling Wilkes something by the mere fact that he has typed the missive. I believe that the "right, left, right, left" reference and the associated numbers are instructions related to the use of a standard typewriter. To that we will return in a moment."

He now pointed specifically to the second part of the message and read out "NO HIDE BIRDIE ID." "I believe there is a clear message here. Moriarty is saying: 'We can now expose the person who has to date been undercover, unrecognised or otherwise hidden from the public gaze.' 'BIRDIE' is his code for the mole, spy or agent he is referring to."

"But what about this word 'ID', Holmes, what does that suggest?"

"The term 'I.D.' has a certain American ring to it – a slang term for *identification.* It is not one which our British policing colleagues have yet adopted with any great enthusiasm, but the Police Department of New York has been pioneering in its work to provide I.D.'s for all of the major felons it wishes to apprehend. Inspector Thomas Byrnes' *Professional Criminals of America* was published in September last year and provides both written descriptions and photographs of the offenders concerned. I only know this because I was asked by the capable Inspector to contribute intelligence to some of the descriptions used in the book. For the purposes of our note, Moriarty is saying to Wilkes that the target's identity can now be revealed."

I was still confused. "So, who is the subject of the note? How could Moriarty be sure that Wilkes would know exactly who to target without risking detection if the note was intercepted?"

"A good point, Moriarty needed to be specific. But this is a clever piece of subterfuge. Alongside the main communication, there is a second, hidden message, which precisely answers your question. Let us now turn to that."

His pointed his long index finger at the main body of the text. "I thought at first that the hidden message was a simple process of letter substitution, with each different character of the 'NO HIDE BIRDIE ID' line representing an alternative letter in a traditional cypher. I was quick to discard the thought though, as there were no obvious solutions and it would have been unlikely that as a mathematical genius Moriarty would have relied on such an obviously easy code."

"Would the message be an anagram in that case?" I interjected, realising instantly that a straightforward anagram was also unlikely. "After all, the number sequence '2, 3, 1, 3, 3, 2', contained within what we believe to be the instructions, do add up to fourteen, the number of letters in the main message."

"That is true, but try as I might, Watson, I could think of no sensible anagram from the letters in the sentence. I did, however, come up with one line that I thought you might like as a medical man –'I'd bid heroin die.'" I ignored the jibe, resisting the temptation to castigate him as I had so often for his casual drug use. Holmes returned to the subject of the typewriter.

"I am convinced that the keyboard will provide the solution to this puzzle," he said, placing his hands in the correct position for typing. "The sales assistant was most insistent that the fingers be positioned accordingly. Now, following the instructions in the note, we move our finger position one key to the 'right' and type the first two letters out as if we were routinely typing the word 'NO'. His fingers struck the keys accordingly and the letters "MP" appeared on the paper. He then tapped a long key at the bottom of the keyboard which he informed me was the "spacebar".

"Now we are instructed to move to the 'left.'" He repositioned his fingers to the left of the standard typing position and typed what would have been "HIDE", being careful to use the spacebar to separate the letters into two words – one of three letters, the second of just one. On the paper, the newly typed words read "GUS W." At this point I remained unconvinced that Holmes" experiment would bear any useful fruit.

Following the same logic and procedure, Holmes finished typing out the short sentence. Having done so, he pulled the newly typed page from the typewriter and retrieved an ink pen from the desk drawer, adding a few words atop the typed sentence.

"Let us see what we now have Watson! Put together, two sentences read: 'No hide birdie ID – MP Gus W not for us.'"

Recollecting the earlier article in *The Times*, the message now made perfect sense to me. "The dead politician Holmes!

The MP for Chippenham East, Augustus Waldringfield – he was found murdered last night!"

"So it would appear, dear fellow. And his demise was at the hands of Wilkes and not the Fenian Brotherhood. That invention was most likely promulgated by Moriarty himself to throw the suspicion off his criminal associates. What you might not yet have read, Watson, is that Waldringfield has also now been linked to the major fraud case involving the Surrey Shires Bank, of which he was one of the directors. I think we can take it that Moriarty or one of his associates had found out about the bank's fraudulent activities, and had then tried to blackmail the MP with the information, threatening to reveal both the crime and the politician's link to it, if he did not bend to Moriarty's will. The outcome of the matter suggests that Waldringfield had refused to yield to the Professor's demands, and Wilkes was therefore instructed by this note to go public with the information about the MP's nefarious activities. Whether or not Moriarty had gone as far as to sanction murder we may never know."

At that point, a heavy footfall on the stairs alerted us to the return of Inspector MacDonald. When he entered the room, the detective looked tired and dejected. "I have bad news, I'm afraid. It seems that sometime this morning, after I had left him to come here, Wilkes received a visit at Scotland Yard from someone purporting to be his legal representative. Having spent just a few moments with Wilkes, the man asked to be released from the holding cell and left the building. The supervising officer said that Wilkes had appeared to be fine at that point and had expressed his confidence that he would soon be released from custody. However, when the same officer returned to check on Wilkes some twenty minutes later, he found the banknote forger in the last throes of death. It seems his visitor had dispensed some form of poison to the hapless prisoner and Wilkes died shortly afterwards. I guess that puts an end to our speculation about the puzzling note, Mr. Holmes."

It was Holmes's turn to look dejected. "That is troubling news, MacDonald, and I can only apologise for having underestimated the extraordinary lengths that Moriarty would go to in covering his role in this sad state of affairs. Doctor Watson will no doubt convey to you over lunch the full details of what we have uncovered, having deciphered the note, and our speculation as to its links to some of the recent stories which have appeared in the press. For my part, I will leave you in his excellent company. I find myself suddenly without an appetite and in need of some fresh London air."

With no further explanation, Holmes left us to the fine spread which Mrs. Hudson had prepared, and we spent the next hour discussing the meaning of the note and the ramifications of the case.

In the two weeks that followed, I saw very little of my colleague, immersed as I was in the celebrations for my wife's birthday. That, at least, had been a great success – the chaise longue being considered a most perfect centrepiece for our new yellow parlour.

When I did eventually feel comfortable to bring up the subject of the Wilkes note, Holmes was demonstrably reticent to discuss the matter in any further detail. With a dismissive shake of the head, he requested only that I promise him two things – firstly, never to make public the strange case of the typewritten missive, and secondly, to never let him forget that Moriarty might one day be the cause of his undoing. It is with more than a tinge of sadness that I convey to you, dear reader, as I sit here reflecting on the terrible events that have occurred at the Reichenbach Falls, I fear I have let Holmes down on both counts.

The Case of the Vanished Killer

by Derrick Belanger

It was a late Saturday morning on the first of October when I heard word of the double murder of the Smith siblings, a crime which held the attention of all of England for a few brief weeks in the waning months of 1887. Although the case is now well known throughout the Commonwealth, the role my friend played in solving the crime has been ignored and credit given to our own Scotland Yard. While England's brave officers deserve their fair share of credit for assistance on this adventure, I believe the murder would still be an unsolved crime, possibly one as famous and with as many outlandish theories as that of Jack the Ripper, if it weren't for Sherlock Holmes bringing the case to a swift conclusion.

The tale begins with me stirring bleary eyed in my bedroom at 221b Baker Street. My wife was overseas visiting her mother in Missouri, and I moved back in with Holmes for a few weeks to spend extra time with my dear friend. I had difficulty sleeping the previous evening as the weather was excessively chilly, and I awakened to find frost on my window and the sun already high in the morning sky. I joined Holmes in the dining room, where he had already imbibed two cups of Darjeeling tea and completed the morning edition of *The Times*.

"Good morning, Watson," Holmes said while folding up

the paper. "You have risen just in time for a breakfast certain to warm you on this frigid autumn day."

Mrs. Hudson had prepared a fine meal of poached eggs on toast, grilled ham that was slightly crispy, and browned tomatoes. We drank orange juice with our breakfast and talked briefly about the recent cold spell which had enveloped all of England. This pleasant start to the day was interrupted by a ringing of the doorbell and Mrs. Hudson delivering Holmes a note.

I could tell by Mrs. Hudson's wide eyes and slight smile that this was no ordinary visitor.

Holmes looked at the note and handed it back to Mrs. Hudson. "Well, Watson," he stated, "it looks like we have a celebrity in our midst. Please, Mrs. Hudson, show the gentleman in."

It did not take Holmes's powerful reasoning skills to know the identity of his guest. Mrs. Hudson opened the door and a man in a rather dour black suit entered. Even out of costume, his notorious Van Dyke beard and long, flowing brown hair clasped back in a ponytail would leave any Londoner no doubt as to the gentleman's identity.

"Thank you for seeing me, Mr. Holmes," the man started in a drawl only spoken by natives of the American West. He turned to me and offered his hand. "Hello, my name is –"

"Buffalo Bill Cody," I said rising from the table and meeting his hand in a firm grip. "Thank you, my name is Dr. John Watson."

"Ah yes," Mr. Cody said as we shook hands then released our grip. "Heard about you. You're the guy writing that novel about this fella dealing with those Mormons," he said, referring to my forthcoming book, *A Study in Scarlet*.

"Let me assure you," Holmes responded, "that the actual solving of the case was not as dramatic as its portrayal in Dr. Watson's telling. Now, please have a seat, and let us know what brings a famous entertainer such as yourself to my residence."

Mr. Cody sat down in an easy chair, and we three pulled our chairs around in a circle. "First off, let me apologize for bothering you on the weekend. Know that I wouldn't be here if it weren't mighty important."

Holmes silently motioned with his wrist for Mr. Cody to get to the point.

"Anyway, I need your help sir, very much sir. You see, this Inspector Lestrade is threatening to keep my whole show from going on tonight. I can't afford to have a cancelled performance, but without my Indians, I'm not sure what to do."

At the mention of Lestrade, Holmes's ears perked up and the detective leaned forward clearly interested in the cowboy's tale.

"Mr. Cody, before I can tell you if I can help you, I must know the details of why Inspector Lestrade, a man I can assure you I know quite well, and a man I have, on many occasions, shown the error of his ways, is interested in keeping your Indians from performing."

"Well sir, did ya'll hear about the murder committed last night?"

"Murder?" I said raising my eyebrows in surprise.

"Yes, Watson," Holmes calmly informed me. "It is the headline of this morning's *Times*. As usual, the article includes all the grisly details, but none of the important aspects of the crime. Last night, or should I say, early this morning, a brother and sister with the last name of Smith were brutally murdered in their tenement building. The building is on Old Montague Street, in the Whitechapel district. There was no apparent sign of a break in. No money was stolen. The brother was found dead with a hatchet in his head, and the sister was found on the fourth floor landing, stabbed to death. At the time of the newspaper's publication, the police had no witnesses and no suspects. I assume that has changed."

"Right you are," answered Cody. "At just about dawn this

morning, this Inspector Lestrade and half of Scotland Yard comes bursting into my Indians' sleeping quarters. They're hollering and screaming that one of my performers is guilty of killing these Smith siblings in cold blood. Fortunately, Red Shirt was there and was able to keep the peace. With all that at six in the morning, after my troop had rightly stayed up late celebrating, we're lucky no fights broke out, and no one got arrested."

Red Shirt was the name of the famous Lakota-Sioux leader who was part of Bill Cody's Wild West show. The press loved the Indian, and he was almost as famous as the cowboy before me. I was baffled as to why Mr. Cody was telling us about how Inspector Lestrade connected the Indians to the murder, and said as much to the gentleman.

"Well, apparently it wasn't no ordinary hatchet that killed that Smith boy. It was a tomahawk they found in his head, and that's not all. They also claim they found a few arrowheads on the floor of the apartment. That was what led the inspector to jump to the conclusion that an Indian had killed the Smiths. And, of course, where else to find an Indian but at my Wild West show?"

Holmes leaned back in his chair for a moment, taking in the description of Mr. Cody's situation. "Lestrade," the detective stated, "does have some rationale for his actions. Can you vouch for the location of all of your Lakota members?"

Mr. Cody's spine stiffened, and I feared my friend had insulted the celebrity, but when he spoke his voice was quiet and serious. "Mr. Holmes, I assure you that there ain't a one of my tribesmen who would commit such a crime. After last night's performance, as I said, they celebrated something fierce. I don't see how any of them would have had the capabilities to trek halfway across London, commit a murder, and return back to camp without anyone, including Red Chief, knowing they had gone missing."

"You admit there was a celebration that evening. In the

"Yes, if you look closely at the family photos you will notice both Donald and Olivia Smith together, holding hands in some of the photographs. The family portrait of all the matriarchs of the family has Olivia's left hand slightly concealed behind her dress. Even so, the edge of a diamond ring is clearly visible. Lastly, while the bed is a single, clearly it has the impressions of two bodies. Yes, indeed Sergeant, the Smiths were not only lovers, they were husband and wife."

As my friend explained his reasoning, I could see the truth behind the words dawn upon Rousseau's face as his look went from one of astonishment to one of being dumbfounded. I sympathized with the sergeant, as I had the exact same feeling, one I've had on many occasions with Mr. Holmes.

"That is truly astonishing, Mr. Holmes. I'm not sure how we could have missed it. Does that have any bearing on the case?"

I awaited a sarcastic quip from Holmes, but he was in a serious state, and merely responded. "I'm not sure as of yet. Come Watson. I'd like your opinion of the bloody footprints."

As we left the Smith residence, I started seeing the faint outlines of the bloody prints. It was just the left foot, in fact just the tip of the left foot. I couldn't make out much more than the man had stepped in a bit of spilled blood which had remained on his foot. Holmes stopped on occasion and observed the footprints with his magnifying glass, while Rousseau complained about the lack of officers on the force. Apparently, one constable sprained his ankle in all the rushing around the previous evening, leaving the Yard with one less patrolman. Eventually, we climbed onto the roof and were met with a burst of sunlight.

The roof was nondescript, except for one fact. The buildings surrounding this tenement were several floors taller than the current one. An alleyway separated the building on the northeast and southeast sides from the next closest residences. Even if a thief could make the leap across the alleys on either side, they would surely smash into the brick walls of the neighboring buildings. The southwest side of the building was close to another tenement, though this one had an exceedingly steep thatched roof. For one to leap onto this roof and work one's way down to the ground seemed difficult. To do so without being observed, impossible.

"Our prey is a skilled devil," Rousseau cursed.

"These are dark dealings, sergeant," Holmes agreed. I noted that Holmes was looking at a scuff mark on the northeast side of the building. What it could mean, I knew not, but I did notice a glimmer of recognition in my friend's eyes.

"It's a shame," Rousseau lamented. "If Lestrade isn't able to crack any of the savages at that circus, then this case may never be solved."

Holmes glared at Rousseau, his mouth turning into a deep frown. "If, by savage, you mean an Anglo man of approximately five feet in height, of a particularly strong and limber body, who is undoubtedly from America, probably New York, and who was associated with the Smiths, then yes, I'd agree with you. As far as the Lakotas from Mr. Cody's Wild West show are concerned, they are completely innocent."

After Holmes's tongue lashing of the sergeant, we made our way back out of the tenement building. "To me, this killer has done the impossible. Yet you are onto something, aren't you?" I asked my friend.

"Remember, cases that seem impossible often have the simplest conclusions. I have noted four possible solutions to the case, but I still need more facts before I can deduce the resolution. For now, I need my Boswell's gift of observation."

"Whatever I may do to assist you, Holmes."

"There is a tavern there," said Holmes pointing to a dingy,

dilapidated ground floor establishment almost directly across the street. "I would like you to interview the barkeep and see if he had any notable customers yesterday evening. Take copious notes, and then send them to me when you are finished."

"Where will you be?" I asked.

"Why, at Earl's Court, attempting to show our dear friend Lestrade some semblance of reason."

I nodded and said goodbye to my friend. I expected him to hail a cab, but I was surprised to see Holmes instead enter the building neighboring the northeast side of the Smith's tenement.

The pub across the way had seen better days. The bar was stained different colors in several areas, crude attempts at covering up its missing chunks of wood. The furniture was a mix of different style tables and chairs from the last thirty years. The lighting was dark, the establishment drab, and the bloated barkeep with three shabby customers were the only people present. I noted that the customers kept their coat collars up and their heads face down in their ale. Not to stay hidden from me, but to stay hidden from the world. Such was the glum life of the alcoholic.

The barkeep, ruddy cheeked and with a crooked smile, lit up when he saw me enter, possibly because of my dress and obvious station in life. I joined the rank group at the counter, ordered a pint, and struck up a casual conversation with the gentleman, who introduced himself as Daniel Spitzer. It was my good fortune to discover the man was not only of jolly spirits but quite a talker. After discussing London's cold spell for a moment, I turned the conversation towards the Smiths.

"That's a terrible business, mind you, what with all that hullabaloo last night. Who would have thought that could happen to a nice couple like that?"

"Couple?" I inquired. "*The Times* said they were siblings."

"Oh, they claimed that they were brother and sister. Not

sure why, not sure what they were fleeing from, really. Oh, don't look surprised. If a couple is pretending to be siblings, you know that they are hiding from someone. It always puzzled me, but I never asked, though I've got an inkling as to what they were running from. You see, the death of the Smiths is terrible for them, but it's also terrible for me," he added with a wink.

"What do you mean terrible for you?"

"No shame telling you that the bar is only a portion of my income. A good chunk of my money also comes from the track, and the Smiths were some of my best clients. You see they bet big, but often lost just as big. I'm not sure where all their money came from, but between you and me, I bet they were swindlers. Nice folks here, always stayed out of trouble, but they had something about them, always looked a little haunted, if you ask me."

Mentioning the tracks and horses led to a separate discussion on the prospects of the thoroughbred Ocean Breeze in the upcoming afternoon race. After placing a small wager with Spitzer, I turned the conversation back to the previous evening, and I was surprised to discover that he had been working during the time the crime was committed. "Yes, sir, I pretty much live here. I have to leave to go down to the tracks on occasion, but there isn't a day that goes by where I'm not here at least fourteen hours. Anyway, last night, guess it would have been after one, people started flooding in. Some even had blood on their clothes. One poor officer looked stunned and shaken, same with two of the men, their clothes covered in blood. I'm guessing they were kicked out by the police before they had a chance to even change their clothes."

"Did you know the two men?" asked Watson.

"I know one of them, Abe Bruder, a jeweler near the Black Lion. Can't miss his flowing beard. Even that had streaks of blood in it. The man badgered on and on with a group of my people. Talked about holding the poor body of Miss Smith as she breathed her last breath. They were most upset, with good reason."

I pondered this information for a moment. Old Montague Street was known as having a predominantly Jewish population. I wondered if I would need to seek out a translator to assist with the Hebrew of the residents.

Finally, I pressed Spitzer again about anything else unusual that evening. He shrugged. "Nothing more than you'd expect. Lots of wailing and crying about the neighborhood and our lot in life. No one struck me as standing out. Everyone was shaken from the murder."

I finished my ale and began to say goodbye when suddenly a thought occurred to me. "Do you know of any Americans who frequent your establishment?" I asked.

Daniel's eyes lit up. "Course I do, know of one man in particular who hails from New York. He's in here all the time."

I was surprised by this bit of good luck and asked for this man's name.

"Course you can have his name. You've been speaking to him for the better part of an hour," Daniel beamed.

Puzzled, I inquired what Daniel meant.

"It's me, you fool. I'm originally from Buffalo, New York."

After my interview with Spitzer, I had my notes sent to Holmes, and returned to our residence. Relaxing, I enjoyed a glass of brandy and continued reading of Miss Nellie Bly's adventures in the book, *Ten Days in a Mad-House*, an appropriate title to reflect upon while sorting this case. Here was a girl voluntarily going undercover to expose the mistreatment of women in Blackwell's Island Asylum in New York. I wondered how many monsters lived in that American colony, and in my mind cursed our luck that Britain hadn't squashed General Washington's rebellion over a century ago. In due course, the brandy worked its effects, and I dozed off only to be awakened by Holmes shaking me a few hours later.

"Wake up, Watson," Holmes insisted. "We are to be guests at Mr. Cody's Wild West Show this evening. Mrs. Hudson is preparing a dinner of roast beef for us, and we should have just enough time to sup before our carriages arrive."

"Holmes, really," I started. "Do you have the solution to this dastardly case? Was it one of Mr. Cody's Indians?"

"I almost certainly do have the solution, and I assure you Mr. Cody's Indians had nothing to do with the crime."

"Well, out with it man," I demanded. "What happened?"

"You will accept my apologies Watson, as I cannot quite tell you the solution yet. There is still one last piece of the puzzle which I shall put in place tomorrow when one of Lestrade's men will join us. I believe he will identify the killer."

"But how?" I insisted. "How did the man pull this off?"

"In due time, Watson," Holmes answered mysteriously. "I believe you will find this evening's performance most enlightening. It took some convincing on my part, but once I assured Lestrade I'd have the murderer behind bars by tomorrow afternoon, he agreed to let Cody's show go on. Personally, I think the inspector just wanted an excuse to go home and finally catch up on much needed sleep."

After a delicious dinner of roasted beef and stewed vegetables, Holmes and I descended the stairs and waited for our coach to arrive. I was taken aback to see not one but three carriages stop in front of our home. Puzzled at why three carriages were needed for two men, I was about to ask Holmes when the answer came round the corner. Jostling towards us was a group of street urchins, dressed in dirty rags and making all sorts of noise as they tramped and jumped excitedly.

Holmes lit up at seeing the rag-tag army marching towards us. "Hello, Thaddeus, hello Barney," he addressed two of the older boys in the front. "Is this everyone for the Wild West performance?"

"Yes, Mr. Holmes," answered Thaddeus, a tall lad, thin – not from his body type but from his lack of nourishment. "There's a dozen of us, sir." He paused then quietly added in a tone of astonishment. "Golly, are we really gonna meet Mr. Cody?"

"Of course you are, lad, as long as we make the show on time. Plus, Mr. Cody has agreed to treat everyone to all the snacks they can eat."

A grand hurrah went up from the children, and then they scrambled into the growlers. I noted how one of the drivers scowled at seeing his passengers, but he kept his mouth shut, and with a crack of the reins, we were all off to the show. Holmes looked rather cheerful. "I wonder Watson, what will be more entertaining, seeing the show, or seeing the expressions of awe on the Irregulars' faces when they see the performances?" I heartily agreed, but inside I wondered what Buffalo Bill Cody would think of his special guests for the evening.

Fortunately, Mr. Cody was as gracious and kind as the stories in the adventure books make him out to be. When we arrived at the fair ground, Cody was there to meet us, dressed in his stage costume, with his gray cowboy hat, tan shirt with fringe, dark riding boots, and his arms filled with a dozen bags of peanuts for the irregulars. After handing out food and shaking hands with the children, the showman led us to our seats. While the giddy children oohed and awed at the spectacle of the show grounds, Holmes asked Mr. Cody, "Did you honor my request?"

"I sure did, Mr. Holmes. Not exactly an authentic portrayal, but I doubt the audience will mind. I reckon you folks are in for one great show. Now, here are your seats. I best get ready."

After the showman had left, I asked Holmes about their side conversation. The detective was distracted, beaming with pride at seeing the boisterous excitement of the irregulars.

"It is tragic, Watson, that my investigative team of children so rarely get to act like children," Holmes lamented.

The irregulars always left me a bit unsettled. The unsupervised children had a wild edge about them, but I conceded that Holmes was correct. It was nice to see all of them excited about a spectacle, not about a morsel of food to alleviate their growling stomachs.

"As to your question, Watson, I asked Mr. Cody to add an act to tonight's performance that I had the pleasure of viewing during rehearsals this afternoon. I believe you will find it both entertaining and of the most interest."

I was taken aback by Holmes's coyness, but I could see he wanted me to show patience. I simply nodded in understanding and left the detective to gaze upon the happiness he brought to our loyal street urchins. Before long, the Wild West show began. It was just as marvelous as the news reported, perhaps even more so.

Cody came charging out in the center of the stage, riding Old Charlie, the famous twenty-one-year-old horse noted as Cody's favorite, who seemed to enjoy the attention as much as his human companion. "Ladies and Gentlemen," Mr. Cody grandly called with a wave of his hat and a bow, "this evening you are in for a feast of the eyes, as you journey thousands of miles across the sea and over the lands, past the Florida swamps and the Adirondack Mountains, to land in the true heart of America, that of the Wild West. Tonight, my friends, you will marvel at the sharp shooting of Annie Oakley, spy an Indian attack on a pioneer stage coach, gasp at the acrobatic feats of Buck Taylor, and witness man conquer nature as a recreated wildfire appears before your very eyes. But enough talking from me – On with the show!"

A huge roar of approval and applause thundered from the audience as a herd of Buffalo rumbled onto the fairgrounds. Both cowboys and Indians worked together to corral the beasts and show a simulated hunt of the now almost extinct symbol of America. This act was followed by the great Annie

Oakley. The sharpshooter known as "Little Sure Shot," threw two clay pigeons into the air. She then hurled herself toward a table where two rifles lay in wait. I expected the dame to pick up the nearest Winchester and shatter one of the fake birds. To my astonishment, the lady leaped over the table, grabbing both rifles and let off two shots even before her feet hit the ground. The pigeons shattered in the air, and the crowd went wild. Holmes was applauding and laughing, but I could see his eyes were on the raucous Irregulars.

After the great Annie Oakley came the stagecoach robbery. The wild Indians, adorned with war paint, whooping and hollering, riding horses bareback, launched a full attack on the circled wagons. The coachmen tried their best but were no match from the overwhelming onslaught of Indian arrows. The actors did a magnificent job falling over, pretending to be dead, and, for added effect, with an arrow emerging from their backs. Just as all seemed lost, a trumpet call came from off stage and the cavalry, led by Buffalo Bill himself, came charging out and drove the Red Men away.

Again the audience seemed to lose their sense of decorum as they called, hollered, and cheered in a way to rival the whoops of the defeated Sioux. Next up came the cowboys. Buck Taylor and his compatriots held races, rode bucking broncos, reenacted daily voyages of the Pony Express, leaped over fallen coaches, and picked up sombreros from the ground while their horses continued at full gallop. Mr. Cody joined the group, riding his faithful companion. He had audience members toss baseballs into the air which he shot from the sky with his Colt army revolver, never slowing Old Charlie who continuously raced around the grounds at a furious pace.

Next came the astounding acrobats of John "The Ranger" Billings. "Ladies and Gentlemen," Cody dramatically started, "you will now witness mankind fighting that most monstrous beast of nature, that terrifying creature which consumes whole towns in its jaws, that horror known as the wildfire." The stage was set at a logging camp in the Rocky Mountains. A ranger station was on one side of the stage and on the other was a tower adorned with a bell to ring at any sign of danger. Two show hands set a pile of brush in the center of the stage and set it ablaze. Suddenly, Mr. Billings, in full ranger gear, burst out of the ranger station. He attempted to get to the bell tower, but the flames blocked his path. He showed concern with his flailing arms and tried several different pathways around the flames but to no avail.

The audience was absolutely silent, and I began to worry that perhaps the act had gotten out of hand, that the fire had shown a life of its own, and perhaps we would be evacuating the building. I looked at the faces of the children in front of me and even scanned the audience to find most faces showing at the very least concern, if not absolute fright.

Just as I was about to suggest to Holmes we move towards the exits to help disperse the crowd, I witnessed the most staggering gymnastic skills my eyes had ever seen. The Ranger grabbed a long, thin yet sturdy, piece of lumber. A cry came up from the audience as Mr. Billings then sprinted straight for the flames in the center of the stage. I felt my heart pounding, *What,* I wondered, *was this fool doing? Would he commit suicide before thousands?*

Then, the miracle occurred. Just as Mr. Billings was about to reach the flames, he jabbed the pole into the ground and used the stick to vault himself over the wildfire and land at the top of the bell tower. The sound of the bell ringing was drowned out by the raucous roars from the audience. We were all on our feet, hooting and screaming for more, and we did not stop our applause even as the fire brigade entered the stage and extinguished the flames.

Our cheers must have sounded for a good ten minutes when, suddenly, what I witnessed, truly witnessed, dawned upon me. "Holmes!" I shouted. "The killer!"

It was about two in the afternoon that following day when an elegant landau arrived in front of 221 Baker Street and both Mr. Cody and Mr. Billings arrived at our doorstep. We warmly greeted the entertainers who made a contrasting pair. Cody with his long hair and whiskers, Billings with his shaved face and closely cropped hair.

"Do you really think you've got the varmint behind this fiasco?" Cody asked. Before Holmes could respond, a wagon pulled to the curb behind where Mr. Cody's landau had just departed, and out stepped Lestrade, and three of his constables. There was a fourth man the group, assisted in removing from the carriage, who had a lame foot and a crutch. The men helped their crippled companion through the front door, and we heard them struggling up the stairs.

"We should help that young man," said Billings.

"Actually, I have a rather unusual request for you," said Holmes and he opened the door to his bedroom. "Please stay here, gentlemen, and await my call to come out. You will hear the conversation I am about to have with the officers of the law, but I ask that you remain silent and do not reveal the fact that you are here until told to do so. As you know, Mr. Cody, I can be trusted."

"If that's what you'd like Mr. Holmes, well, okay then." Cody assented, and the two men entered the bedroom after which Holmes closed the door behind them.

Shortly thereafter, the constables finally reached the door to our sitting room. Holmes warmly welcomed them in and offered a couch for the lame officer to lay upon. After they entered, I noted that Holmes closed and locked the door behind them.

Rousseau was one of the men present. The other two affable men were introduced as Constables Holly and Tiller, both young officers whose forms didn't quite fill out their uniforms, giving them an unintended comic charm. The lame officer on the couch was introduced as Constable Fowler, a man closer to my own age with coal black hair and a crooked nose.

"Really, Holmes," Lestrade complained, "I don't know

why you couldn't have gone to Constable Fowler's residence. Forcing him to climb those stairs is beyond my reasoning."

"As I find is almost always the case," Holmes muttered, but Lestrade did not respond, either because he ignored my friend or did not hear him.

"Constable Fowler, like Rousseau, was an officer at the scene of the crime Friday evening. Watson, if you recall, he is the officer that Rousseau informed us had sprained his foot that night. I believe that Fowler witnessed the murderer as he fled from Old Montague Street."

Fowler shook his head. "Mr. Holmes," he replied, "if I can help in any way, I will. It was the dead of night, and I did not see anyone flee from the crime scene. I only arrived quickly because I reside on Old Montague myself. There were quite a few people running about, but I can't say I saw someone fleeing from the area."

"Fowler, please look over these photographs of members of Mr. Cody's troop. I believe there is someone you will recognize," Holmes insisted and handed a pile of promotional photographs from Cody's show to the officer.

The constable took the photographs from Holmes and began looking them over. The collection was a menagerie of men, both Red and White. With each turn of the pictures came a shake of the head from Fowler. Finally, he reached the end of the pile and held aloft one picture of a bald strongman. "Possibly him, although he would have had a wig on, but there's something familiar about him."

Holmes looked crestfallen. "That man is Melvin Brady, a former member of Mr. Cody's troop, who never made the voyage to London. I did not mean to include his picture in the mix. Ah," Holmes perked up. "There is one more photograph." He removed a small, folded paper from his pocket and handed it to the injured man.

Fowler looked at the photo and his eyes bulged from his face. With a swift motion, the invalid was on his feet and dashing towards the door. He grabbed at the handle, attempting to turn it, and finding it locked.

Realizing his situation, the fiend turned towards Holmes. Wild eyed, teeth clenched like a wounded animal, he sprang at Holmes with an inhuman growl. He made it but three steps before Rousseau, Lestrade, and the other constables had grabbed him and thrown him to the floor.

"Holmes, what on earth is going on?" asked Lestrade, after the officers had restrained Fowler with some rope.

"Cody, Billings please come out now," Holmes called. "I believe you will recognize Mr. Wendell Finke, a former employee of the Wild West show."

Lestrade was stunned to see the two showmen step out of Holmes's private room, and I noted a slight reddening of his features, tightening of his jaw, and clenching of his fists. "Really Holmes!" Lestrade growled. "Did we need these theatrics?"

Holmes did not answer the Inspector's question. He waited as both Cody and Billings looked over the still struggling form of Finke. I saw a slight recognition in Wild Bill's face, but Billings clearly knew the man before him. "Finke," Billings gasped. "What have you done to yourself?"

"Only what needed to be done to give what those two had coming to them!" spat Finke.

"Mr. Finke was a member of Mr. Cody's Wild West show," Holmes explained to Lestrade and the other officers. He handed them the last photograph he had shown to Finke which revealed the man in full cowboy regalia, but with blonde hair and a straight nose. "He was the assistant to Mr. Billings and a noted acrobat. After the troop arrived in London in the spring, Mr. Finke was part of the show until the end of April, when he abruptly quit."

"That's right," Finke blurted, then held his tongue. The man was fuming, and we were not sure whether he would speak more, yell at us, or struggle against his bindings, or perhaps do all three at once.

Finally, with a heavy sigh, Finke seemed to decide that

since he was caught anyway, he should tell his tale and explain his actions. "I had finally tracked down those Smith crooks. I had stumbled upon them in London. They had taken everything from me, the devils. I met them in New York, at my mother's funeral, though they weren't called Smith then. Then it was Roger and Mary Corbin. Roger claimed to be a stockbroker, claimed he could double my inheritance by investing in a horseless carriage company. I fell for it. I was the rube, I was. They took everything and fled. That was ten years ago almost to the day.

"Finding myself destitute, I sought out work, jobs that allowed me to move around as I tried to track down the Corbins. I almost caught up to them once in Chicago, but they disappeared again before I could find them. They always left rich men poor in their wake. Roger was a gambling man of the worst kind, the kind that does not know when to stop and always loses.

"Finally, in the fall, I joined Mr. Cody's troop. I had given up on tracking down the Corbins. Their trail had gone stale, and I had moved on. Then, as fortune would have it, one day I was exploring London and ended up in a tavern on Old Montague. Who should I see making a wager with the barkeep? Why, Mr. Roger Corbin. I saw him, but he did not recognize me. I followed the man, found out where he lived, who he was, that he hadn't stopped his wicked ways."

"That's when you decided to murder them?" Lestrade demanded.

"No. It had been years since I had seen them. I tried to put them out of my head. Tried my best, but I couldn't stop thinking about what they'd done, how they were still swindling people. After a few weeks, I decided to seek my revenge. I quit Mr. Cody's show and became a constable. It was easy enough. There's quite a shortage of us." He motioned to the other officers present. "Anyway, I took lodging in the building next to the Corbins, now Smiths. I dyed my blonde hair black, and even got my nose smashed in a proper tavern brawl. I needed to make sure the couple wouldn't recognize me. As an officer, I occasionally entered their tenement building. I noted how tight the hallways were, how crammed the stairwells. If I were to kill the couple, I most surely would be seen fleeing, especially if I was wearing my police outfit."

"But," Holmes interrupted, "you were an acrobat, a skilled knife thrower, and a man who knows how to walk a tight rope, or vault across a pit of fire. You will recall, Watson, that after inspecting the home of the Smiths, we wandered up to the building's roof, and I noted a scuff mark in the in the roofing overlooking the northeast side of the building. My first thought was that someone had laid a pole or thin ladder across the two buildings and that there were even possibly two assailants, one to hold the pole while the other scurried across it. The person who scurried to the other building would have to be someone who was extremely athletic. From the bloody footprints I noted the man's gait and knew he had to be about five feet in height, the exact height of Mr. Finke. I also deduced that the man who killed the Smiths was someone that they knew, most likely from America, as one of the photographs of the couple in front of The Statue of Liberty, was crumpled slightly and off to the side, as if the killer had stared long at the image before discarding it. I also knew that the man had to be Anglo. Otherwise, someone would have noted a man of a different race, especially a Lakota Sioux, approaching or fleeing the tenement building.

"Extraordinary, Mr. Holmes," remarked Rousseau. "Still how did you find that Finke was our man?"

"Ahh, well after Watson and I left the Smiths, I went to the tenement on the northeast side of the building. If the assailants had escaped via the rooftop, there was a good chance they would have been seen returning down the stairs to their lodgings. I inquired with the building supervisor about the building tenants. He mentioned Officer Fowler.

It dawned on me that a constable would have the means of committing the murders, return down to the street level, and cover up his tracks. I knocked on the officer's door, pretending to be a reporter for The Times. I noted the man's features and when I visited Mr. Cody's grounds I stumbled upon Mr. Billings practicing his wildfire act. After seeing the pole vaulting, I realized one man could easily have committed the crime. I inquired with Mr. Billings about current and former members of the Wild West show capable of completing the pole vault. When he showed me the picture of Mr. Finke, gentlemen, the case was closed."

"But how on earth did Finke get a vaulting pole?" Lestrade inquired.

"The missing pole!" suddenly Billings called out in shock then turned to the bound Finke, "You stole it!"

"That's right," Finke snarled. "I returned to the showground as an officer of the law. I stole the pole and returned to my building, then the next day, I went to the roof of the Smith residence and stashed the pole, ready to finally enact justice."

"But the pole?" Lestrade puzzled. "How did you transport such a large pole?"

"I believe Mr. Billings can answer your question," Holmes interjected.

"Yes," answered Billings. "The pole is an invention of my own. I found bamboo bends quite easily and can achieve greater heights than hard wood; however, it is still difficult to transport an eight foot piece of wood. I created a five piece version where the pieces screw together to make the pole, quite similar to the newer cue sticks."

"Then everything was set," continued Holmes. "Finke entered the building in his police uniform. The Smiths, seeing a constable at their door, invited him in. Finke then dispatched the Smiths, climbed to the roof, removed his shoes, tossed them into the alley below, vaulted over to his own building, and then descended the stairs to his room where he put on new shoes. The accoster quickly went to the alley where he gathered the bloody shoes and the stick, which he disassembled, hid them in a bag or beneath his uniform, and then stashed them away in his own apartment. I would not be surprised, constables, if you were to find the materials still inside Finke's residence."

Lestrade looked stunned at all that had been revealed before him. "I assure you Mr. Holmes, that my men will search his room after we bring him back to the Yard."

"Before you take Mr. Finke away, I do have one question for him.

Why did you set up Mr. Cody's Lakota-Sioux?"

"I know those men, barbarians they are," grumbled Finke. "I figured there wasn't nothing I did to the Smiths that those warriors hadn't done a thousand times over to settlers. If an Indian hanged for the crime, so be it. There's a saying in America, that the only good Injun is a dead Injun."

Holmes's face was filled with absolute revulsion at Mr. Finke. "I believe in your country, just as ours, all people are created equal, and all people are equal in the eyes of the law. You chose to take the law into your own hands. You committed a crime and now must face the punishment."

Finke lashed out with harsh words at my companion, words I cannot repeat in the confines of this narrative. My dear friend just stood quietly as the constables hauled away the murderer.

"I'm glad that's over," I said to my companion as the wagon took Finke away.

"I agree, Watson. Finke believed he was serving a perverse form of justice. In the end, he was actually a worse criminal than that of the Smiths. I believe he will learn true justice when he hangs from the end of a rope. And now, Watson, onto another puzzling dilemma," my friend stated.

"I hope it is not another grisly murder," I stated in astonishment. "No, no, I was deciding whether I should order the quail or the flounder at Simpson's this evening."

The Adventure of the Aspen Papers

by Daniel D. Victor

Nine-tenths of the artist's interest in [bare facts] is that of what he shall add to them or how he shall turn them.
– Henry James, *The Art of the Novel*

I

Mrs. Hudson recognized a man of noble bearing when she saw one. Those were the visitors she most often reserved for herself to introduce, leaving to the boy in livery the task of announcing the guests she deemed less important. As a consequence, when she appeared at the door of the sitting room one morning in late October of 1887, both Sherlock Holmes and I looked up with great expectation. Sensing the drama her presence created, she smoothed down her skirt, cleared her throat, and proclaimed, "Mr. Henry James."

It wasn't that I thought she'd actually recognized the cerebral American author of *Roderick Hudson* and *The Portrait of a Lady. Rather*, it was the man himself who presented quite the authoritative figure. He appeared to be in his forties, with piercing light-grey eyes, a high forehead, and thin dark hair at his ears that accented a balding pate. Combined with his short grizzled beard and sensitive mouth, his features conveyed a sense of dignity, perspicacity, intelligence. What's more, having recently moved to London from the States, he was attired in a smart, three-piece English suit, a gold chain stretched taut across his waistcoat. Taken as a whole, his was an image destined to command respect from anyone, even those like Mrs. Hudson, who had never heard of him – let alone his reputation.

"Mr. Sherlock Holmes?" said our visitor to my friend, somehow aware of which of us to address.

Holmes bowed slightly, introduced me, and indicated that James take a seat.

No sooner had we settled ourselves than he addressed us. "Gentlemen, I come to you – I come to you – with a problem."

Let me say from the start that for so accomplished a writer, Henry James had the startling tendency to hesitate and repeat – almost to stutter – when he spoke. His manner of speech seemed less a bumbling with words, however, than the rehearsing of finely-tuned sentences. To spare the reader superfluous repetition, I have striven to minimize this characteristic.

In point of fact, James' voice was rich and melodious, almost mesmerizing; and I was pleased to observe that Sherlock Holmes was immediately engaged. As I have reported elsewhere, the previous spring had been a difficult time for my friend. He'd been worn down by the months he'd devoted to resolving the matter of the Netherland-Sumatra Company, not to mention the unpleasant business near Reigate in Surrey where ironically he'd gone to regain his strength. To see him devote his complete attention to Henry James was most reassuring indeed.

I hoped it would be equally reassuring to James; for as he sat drumming his fingers on the velvet arm of the chair, he certainly looked in need of some sort of aid.

"You don't mind if I smoke," said Holmes. It was more of

a statement than a question, and it left to me the obligation of offering James a cigar.

"Not today, Doctor," said he, waving off the suggestion. "I'm – I'm in need of quick answers. This is not a social call."

Holmes flashed a smile as he filled his briar with dark shag. "How can I be of service?"

"It's a moral issue, Mr. Holmes," said James and immediately got to the point. "An acquaintance of mine has gone missing. Since I'm the one responsible for having gotten him into a sticky situation, I feel responsible for finding out what's become of him." He placed one hand on top of the other, interlocking his fingers in the process. It was as if he was signalling the complexity of the story he was about to tell.

"Pray, start at the beginning," said Holmes, blowing a blue cloud upward.

"The acquaintance in question, gentlemen, one Thomas Warren, arrived in London from New York at the end of the summer. He's an aspiring young academic, though a bit headstrong and compulsive. He's a professor – an instructor – at the University of Virginia, and the two of us have exchanged some correspondence. He hopes to advance his career through a biography of the American poet, Jeremy Aspen – Jeremy Bishop Aspen."

"Jeremy Aspen," I repeated. It was a name unfamiliar to me.

Holmes, who took little interest in poetry, showed no recognition at all.

James pulled at his beard. He resembled a frustrated instructor, annoyed that his students had not remembered his previous lecture. "Aspen was famous for the romantic poetry he composed at the turn of the century. His devotees call him 'The Orpheus of the New World'. A few months ago, I learned through my arcane literary connections that a former paramour of Aspen, a woman named Olivia Borden, is rumoured still to be living in London. I forwarded this information to Professor Warren, and so great – so intense – was his interest that he dropped everything he'd been doing and immediately sailed to England."

"Quite the dedicated scholar," I chuckled.

A frosty glare quieted me. "I thought so too, Doctor; but he's gone beyond so benign a description. He considers Aspen a veritable god. More to the point, he's obsessed with the idea that Miss Borden will further his career. He believes that not only could she be a fountain of knowledge regarding Aspen, but that she might actually possess letters of an intimate nature from Aspen himself. Such a find – such a discovery – would elevate Warren's career in an instant."

"The paramour of a poet who wrote so long ago?" said I. "She must be well advanced in years."

"Close to ninety, I should imagine," said James, waving away Holmes's smoke that had begun to envelop us all. "Her age explains Warren's haste. He rightly fears that she could die at any moment, in which case *his* moment would dissipate as well. Little is known of the years Aspen spent away from his home in New York, you see. Oh, we're well aware that he lived for some time in England – but nobody knows the details. The scholar – the researcher – who furnishes such information would certainly receive grand honours, and now Warren – thanks in great part to my encouragement – believes he can get the answer from this old woman, a lady with whom Aspen supposedly fell in love over seventy years ago. Warren thinks she must be the reclusive muse that scholars have been seeking for years."

"If these letters exist," I observed, "I imagine they'd be worth a fortune."

"To be sure, Dr. Watson," said James. "Thomas Warren's quite right. The discovery of such a woman would go far to establish his career. He can't afford to miss out."

"And how well has he succeeded?" Holmes asked.

"That's just it. I don't know. Not long after he got here, he wrote me a lengthy letter. He said he'd established that the old woman really does exist and that he'd been able to track her down to a run-down manor house in Southwark called The Hollows. She lives in rented rooms there with her niece."

Holmes exhaled another blue cloud. "You're a literary man yourself, Mr. James. Hasn't this singular information from Warren sparked a similar curiosity in you? Why haven't *you* met the woman yourself, for example?"

"A fair question, Mr. Holmes. Aspen, you see, is Warren's province. It's true that I did go there – to The Hollows – once – but only after Warren had gone missing. That's when I met the niece, a middle-aged spinster type, quite plain and matronly. I learned very little. Indeed, most all that I'm telling you I gleaned from Warren himself."

"Pah!" Holmes snorted. "Little comes from second-hand tales."

Henry James arched his eyebrows. Accomplished writer though he might be, I was certain he was unused to people discounting his narratives.

Nonetheless, he ran his hand across his balding head and continued. "Warren wrote me about an overgrown garden within the grounds. Apparently, he managed to convince the niece of his love for flora. More important, he convinced her of his need for seclusion. He told her he was a writer, you see, and required peace and quiet in order to compose. It was the grotesqueness of just such a garden, he told her, that soothed his soul. And I should imagine that she believed him."

"Quite so," murmured Holmes, the pipe clenched firmly between his teeth.

"The niece told him that her aunt craved money; and in the end, he offered the old woman much of his life savings for two rooms. He paid for three months the amount it might have cost him to stay in an exclusive flat for a year – that's how important the Aspen papers are to him. She agreed; and he delivered the money to her in gold in a bag of *chamois*-leather. Or so he told the story. Accompanied by his manservant, he moved in soon after and seemed to be getting along. I myself had just returned from a lengthy stay in Italy – Venice and Florence, in particular – and have been quite busy with my own writing. Quite frankly, I didn't think much about not having heard from him."

"How long has it been?"

Henry James looked to the ceiling the way some people do when they calculate sums. "It's three months since he moved into the house, the Hollows. But when I received no answer to a letter I sent him a few weeks ago, I myself went down there – to Southwark. That's when I encountered the niece. Rita Borden – Miss Rita, she's called. At first, she sounded worried. She said that she didn't know what had become of Mr. Warren – that he seemed to have disappeared. And that was all. Then she said she didn't want to talk to me. It was quite strange, really. She seemed both reticent and direct at the same time. All around, I must tell you, it was not too inviting a place."

"And the old woman – she still lives?"

James flashed a quick smile. "Yes – as far as I know. Though I for one never got to see her."

"And the Aspen papers?" Holmes asked, taking the pipe from his mouth. "I assume that while Warren was living at The Hollows, he never stumbled across them. If he had, I suspect he would have shared that knowledge with you."

"I don't know, Mr. Holmes. At the beginning of all this, I would have expected him to tell me of his discoveries. Now I'm not so sure. When I asked Miss Rita about his work, she shut the door in my face. That's when I thought of turning to you."

Sherlock Holmes put down the briar and smiled at Henry James.

Good fortune was smiling upon the writer as well. Appealing to my friend's talents was a sure-fire method of engaging his services.

"I would like it very much, Mr. Holmes, if you could go to Southwark – to the house – and find out what's become of Thomas Warren. It was I, after all, who set him off on this course; and it will be I who'll feel culpable should something tragic have happened to the poor fellow."

James reached into his inside coat pocket and produced a wallet. "Let us see what I can uncover before we talk finances, Mr. James.

Perhaps there will be very little mystery at all. What say you, Watson? Are you set for a drive to the Borough in search of a missing scholar this afternoon?"

I readily agreed. The pageboy could take a message to my wife, who was more than understanding when it came to matters involving Holmes. As for my surgery, I had no patients scheduled for the next day and could easily be spared.

"Dr. Watson and I will look into this matter, Mr. James. It seems quite the curious puzzle."

Shaking hands with Holmes and me, Henry James offered a formal nod. Then he turned and marched down the seventeen stairs to the outer door, his footfalls ringing steady and certain.

II

A hansom carried us to London Bridge and over the river into Southwark. As per James' instructions, we took the specified turnings below Long Lane and soon found ourselves in a low, wooded area where the abundance of foliage obliterated the afternoon sun. A final bend in the roadway brought us to the aging manor house known as The Hollows. Draped in darkness by the shade of the massive oaks that surrounded it, the structure appeared to be a single square – its two tall chimneys rising like bookends at each side; its once honey-coloured walls turned black by a century of soot, grime, and neglect. The curtained windows looked dark; many on the ground floor were barred. A rusting metal fence framed the primordial landscape, presenting to the unlucky visitor a tangle of gnarled and overgrown hedgerows.

Our driver pulled his horse up before the access road. The metal gates, mired in damp soil, might gape wide for eternity.

"Do you know this place?" Holmes asked the man.

"Aye," said he, pulling down the front of his cap as he surveyed the gloomy scene, "but just to pass by. Nobody in there but a pair of daft old ladies. There's some what calls 'em witches, but that's just a tale. They live in a couple of rooms downstairs; the rest of the place stays empty."

Holmes nodded and instructed him to wait: paying for the added time would be far easier than trying to hail another cab on this deserted road.

With a dank, cloying smell attacking our nostrils as soon as we set foot on the broken flagstones, Holmes and I quickly negotiated the irregular pathway through the unruly grounds. It came as no surprise to encounter neither bell nor knocker when we reached the entrance to the house, and Holmes pounded on the massive oak door with his fist.

After a few moments, it was opened but a few inches by a short young woman dressed in a blouse and skirt of white linen. She stared out at us suspiciously from beneath a single eyebrow extending above both eyes. Her black hair hung in a plait down her back to her waist.

"Si?" said she in Spanish through the small gap.

"Is your mistress in?" Holmes asked, but already we could sense someone else approaching behind her.

"Yes?" this latter asked, stepping in front of the maid and opening the door a few inches wider. She was a heavy-set, middle-aged woman draped in a formless dress of navy blue. "Rosa doesn't speak much English. What do you want?" She wore her dark hair tightly wound in a bun, its severity accenting her aquiline nose; and she stared at us with wide-set eyes. This was obviously the matronly niece,

Rita Borden, about whom Henry James had spoken.

"Yes?" she asked again.

"You are Miss Borden? Miss Rita Borden?"

"I am Miss Rita. And who are you, I should like to know?"

"My name is Sherlock Homes, and we're looking for a gentleman who lodges here, Mr. Thomas Warren."

"Oh," said she. "He's gone. Left suddenly, he did, without even taking his man. I haven't seen him in days – though it seems much longer."

There was sadness in her voice. But suddenly, just as Henry James had forewarned, she countered, "And what's it to you?"

"I'm a colleague of Mr. Warren," Holmes lied.

"You're another book critic then?" said she with a touch of venom.

"Not exactly. But we haven't heard from him in months, and we are concerned about his welfare."

She smirked. "He said he was interested in our garden. That's what he told my aunt. He said he wanted to rent a room, but she told him no."

"And yet I understand that he did secure lodgings here. What changed your aunt's mind?"

"Money, of course. Lots of it. Say, you do ask a lot of questions. I don't know why I should be telling you all this."

"To help find Mr. Warren, of course."

Holmes seemed to be offering hope, and she brightened a bit at his response. "My aunt gets a trifling amount each year from someone in America – hardly enough for us to live on. That's why she accepted a lodger. She wants the money for *me*."

During the course of this discussion, Miss Rita had allowed the door to open wider, and it was through this larger gap that I gazed upon the ancient woman herself. The maidservant had pushed towards the door a three-wheeled Bath-chair. Staring up at us from its brown, wickerwork seat was a decrepit little figure cloaked in black – or in what must have at one time been black; her dress was now a faded dark-grey, worn shiny by many years of wear. Sitting hunched over like that, she could have been a hundred years old.

Henry James' estimate, however, was probably nearer to the mark. She had to be close to ninety – infirm, frail, desiccated. Breathing seemed to be a chore as well. But it was not her cadaverous form that caused the most alarm. That distinction fell to a black veil of tightly drawn lace that covered the upper half of her visage, leaving visible only her withered lips and skeletal jaw. It was as if she was wearing a ghastly mask. Worse, in the darkness of the room, though you could barely discern her eyes, you still had the sense that they were boring right into you.

"Who's there, Rita?" she called in a grating voice. "Who's come to disturb our afternoon?"

"Two men looking after Mr. Warren." Her tone was matter-of-fact. "Show them in, dear. *They* might have money as well."

Miss Rita led us into a large sitting room, the thick green-velvet curtains pulled shut before a row of French windows. Heavy crossbeams ran across the ceiling, and oak panelling lined the walls. Although white sheets covered most of the furniture, a few wooden chairs and a low mahogany table stood open in a far corner, illuminated by a pair of yellow candles. One got the feeling the room had looked like this for ages.

The old woman leaned forward and gestured for us to sit down. "We're looking for Thomas Warren, Miss Borden," Holmes said as soon as we were seated. "We know that he roomed here for months and has now disappeared. We were hoping you might shed some light on the matter."

Below the unyielding vizard, the old lady worked a small smile – a sort of smirk, actually.

"He came here under false pretences," she rasped. "He said he valued our old garden. He said it was exactly the kind of quiet place he was looking for in which to do his writing. He said he'd seen it through the fence and wanted to revive it. All it needed was some work, he said. He promised to find some geraniums or 'Jack Frost' that would flourish in the shade. He festooned the house with flowers. For weeks on end he played his game, and only lately did he show his hand."

"He talked to me of plants and nature as well," added Miss Rita. "At first. Then he moved on to art and books. It took him months to get round to talking about the research he did on writers. And when I asked if he knew about Jeremy Aspen, he said he didn't know the name. Didn't know Aspen was a poet, he said. The rogue was lying, of course. In point of fact, he knows lots about Aspen. But it was only last week that he finally began asking about him. He said that since he did research on other writers, he might as well enquire about Aspen. He wanted to know if my aunt might have some papers or letters concerning the man."

"As if I would leave Mr. Aspen's papers lying about," the old lady said. "Once I realized that's all he was interested in," she added in a confidential whisper, "I told him he would never get them from me." In a sudden burst of energy, she hissed, "If I had any such papers to give, that is." This last utterance seemed to have tapped all of her strength; for after saying the words, she dropped back in her wickered chair and appeared to fall asleep.

Miss Rita gestured sympathetically at her aunt. "It's late," said the niece, rising and moving towards the entrance hall.

When she opened the door, we could see a finger of late-afternoon sunlight poking its way through the leaves. "I fancy you won't be nosing round here again," she said, her wide eyes registering a degree of triumph as she closed the door.

"That was no great help," said I as we walked along the broken flags. "Not only did we learn nothing about Warren, but we haven't even determined that the Aspen papers are real."

"Did you not notice, Watson, how Miss Borden spoke of the poet as 'Mr. Aspen'? When one refers to public figures that one doesn't know, one generally calls them by their surnames only."

"I've never thought of the matter."

"Well, please do. We say, 'Shakespeare wrote' or 'Shakespeare said'."

"Of course, now that you mention it."

"But when one speaks of an acquaintance, one employs a title like 'Mister'."

"And the old woman called the poet 'Mr. Aspen'."

"Precisely, old fellow. I'd be willing to wager that a relationship between Miss Borden and Jeremy Aspen is more fact that fiction."

"Then how do you explain Warren's disappearance? If she's the right lady, why would he have left?"

"Since I expect him to return, the reason doesn't concern me. No doubt, he was frustrated. He'd spent months cultivating his relationships with the two women and saw nothing come of it. As long as the papers are here, however – not to mention his manservant – he'll be back. The Aspen papers are too important for him to abandon."

The hansom stood where we'd left it; the sorrel horse was impatiently pawing the dirt.

"Back to Baker Street, if you please," Holmes instructed the driver as we climbed into the cab. To me he said, "I shall speak to the Irregulars." He was talking of the young street Arabs whom he frequently hired to provide information from the byways of London. "They can keep an eye on The Hollows for us. That way, when Warren does return, we shall know."

The carriage took off with a jolt, and Holmes leaned over to me. "After I instruct the boys, Watson, I think a dinner in the Strand might be in order."

I smiled in agreement, but Sherlock Holmes was already staring out the window submerged in thought. I don't imagine he noticed the pink and purple swirls of sunset painting the sky.

III

"Dead!" came the cry as the street urchin burst into our sitting room the next morning. We were just finishing breakfast when he gave us the news. "There's somebody in that house what's died! Popped their clog, didn't they? Hopped the twig!"

Sherlock Holmes put down his coffee and rose to meet the lad. "Who?" he demanded.

"Dunno, do I?" said the boy, brushing a lock of dirty brown hair from his eyes. "But I seen the wagon arrive. Only there was no black feathers on the horses. And no coffin inside. Just a bloke in a tall hat and black togs. He went into the house."

Sherlock Holmes was already donning his coat.

"Come, Watson! There's not a moment to lose! We must get to the body before it's taken away. That was the undertaker the boy saw – come to make final arrangements with Rita Borden."

Thomas Warren must have kept his own watch on The Hollows. For no sooner had the old lady died than Warren returned. In all probability, it was his manservant who'd informed him of her death. In any event Warren was already there when we arrived.

Rosa admitted us, and Holmes and I introduced ourselves in the sitting room. In black suit and sombre mien, Warren certainly dressed the part of a concerned mourner. Attired for a funeral, he had obviously packed his luggage for England contemplating the possibility of bereavement. Yet with those dark, penetrating eyes and black hair combed straight back, he appeared more dashing young suitor than heavy-hearted scholar.

"We're here at the behest of Henry James," Holmes

told the professor. "Mr. James is concerned with your whereabouts and the progress of your business."

"I'll contact him when it's appropriate," Warren said without much concern. "'*Comme il faut*', as the man himself likes to say."

Holmes and I exchanged glances, but fell in line behind Warren as he crossed the sitting room and, passing through the door to the ground-floor sleeping quarters, made his way to Olivia Borden's inner sanctum. It was there that Miss Rita stood beside the bed, the diminutive body of her aunt lying before her.

The late Olivia Borden commanded the centre of an anachronistic tableau. With her veil no longer in place, one could see the prominence of her aquiline nose and the roundness of her skull. Wrinkled hands folded on her chest, she was clothed in luminescent white, a dress most probably kept hidden away for this particular occasion. The threadbare quilt upon which she rested had yellowed over the years; and the bed itself, of Regency design, might have come from another century. Redundant hairbrushes and depleted unguents adorned the dressing table, and a mirror replete with spidery cracks presided over the futile homage to vanity. Atop the nearby chest of drawers, a japanned wooden box that could have contained any number of rings or necklaces or letters stood conveniently open – open and empty. With dusty white drapes covering the windows, the whole scene, illuminated as it was by floor-candelabras on either side of the bed, seemed a setting from some antique mystery play.

Warren had positioned himself next to Miss Rita and bowed his head. Despite his show of sympathy, I felt certain that his concern dealt less with the dead woman than with the papers she'd been suspected of possessing, the same papers presumably now in the custody of her niece.

We took our cue from Miss Rita and, following a decent period of respect, prepared to exit. I made one last visual sweep of the chamber, hoping I might detect evidence of someone's final frantic search for the missing papers. But there appeared no signs of disruption.

As I turned to leave, however, Holmes caught my arm. "Watson," he whispered. "Engage the others in conversation. I need time in here to examine the scene."

"I wonder," he now said to Miss Rita, "if you'd mind giving me a moment alone with your aunt. Many people will tell you that I am a private person who prefers to keep his personal thoughts strictly between the deceased and himself."

"You hardly knew the woman," she scoffed, but Holmes seemed sincere; and fortunately Miss Rita, no great master of recognizing deceit, needed no further convincing. For his part, Warren seemed eager to talk. Indeed, no sooner did we find our places in the sitting room than he began discussing what he knew of the elder Miss Borden and Jeremy Aspen.

"Looking at that old woman," said he, "you wouldn't think her to have been a beautiful, vivacious, even rebellious young lady. But she must have been all those things. It would explain why Aspen was attracted to her. For that matter, I often wonder how they met."

Miss Rita shrugged. "He came calling on her."

"But that's my point," said the professor. "Aspen was an aristocrat; Miss Borden's background was more modest. My guess is that she must have been connected to someone with whom the poet had dealings here in England. She could have been a governess to a child of one of Aspen's friends. Or the daughter of someone he'd employed – a secretary, perhaps, or a portrait painter. Americans love to have their images immortalized by English artists. Whatever the circumstances, she attracted the man – so much so that she became the object of his love. She was, after all, 'l'ange' in his cycle of love sonnets."

I shrugged my shoulders, hoping that the conversation would prevent the others from wondering what Holmes was up to.

Suddenly, Warren's eyes flashed, and he changed the subject. "I think she hid the papers somewhere." He pointed at a tall mahogany secretary's desk with brass fittings. "That was my first choice. I'd always suspected it was locked, but I couldn't be sure. Not that I would ever steal them, mind you; but a few weeks before her death, I finally worked up the courage to see if the desk would open. I was just about to test the lock when the old lady interrupted me."

"Why," Rita cried, "that must have been just before you left."

"In truth," Warren said, "she gave me quite the fright. 'Stop that!' she'd rasped while teetering on a cane in the doorway – all those months and I didn't even know she could walk. In such a fury was she that she tore off that infernal mask and threw it to the floor. That was when I saw her magnificent eyes."

"My word," I barely whispered.

"They were wide and deep and full of hatred. And yet, strange to say, they also filled me with a kind of comfort. For looking into those extraordinary orbs, I somehow felt closer to Aspen. Her rage at me was a short-lived imitation of the torrid flames that must have burned so brightly when she was in his arms, a fiery passion that I thought had been all but extinguished."

Warren's own eyes were wide open now, a man staring full-on into a vibrant past.

"'I know what you're looking for,' the old woman screeched, ' – why you've come here.' She nodded at the secretary desk. 'Go ahead and look inside, if you must.' Reluctantly, I tried the lid and, discovering that it was unlocked after all, lifted it open. I expected to discover nothing, and nothing is precisely what I found. The old woman stared triumphantly at me. It was when she turned and hobbled back to her room that I realized she would never be giving me the letters. Only when they passed to

Miss Rita might I have a chance of securing them. Mortified – and not a little angry – I left the house the next day."

Miss Rita sat open-mouthed. There was obviously a lot about her aunt she'd apparently never got to know.

Just then Rosa entered the room with two large vases of Calla lilies. "I ordered them," Warren said.

A look of admiration appeared in Miss Rita's wide-set eyes. I couldn't say whether she'd ever had a social engagement with a man, but she was certainly appreciative of Warren's gesture.

I, on the other hand, was more cynical. With the papers as Warren's goal, I couldn't help regarding all of his acts as empty motions. They were designed to get Miss Rita to share her aunt's literary trove with him. In fact, I was beginning to suspect that the letters had motivated the behaviours of everyone in that house. Perhaps the old woman had been dangling them in front of the professor to unite him with Miss Rita. Or perhaps the middle-aged spinster herself was hoping to inherit them and use them to entice the man.

Holmes's return interrupted my thoughts. He arrived in the sitting room just as Miss Rita was rising to help Rosa set up the flowers.

"It's a bit stuffy in here," he observed, striding to the green-velvet drapes. Drawing one of them aside, he opened the French window an inch or two. Then he turned back to Miss Rita. "One last question, if I may. Did your aunt write a will?"

Miss Rita looked down. "No. She had nothing to leave me." "Except for the papers," Thomas Warren muttered.

Holmes glared at the professor, but all he said was, "Don't fail to let Henry James know that you're safe." Then he motioned for us to leave, and once more we expressed our condolences to Miss Rita.

"If you don't mind my asking," Holmes said to her as we were about to exit, "should I want to pay my respects yet again, when will the undertaker come for your aunt."

"At nine o'clock tomorrow morning."

With Holmes nodding at the information, we left that frightful house and hurried back to our waiting hansom. I climbed in as under darkening skies my friend exchanged a few words with the driver. Then Holmes joined me, and we began our journey back to Baker Street. Or so I thought.

IV

After we'd made the first turn that hid us from The Hollows, the cab came to an abrupt halt. The horse whinnied in protest, but Holmes stepped out and bade me follow. He dropped a healthy number of coins in the driver's hand, and the two of us stood out in the road listening to the clink of the horse's hooves diminish as the hansom disappeared in the darkness.

"Should anyone be watching," he explained, "I wanted it to appear that we'd left. The old woman was murdered, Watson; and I fear there may be more violence yet to come."

"Murdered?" I cried. "But she looked so peaceful, Holmes. What makes you say such a thing?

"You know my methods, old fellow. As soon as I was alone with the body, I drew my lens and examined the corpse. It was absurdly simple to discover the bits of down in Miss Borden's nostrils, the tiny feathers she must have inhaled gasping for her final breaths with a pillow held down over her face."

"Who committed this heinous act?"

"That is what I hope to confirm tonight."

"But, Holmes, surely we must inform the police."

"We don't have the time," said he, shaking his head. He then motioned me to follow, continuing his explanation as we moved down the dark road towards The Hollows. "We know that Olivia Borden's body will be collected by the undertaker tomorrow morning at nine. I fear that the immediacy of that appointment may precipitate some harmful action."

"You think that Miss Rita is in danger then?"

Holmes smiled. "On one level, I think not. The death of the old woman leaves the niece as the sole link to the papers. Anyone seeking the papers would be foolish to silence her."

"Unless," I added, "the miscreant has already acquired them."

"If he had acquired them, Watson, he would no longer be here." We were approaching the house now, and Holmes lowered his voice. "When I searched the old woman's room, I spied some sheets that appeared dishevelled on the far side of the bed. I immediately ran my hand beneath the upper mattress."

"Did you find anything?"

"A single scrap of very old foolscap containing a few strokes of faded ink. But even so small a morsel was enough to suggest that somehow the withered old woman had mustered the strength to hide the papers between her mattresses."

"Surely such a hiding place could not be secure. When Rosa changed the bedding, she'd discover the cache."

"You're right, of course," replied Holmes. "Perhaps Olivia Borden had originally kept them in the secretary desk just as Warren suspected or even in the japanned box so conveniently left open for us. But move them she did, and somehow – maybe with Rosa's help – hid them beneath her mattress. In any case, I suspect that by now Rita has found her aunt's hiding place – or may even have been given the papers. In any case, Rita's probably the only one who knows their current location."

I was about to respond; but we had reached the metal fence, and Holmes put his finger to his lips. In the darkness, we slipped through the open gates and tiptoed to the garden at the side of the building. It was here that we encountered the French window that earlier Holmes had so presciently left open. Although we could see nothing of the sitting room through the curtained glass, we could hear quite clearly the conversation that was going on inside.

"I thought that you liked spending time with me," Miss Rita was saying to Warren.

"Of course, I do," said the professor. "I enjoy your company. Remember those summer evenings out in the garden?"

"Yes," she sighed. "They were grand." You could hear the longing in her voice. "For years I've been imprisoned here with my aunt. And then you came round, someone who took an interest in me."

There was a moment of awkward silence. I imagined Warren dwelling on her final few words. "Now listen," he said at last. "I don't believe I've ever acted in an ungentlemanly manner towards you."

"I thought that the flowers –"

"They were intended for your aunt as well as for you."

"So you might get the papers. Perhaps that's what my aunt was thinking all along. In the end, bringing the two of us together must have meant more to her than spending her final hours with her niece."

Warren wouldn't give in. "I should imagine that all along her plan had been to give me the papers."

"No!" said Miss Rita firmly. "She never wanted outsiders to get their hands on them." There was a pause of a few moments during which Miss Rita must have been fashioning her most convincing smile and most flirtatious voice. "Now if you were a relation...."

The word could have but one meaning. "Me – and you?" Warren spat out.

"I've liked our time together."

"But for the rest of our lives? Not even the receipt of all your aunt's papers would be worth such misery!"

We heard her gasp and then the rustle of clothing and the stomp of heavy feet. Warren had obviously stood and was about to make a grand exit up the stairs to his room. "I'll be leaving in the morning!" he shouted. "Early!"

Muted sobs filled the silence.

Sitting on the damp ground by the open window, we managed to stay awake through an uneventful night. With only the routine activities of nocturnal creatures to distract us – mice scrabbling among the tree roots, crickets drumming their songs, an owl hooting his displeasure at our presence – we had to wait until the next morning for human passions to become enflamed.

Sometime before dawn, Holmes reached inside the window and, adjusting the green-velvet curtains that had blocked our view, created a gap of about half-an-inch through which we could peer. The morning activities in the house played out before us as if we were attending the theatre. Off-stage, the clatter of dishes and clanging of pans announced that Rosa was preparing breakfast in the kitchen. At half-seven, Miss Rita made her entrance from the sleeping quarters on the ground floor. Dressed in austere black, she was prepared for her meeting with the undertaker. At almost the same moment, as if he'd been waiting, Thomas Warren emerged from his chamber and hurried down the stairs. Despite his threat to leave before the removal of the body, he wore the same black suit we'd seen the previous day. Miss Rita turned at his approach, a melancholy look colouring her down-cast face.

"I'm sorry," Warren said, reaching for her right hand. "I've been cruel. I should have taken your proposal more seriously last night."

She raised her head.

"In fact," he said, sounding full of contrition, "I've given myself the chance to examine your offer once more, and I believe I now see much wisdom in its implementation. I owe my career to the securing of those papers; and while I did all I could in the most proper way to obtain them from your aunt, I believe she never seriously appreciated my efforts. I think that for as long as she lived, she intended to use those papers as bait to bring me closer to you."

Miss Rita's wide eyes looked even wider. And more melancholy.

Perhaps she sensed what Warren was about to suggest.

"In fact, I believe we should honour your aunt's wishes and agree to such a union. I believe she intended for you to do with them exactly as you had proposed to me last night. I am, you see, quite prepared to accept your aunt's papers – the Aspen papers, if you will – as a dowry."

At some point during Warren's last few words, Miss Rita's left hand had begun a slow journey upward until it was covering her now open mouth.

"Why, what's the matter?" asked Warren. "I know it's what you want. Everyone will be pleased. You will get a husband; I will get the letters; and your aunt's memory will be honoured."

Miss Rita lowered her head.

"What's the matter?" Warren asked again. His eyes signalled fear; his tone had grown desperate.

"Oh, Thomas," she said slowly, "I burned the papers last night.

Once you refused me, I saw no point in keeping them."

"You burned them? The key to my life's work?"

"I was going to have them buried with my aunt," she explained, realizing that she'd also destroyed any future she might have envisioned with this man. "But you made me so angry last night that I burned them one by one. It took a long time."

Warren's eyes began to bulge. "After what I've already done?" he muttered, his face turning dangerously red.

"What?"

"And to think," he snarled, "I almost found you charming."

"We can still marry," Miss Rita urged. "You'll see. I can make you a good wife."

Thomas Warren glared at her. The silence seemed

interminable. In the end, he threw back his head and laughed. It was a loud, raucous laugh, but it slowly transformed itself into a maniacal shriek. Suddenly, he was upon her, his white fingers tightly gripping her throat.

Without a word, Holmes sprang up, jerked open the French window and raced towards the struggling pair. Wrapping an arm around Warren's neck, he yanked him off the poor woman, who fell heavily to her knees on the hardwood floor.

In an instant, I had joined Holmes; and between us we managed to wrestle Thomas Warren onto one of the sheet-covered armchairs. Rosa ran out from the kitchen to see what the trouble was. She helped her mistress to stand, and Holmes ordered her to go out in the street to find the nearest constable.

"*La policía!*" he instructed.

Soon we heard the blast of a police whistle, and within the hour Inspector Gregson arrived at The Hollows.

Not long thereafter, we had the satisfaction of seeing Thomas Warren charged with the murder of Miss Olivia Borden – whom he confessed to smothering after he'd secretly returned to the house – and the attempted murder of Miss Rita Borden. Between two uniformed officers, he was marched to the police van, which immediately drove off in the direction of Scotland Yard.

As it clattered down the road, it passed the undertaker's hearse, which was just then approaching the house.

V

The following afternoon, Henry James joined us for tea at Baker Street. Holmes had sent a request to the writer at his rooms in De Vere Gardens following Warren's arrest, and James eagerly accepted. In addition to the tea, Mrs. Hudson set out small chocolate biscuits and a few of the sugary doughnuts James was known to enjoy.

Sherlock Holmes reported the details of the case to our guest as we sampled our tea.

"Good Lord," said James, when Holmes had finished. "I had no idea my letter regarding Jeremy Aspen would create – would weave – such a tangled skein."

"More tangled than you can imagine, Mr. James," Holmes observed. "For it is my conjecture that the Aspen papers contained more value of a personal nature than even your world of *belles-lettres* could estimate. I have no valid proof, you understand; but judging from my own observations – the similar facial structures, the widespread eyes, the curved nose – not to mention the concern that Olivia Borden expressed regarding her niece's welfare – I can only conclude that a major topic of the correspondence between Jeremy Aspen and his mistress was the welfare of their child – a daughter I believe to be Miss Rita Borden."

At this revelation, the doughnut Henry James was poised to devour fell onto his plate.

"And does Miss Rita know of your conjecture?" I asked.

"Only if she read the letters before she burned them – and, of course, only if my supposition is accurate. Based on so little evidence, it is certainly nothing I would share with her."

James took a small bite of the doughnut he'd dropped. "So," he said after finishing the morsel, "in addition to the tale – the mystery – surrounding the Aspen papers, we also have a story dealing with the secret love-child of a writer and his mistress. Not to mention the cunning machinations of a so-called scholar."

"Just so, Mr. James," said Holmes.

The author didn't respond for a moment. Staring off as they were, his grey eyes suggested his mind was somewhere else. If my own writing experiences were any model, I imagined him already at work, composing in his head some sort of novel dealing with the bizarre triangle of old woman, forlorn niece, and obsessed academic.

"One writer to another, Mr. James," I dared to say, "quite a story, is it not?"

"Indeed, Dr. Watson. Perhaps one we might both attempt to record – each in his own fashion, of course."

"An excellent suggestion," said I, already devaluing my factual narrative when compared with the intimate psychological embellishments so typical of James' fiction. His ornate and methodical style could perfectly reflect the labyrinthine twists and turns of a mind diseased.

"I would, of course, purge the story of obvious references," said he. "And shift the scene of the adventure to somewhere outside of London. Maybe even outside of England." Suddenly, he clapped his hands together, the notion of subterfuge obviously gaining in appeal. "Who knows?" he cried. "Perhaps I'll even fudge or doctor my notebooks – change Jeremy Aspen to Byron. Or Shelley."

Holmes nodded in appreciation. He often worried about the inadvertent but harmful revelations that occasionally found their way into my own accounts of his cases.

"I shall walk – no, I shall drive – to the National Gallery this very afternoon and look at landscapes for inspiration. Turner's watercolours of Venice might be just the thing!"

Sherlock Holmes poured himself more tea. "I envy you, Mr. James. The world of detection offers no such escape. My boundaries are limited by the rules of logic and the confines of reality. The detective cannot go willy-nilly where inspiration calls him."

"Ah, yes, Mr. Holmes," said Henry James. "But it is the claustrophobia created by such rules that leads the literary artist to the world of fiction. Imagination trumps reality every time."

Such abstract arguments usually make my head spin. But on this occasion, I was ready to do battle. "I – I take your remark as a challenge, sir," said I to Henry James. "Let us each report the story of the Aspen papers in our own manner and leave it to posterity to judge who has rendered the stronger case."

With a smile, Holmes pointed first at the gasogene and then at the spirit case. I understood his gestures and, producing three glasses, mixed the sparkling water with brandy. Once everyone was served, we hoisted our drinks.

"To the judgment of posterity," proclaimed Sherlock Holmes. "Hear, hear," Henry James chimed in, and then the three of us emptied our glasses.

The Ululation of Wolves

by Steve Mountain

The wolf howled.
He knew when his leader was dead. The crisp, red, warm smell of life was becoming tinged with the acid, blue, icy smell of death, creeping like a snake through the early spring air. Ahead lay a time of uncertainty.
– a new leader would have to be chosen.
One by one, more wolves joined the mournful lament.

Sharing accommodation with Holmes was never dull. We had been at Baker Street for seven years, and yet still I could rarely predict at the start of a day what would have come to pass by that day's end. One day would perhaps herald the start of a protracted adventure, another would end having resolved a seemingly intractable problem in a matter of hours due to Holmes's genius. My least favoured, of course, were those days when nothing happened and which led to monotony and depression, and the inevitable arguments over his use of various substances to ward off the effects. But whether with work or without, Holmes had become a rare attraction, no part due to my efforts (I felt) once my reports of his successes had started to be published.

This day had started typically enough; Mrs. Hudson had

brought our breakfast and Holmes was settling down after reading the newspaper when we heard a commotion in the street. Holmes rose to see what was unfolding below.

"Someone in a hurry!" he exclaimed, returning to his seat. "I wonder what he wants of us?"

"Perhaps nothing at all," I replied. "It is entirely possible for people to have business of their own without conferring on them the need to make use of your services."

He smiled, a slight look of pity on his face. He seemed to be counting under his breath.

Shortly there was a violent knocking at the door, which we heard Mrs. Hudson open. Holmes looked to me and rubbed his hands. "Adventure?"

"How did you know – as if I should dare ask?"

He passed me a telegram as he rose. "This was delivered earlier, whilst you were getting dressed."

I read it quickly, and gave it back. "Adventure indeed, Holmes. Mr. Reynolds appears in desperate requirement of you."

"I think perhaps his desperation stems from an understandable lack of progress with more conventional means of investigation."

Shortly afterwards, our guest was sitting in the chair facing me, flushed and breathless from his exertions in reaching us from the station in under ten minutes. Holmes stood over him.

"Brandy?"

Reynolds politely accepted Holmes's offer and took the glass with trembling hands. He seemed to relax slightly. I made to offer a cigar, but was declined. Holmes walked back to the window and looked down onto the late morning bustle of Baker Street. The spring sunshine was streaming through the bay, against which he then half drew the curtain and returned to his seat. Dust hung in the air. Our visitor drew a deep sigh.

"So," said Holmes, "Tell me what brings you from

Ellington House.

Your telegram spoke of great urgency."

"Nothing less than murder, Mr. Holmes," replied our visitor. "But the local force are at a loss," he added. "So they have sent in the Metropolitan force, led by an Inspector Lestrade I believe –" Holmes coughed quietly –"but all I know is that from the good Doctor's account, we need *you*, Mr. Holmes, to solve this." Holmes raised an eyebrow.

My pride was short lived. "The good Doctor's account paints my successes in an overly dramatic light which I fear the reality may fail to live up to," replied Holmes. "There have been situations in which I have had to admit defeat or error."

Reynolds laughed. "Not so, Mr. Holmes! I know some of those with whom you have had dealings. We gentlemen's gentlemen share many secrets, I can assure you."

Some colour came to Holmes's cheeks. "Pleasantries aside, then, tell me what troubles you. From the beginning." He sat back in his chair and lit his pipe as Reynolds started to recount his tale.

"I am – was – Sir Cedric Wolfe's valet."

"The Director of the London and Colonial Bank," interrupted Holmes.

"As you say, Mr. Holmes. I have been in my post these past eleven years and can vouchsafe my master as being a man of honour and deserving of total respect."

"The perfect master, then," I opined.

"In many ways, yes, Doctor," replied Reynolds. "He was seen by some to be a hard man, cold even, but fair. He had responsibilities which he took very seriously, and sometimes I felt these weighed heavily on him. Like all of us he had his ways but, indeed, a better master I have not served in twenty years. He was always the gentleman to me."

"We all know about little ways, don't we, Holmes?" I said. Holmes waved my comment aside impatiently, although I caught a glimpse of a wry smile.

"When you say, 'ways', what do you mean?" Holmes enquired. "In detail, please."

Reynolds thought for a moment, as if marshalling his thoughts. "He was a pedant, Mr. Holmes. Everything he used had to be under his control – stamped, embroidered or engraved with the family crest, even down to the linen, crockery, cutlery; the curtains were made specially with the crest within the woven design. Visitors have to sit at specific places at table. You could set a clock by his routines.

"I have started rather negatively I fear – please forgive me. Mr. Holmes, my master was a great man, rich of course through his work, but generous in equal measure to those to whom he chose to show liberality. Always on his terms, though! The Ellington estate is only small, some two hundred acres of Buckinghamshire park and farmland, and so has only a small number of house and estate staff. He cared passionately for the good of the estate, which he inherited from his father some eight years ago, and he his father before that – six generations in all, Mr. Holmes." He paused; Holmes drew quietly on his pipe.

"Perhaps he cared for the estate more than he cared for those closer to him in familial ties – but that was the measure of him. As to his 'ways', well, as I said everything had to be just so, and he was unnerved and became anxious and upset if anything was different or out of place. He was an insecure man, Mr. Holmes, and afraid of the dark. Not insecure in his profession, of course," he added quickly, "in which he was peerless; but he oft spoke to me of various fears. And...." He paused again. When he next spoke, I thought I detected a slight air of reserve in his voice. "He kept the menagerie his grandfather started half-a-century ago."

"A zoo? What animals?" I asked.

"Only one species now, Doctor. In former times it included big cats, for the old man spent long in Africa. But now, only wolves, and they unpenned. I think it is supposed to be a play, a poor one in my humble opinion, on the family name. I must admit to that collection being the one distasteful feature of my life serving him. One becomes almost a prisoner in the House and estate, there being a high wall running the full length of the boundary, and just the one gate as entrance, from the Bicester Road. A second wall surrounds the House, closer in, and the wolves have free run between the twin circuits of the walls."

"That would certainly play well to a fear of anything out of the ordinary," mused Holmes. "He would feel secure knowing he was so well guarded...."

"Indeed, Mr. Holmes," continued Reynolds. "I am not being disrespectful of my late master when I say that his bond with them was almost unnatural. He spent long hours studying them, and walking alone in the fields in their company. I believe they accepted him as one of their pack, or even the leader – they were all hand reared of course, so tame to a degree. But only with him, Mr. Holmes. Any stranger, or other member of the household who went out there without precaution, was in some danger. And that is what has got the local force so lost as to a solution to his murder. Despite the walls, despite the wolves running free. How could anyone have got in and done the deed? So the constabulary consider the murder must have been committed by someone already in the House. Inspector Lestrade concurs with this view."

"I expect he does," said Holmes. "It makes eminent sense. But it cannot be as simple as that, for otherwise you would not be here. Now, although I have of course read the account of the affair in the newspaper after I received your telegram, I would like to hear it in your own words."

Over the next hour, Reynolds explained to us the events of that fateful night at length. Holmes stopped him at a number of points to clarify details, whilst I made hurried notes.

Two days earlier, on the evening of the 22nd March (so Reynolds recounted), all had seemed tolerably well. His master had followed all his usual habits, although he seemed troubled, by what he would not share. After dinner at six he had taken leave of the household – his wife Lady Elizabeth, their teenaged son Thomas and daughter Sarah, together with their guests – a Mr. Wilson, who was an old school friend; Mr. Graham, a neighbour from the village; and Mr. Turner, a business associate who had been dealing with a land transaction on the Estate. Sir Cedric had gone straight to his room and, as was his custom, locked the door to conclude business affairs for the day in solitude.

For the rest of the evening, they had all retired to the Games Room. From about seven, the gentlemen, including Thomas, were left to continue whilst the two ladies took their leave for the kitchens to plan with the staff the meal for the following day – a special luncheon to be given to welcome Colonel Sir Jerome Russett to the village upon his return from the colonies. This concluded, the ladies had retired to the Drawing Room where they were later joined by Thomas, and passed the rest of the evening sewing, the boy reading quietly in a corner.

At nine, Reynolds had himself withdrawn to his chamber – a room next to that of Sir Cedric, and through which anyone wishing to communicate with his master would have to pass. At about eleven, it was reported that the children had retired to their rooms and Lady Wolfe to hers, and come midnight the rest of the household and their guests were in their beds. The Butler, Maddison, had reported that when he did his final rounds of the House all the doors and windows were secure.

"At seven yesterday morning, I rose and started to prepare my master's clothes and breakfast. As by usual custom, it was Lady Wolfe who, at eight, went to her husband's room with the breakfast I had prepared, and...." At this point Reynolds' voice broke. My further offer of brandy was gratefully accepted. Holmes drummed his fingers on the arm of his chair whilst the man regained his control. ". . . They couldn't open the door. Normally my master unlocked it when he awoke."

"Did you check it was unlocked when you arose?" asked Holmes.

"I admit I had not checked whether it was locked or unlocked. I do not check it every day by rule, for there is no need to do so. That is how the house works, Mr. Holmes – he always unlocks it. That is the routine. We had to break down the door. He was sitting in his chair facing the fireplace, back to the window. The fire was dead...and so was he. He had been stabbed. My mistress was hysterical and took to her bed."

"That tallies with the newspaper account," said Holmes. "Unusually accurate for a change. Please, describe the room. Just so I can clearly picture the setting."

Reynolds seemed taken aback. "Well, Mr. Holmes, it's just an ordinary bedroom, simply furnished. On the ground floor; my master worked and slept in that room all the time I have been in service. A large fireplace, which was prepared and lit at five-thirty each evening at this time of year. A writing desk. A bedside table, with his supply of candles for when the nights are dark – the House will be late getting an electricity supply, for he did not hold with it. French windows to the gardens, which are locked out of use, even in the summer. Curtains always half drawn; he would sometimes watch the wolves roaming the grounds before retiring to his bed. Please believe me when I say that nothing was out of the ordinary to any previous day."

"So what has got our professional friends so baffled?"

"We know he was alive for some time after ten. But everyone in the house was accounted for at and after that time. And no-one could get in from outside without falling prey to the wolves; or at the very least, rousing them, which would have been heard. I was in the room next door, and heard nothing. No-one came through my room."

"Ten?" I asked. "How do you know?"

"He lit a candle after that time. His candles are custom

made to burn for exactly...." He saw Holmes's quizzical glance, so he corrected himself. "Near enough, give or take maybe ten minutes, for ten hours, and the candle was burning low as we entered the room at eight yesterday morning. We know no-one entered his room – it was locked and his key was on the bedside table. No-one went through my room once I settled down to my end of day tasks at nine. No-one was out of sight of anyone else at any time when he could have been killed. And yet, he is dead."

"There is no duplicate key?" asked Holmes.

"Only one that I hold, in case of emergency. I can vouch it was not away from my person all night."

"Could not someone have got into the room from the window?" I asked. "He slept on the ground floor, you say." Almost as soon as the words were out of my mouth, I knew the mistake I had made.

"Locked and bolted out of use, as I said, and all the glass intact. And of course the wolves...."

"Keep up, Watson!" interrupted Holmes impatiently. Then to our visitor, "What do you know of the three guests?"

"Turner has been dealing with matters of the Estate – land sales, lettings, purchases – for as long as I have been at the House. His father before him held the same station, with the elder Mr. Wolfe. My master looked after him and his family well. Graham owns the lodge next to Ellington House, and has been a family friend for many years. He is a regular visitor and takes great interest in the well-being of the children. I admit I don't know much about Wilson, but he and my master seemed to get on very well. They had not met up these past twenty years, evidently. He was fascinated and frightened in equal measure by the wolves."

"What did your late master think of Mr. Graham's interest in the children?" I asked.

"I have never detected any concern on his part."

Holmes turned to me with a twinkle in his eye. "Your thoughts?"

I took a deep breath, and looked to Reynolds with a resigned smile. "He does this, just to show how good he is. Inevitably, whatever I say will be wrong."

"Far from it, my dear fellow!" interrupted Holmes. "But I do value your often refreshing views."

"Very well. We know nothing about this man Wilson. What brought him to the House just at this time? Surely suspicion has to fall first on him. Somehow he got into Wolfe's room and did the deed during the night."

"Very well; but how, Watson? That is what I am after."

"That's your job, Holmes," I replied. "You will draw me no further."

"Well, a fascinating diversion awaits us," said Holmes, suddenly warming to the task. "I think we will return with you to Ellington House. Let's see if we can help the local constabulary – and our friend Lestrade

– make some progress. But first, gentlemen, I need to spend a little time making use of 'Who's Who' and see if my library holds any clues. You may order a cab to the station for one hour's time, Watson. And there will be a telegram to send shortly."

Ellington House was reached by a short ride from the village station. The afternoon sun was starting to set behind the trees as we were driven along the curving driveway through park lands until the House came into view. It was not a large house, as such houses go, but, reflecting the reported character of its pedantic owner, not a blade of grass seemed out of place. Nonetheless, and perhaps unsurprisingly, an air of gloom seemed to hang over it. Off to the left, I noted we were being watched – two wolves lay under a stand of trees. Other shapes moved furtively in the bushes away to our right. On the light wind a single howl echoed around the gardens.

We came to a second gate, which was unlocked by Reynolds. A short ride onwards, and we were greeted at the front door of the house by Maddison. Most of the other staff had been given leave of absence, so only the family, their three visitors, and a young policeman from the local constabulary were about, along with Lady Wolfe's maid and the cook. Lestrade, or anyone else from the Metropolitan force for that matter, was no-where to be seen.

Holmes was led into the Games Room and had a short conversation with each of the three guests in turn. Turner was open and affable, but I thought the man Graham looked uncomfortable on questioning about his interest in the family; his statement that such interest was only made in light of Sir Cedric's coldness towards them, and his concern over their future education and well-being, seemed forced and unlikely to me, whilst Wilson seemed a most disagreeable sort, furtive and secretive.

"It's those blasted wolves, Mr. Holmes!" he exclaimed. "I'm sure one of these days no good will come of keeping them so unnaturally. Howling and calling to one another as they do, it's enough to put anyone off their game. Or their meal." The glass of whisky he held betrayed the shaking of his hand.

"Well, no good has come, Mr. Wilson. They seem quiet enough now," replied Holmes.

"Yes, I suppose so," he blustered. "But they frighten me, and I'm not sorry to say it. How anyone could go wandering about after dark knowing those things were around is beyond me. Only a ghost would want to do so."

The man who had been introduced as Turner sighed. "I tell you, no-one else saw it."

"What did you see?" asked Holmes sharply.

"I saw a figure moving across the lawn, after dark, whilst I was taking a break from the game. I'm convinced it could not have been anything from this world."

"No-one else saw it, Mr. Holmes," replied Turner, "even though he called me to the window. I think it was the drink playing tricks."

"I was as sober as any man!" exclaimed Wilson. "I did

see it I tell you! A ghostly figure, making quickly towards the outbuildings."

"Come, my friend," soothed Graham. "Take no heed. If you say you saw it, well, I believe you."

Turner snorted. "You were trying to put me off my game," he retorted to Wilson. "The boy was slowing us down, and you could see how that was affecting me."

"Gentlemen, please!" exclaimed Reynolds. "We have all suffered a great shock, and Mr. Holmes is here to help. Have respect, please!"

Holmes seemed satisfied of his enquiries. Wilson looked especially discomforted, and my suspicions of him grew. This story of his seeing a figure outside was clearly meant to distract attention, and once we were out of the room I shared this with Holmes.

His only reply was, "It may be of interest, Watson." I decided not to tempt Holmes's disapproval further by repeating my growing conviction that Wilson was somehow involved. Holmes would get to the truth, I knew.

Holmes spent a few minutes talking to the cook, and then, the interviews seemingly complete, spent the next half hour or so subjecting Sir Cedric's bedroom to a minute examination. The room had been sealed by the police as soon as they had arrived. On hands and knees, or even on occasion almost lying flat, he worked his way across the floor; and as he went he picked up various small items that had fallen on the carpet; here a few hairs, there a short piece of string. All went into an envelope. When he had finished he went to the window, checked the lock and bolts, and stood quietly looking out over the lawn towards a lake as the sun set, the curtains half drawn as usual across the French windows. He was seemingly in a world of his own. At one point he looked again at the contents of the envelope. Reynolds and I waited patiently.

"Was there anything – anything, mark you – out of the ordinary that night that you have not shared?" he asked at length. Reynolds thought long and hard. "I don't think so, Mr. Holmes," he replied. "There were the three guests of course in the house, so the routine was different in that respect....Ah, there was one thing which they commented on. Especially our Mr. Wilson. The wolves broke into howling at about eight. Only for a short time – I remember thinking they must have caught a deer, perhaps."

Holmes eyes were suddenly bright. "That is most suggestive, is it not, Watson?" he said. Regrettably the mystery was lost on me. He fell into silence again. "I would like to speak with her Ladyship, please," he then continued.

A few minutes later the lady was duly ushered into the room. Her eyes were red with crying; with her, her daughter also came for support. They sat together on the edge of the bed, holding hands.

"Please accept our sympathy in your sad loss," I said. I caught Holmes's sideways glance. "I know you wouldn't say it," I mouthed silently to him.

"Indeed," added Holmes. "Please, Lady Wolfe, I will not keep you a moment. I have but one question, just to clarify my thoughts you understand – you were with your daughter all evening once you had left the gentlemen to their games, yes?"

"Yes."

"All evening?" There was a definite emphasis on the 'all'. "As I said, yes."

"Oh. Then that is very sad," replied Holmes.

She looked at him in shock – and I likewise. "What do you mean by that, Holmes?" I muttered quietly. "Of course it is sad. This dear lady has lost her husband, and the young lady her father, in the most awful circumstances."

Holmes ignored my protestations. "Thank you, that will be all," he said, and dismissed them with a wave of his hand. When they had left, I addressed him angrily. "Do you really not understand the effect your thoughtless behaviour has on people, Holmes? The ladies need our sympathy and support, not your rudeness!"

"Perhaps they do," said Holmes. "But the case is all but solved nonetheless. I know who, and I know the when and broadly the why. I just need a few moments to determine the how." He produced a telegram from his pocket. "This is the response to the telegram I asked you to send whilst we were in Baker Street."

"Yes, I know it full well," I replied. "It came as we were leaving."

"It holds some interesting information about Colonel Sir Jerome Russett."

"You mean, he did it? But how? He wasn't seen in the house that night."

Holmes sighed. I could feel the approach of another assault on my already battered pride. "Watson, sometimes your inputs are most valuable. Other times – No, he did not do it, but he is the reason for why it was done."

"Pray, then, tell us," said Reynolds.

"First I must have a quiet word with the constable," said Holmes. He left the room; Reynolds and I exchanged glances whilst we waited. He returned a few minutes later, smiling broadly. "Capital! So, now, let us join the others. We have an old friend joining us as well."

Lestrade had just arrived, and was having his coat taken by Maddison as we entered the Great Hall. "Well, Mr. Holmes," he said, "I heard that you had been engaged, and I have to say that on this occasion I would be somewhat grateful of any assistance you can offer."

"This is a change, Lestrade!" I exclaimed.

"Come, come Watson," replied Holmes, "Do not be so harsh on our friend. Do not worry, Lestrade, I will not take this as a sign of your desire for regular use of my meagre talents. I am always ready and willing to help, as you well know, should help be requested. The story Mr. Reynolds has unfolded today merely piqued my interest."

"And I am glad of it, Mr. Holmes," replied the policeman.

"I cannot make head or tail of how the deed was done. From ten in the evening no-one was out of sight of anyone else, and yet murder was committed. After I was summoned, I spent most of yesterday and again today trying to see how it could work, but...."

"Have no fear, Lestrade," continued Holmes. "I believe I can help you with the solution, although of course the credit will be to the Metropolitan force. I have no desire for fame." I coughed quietly. "Beyond what has already been thrust upon me by the good Doctor of course," he continued, barely breaking his stride. "But first, a quiet word please."

Holmes and Lestrade left the room for a few moments and I heard snatches of a whispered conversation outside the door. "Arrest...walking...ghost...."

They returned and Lestrade took the constable aside as Holmes started to speak. "Key to the solution is that the murder did not take place when you think it did. Not at or after ten. It took place earlier. And if you ignore the supposed time of the murder, other opportunities present themselves. What I needed was a motive. Once I had that, then I merely had to construct the events of the night to place the murderer in the right place at the right time."

"So what is the motive, Holmes?" I asked.

"It is the oldest motive, I am afraid, Watson. But we will come to that."

"But, Mr. Holmes, I don't understand." Reynolds' voice was flat, shocked. "We know the murder could not be earlier than ten. The candle. It had not yet gone out as we broke the door down at eight in the morning. It is a ten hour candle. Even allowing for a few minutes' variation in the manufacture, I'm sorry, but you can't get the murder to happen earlier than when I was in my room next door to Sir Cedric. There just is not the variation in the candles to do that. I tell you, Sir Cedric was a man extremely upset by anything out of its usual routine. Samples were regularly tested. A candle burning longer than ten hours would have driven him mad."

"Nevertheless it had to be so," retorted Holmes. "Watson is familiar with my methods. Test everything. What is left after disregarding what does not fit the facts has to be the truth. The murder took place at about eight, not ten."

"How so precise?" asked Lestrade. "The wolves," replied Holmes.

"I'm sorry, Holmes," I interrupted. "Are you saying that you can pinpoint the time of a murder by the actions of the wolves?"

"Most certainly. Both Reynolds and your cook report that they broke into a veritable ululation of howling at eight. They knew their pack leader – for that, in effect, was what Sir Cedric was – had met his end."

"You are going to have to explain this, Mr. Holmes." Lestrade was clearly at the same time both impatient to know the solution, yet clearly in awe of Holmes's intellect.

"First, may I say that Master Thomas of course is totally innocent of any involvement in this sad chain of events." He turned to Thomas. "You joined your mother and sister in the Drawing Room when?"

"About eight thirty, sir. After our 'best of three' on the billiard table was concluded."

"So you see, the murder could have been committed at any time between the ladies leaving the Games Room at about seven, and eight thirty. By nine you were in the room next door to Sir Cedric, and would have heard if anything amiss was going on." He saw Reynolds' blank expression. "You see, between the time the ladies left the cook and until Master Thomas joined them in the Drawing Room, the two ladies were on their own."

Reynolds was shaking his head. "No...."

"But yes," replied Holmes. "You asked for a motive. Lady Wolfe loves the Colonel. But there is more to it than that. Have you noticed how alike Master Thomas is to his father, but Miss Sarah is not, nor strongly to her mother?"

"Yes, but that is common, Holmes," I responded.

"But *'Who's Who'* did lead me to a *Times* article about the Colonel.

An article which includes an illustration." "Stop! Enough!" exclaimed the lady.

"No, it must be out," replied Holmes. "Did you never tell your daughter that the Colonel was her father?"

The room was in turmoil for a moment. The young constable standing behind the chaise longue on which the ladies were sitting moved closer to it on a motion from Lestrade. Holmes waited for us to settle. Reynolds was shaking his head.

Lady Wolfe did not speak for a long time. Her daughter fixed her in her gaze, whilst the son sat groaning on a chair and buried his head in his hands. Finally it was the younger woman who spoke. "Mother told me the night my...father died. Just after dinner."

"When I learned the Colonel was coming back to the village," Lady Wolfe interrupted, "it was all I could do to plan for our future life together. I knew eventually my husband would find out about us, and thus we would be in danger. I have not loved him for many years, Mr. Holmes."

"So you killed him," said Holmes.

"He could be a brute if roused," she answered simply. The daughter nodded. "If once he had found out about us, please believe me, I knew it would then be my body you would be finding. I had to kill him before the Colonel arrived."

"That's not the master I know!" protested Reynolds. "He would never have acted in such a way!"

"But he would, Reynolds," replied Lady Wolfe simply. "He was not the saint you believe him to be. Not a bad man of course – I loved him once – but cold and dismissive to me, and others. You must have seen that. He loved his wolves more than any of us."

"I have hated him for years," added the young woman,

"and I'm glad I am free to say that now." Reynolds gasped.

"To others outside the family, Reynolds, your master was caring and attentive," said Holmes. "But it is sometimes the way. To those closest to him all he had left was a coldness, leaving them starved of love and affection...." He let the words tail off, and then continued sadly. "It does happen in families, sometimes...."

"No!" continued Reynolds. "It will not do. Even if the ladies were on their own between seven and eight-thirty as you say, you forget the candle. There is no way you can possibly get it to be alight at that time. I'm sorry, Mr. Holmes, but on this occasion I believe you are in error."

Holmes's response was measured. I knew from experience he did not like his deductions to be questioned in such a manner, and saw his knuckles whiten slightly. "So how did the night's events unfold, I ask?" he said quietly. "Well, when the ladies left the gentlemen to their game, we know they went to the kitchens, ostensibly to discuss the meal arrangements for the Colonel's visit. Doubtless as a result of my more informal questioning, Lestrade, the cook now recalls that Lady Wolfe went outside for a few minutes, complaining of a headache and needing to walk in the fresh air. You missed that, and I am afraid as a result you made your enquiries more difficult than necessary, for on that one piece of information the whole matter rests.

"Lady Wolfe merely needed an excuse to go outside. Her route took her along the north side of the House, the same side as the Games Room. She was the so-called 'ghost' seen by Mr. Wilson, although he did not recognise her because of the lack of light. But note, she was seen walking with purpose and speed, not with leisure, towards the outbuildings. There is only one building along that frontage that can be reached without venturing into the wolves' enclosure – the ice house. That was the point at which I started to realise how she had committed the murder of her husband."

"She may have wished to choose a joint for the meat

course," I responded. "I know that's what my mother used to do."

"But in an establishment such as this, Watson, that is the cook's job – to choose the joint of meat for approval. Lady Wolfe went to the ice house for a very specific reason, did you not, madam?" The lady nodded. "You then made your way to your husband's room, whilst your daughter went to the Drawing Room. You had agreed to act as alibi for each other. So sad; involving your daughter in your crime."

"I'm not sorry," the daughter said quietly.

"But Sir Cedric's room was locked, Mr. Holmes!" exclaimed Reynolds. "I have the key, here." He held it up. I understood his motive, for I would do the same; trying to find a way of upholding the family honour in the face of what were becoming overwhelming odds.

"I had a copy made," whispered Lady Wolfe, "from my husband's key." Reynolds was crestfallen.

"So," continued Holmes, "you entered his room and killed him. He was sitting by the fire, back to the door and the window, and probably didn't hear you or see you coming. When the deed was done, you locked the door behind you, hid the key, and joined your daughter in the Drawing Room before Master Thomas arrived." She nodded. "Which brings us to the time of death. The evidence is most compelling for eight."

"Probably," she replied. "I didn't really look. All I knew was that I had to be back in the Drawing Room before Thomas came to join us. I knew they were playing best of three, so yes, perhaps eight was the time."

"Remember too," continued Holmes, "that the heat of the fire would have kept the body warm, so we cannot rely on that for an accurate assessment of the time of death. And we have evidence provided by the wolves."

"But the candle, Holmes," interrupted Lestrade. "We come back again to the candle. With respect, this scheme just does not work. It was still alight at eight in the morning."

"To which I reply, the ice house."

Lestrade looked blank, but all suddenly became clear to me. I remembered, almost from nowhere, something that Holmes had spoken about some years ago, in the early days of our acquaintance. "Of course!" I exclaimed. "Why, that's wonderful, Holmes!"

"Come, Watson, explain to our friends!" said Holmes. "You have spent long enough complaining about the experiments I undertake in our lodgings. Now you see why I invest my time thus."

My chance to redeem myself had come. "If you freeze a candle, it slows the rate of burn. So a ten hour candle could easily burn for a couple of additional hours."

"Splendid, Watson!" exclaimed Holmes. "I knew I could rely on you. Lady Wolfe had previously secreted a packet of candles in the ice house, which although is outside the main house is within the second wall and so safe from the roaming wolves. That is why you thought Sir Cedric was unsettled on the night of his death, Reynolds; he became aware somehow of the theft and being the kind of man he was, this would weigh on his mind. His security had been broken; how could that be? No doubt he started to suspect everyone of some hand in it.

"So armed as I was with that knowledge, I tested a scheme of events whereby the time of lighting the candle now moves earlier, to eight or thereabouts, and found no lack of supporting evidence. The final proof I needed was in what I picked up from the carpet." He took the envelope from his pocket and shook out the contents onto a side table. He showed a short piece of string to Reynolds. "You see here, a trimmed candle wick."

"I'm sorry...?" breathed Reynolds.

"To ensure a slow burn, the trick is to trim the wick close to the candle. The flame burns small and slowly, and together with the frozen wax gives plenty of time for the murder to take place whilst young Thomas was together with your visitors, and before you went to your own room, Reynolds."

I suppressed the urge to clap, but doubtless my face displayed enough of my emotions.

"But I am very disappointed nonetheless, in everyone," continued Holmes abruptly.

"Why, Holmes?" I asked, now suddenly unsure of what had been missed.

"Simply the candle itself," he replied. "It was obviously intended to mislead our professional colleagues into thinking that the time of death was after ten when Lady Wolfe was in others' company. And yet, two nights ago the moon was full and the weather was clear. We know the curtains were half drawn. So what with the firelight and the moonlight, why would he even need a candle? There would be enough light in the room to not need any other, even for someone scared of the dark."

"Of course!" said Lestrade. "How did we miss it?"

"Because you take what you see on face value. Let that be a lesson, especially to your colleagues in the local constabulary. As soon as I verified that the room was as it had been found, and seeing it faced full south, I knew the candle was the key to solving the case."

Lady Wolfe gave a cry and buried her face in her hands.

"It is a great irony, of course, but oftentimes it works thus. If the candle had not been lit," continued Holmes, "it would not have been so easy to solve this case. But now it seems you have another account to add to your collection, Watson. A good day's work, if I may be so bold."

The Case of the Vanishing Inn

by Stephen Wade

From time to time in these memoirs of my life with Sherlock Holmes, there emerges a case which has been eclipsed and consequently forgotten. This may be the result of accidental omission, or perhaps by an oversight by my good self, a man as fallible as the next, in spite of my desire to be meticulous in the chronicling of the remarkable detective work effected by my singular friend. This case is exactly that: it was a pleasure to discover my notes when revising some of my stray papers, and I assemble the narrative now, not without a little sense of personal pride at my part in it.

Holmes was away at the time. It was in early June, 1888, soon after the business with the King of Bohemia, and I firmly believe that the encounter with Irene Adler had been a strain upon Holmes's normally robust constitution; he had, of course, performed exceptionally well in that case. Whatever the reasons for his absence throughout that month – and I forget what called him away – the result was that I was left in sole charge of matters at Baker Street. The strange and challenging events of that month return vividly to my memory now that the writer in me attempts to retrieve them from the great backward and abysm of time, as the poet said.

It began with Inspector Lestrade arriving. Now I am aware that in the pages of my memoirs this little man tends to be depicted with less than flattering descriptions, and with some rather demeaning imagery. But to a certain extent he excelled himself in this adventure, and I value him a little more highly now.

I saw him arrive in a hansom cab across the road, as I was finding it hard to settle without the comforting presence of Holmes, silent though he would have been, at the breakfast table. I was staring out of the window, with no other motive than to relieve the tedium of being the sole inhabitant of that wonderfully intriguing lair of the great mind that was Sherlock Holmes.

A bare minute later Lestrade was shown in, and he was not alone. Behind him was a thin, athletic young man with a mere shadow of hair on his face where a beard would eventually flourish, given time. He was almost twice the height of Lestrade and crouched somewhat when addressed, so as not to seem distant and overbearing. He had rich brown hair, as I saw when he doffed his hat on being introduced, and a winning smile, conveying the optimism and joy of youth.

"Ah, good morning Dr. Watson. The sun is out and the day bodes well...and I must introduce you to Detective Constable Lees." The little man turned and nodded upwards. Lees shook my hand as Lestrade began an encomium on myself and my friend. "Lees, I want you to remember this place. Fix this address in your bobby's memory, and look upon it as your most fruitful resource in times when failure rears his ugly head. This is the office of Mr. Sherlock Holmes, a man whose talents have helped me solve a few complex cases, though I had done the hard work myself...yes...he has stepped in and offered a contribution."

A contribution, I thought, but held my tongue. Why, the little rogue was claiming to be far more than he was. He had the cheek to press the point. "Now, Dr. Watson, I have a special role just now. I have been given the task of teaching young Lees the ins and outs of trapping the bad 'uns of this great city of ours...and there are bad 'uns a plenty, as the doctor knows...." He looked at me and added, "Dr. Watson is not averse to firing his pistol at a desperate villain if extreme action is needed, oh no, a good man in a fight is your doctor. He's played his part in my cases, haven't you, Doctor?"

I had planned to offer them tea and crumpets, but I changed my mind after that last statement. The rat-faced upstart was playing the lead part in a sordid little farce, particularly to impress the young man who stood there, mouth almost dropping in awe as Lestrade gave his most audacious falsehood, "Now Lees, Holmes and Watson have more than once been behind me in some shadowy den of evil as I led the way, anxious to protect my civilian charges, useful though they sometimes prove to be."

That was too much. There was a rage building in me and I fought for self-control as I hinted that they must be very busy men and so on. But the little man smiled at me and said, "Oh, not before I tell you how I wish to recruit you for a mysterious appointment tomorrow."

"Do go on," I droned, expecting some ridiculous monologue of lies. "Dr. Watson...read this if you please." He handed me a sheet of paper which had been crumpled and creased in his coat pocket. It read:

> *Esteemed Inspector Lestrade,*
>
> *There is an instance of danger to a royal personage. Your talents are required. Be at the Old Charger Tavern, Poland Street, at seven tomorrow.*
>
> *You must come alone.*
>
> *One who cares for Britain*

He searched my face for a response and asked, with a note of swelling pride, "What do you make of that, sir?"

I decided to pander to his self-regard merely to have some sport. "Now, Inspector, this person asks particularly for you...not any Scotland Yard detective you see, but yourself! That is mighty complimentary. Of course, we know who the royal person is...."

He winked at me. "It's the Prince of Wales o'course. He loves to go down with the common people...he'll be in disguise, and creep in there for some female company...."

"He's right, Lees, listen to the man!" For what seemed like several minutes he beamed and then put his hands to his coat-lapels and swaggered so unashamedly that he needed a dash of normality, but I kept a straight face.

"Now Dr. Watson, I'm not going alone – I'm taking young Lees here, aren't I?"

"You are, sir, Mr. Lestrade, sir. I'll be there...to learn."

The young man, who had minded his manners and said nothing so far, had a broad northern accent, probably from Yorkshire. Holmes would have known which town he hailed from, and perhaps even how long he had resided in London.

"Nobody knows Lees, you see. He can come along and be...well, be invisible, I reckon!"

"I can step into a crowd and hide, in a trice, Mr. Lestrade. He's taught me everything about being a detective, Dr. Watson. He is a...well, He's an *eminence grise!*"

Lestrade was not sure whether or not he was being insulted. But he decided to pretend to understand and put on a false smile. "Yes, I am...one of those. See, Dr. Watson, these young Bobbies now, they've done more school now... see, He's quoting Latin. Now me and my mates down Lambeth, when we was learning, we had the school of the street."

Amused though I was with all this, I had to make a point. "Inspector...there's just one little detail about that letter...I have never heard of a public house called the Old Charger. Though it is some time since I was in Poland Street."

"Oh yes, well now there's a job for young Lees. Lees...go and find the place in Poland Street now...immediately, and report back to me at the Yard. Doctor Watson, I will see you there tomorrow at seven, right?"

Young Lees left in some haste, muttering the name of the inn, and then Lestrade did a little bow before putting his hat on again and saying, "Oh, and...bring your revolver, would you, old mate?"

The truth is that, after Lestrade left, I pondered the letter and I decided that it was probably written by some deranged anarchist, or perhaps a drunken poet, some person of that category. After all, why would a member of the royal family visit a rough place in that part of the city? I was not convinced by Lestrade's thoughts on the Prince of Wales. The thought of the Prince turning up there was ludicrous. But whatever the truth of the situation, I could not let him down; he was an old and valued acquaintance, when all said and done.

At five minutes to seven the next day, I turned into Poland Street off Oxford Street and looked around for the Old Charger. I thought I knew most London drinking-places, but that was a new name to me. However, to my surprise, after a steady walk of a few hundred yards I stepped across the road, having seen an inn-sign, and there it was: a splendid though well-worn picture of a grand old black horse swinging in the breeze.

The main saloon was packed with what were clearly the flotsam and jetsam of society: most were dishevelled and loud, some of them swaying around as if already worse for a superfluity of alcohol in their ravaged bodies. One or two young women were ensconced by the one long window, and a gaggle of stolid old men, ruddy faced and miserable, sat in one corner. Nobody appeared to notice me at all, and I ordered a glass of beer, with a polite enquiry to the landlord, who was a fat, happy soul with a greyish apron swathed around his middle and a wet beard. I asked if there was another room.

"Oh yes, upstairs of course, sir...we tends to get the more better types of coves what sits up there." As I listened, I could see no Lestrade or Lees anywhere in the mass of people milling around. "Tonight, as a matter of fact, it's occupied by a private club of gentlemen...leisure after their labours, as you might say."

"This must be a new establishment?" I asked. Holmes would have wanted facts, so I emulated his approach.

"You're quite right, guv'nor. We been here just free weeks. Is it free weeks, Lizzie?"

He addressed the question to a beautiful young woman who was serving a man with a pint of best mild. "Yes, about that father. Seems longer."

"You're very popular," I followed up, "Do you own the place?"

"Oh no...a foreign gentleman has it. German cove... Kurs...Kust...what's he called, Lizzie, the German mister?"

"Kunstlich" she said, with a smile that would have been alluring to the most steadfast gentleman out for a frisk, as Dr. Johnson would have put it. "Maurice...He's Maurice to me anyway. A very pleasant man he is, cultured!" In fact, I could have been out for a frisk, as there seemed to be nothing to disturb the gaiety of the place. It hardly appeared to be a site for an assassination.

I sipped my beer and started to look around when a bearded, middle-aged man came next to me and gave his name, holding out his hand as he spoke. "Good evening, sir...I am Harry Devaney!" He was square and solid, every inch the well-to-do city type, I thought, and it was strange to see him in a rough-house like that. His handshake was strong and firm, and as his drew back his hand, I noticed some inky stains on the fingertips. For a second, I felt a thrill of satisfaction as I considered that I had produced a Holmesian deduction. He would have been proud of me. Ink stains on the finger tips would suggest a literary man perhaps, or a man in a clerical position in the City of London; but surely, I recall reflecting, an investor would not tend to acquire such black marks. He was not, I concluded, what he seemed to be. I was a little discomfited and at that moment, thoughts of some kind of threat to a royal personage appeared to be a little more possible.

I gave my name. "Oh, a doctor...well, I feel comfortable in the company of a medical man...I have a weakness of the heart, sir. Too much strenuous work in my youth, when I was a railway manager...out in the shire I was. But now I'm not so active...."

"What is it you do?" I asked, determined to make a mental note of it, in case there were to be developments. If any criminality was to emerge, then, as experience told me, it was the more educated characters one had to watch closely.

"Oh I'm an investor. I now invest in the locomotives, rather than arrange for their tracks and their routes across this fair land!"

That was an elusive nomenclature, I reflected. An investor could be anyone, from a member of the new rich to an outright swindler. But he talked volubly and entertainingly, and I listened, and in the course of that conversation, I spotted Lestrade and Lees. They came in separately, Lees perhaps ten seconds after his superior. The young man melted into the crowd, and Lestrade walked to the bar and had to force his way to a spot where he could order a drink.

Mr. Devaney still wanted our talk to continue, and I was struggling to think of a reason why. Surely, I thought, such a man would be drawn to other men of finance in his out-of-office time, and not to a medical man. He continued with his talk of the time when he organised the extension line from East Grinstead to Lewes, and he had no thought that I might find that subject tedious. However, as he spoke, I scrutinised his features further, and it struck me that his beard and full moustache were a deep grey everywhere except for a strange hue across the tips of his moustache which suggested black, wiry texture, as if frayed or damaged. I pondered on what activity might cause such a strange shade and banding across the hairs.

Here was a man who appeared to be a penman of some

kind, and indeed also a man whose mouth and lips were subject to some kind of discolouration. He was, in short, a puzzle.

Then my reflections were disturbed by an almighty commotion, as there was a crack as a table overturned and crashed onto the floor-tiles, and there were shrieks of anger. Someone called out, "Hands off my gal, you young scab!" I looked across, to see a bullish, squat man grabbing hold of Lees' collar, though he had to stretch somewhat, being a foot shorter. He then let go and swung back an arm ready to strike. But Lees blocked the jab and the man was pushed back. A young woman squealed, "Jim...he touched me...He's a foul swine he is...you get him!"

I went over, but hands held me back and someone shouted, "Let 'em fight!" The crowd moved back and created a space large enough for the two men to face each other. I couldn't see Lestrade anywhere, and I assumed he was stuck fast in the crowd, as I was. Voices screamed encouragement and insults, and the muscled man, who looked like a navvy, squared up to Lees, who crouched a little and put up a guard with his arms and fists. I could see immediately that the young detective was familiar with the pugilist's skills, and my surmise was soon shown to be correct. As his opponent approached, looking fearsome and swinging another punch at his man, Lees again blocked, but this time he brought an uppercut to the man's jaw and the fellow reeled back, with a scream of pain.

A voice called out, "Four to one the bull!"

Another echoed, "Even money the tall one...even money!"

I was disgusted at the corruption and depravity of mankind that they could take bets in such a demeaning situation, but of course, it was nothing new; I had seen such despicable low behaviour out in Afghanistan, and my time with Holmes had confirmed my opinion that there is a degenerate class beneath any scrap of decency and right-thinking in our dear Queen's realm.

Another assault from the shorter man ended in his taking a fist directly in the face and blood spouted from his nose. He yelled like a stuck pig, and a crowd of men gathered him up and restrained him from any further injury; he was patently second-best. A tall man was elected to go to Lees and raise his arm. "I declare this young fellow the winner!" he shouted. Everyone needed more drinks and there was a press against the bar. As this happened, I saw Devaney go to a door and walk through, with Lestrade by his side. The latter looked back and he saw me. I could tell by his demeanour that he wanted me to follow.

But this was followed by a deep frustration; the landlord saw me and stood in my way. "No, sir, as I said, there's a private party up there. The German gentleman has the room."

"But I have just now seen two men go through, and I assume walk up the stairs!"

"They are his friends, sir...now please...have a drink on the house!"

Terrible fears infested my imagination then. He ushered me to the bar, and he poured me a drink. Not far from me now, Lees was being offered drinks by a dozen men, and he had to refuse. I could see that he also wanted to be upstairs, knowing his Inspector was up there, and perhaps in trouble.

I put my mind to work, and thought more upon the man, Devaney. My poor brain battled to apply the ratiocination Holmes had spoken of when I first met him, in his talk of the writer Poe. What would stain a man's fingers and make that mark on his moustache? I pictured the moustache and the odd colour on the band through it, and the realisation came, like a rising sun. By heavens, he was a scientist...the marks were burns! A man who had such ink stains permanently on him, and burn-marks on his facial hair – well, that man experimented with something dangerous. He could be the anarchist, I concluded. He had to be stopped. He would be, logic suggested to me – a man who manufactured bombs!

As I determined on drastic action, I was aware that the landlord had been called over to the window by one of his friends, and I moved smartly to the door again, only to find that, as I opened it and walked through, there was a large, sturdy man in my path.

There is a slight shiver of regret when I record this in this account of such a difficult and testing case, but at that instant I had to make a quick decision to apply some violence. This is not my habit of course, but I was sure that Lestrade was in danger. I took my revolver from my side-pocket and brought up the stock heavily on the man's temple. He fell over, and I struck him once more, so that he was unconscious.

Behind me, to make the atmosphere of fear and disquiet even worse, I heard another furore, as if a second fight had ensued. But I could do nothing but run upstairs. My heart thumped so that I felt the beat in my throat, and as the gun was still in my hand, a part of me felt certain that I may have to use it, and perhaps do so to save a life.

However, when I reached the top of the stairs, the door was partly ajar and I heard conversation. My immediate impression was that the talk was civilised, and so I stopped to listen and to observe through the space between door and jamb. A handsome, tallish man was speaking, and with a German accent. That was, I concluded, the Herr Kunstlich the young lady had spoken of. He was speaking to someone nearer to the door, at the side of my vision, and I squinted, just able to make out that the man was Devaney, and he was bending over a tripod on which was perched a photographic camera.

As my eyes switched to see the right-hand side of the room, I felt a start of astonishment as I saw Lestrade with a man by his side who pointed a gun at the detective's head. Between them, sitting on a couch, was a woman with long, rich, black hair and bared breasts, slouched in a most indecent position. Why, I thought, she could be one of the worst harlots who haunt the Haymarket, and here she is, involved in a group of characters who want to kill Lestrade.

"Mr. Lestrade, my offer is a generous one. I am the sort of man who buys everything he wants, and on this occasion I wish to buy a policeman. In fact, I wish to buy you. My dear friend with the camera here, now he will take this picture. It will be a very tasteful *carte de visite*, showing your good self having a little recreation...and enjoying it of course. If you don't act at your ease and give this young lady some of your favours...for our lens...then I'm afraid tonight will be your last night on this earth, and a bullet will despatch you into eternity."

"No, you can't do it! This is wrong...I'm an officer of the law!" Lestrade was hardly presenting the most gallant and admirable qualities of the British gentleman who gained an empire for us. "Who the devil are you anyway, you German fiend!"

"Ah, no matter," the man said, walking gracefully a few steps away from Lestrade. "Let's simply say that your friend Mr. Sherlock Holmes knows very well who I am...he is, in fact, the one person in the world I most wish to see flourish, for he brings the kind of excitement that life very rarely offers one...this kind of excitement I would say, *naturlich*, a scene in which Death flutters his black cape and makes the shivers of fear run through your intestines, *nicht wahr*?"

I recall the devil's words most perfectly. My mind worked hard to try to define who he was, and why he spoke of Holmes. I still clutched the gun, but I expected at every second to have someone rushing behind me to clutch at my legs and drag me back, away from any opportunity of saving poor Lestrade from his imminent fate.

"Inspector, all I ask for is a little information. This is a very big city, and any businessman such as I has to have feelers out in every little back alley, as well as in the grand thoroughfares. You would be the perfect man to supply such information. So, my friend, if you wish to live, and walk into Scotland Yard tomorrow in this beautiful June weather, you must vow to be one of my little purchases, and this gentleman here will take a picture of you with Lisette here, my little female entertainer. She spends all her time learning how to please sporting young men, the sons of lords...oh yes, your fate will be in safe hands. *Lestrade and the Siren Lisette.* That will be written under the picture. *'Lestrade and the Siren Lisette enjoying each other's charms'*, it will be written. All the world will know, Inspector...time for you to decide now!"

The German voice, precise and menacing, was eating into my sensibility now, and I was caught between action and sheer paralysis. As he spoke, he was moving more and more to the left, well away from my line of sight.

There was a cacophony behind me, in the downstairs room, and then I heard shouts indicating that there was another fight in progress. I distinctly heard Lees's name shouted yet again. At this stage in my account, I must confess to a certain degree of dithering on my part, but when there was the sound of footsteps behind me on the lower stairs, necessity dictated my action, and I burst into the room. At that very instant, there was a horrific explosion and a dazzling spasm of light across the room, emanating from my right. I lifted one hand to protect my face and the other was free to pull the trigger of my revolver.

The second I saw Lestrade dive to the ground and the gunman beside him move, I fired; astoundingly, in the moment it took to make that decision, someone grasped my legs in a rugger tackle and down I went, hitting the floor hard.

I must have passed out momentarily, because when Lestrade's face was above me, shaking my shoulder and asking if I could see him, I sensed that all was comparatively tranquil again. When I managed to sit up, I looked around and asked the officer where the people were.

"Oh, they hopped it out. The German...he went downstairs, and the others went after him...the lady is still cowering behind the couch, and she's sobbing, sir...if you're up to it, you should attend to her, like."

The transformation was beyond belief. The room was bare except for a camera and tripod and the couch. I managed to look at the young woman, and happily she was merely in a state of shock and nervous alarm – not at all surprisingly. When she was sitting up and relatively calm, I saw that Lestrade had gone downstairs and I followed him.

In all my days working against the criminal fraternity of our great capital city, I have never been so astounded. The room downstairs was completely empty, except for Lestrade bending over Lees, who was severely injured, lying on the floor by the window. "Dr. Watson, come and have a look at the boy, quick!" Lestrade called.

The young detective was badly bruised and cut about his face, but I could detect no evidence of fractures; he had been, as I was, unconscious, and was muttering about there being "three of them...in the fighter's gang. Too...too much for me...."

I insisted that Lees be taken to hospital, and Lestrade went to find constables and attend to that. I looked around, and it was as if there had never been a human presence in the place; where there had been the bar, there was simply a wall and a table; the seats and small tables by the window were gone also; I ran outside and expected to see the sign, indicating the Old Charger, but there was nothing to see. There was Poland Street, as it always was, except for the inn I had visited the previous night.

Lestrade came back with several policemen, and Lees was carried outside to a cab. Lestrade directed one of the policemen to go upstairs and comfort the young woman.

"He was a regular hero, our Detective Constable...should be commended!" Lestrade said.

"Inspector," I asked, still dumbfounded at what was around me, "Who was the German?"

"Wish I knew, sir...him and that photographer cove, they was very close. My God, Dr. Watson, the man said he wanted to buy me...oh by Heaven! The camera...."

His face had the appearance of a man in sin who had seen the revelation of some mighty truth, and he ran upstairs. I followed, full of curiosity to see what had alarmed the man.

"Here we are. The camera...there's still the plate in it! What relief, Dr. Watson. "

I inspected the camera and when I looked around I saw what had been the source of the blinding light. It was the flash powder of course, and that explained Devaney's inky fingers and singed moustache. I explained that to Lestrade.

"Oh yes, I seen these before today, sir, the flash powder is very dangerous. Burns you, it does. This is a most risky business, this picture-making. I don't hold with it." He went to the machine and slid out a plate. "On this fiendish thing there's a picture of me with that...that young lady over there." We looked at her, now wrapped in the constable's cloak and trying to smile.

"To think...I could have been...what's that word...." "Compromised?" I ventured.

"Ruined, I think, puts it more exactly, Doctor."

"Who on earth was the German? " I asked, expecting no answer. "Well, one of 'em called him Maurice...well, Mauritz, German variety of Maurice."

"What about that plate? What's on it?" My question caused a stir on Lestrade's face. "Well, nothing now guv." He hurled it to the floor and stamped on it.

My mind was now working hard, turning over all the facts, and trying to assemble them as Holmes would have done. Maurice Kunstlich...what or who was he? "How's your German, Inspector? Mine is very feeble I'm afraid...I recall a problem with the word *Rache* at one time...."

He called the constable across. "My ability with other tongues is limited, but Hesslam here has a German dad...."

"The man was given the German name," he said, with instant understanding, "Well, that would be Maurice Arty in English, sir. Ridiculous name, sir"

Maurice Arty...Moriarty. My God! At that moment, I had the awful realisation that I had been in the presence of the fiend himself, the deadly enemy of my dear friend Holmes. Worse still, the thought struck me, there had been a picture of him on that plate, now shattered and useless, at our feet. Holmes was never to know that fact. I persuaded myself that there would simply have been a blur, as the man had stepped out of the picture before I shot at his minion.

I rather think that my losing the notes of this case is perhaps the result of my embarrassment at missing a unique opportunity of trapping an image of the man whose machinations often gave Holmes and myself sleepless nights, and more than acceptable amount of worry.

Then, something dawned in my mind that night, as I sat in my armchair, working out the amazing disappearance of that inn. I said the words aloud. Moriarty knew that Holmes was away! My brooding, cerebral friend would have seen through his German identity in a second. As for Lestrade: well, I never saw him stretch the truth of his life in front of younger officers again. He reverted to his usual crass, thoughtless self, but it has to be said that he behaved with courage and self-control.

I have only once walked along Poland Street since that strange evening. I recall stopping to look at the wall on which the inn-sign hung. I blinked, took stock of who and where I was, and for a second I heard the sound of laughter and drunken jollity behind that solid stone. One day, I resolved, I shall relate the whole affair to Holmes. But for now, let it lie.

The King of Diamonds

by John Heywood

Sir William Voigt, owner of a quarter of the world's diamond mines, was not a man to hide his light under a bushel. He wore diamond-encrusted jewellery with the flamboyance of a Maharajah, and so great was his wealth that it earned him the sobriquet of The Diamond King among the English press. It can have surprised nobody that when such a man lost his life in a wood on a Norfolk estate, the tragedy was recounted in the greatest detail. But interest in the sad event was not to last: before the week was out, new tales of death and scandal were vying for the attention of the public, and curiosity about the millionaire's murder withered away as suddenly as it had sprung up. Soon, perhaps, Sir William will be quite forgotten, and against that day I wish to record here a brief sketch of the events surrounding his death. The newspaper reports at the time were partial and misleading, for it is seldom within the powers of the reporter to delve under the surface of the disaster he recounts and unearth the twisted complexities beneath. My friend and colleague Sherlock Holmes, however, has made it his life's work to shine a light upon these dark secrets, and he seldom did so to greater effect than when looking into the death of the King of Diamonds.

The summer of '88 had lasted long and late; in early October of that year, the streets through which I passed on my way home to Baker Street still glowed warm in the light of the setting sun. Within a day or two, however, the season turned, and the golden light of summer was replaced by morning mists and darkening afternoons. Now, instead of strolling home in comfort, I and a thousand others like me hurried homewards through the damp streets, each of us huddled in his great-coat against the biting air. It was on one such evening that the case I am about to relate began. I had returned home to find that the landlady Mrs. Hudson had set a fire, the first of the autumn. Sitting by it was Holmes, his heels resting upon the coal-scuttle, so absorbed in some black-letter tome that he continued to read without so much as a glance at me or a word of greeting. Not that I had the least objection to my friend's unclubbable ways. After a busy day at my practice, I was looking forward to a few hours of quietness, and so I was happy to settle myself in the other chair by the fire and read the paper. The evening proved as pleasantly uneventful as I had hoped. From time to time a few words of conversation would flare up between us, much as a few flames would occasionally shoot from a log, only to die down again into a steady glow. One of us might shift to a more comfortable position in his chair, and then settle again, as the burning logs once or twice collapsed into the embers and then continued to burn quietly in their new arrangement. The lines of print swam before my eyes, the paper fell from my hand, and I was drifting into sleep when my drowsy reverie was interrupted by a knock at the door.

"Come in!" I heard Holmes cry. The door opened to reveal a lady dressed in a most curious manner; heavily veiled, she wore a broad-brimmed hat trimmed, as was her collar, with silver astrakhan, while the skirts of her dark top-coat were so low and full that they brushed the floor. After hesitating for some seconds in the doorway, the lady rushed impetuously into the room, only to bridle suddenly and stop dead in her tracks again. She lifted her veil, and her glance, flickering between us, finally alighted on my friend:

"Mr. Sherlock Holmes, detective?" she asked. Her manner of speech was as curious as her appearance and behaviour. It was evident that she was not a native of this country. Stepping up to Holmes, she clasped his hand in both of hers. "Mr. Holmes, help me, I beg you. My brother's life is in jeopardy. The Diamonds King is dead! And they say –"

"You are very disturbed, madam. Please calm yourself," said my friend, guiding her to a chair and bidding her sit. "The *sal voltile*, if you would, Watson. Now," he said, turning back to her, "when you are ready, you will tell me about the Diamond King and your brother, and what danger it is that brings you here." He gestured in my direction. "This is my friend and colleague, Dr. Watson, and my name you know. There, of course, you have the advantage of us."

The lady sat upright, grasping her bag in her gloved hands and clenching her teeth as she struggled to control her feelings.

"Good evening, Dr. Watson and Mr. Holmes. I am Miss Maria Oblonsky."

"Good evening, Miss Oblonsky," I answered. "It so happens that I have just been reading about the Diamond King. It's a bad business. Have you heard the news, Holmes?" I asked, retrieving the paper from the floor.

"No. You had better enlighten me. If you will read out the report, Watson, I shall be much obliged, and Miss Oblonsky will then tell us what she knows of the matter, and how she and her brother come to be involved."

I turned to the page headed "A Dreadful Murder at Carre Castle" and read aloud from it.

> *A tragic event has taken from us one of the Empire's greatest men. Sir William Voigt, better known to many as the King of Diamonds, was as familiar a figure on Change as he was at Monte Carlo, and was also a fine sportsman, who bagged, it is said, more head of game than any man living. It is our sad duty to report that "The King of Diamonds" is dead.*

> *Sir William Voigt met his death shortly after midday today on the Norfolk estate of the Marquess of Ambleside, during a weekend shooting party. Among the exalted guests were the writer Mr. Peake Aubrey, General Sir Arthur Lamb, General Oliphant, and other prominent public figures. This morning's shoot started after an early breakfast and was to continue into the early afternoon, with the marksmen taking their luncheon in the field. Sir William ate with his fellow hunters, and soon afterwards complained that he was unwell. It became evident that he was in great pain, but all attempts to help were in vain; within a few minutes he was dead.*
>
> *It was immediately suspected that the luncheon he had just ingested was the cause of his death, and we are informed by Inspector Shaw of the North Norfolk constabulary that poisoning, accidental or deliberate, has not been dismissed as a possibility. "An inquiry is in hand," said that officer. "The circumstances surrounding Sir William Voigt's death will be investigated fully, and I am confident that if there has been foul play we shall find it out."*
>
> *We have little doubt that Inspector Shaw is correct, and that further details of this dreadful event will come to light over the next few days, details which are yet shrouded in much darkness. Readers may be assured that this journal will be second to none in laying before them all the circumstances behind this unhappy event as they emerge.*

"Now, Miss Maria Oblonsky," said Holmes, "perhaps you will be kind enough to tell us about yourself. Beyond the obvious facts that you have only been in this country for a few weeks, that you work as a seamstress, and that you and your family have seen better days, I know little about you.

She looked at him in astonishment. "How do you know these things? How do you know that I am seamstress? How that my family were once more rich?"

A smile of satisfaction briefly passed over Holmes's features at the amazement that his powers of observation and deduction had produced. "The signs are obvious enough to the practised eye. You have pronounced marks around the tips of your index and middle fingers," he observed. "They are the marks, common amongst seamstresses, made by the constant use of a thimble. Incidentally, that the marks are on your right hand proclaim you to be left-handed. If you wish to preserve your secrets from the eyes of men, you would do well not to remove your gloves. The hands have much to tell those who can hear."

"And my family? That we are not rich now as before?"

"There are many signs. These gloves, for instance," he answered, picking them up from the table. "They are of fine kid, and fitted to your hands by the glove-maker." Holmes rose and took the lady's hand in his own, splaying the fingers as though she were a patient in a public ward. "I observe that the index finger is slightly longer than the fourth; a most unusual proportion." He held the glove against her hand. "Precisely the same proportion here, you see," he pointed out. "This glove was certainly made to fit that hand."

"You are as clever as they say, Mr. Sherlock Holmes; but how does this tell you that my family fell from fortune?"

"It is simple enough. The glove, though of excellent quality, is now old and worn. See here, where scratches on the surface have been carefully dyed, and here, where a break in the seam has been mended in thread of the matching colour. Bespoke gloves of the best quality, many years ago, but not enough money to buy new ones now when they are needed, although the owner," he added with a nod towards the lady, "still has proper pride in her appearance. What else can that mean, but a reversal of fortunes?"

Not unnaturally, she seemed downcast by this reminder of her present state. "It is quite true. I have lost all I once had."

"Not all, Miss Oblonsky. As I said, you have not lost your pride." Holmes dropped her glove on to the table and resumed his chair. "Now, let us concentrate on the matter in hand," he said. "Pray be kind enough to tell me about you and your brother, and what brought you to this country."

"My brother Peter and I have good education, and we come from good family, very old family, but, as you see, not rich like in the days before Uprising. Little by little we lose everything, and then we have no money. My brother Peter Oblonsky comes to your country since fourteen years. It is very difficult for Peter. He pulls cart at market, but still he sends some money home for us. Then he works footman, and because we come from good family, he knows to be footman and to wait at table. He does not serve port in sherry-glass and so. Then he is manservant to one man, which is for two years, and now he is valet to Sir William Voigt."

"When did your brother Peter enter Sir William's employment?" asked Holmes.

"This is three years ago, in the same year that Mother dies. In Warsaw, I am lucky to find work. You know already that my job is seamstress. Peter writes to me that there is work for seamstress in London and also for domestic staff, like he is. He thinks that there will be place for lady's maid, or perhaps I find position as governess. So two months ago I come to England. Peter finds for me small room in Covent Garden, which is not garden, but streets and alleys."

"You have given me a very clear account of your background, Miss Oblonsky. Now, tell me what happened in these last few days."

"Last Wednesday afternoon, Peter and I meet. We meet on Wednesday afternoons, because they are his afternoons off work. Peter tells me that he will go with Sir William to Norfolk, to the castle of Lord Ambleside. Then on Sunday, they will return to London. Peter wants me to see England, which he says is in many parts very beautiful, not like Covent Garden, so he pays for me to take train to Norfolk, and he pays for room in the inn so I may be near him in Norfolk. One day, Peter has free time, so I meet him and we go for walk near where he stays with Sir William. He is right, the country is most beautiful. That day is Thursday. The next time I will meet him is Saturday. Two o'clock we will meet, at the South Lodge gate, but when I come to gate I see another man is there waiting instead. He asks me if I am Maria, and he tells me that there is something wrong. He says that Sir William Voigt is dead and Peter cannot come to meet me. He tells me that Peter is in police prison for killing Sir William. This I cannot believe. I ask how Sir William dies, and he says that he is poisoned. Sir William eats sandwich and dies. The person who makes sandwiches for Sir William is Peter. And they search Peter's room and find hidden there jewels of diamonds that belong to Sir William, the Diamond King.

"No mention of an arrest in the paper," Holmes said to himself. "So the theft was discovered and Oblonsky arrested after the newspaper reports were despatched. Now, Miss Oblonsky, tell me about your brother's relations with his late employer. Do you know of any difficulties between them?"

"My brother was very pleased to have his position with Sir William."

"He never complained to you about his master?"

"But yes, I must tell you that he did sometimes tell me that Sir William was a difficult person to please, and demanded much of him, but then also Sir William can be very generous and kind. You must understand that Peter is gentle man, very good man, and I know that he will never, never try to hurt or kill, never. Please, Mr. Holmes, you must help save my brother. I know that he is not guilty of this death. I know it. Please, will you help?"

"I will see what I can do, Miss Oblonsky. But you must understand that I am not in the position of a lawyer who represents his client's interests. My task, if I undertake to investigate this matter, will be to find out the truth, whatever it may be. I ask you to bear in mind these points: that your brother, apparently, prepared the sandwiches that poisoned his employer; that very valuable property of the dead man was found hidden in your brother's effects. If I should find the truth about Sir William's death, it may not be what you believe and wish it to be. You do understand that?"

Miss Oblonsky rose from the chair and stood straight, her back straight and head high.

"I ask no more than that, Mr. Holmes," was her reply, given with something of the pride to which my friend had alluded. "Your words are great relief to me. I have no friends in your country except my poor brother, and if Sherlock Holmes is investigating this death, I know all that may be done is being done."

Holmes acknowledged her words with a shallow bow. "I shall look into the matter, Miss Oblonsky, and see what I can find. If I have any news for you, you shall hear it within a day or two. You have done well to come to me, and there is at present no more that you can do. Leave matters in my hands, and try to set your mind at rest. In the meantime, I wish you a safe journey back to Covent Garden."

Closing the door behind the lady, Holmes stepped briskly over to the book-case, pulled out Bradshaw and the atlas, and carried them over to the table. He spread them open and turned up the lamp. "Let me see – Carre Castle... it is rather off the beaten track...Brailston Thorpe will be the station." He turned to Bradshaw and ran his finger down the column: "A train leaves Liverpool Street at 8.48. Will you be accompanying me, Watson?"

"If you wish. I have nothing planned for tomorrow."

"Capital! I shall tell Mrs. Hudson that we breakfast at seven."

From the station at Brailston Thorpe, we took a four-wheeler, and across the flat landscape we saw, far away in the distance, the turrets of Carre Castle rising from the low-lying mists. It was a further half-hour's drive before we reached the South Lodge, where we turned in and drove on to the main gates. The castle, which we had seen floating in the distance like a vision of Camelot, now loomed heavily over us, massive and grey, its turrets and mullions rising far above our heads. As we entered the Great Hall, we seemed to be in another age, for suits of armour stood sentinel by the doorway, and tapestries and old weapons of war hung upon the walls. They brought to my mind fabled days of yore –"old, far off, unhappy things, and battles long ago." I said as much to Holmes, but the romance of the past had no place his heart, and in response he merely asked a maid who was working nearby where Inspector Shaw was to be found. "The police are working from the gun-room, sir," she answered. "Down that corridor there and to your right."

We found the gun room easily enough, but our knocking went unanswered, and when we entered we found ourselves in an empty room. There were no guns to be seen; they were, no doubt, behind the stout locked cupboards that lined one side of the room. Nor were there any people in the room. An aged dog approached us, slowly wagging its tail, and, having made itself known to us, wandered off again to slump down in its basket. We saw no other sign of life.

"The enquiry does not appear to be proceeding at full pelt, does it?" said I. But I spoke too soon, for at that very moment a door on the opposite side of the room flew open and two men strode in.

"Monstrous!" cried the first man. "How am I to make a report when half the witnesses have fled to the four corners of the earth? 'Tis beyond me."

"Yes, sir," answered the other, leaning forward to brush some cartridges off a rough table with his sleeve. The first slammed down a heavy ledger onto the table and, looking up, caught sight of Holmes and myself. He glared at us across the room.

"How may I help you gentlemen?" he asked, in no very friendly tone of voice. We introduced ourselves. "Inspector Shaw, of King's Lynn," he responded. "We're honoured, I'm sure, to have you here, Mr. Holmes, but I'm afraid you've missed the boat this time. We already have our man, safely under lock and key in the station."

"Yes, so I heard," replied my friend. "Commendably speedy of you. However, I am privately retained to look into this case. I hope it will not inconvenience you if I do so?"

"Not at all, I'm sure," was the muttered answer.

"Thank you, Inspector. I suppose you have little doubt that it was the prisoner Oblonsky who killed Sir William?"

"No doubt of it."

"Poisoned the sandwiches, I hear. The police surgeon examined the body?"

"He did. Found enough arsenic in the body to kill a horse, and enough in what were the rest of the sandwiches to kill another horse. Now, a good supply of arsenic is kept in a locked cupboard in the scullery, as rat poison, and what would you think? Most of it is missing."

"Has the cupboard been forced?" "I don't think so – Constable?"

The constable pulled a notebook from his pocket and consulted it. "No, sir. 'Cupboard door locked, remaining powder on shelf.'"

"Any idea as to the motive?" continued Holmes.

"Motive? There's no mystery there – theft. The greater part of Sir William's personal jewellery was missing, and we found several pieces hidden in Oblonsky's bag – some shirt studs and a tie-pin. All set with diamonds, of course. Sir William was no fool, and when he missed his jewellery he would guess who had taken it. Oblonsky had to silence him."

"And the other stolen jewels?" asked Holmes. "Where were they?"

"We haven't found them yet. We've searched the man's room, of course. It's my guess that the sly fellow has hidden them in some other part of the castle. We may never find them."

"I wonder why he did not hide all the jewellery in that way, then." "Because he didn't have time. He had to leave his room to prepare for the morning shoot before he had finished hiding the jewellery. Or perhaps in his hurry he simply overlooked them."

The inspector shot Holmes a knowing glance. "I can guess what you're thinking, Mr. Holmes. You're thinking, 'This is all well and good, but it's just supposition. Where's the proof?'"

"Ah! You are right, Inspector Shaw. I was thinking something along those lines."

"'Tis a question of access," explained the Inspector. "You'll be wanting to make your own enquiries, of course, but here's my advice. We have three vital items in this murder: the arsenic, the jewellery, and the sandwiches. Who had access to all three? A simple question, but 'tis sometimes the simple questions that count.

"Now, I'll be getting back to my report. 'Tis a shame you weren't in time to catch your man. We beat you to it this time, Mr. Holmes!"

"Nonetheless, I'd like to have a word with Oblonsky. Perhaps you'll be good enough to write an order to your man at the station.

"But before we go to the station to see Oblonsky," said Holmes as we left the gunroom, "there are one or two other people here I'd like to speak to. It would be as well to hear what the butler can tell us, first of all. He's likely to be as well informed as anyone about yesterday's arrangements."

The butler was in his pantry, a stout, dignified silver-whiskered man named Meades. Holmes had guessed rightly, for although the butler had remained in the castle during the shoots, he was, nevertheless, aware of the whereabouts of the guests and servants at all times. The sport for that day, he told us, had taken place in the lower Midden woods, a part of the estate that lay at such a distance from the castle – some twelve or thirteen miles – that it had been decided that the guests would not return for their luncheon, but would take a light meal in the woods, and return to the castle late in the afternoon. The eight guests and their host, Lord Ambleside, formed three groups of three Guns for that morning's shoot, stationed some two or three furlongs apart. Sir William's group also included the novelist Peake Aubrey, and Lord Henry, Lord Ambleside's son.

Oblonsky had prepared Sir William's food in the kitchen in the morning, and then accompanied him on the shoot. It was not unusual, Meades explained, for a valet to prepare his master's outside meals in this way, as he would know better than the castle staff the gentleman's requirements. The regular staff did, however, prepare the food for Mr. Aubrey and Lord Henry, who were not accompanied by a manservant. Oblonsky used the same kitchen as the regular staff, but on being asked exactly where the various servants were working, Meades regretted that he was unable to say. Nor was he well placed to give first-hand information about the arsenic, advising us to apply to Mrs. Olds the housekeeper on both these subjects.

He did, however, give precise information about the times at which events took place. He assured us that Oblonsky must have gone to the kitchen before nine o'clock to prepare the sandwiches required by his master, the shooting party having left the castle at ten past nine in the morning. As to the time and circumstances of Sir William's death, the butler, having been at the time in the castle itself, twelve miles from the scene of the tragedy, was able to give us only an indirect report. He had been informed, however, and had no reason to doubt, that nothing out of the way had occurred within the Voigt threesome until Voigt ate the sandwich served him by his valet. Shortly after eating the sandwich, he had fallen to the ground in pain, and within less than a minute was dead. There was little doubt that it was the sandwich that had poisoned him, for one of the dogs, in the confusion, snapped up one of the fallen sandwiches, wolfed it down, and quickly met the same fate as Sir William.

The dreadful event had, of course, brought to a premature end the weekend's sport, and many of the guests had already left or were on the point of leaving. The two Guns who had been of Sir William's party, however, remained; Lord Henry and Mr. Peake Aubrey.

"Those two," asked Holmes; "are they still at the castle?"

"They are, sir. I am given to understand that Lord Henry will be staying for some little time. Mr. Aubrey will leave us this afternoon."

"At least are still here. Many of the guests seem to have left already.

Indeed, a carriage on its way out passed us as we came in."

"Yes, sir. That would have been General Oliphant and his party. You will readily understand that the misadventure has brought the sport to an unexpectedly early end. Only Mr. Aubrey, Sir Lumsden Grey and General Lamb are still at the castle."

"And Lord Henry?"

"Indeed so, sir. I was thinking of the guests only." "Where am I to find Lord Henry and Mr. Aubrey?"

"Mr. Aubrey, I believe, is in the library. As for Lord Henry, I cannot say with any certainty, but he is often to be found in the billiards-room at this time of the day."

In the billiards-room, we found two young men in the midst of a frame, one stretching over the table to play a shot, the other leaning against the back of a chair with his hands in his pockets, watching his opponent. The onlooker identified himself as Lord Henry and his friend at the table as Mr. Walter Willoughby. "Fire away with your questions, Mr. Holmes," he said. "We have plenty of time, I'm sorry to say. Willoughby's well into his stride, and once he gets going like this there's no stopping him."

Although he responded willingly enough to Holmes's questions, Lord Henry's answers were something of a disappointment, for they told us nothing we did not already know. I shall, therefore, not weary the reader with every question and answer that passed between Sherlock Holmes and Lord Henry. Suffice it to say that the young man's account of events only confirmed what we had heard before.

Mr. Aubrey, who, as the butler had predicted, was to be found in the library, had, at first, equally little to tell that was new. After the morning's shooting, Sir William, he said, had settled himself on his shooting-stick in a clearing and taken a sandwich from the little hamper presented by his valet, Oblonsky. He had offered to share the sandwiches with his fellow Guns. "A dashed close shave," as Aubrey put it, for had the sandwiches not contained mustard he would have accepted Sir William's offer, a decision which would surely have proved fatal. Soon Voigt complained of feeling unwell. A minute later he was grimacing in pain and wavering on his seat; and then he crashed to the ground, clutching his stomach. Within a minute he was dead. In these matters, Aubrey's answers, like Lord Henry's, served only to corroborate those accounts of the morning's events that we had already heard, but on the topic of his fellow guests, Aubrey was more informative. Asked to describe them, he pondered a moment, pushed back a lock of hair from his forehead, and settled back in his chair.

"I have no interest in tittle-tattle," began the novelist, "but as a simple spinner of tales, I take a keen interest in the foibles of my fellow creatures; and I may say that I am a seasoned traveller in the ways of the human heart. Of course," he added, "you gentlemen understand that these observations are not to be repeated willy-nilly. They are of a private nature.

"Youth first: Lord Henry. I've known him since he was a boy, and he's become a very pleasant young man, though whether he'll measure up when he becomes Marquess, I don't know. Well, that day is a long way off, we all hope. Perhaps he's rather in his father's shade at present. I know nothing of his friend, Willoughby, I'm afraid.

"Two other young men, the Mainwaring brothers. Hugo is a charming fellow, but his brother Ralph is quite another kettle of fish. He was drunk most of the time. In fact, he had to cry off the shoot. Rude to the servants, too. To be frank with you, he's a blackguard of the first water. Why Ambleside keeps inviting him I cannot imagine.

"Now, General Lamb. I hadn't seen him since Majuba, but he's the same as ever: a fine old soldier. He fell out with Voigt after dinner, you know. I don't know what it was all about, but voices were certainly raised. The port was flowing rather too freely, I dare say. There was another General, too, Oliphant. He was quite unlike one's idea of a military man. Very quiet. I could scarcely get a word out of him, and he looked as if he'd spent his life at a desk. Rotten shot, too. He kept himself to himself." Aubrey counted off the guests on his fingers.

"That's six. There were ten Guns in all. Well, poor Voigt, of course. I was with him and Lord Henry, you know. Saw him die." The writer's flow of words dried up for a few moments. "We spoke about that. As to the man himself, I hadn't met him before, but of course with a man like that, his reputation precedes him. He was a touch vulgar, it must be said, red of face and loud of mouth, though one doesn't wish to speak ill of the dead. He was very friendly and gregarious, though. You couldn't help yourself liking the man. Now, who else? Your humble servant, of course, and there's Ambleside, our host. I have no secret information for you there, I'm afraid. Just a very fine gentleman of the old school. That's nine. Who else?" He rubbed his jaw as he tried to call the last Gun to mind. "Grey!" he cried. "Lumsden Grey. How could I forget? I was at school with him. He's in the Privy Council now, if you can believe me. I let him have a few home truths about his damned government, and he had to admit I spoke a good deal of sense."

"Thank you, Mr. Aubrey," said Holmes. "Tell me, do you

know if any of these men had some quarrel with Sir William? Or of any other enemies he may have had?"

"Enemies? A man like that probably has enemies in three continents. He won't have built up the world's biggest diamond business without treading on a few toes. And I'm not only talking about personal enemies. There are those who can't bear to see a man do well – anarchists, socialists, nihilists – they hate to see any man make his way to the top."

"You think this was a murder motivated by envy?" The writer shrugged his shoulders.

"Why not? We all know of the outrages these monsters perpetrate. They are not above killing innocent people, Mr. Holmes. Indeed, they glory in murder. The fouler their misdeeds, the louder they boast of them. You know who I mean: anarchists." He moved a little closer and lowered his voice. "Oblonsky is one of them!" he hissed.

If Lord Henry had given too little information, Mr. Peake Aubrey had perhaps given too much.

"What do you make of it all, Watson?" Holmes asked me as we left the library. "Who might have been enemy enough of Voigt to kill him? Any idea?"

"Well, perhaps if Oblonsky is indeed an anarchist – or if Voigt has made an enemy who crossed his path here – or – dash it, Holmes, I don't know. It all seems so vague and confusing; I'm afraid I'm quite in the dark."

"I'm with you there, old man; all this seems to be leading nowhere," he said, shaking his head. "Let us hope that a talk with Oblonsky will shed some light on the matter. But before I speak to him, I'd better have a word with Mrs. Olds, the housekeeper. I'd very much like to see her poison cupboard and find out who had access to it."

Mrs. Olds was in her scullery, in a cap and apron, sitting at a plain deal table on which was heaped a score or so of freshly shot birds. A kitchen maid stood by as the housekeeper ran a thick finger down the columns of the game-book that lay open before her, no doubt checking that the records and the bag matched. At our approach, she pushed the book aside and rose to her feet.

"The arsenic? I wish I'd never set eyes on it, that I do. It's kept in that cupboard in the corner there."

Holmes strode over to it and bent over the lock, running his fingertips over it and examining it through his pocket lens. He turned to the housekeeper.

"The key, if you please."

She took a key from her apron pocket and unlocked a wall-cupboard. From the row of keys inside she selected one and handed it to Holmes. He glanced at her keenly.

"Is this key always kept there?" "Yes, sir."

"And who has a key to the key-cupboard?" "Mr. Meades and myself."

"And the key to the poison cupboard is always kept locked in there?"

"Oh yes, Mr. Holmes!" "On no, Mrs. Olds!"

She looked at him in astonishment.

"Now tell me the truth," he continued. "Why was the arsenic cupboard left unlocked yesterday?"

His certainty and hawk-like gaze were more than a match for her feeble protests, and she gave up her pretence. "I can't say, sir, really I can't. It was locked first thing yesterday, but on these busy days a person can't always keep an eye on everything at once. All I can tell you is this; when we were cleaning up after luncheon yesterday, there was the key left in the cupboard door."

Holmes and I left the kitchen and came back up the stairs. I was still struggling to make sense of the case.

"So anyone in the kitchen could have slipped into the scullery when it was empty and taken the arsenic, with no-one any the wiser."

"Exactly," Holmes agreed. "We have not narrowed the field much. In fact, I don't seem to be making much progress at all."

"What do you intend to do?" I asked.

"I intend to see Oblonsky. Perhaps he will be able to cast some light on this murky business."

A two-wheeler awaited us at the stables, and soon we were rattling along the misty lanes to the village of Carre and its police station.

The sergeant in charge carefully wrote our names in his ledger and walked with us down to the cell, locking the door behind us once we had entered. Oblonsky was a small man with thick hair greying at the temples. He was neatly dressed, but his jaw told me that he had not shaved since his imprisonment the previous day. He was sitting on a bench that jutted from the wall, his hands clasped before him. On our entrance, he jumped briskly to his feet and gave a short bow. Holmes explained that we were there at his sister's behest, at which the prisoner expressed his gratitude and assured us of his innocence.

"In that case, Oblonsky, there is good reason to hope that in a few hours the charges against you will be dropped, and that you will walk from here a free man." So said my friend; but his words brought little cheer to Oblonsky, who received them with a weary shake of the head. "I have held back nothing from the police, I assure you, and yet here I am," he said, indicating the walls around him, "a prisoner, to be tried for murder." Again he shook his head and cast his eyes to the floor of his cell.

"Come now, do not be downhearted," insisted Holmes. "Although things seem black from your police-cell here, the case against you is much weaker than it appears. There is every chance that you will soon be free. But if that is to happen, you must give me the information I seek as fully and accurately as you can. It is of the first importance that you do not pass over some detail because you think it trivial. You must allow me to judge what is germane to your case, and what is not."

Holmes pulled up his chair and leaned forward, so that he was looking his man squarely in the face. "Firstly; are you a member of any political society?"

Oblonsky looked somewhat taken aback by the question, and I confess that I shared his surprise. "I gave my word that I would tell you the truth," he said, "and so I will. Yes, I am a member of a group for progress in the world."

"The name of your group?"

"That I cannot tell you, because we have no name. It is safer thus, and more in keeping with our beliefs."

"Well, would you say your group is nihilist? Anarchist?"

"No, not nihilist, no!" Oblonsky spoke with passion. "We abjure them, their despair, their violence, their bombs and killings. We are not nihilist. Anarchist?" He inclined his head one way, then the other. "Perhaps. We oppose ourselves to violence, whether done by the greatest nations or by the meanest person. We hope for a day when there will be no money, no property, no distinctions of rank, no need for prisons and armies. We meet to discuss how this may be achieved."

"So you look forward to a day when there will be no man and no master?"

"We do, Mr. Holmes."

"I take it that you kept your views on social matters from your master."

"But no, I told Sir William my beliefs. One day he found some papers recording our discussions, and he asked me about them. He was insistent that I tell him. So I told him."

"What was his response?"

"He laughed loudly and slapped me on the shoulder. 'You're a rum bird, Oblonsky,' he said."

Homes then turned his attention to the events of the fatal morning, beginning with the point-blank question, whether Oblonsky had introduced poison into the sandwiches. The valet repudiated the suggestion categorically, swearing that he had no idea how the poison had been put into the sandwiches, except that he had not done it himself.

"Well, somebody did it," was Holmes's blunt reply.

"Now, what can you tell us about the diamond jewels that were found in your bag? Did you steal them?"

"I did not," he assured us.

"Do you have any idea how they came to be there?"

"None."

"Somebody put them there." Holmes got to his feet and paced the little cell two or three times. He turned to the prisoner: "You understand, I'm sure, that these two questions are at the crux of this case. If we can answer them, you will be a free man. If not, your life will be forfeit. So let us do all we can to find the answers. I believe you and Sir William arrived at the castle three days ago, did you not? What rooms were you given?"

"We arrived on Thursday evening and were put in the East wing, Sir William on the second floor, and I on the third."

"Who else was in the East wing?"

"General Lamb occupied the room next to Sir William."

"I see. Was anybody else on the third floor with you?"

"Yes, General Lamb's manservant Griggs. He was on the upper floor, as I was. Our rooms were opposite each other on either side of a narrow passage. His room looked out on to the parterre, mine on to the courtyard.

"At first, Griggs and I did not hit it off very well. He held himself deliberately aloof, not acknowledging my presence at all. It was uncomfortable. But soon he became more friendly towards me, helping me in my duties at times. We were on good terms in the end."

"When did you first notice this change of attitude in Griggs towards you?" asked Holmes.

The prisoner glanced upwards as he tried to recall events to his mind. "It was the day before yesterday, in the evening, when he and I were both in our rooms, preparing for the following day. I was fetching Sir William's hip-flask and luncheon case, which would be needed in the morning. Griggs was also busy preparing for the day ahead. He had left his door open, and as I left my room I glanced through the open door and caught his eye."

"What was he doing?"

"Exactly what, I cannot tell you. There are a thousand little things that a manservant must attend to in good time if everything is to go smoothly. Just which of these so many tasks occupied Griggs at that moment, I do not know. Unpacking some piece of equipment or clothing, I should say, for when I saw him he was kneeling at a small open case. My sudden appearance at his doorway surprised him and he gave a start. I made a remark to the effect that we both alike had much to do in our line of work. He fully agreed, and for a few moments we shared our experiences. It was from that time that relations between Griggs and me became warm. The bond between men who work side by side is naturally strong. Many laugh at this truth, but I believe this bond has a place in every heart, and the warmth that briefly grew up between myself and Griggs is an example of it."

"Cast your mind back to that moment when you caught sight of Griggs and spoke with him. Was there anything remarkable about it?" asked Holmes. "Please think carefully."

The valet frowned, thinking over the question. "No, sir," he finally answered. "Nothing at all unusual. I had gone into Sir William's room first, and then into my own, to fetch what was needed for the next morning. I left my room hurriedly to return to Sir William's room, and it was then, as I was hurrying to the stair, that I saw Griggs and spoke with him. When I was finished in Sir William's room, I went down to the servants' hall to complete my tasks."

"And then?"

"And then I returned to the East wing. As I came up the stairs, Griggs, hearing me return, opened his door, and we had some talk before retiring. He had been giving my earlier words much thought, he said, and they had given him a new understanding. Nothing must stand between two comrades;

not the power of law, nor of wealth, nor of social degree. However strongly these chains might bind a man, he should never betray his fellow.

"I was touched by his sincerity in these new-found beliefs, and we clasped hands and swore loyalty to each and all our fellow men. So we parted as brothers."

"The next morning, I rose at half past six and made Sir William his coffee. I laid out his clothes and equipment for the shoot, and at about a quarter past eight went down to the kitchen. A table was set aside for the use of us visiting staff, where I was able to make a luncheon for Sir William and for myself."

Holmes closed his eyes and frowned in concentration.

"I entered the kitchen," continued Oblonsky, "and went to the cupboard and safe, whence I took what I needed for the luncheon sandwiches."

"You did not bring your own supplies?"

"No, I took what I needed from the castle provisions. For instance, there is at all times a pat of butter in the dairy safe, from which I helped myself. I also cut the bread for the sandwiches from the loaf in use at the time; there is always a loaf available. And so with the ham, salt and pepper, and parsley. Only the mustard I prepared myself. Sir William liked a particular mixture."

"I see," said Holmes. "You say that you visiting servants had your own table, but shared the general supplies?"

"Exactly so, sir."

"Were you alone in the kitchen?"

"Not at all. The kitchen was a busy place, with people passing to and fro, fetching and carrying constantly."

"Let me see," said Holmes, his eyes still closed as he painted in his mind's eye a picture of the kitchen that morning. "You were sitting at the table, others bustling around you on various errands. Did you stay at your table all the time?"

"No, I had to leave the table several times. I had to fetch

the bread, the butter, the ham, and the mustard ingredients."

"Were you alone at the table?"

"No. Wilkins, General Oliphant's man, was there too. He left before me, but I was soon joined at the table by Truman, Sir Lumsden's man, and Griggs, my neighbour. We were quite a party!"

"While luncheon for many of the Guns was being prepared by the castle staff?"

"That is correct, and of course luncheon had to be prepared for those not at the shoot, for the family, and for the castle staff too. It was a very busy morning in the kitchen. We at our table had to speak up to be heard above the noise and chatter."

"Some of that chatter coming from your table, I suppose. What did you talk about? The day's duties?"

"No; our duties were all decided, and gave little opportunity for debate. Sporting matters, as I recall, were the topic of much of our talk – the prize-fighters of this country and America, and the St. Leger. Two at the table having recently been successful in their bets on the race. We talked about the Whitechapel killings, too, as do people up and down the country; although surely you, Mr. Holmes, know more than any about those ghastly murders?"

"And where else did your conversation lead you?"

"Our conversation turned from the murders to the perfect sandwich, and how it should be made. It is strange, is it not, how talk at a table flows, twisting this way and that?"

"What was your view on the sandwich question?"

"I favour ham sandwiches," replied the valet. "There I am at one with my employer – or was at one with him, I should say."

"Tell me about the sandwiches you made, that killed Sir William.

Where did you put them?"

"I wrapped them and put them into Sir William's small hamper."

"Where did you put the hamper? Is there any way that the luncheon could have been interfered with?"

Oblonsky shook his head. "The hamper went into my satchel, which I carried at my side until I offered it to Sir William. I have been sitting here in this cell racking my brains, but for the life of me I cannot think of how anyone could have tampered with those sandwiches.

"What am I to do, Mr. Holmes? I swear to you that I did not kill Sir William, and yet I prepared the food that poisoned him. The police think me an anarchist, a man who would kill for his beliefs. How can I hope to escape the gallows? What will become of my sister?" Oblonsky's head fell forward and he covered his face in his hands.

"The outlook is not so bleak as you fear," my friend answered. "Do not despair; many men have been arrested only to be released later without facing a charge. Assure yourself that though you languish here, I shall be doing what I can to discover the truth behind Sir William's death." Holmes stood up and buttoned his coat. "Come, Watson. There is no time to waste. I must be back at Carre Castle before the last of the guests have gone."

The mists we had seen earlier in the day drifting around Carre Castle had now quite vanished, and the enchanted England of King Arthur had vanished with them, leaving in its place the real England of today: gardeners working in the grounds, a pair of bays being harnessed, and, strolling between the hedges of the parterre, the figure of Lord Henry's friend, Mr. Willoughby, smoking a cigar. Holmes did not wait to admire the view, however, but entered the castle immediately, and strode briskly down to the gun-room, where we found Inspector Shaw. "Ah, 'tis Mr. Holmes!" said he. "How was your talk with the prisoner, sir? Did he confess?"

"He did not."

"He'll maintain his innocence to the end, I dare say." "I dare say he will."

The inspector glanced shrewdly into Holmes's face. "You still believe that man to be innocent, do you not? I should like to know how you propose to clear his name. I must warn you, Mr. Holmes, that once we have our man, we're not quick to let him go. We may not be flashy, but we are dogged."

"An admirable virtue, inspector."

"We like to think so. May I ask you, Mr. Holmes, as you don't think Oblonsky was responsible for Sir William's death, who the devil was?"

"I prefer not to air my suspicions until they are confirmed."

"That's all very fine, but when might that be? You know, don't you, that half or more of the guests have left already, and the ones still here will be leaving this afternoon? No good having your suspicions confirmed after the bird has flown, I'd have thought."

"There I agree with you, inspector, and I assure you that the question will be decided, one way or the other, this afternoon."

"And how do you propose to arrange that?"

"Before I answer your very pertinent question, let me first put a question to you: what is the most damning evidence against Oblonsky?"

"There's a deal of evidence against him; but the diamonds found in his bag seal it for me. Circumstantial, you may say, but I'd call that a powerful circumstance."

"You agree, then, that the thief of Sir William's diamonds is in all probability the murderer?"

"Certainly I do. Why do you think we have Oblonsky in custody?" "Well, then," said Holmes, "you will surely agree that we would do well to find the missing jewels, for when we know who has the diamonds, we will know who is behind Sir William's death."

A smirk of complacency appeared on the policeman's face. "I'm afraid you've not quite grasped the facts, Mr.

Holmes. The missing diamonds, as you call them, are no longer missing. They were found in the effects of the man Oblonsky and are now in police custody in Carre station."

"Some of them were found, as you say, but others are still missing." "The fact remains that diamonds belonging to Voigt were found in Oblonsky's bag. That's the fact, whatever your theories say. Oblonsky says he doesn't know how they came there. Well, I do."

"Perhaps you're right, Inspector. Still, I shall carry out my simple plan: I shall make a search of the luggage before it leaves the castle today. I don't want to miss the opportunity while I have it."

"I wish you good fortune hunting for those other jewels, Mr. Holmes," said the policeman. "You'll need it."

"Thank you, Inspector. Come, Watson, let us take a turn outside. The cold air may sharpen my wits."

So we left the inspector muttering about needles in haystacks. For a few minutes we walked in silence, the gravel crunching under our boots and our breath hanging like smoke in the cold air. I was the first to speak: "Are you still in the dark, then?"

Lost in thought, he walked on for a good many paces before answering with the distracted air of a man suddenly woken from sleep. "What? No, there's little mystery about how and why the Diamond King met his death. My problem now is to prove the matter to the satisfaction of the police, so the real murderer can be taken and Oblonsky released. As the inspector kindly reminded us, time is not on our side."

"How did you find out what took place yesterday?" I asked him. "Was there some clue I missed? I can't fathom this business myself, I freely admit."

"My dear fellow, I found out by asking Oblonsky, who obliged by telling me. Though the importance of what he said was not apparent to the man himself – nor to you, I gather," Holmes added, with a sly sidelong glance at me.

"I'm sorry to say it was not. Tell me, what –"

Holmes stopped and put his hand on my arm. "Hush! Do you hear that?"

It was a faint rasping sound, repeated regularly every second or so. "I think the help I'm looking for may be close at hand," said Holmes, and sped off at such a brisk pace that I could scarcely keep up. We were hurrying alongside a bank of tall hedges that hid the castle from view. Rounding it, we found ourselves in a large yard, on three sides of which the stables were ranged. In a corner, smoke was rising from a pile of damp leaves, and beyond it I spied the source of the noise we had heard: a man in the doorway of one of the stables, sawing wood to repair the shaft of a cart that stood by.

"Excellent!" exclaimed Holmes. "There's the fellow I need. Now, Watson, it is of vital importance that the servants of the remaining guests attend me in the gun-room in twenty minutes from now. Will you ensure that? Thank you. Do not fail me. I shall meet you there in twenty minutes."

I carried out Holmes's instructions, and at the appointed time the following people were assembled in the gun-room, besides myself: Inspector Shaw and his constable, Griggs, valet to General Lamb, and Truman, Sir Lumsden's man. We were an awkward, silent group, not knowing what to say to each other, and the few minutes we were together there passed painfully slowly. It came as something of a relief when the door was flung open and Holmes strode into the room. Throwing down his coat and hat, he perched on the edge of a bench and began to question the servants about their movements and those of their masters. The answers he received were not very enlightening, serving merely to confirm what we had already heard, and offering, so far as I could tell, no new information to throw light on the mystery. After a few minutes, Holmes turned to Shaw.

"Do you have any questions for the men, Inspector?" Shaw shrugged and shook his head.

"Nor I. Bye the bye, Inspector," he added, as we left

the room, "I'll be carrying out that search of the rooms in a quarter of an hour or so. Just the servants', I think, don't you?"

Shaw darted an angry glance at Holmes, and moved his hand side to side in a furious gesture of negation, demanding immediate silence. I could well understand the inspector's anger, for it was most likely that the servants, only a few yards behind, had heard his words, and a search would be rendered quite pointless were they alerted to it. But my friend failed to notice the inspector's warning, and indeed made matters worse by continuing, "Watson, you'll help me, won't you? I'll start with Truman's room, and then we can go on to Griggs'."

I, too, tried to signal to Holmes to remain silent, although by then any harm was already done. Once we turned the corner in the corridor, however, Holmes changed utterly. The absented-minded Holmes who had strolled down the passage with us suddenly tautened in every sinew. Throwing at us a glance of the fiercest concentration, he put his finger to his lips, and, whispering in a hiss, "Follow me!" sped down the corridor. He turned, raced through a dining-hall, and then into another corridor. I realised, as I struggled to match his pace, that we were now in the East wing, at the foot of the stairs. Up he galloped, we following him as close as we could, when we met the carpenter with his tool-bag coming down, the same man whom I had seen half-an-hour ago in the stable yard. "Is it done?" asked Holmes.

"All done as you asked, sir."

"Good man!" he said, and hurried on. We ran up the second flight of stairs and found ourselves in the narrow passage Oblonsky had spoken of, with doors on either side. Holmes opened one of them. He stepped inside first, and, again enjoining us to silence with a finger to his lips, ushered in the three of us: myself, Inspector Shaw, and his constable. The room we entered was as dark as a cupboard, and not much larger, its ceiling sloping down almost to the floor. It smelt of staleness and dust, and was full of boxes, trunks, upturned chairs and other jumble. The floor was of rough planks. There was no window, but the darkness was pierced by a single beam of light in which motes of dust swirled as we disturbed the air. Holmes beckoned us over to show us its source: a hole freshly cut in the wall at about four feet from the floor. I bent down and peeped through. I saw a small room, plainly furnished, lit by a dormer window in the slope of the ceiling. Under the window was a narrow bed, and a small table with a candle and a box of vestas upon it. A fireplace stood in the opposite wall and a cupboard in the alcove. On the floor lay two cases, the lids closed.

"Griggs' room," whispered Holmes. "He will be returning to it at any moment. Absolute silence is essential! The creaking of a floorboard might be enough to alarm him. Constable, do you stand by the door, and be ready to block his escape when I give the signal."

We did not have long to wait before we heard footsteps coming up the stairs and along the passage towards us. The steps ceased, and we heard a door-handle turn. I peered into the bedroom. At first I saw nothing, only hearing the sounds of hurried movement and a step on the wooden floor, for the door was not visible through the peep-hole. Then a figure came into view; it was the manservant Griggs. He glanced about him. Had he seen or heard something to arouse his suspicions?

For a few moments he hesitated. Then, crouching down to the floor, he plunged his hands into one of the cases and started flinging out clothes left and right. He pulled out a small packet which he pushed into his coat pocket, and then returned to the search, rummaging frantically until he pulled out another packet. I felt a touch on my shoulder. Holmes was signing me to let him watch. I moved aside, and he bent down to the spy-hole, too dark a figure to make out except for where the light shone in a bright circle on his predatory eye. His hand was up, ready to give the constable the signal.

We waited breathlessly, not daring to move.

Suddenly Holmes dropped his hand, and the policeman rushed out, followed by the rest of us. He flung open the door, and over his shoulder I saw Griggs leap to his feet and snarl like a cornered animal. Griggs rushed to the little window, flung it open and, to my unspeakable horror, leapt out before the constable could stop him – out into a sheer drop of forty feet to the ground. I could scarcely believe what I saw when the constable immediately dived out of the window after him, and was gone.

I ran to the window and saw the manservant and the policeman running away from me down a roof valley six feet below the window-sill, the roof sloping up on one side and on the other side a crenellated parapet. The policeman was gaining on his quarry, but before he could catch him Griggs scrambled up the roof towards its apex, grasping at a chimney-stack to help pull himself up the steep slope. The constable seemed about to follow when Griggs' feet above him, scrabbling desperately to grip on the slippery roof, dislodged several slates. The policeman shielded himself from them with his arm as they slid and clattered down the roof and over the battlements. Griggs managed to grasp the ridge and began hauling himself upwards. I was about to climb out to help when, with a cry of, "The other side, man!" Holmes dashed out of the room and across the passage into the opposite room, Oblonsky's.

We opened its window and I started to clamber out when I instantly froze; on this side the roof had no parapet, but only a gutter and the forty foot drop to the courtyard. I glanced sideways up; silhouetted against the sky was the figure of Griggs, perched on the ridge of the roof. He held something in his hand, which with a vile oath he flung down at the policeman on the other side of the roof. He reached down to pick up another missile and aimed again, but this time leaned so far back for his throw that he lost his balance; waving his arms and clutching wildly at the air he slowly toppled backwards towards us and, with a hideous wail, slithered head-first down the roof, over the guttering, and out of sight.

We stood in the courtyard. On the ground behind us lay the body of Griggs, covered by a blanket, with the constable standing guard over it until the police surgeon should arrive. Inspector Shaw, showing little of his earlier hostility, was discussing the case with Holmes.

"We were convinced at first that Oblonsky was our man, I'll grant you," he admitted. "Of course, we would have got round to Griggs soon enough, have no doubts on that score. But you were the quicker, Mr. Holmes, I won't deny it. When did you first have doubts about Oblonsky?"

"I never thought him a suspect. From the outset it seemed most unlikely to me that Oblonsky was the culprit."

The inspector twisted the end of his moustaches as he tried to make sense of this remark. "But it was he who poisoned the sandwiches," he said.

"Was it?"

"Well, he prepared them. Much the same thing."

"Not quite the same thing, but I grant you that everyone must have known that, as Sir William's valet, he was the one who prepared those sandwiches."

"Exactly."

"As you say, exactly. Tell me, Inspector, if you wished to murder a man, would you do it in the one way that you knew would immediately establish your guilt in everyone's eyes?"

The inspector frowned thoughtfully. "Well," he continued, "but what about the diamonds in his bag?"

"There again, is it likely that a murderer would leave such incriminating items in his own luggage? No, they were placed there by somebody else.

"So I started with the likelihood that Oblonsky was not the murderer. Was there anyone else I could eliminate? Well, the guests were unlikely suspects. The theft of the poison from the scullery cupboard pointed to a servant. In the bustle of the kitchens, a servant might have found his way into the scullery without attracting much attention, but not a guest. One can hardly imagine General Lamb or the Marquess appearing in the kitchens unnoticed. So, a servant other than Oblonsky was indicated.

"But further than that, I was at a loss. It was not until Oblonsky told me of the singular change in Griggs' behaviour that I had my first positive clue. Griggs' coldness, even hostility, had turned to an astonishingly warm friendship in an instant, it seemed. When had it changed so suddenly? When Oblonsky had looked through the doorway and seen Griggs rummaging in a suitcase. It was from that moment that Griggs had sworn undying loyalty to the principles so dear to Oblonsky's heart. Oblonsky himself was clearly unaware of the significance of that moment. He had seen Griggs rummaging in a suitcase and, naturally enough, thought little of it. Yet it was evidently of the greatest importance to Griggs, if he changed so suddenly from the moment he was spotted. What was his secret? I asked myself.

"Someone had stolen the diamond jewels from Voigt. Suppose that person was Griggs, I wondered, and that what Oblonsky had seen unawares was Griggs secreting the stolen jewels in his case. Griggs, surprised in his guilty act, did all he could to placate Oblonsky for the time being by claiming a kind of brotherhood with him. For the time being only, for while Oblonsky lived, Griggs was unsafe, as he thought. When the conversation in the kitchen turned to sandwiches, and Oblonsky announced his preference for ham sandwiches, Griggs leapt to the conclusion that Oblonsky was preparing ham sandwiches for himself. Here was an opportunity to silence Oblonsky permanently, he thought.

Seizing his chance, he used the confusion of the kitchen to make his move, adding the arsenic to the mustard when Oblonsky had stepped away from the table. He was lucky enough to find the rat poison in the cupboard that should have been locked. He prepared the lethal mustard, with what results we know, and put some of the less valuable jewels he had stolen into Oblonsky's case to incriminate him.

"No other hypothesis fitted the facts, but proof was lacking. The other diamonds beside the tie-pin were, I guessed, hidden somewhere in Griggs' effects. I therefore announced a search of the servants' rooms, making quite sure that Griggs, in particular, heard me, and I waited for him to lead us to the hidden jewels. A crude stratagem, perhaps, but it served its purpose."

"Ah, now I see!" exclaimed Shaw. "You had me there, Mr. Holmes, I can't deny it." He smiled as understanding dawned, but a moment later he was frowning again and pulling on his moustaches. "Wait a moment," he said. "Why bother to use any of the jewels at all to implicate Oblonsky? Although the poisoned food didn't kill the intended victim, the fact that Oblonsky prepared it was enough to have him arrested and out of the picture."

"We'll never know now," said Holmes, with a nod towards the body under the blanket, "but my guess would be that he was simply trying to be clever. He held in his hand more wealth than he could dream of, so he could afford to use some of the lesser jewels to add to Oblonsky's apparent guilt."

Shaw shook his head in despair. "The Diamond King, they call him, one of the richest men in the world. They say an army of thousands protects his diamond trade. And what becomes of him? Another man's servant steals his beloved diamonds from under his nose and then kills him by mistake."

Our trap drove up. Opening the door, Holmes turned to the inspector.

"I take it you'll be releasing Oblonsky without delay?" "I will indeed."

"Then my business here is finished."

Holmes and I climbed in, the driver flicked the reins, and we set off for Brailston Thorpe. As we turned into the main drive, I saw a group of four or five men gathered under one of the vast elms that lined the drive on either side. Two of the men were on horseback. One of those on foot gave a signal to the driver to pull up, and walked over to us.

"Mr. Sherlock Holmes?"

"That is my name."

"Perhaps you would be good enough to step over here. Lord Ambleside would like to speak with you."

As he approached the group, the man on the tallest horse turned towards him and looked down. "Mr. Holmes, the detective! You have been looking into the death of my friend Voigt."

"I have, my Lord."

"It was his servant, they tell me." "It was General Lamb's servant."

"Another one? What a damnable business! Is he under arrest?"

"He is dead, my lord."

"No, the servant, the one who killed Voigt."

"He is dead. He fell from the roof not an hour ago."

"The roof? What was he doing on the roof?" He raised his hand to forestall an unnecessary answer. "Well, it doesn't much matter now. I won't keep you any longer, Mr. Holmes. Rat poison!' he sighed. "What a beastly way to go!"

The Marquess turned back to his group, leaving Holmes and me to continue our journey home.

The Adventure of Urquhart Manse

by Will Thomas

"Mr. Holmes," our visitor said, "I must ask you to listen to my story in its entirety, without question or comment until it is done. Afterward, I will readily answer anything that you may ask. If you can accomplish this feat, I assure you, you will have succeeded already where Scotland Yard has failed."

Sherlock Holmes raised a brow in her direction, and eyed her speculatively. She was a comely young woman, almost too young to have the word Mrs. in front of her name.

"Very well, madam," he said.

"And you, Doctor, do I have your word as well?"

"You have it most readily, Mrs. Urquhart. Now pray tell us your story."

"Very well," she said, and sat back in the basket chair in our sitting room. She was petite, and smartly dressed, but there were dark circles under her eyes signaling sleepless nights. Something of significance was troubling her.

"First of all, I grew up in Tunbridge Wells, the daughter of a merchant sea captain, Daniel Cavell, who went down with his ship in the Indian Ocean off of Borneo when I was six. Since then I have lived with my mother, or did until I was married last year.

"I met Alexander Urquhart at the garden party of a friend, which he admits to having been dragged to by his brother, Andrew. Alec and I were attracted to each other immediately, and within a month our courtship began. The family lives in an old estate named Urquhart Manse, on the Old Kent Road, outside of town. It is set back among trees, and has fallen on better days. Alec invited us there for lunch one day. It was a gloomy old pile, in need of a woman's touch. While we were there, mother and I had the chance to meet Andrew, his younger brother. He must have been younger by mere minutes, for the two were twins."

So far, Holmes was keeping his promise to her, but was writing furiously upon his cuff with a small, silver pencil.

"Alec works in London as a stock-broker, but Andrew – I'm afraid he doesn't do much of anything. He claims to be an actor, but on most days he makes small repairs on the estate which, frankly, he has no skill in making. Both he and Alec are tall and red-haired, but while Andrew is clean-shaven, Alec has a becoming moustache.

"We were married before Christmas, and I moved into the manse. Sometimes I think there is an air of tragedy about the place. Alec admitted to me that he had assumed he and Andrew were the last of the family in his line, but that my arrival had given him hope for the future. I took the house in hand, trying to brighten it up a bit, but I have been aided in no way whatsoever by the housekeeper, Mrs. Petrie. She is a dour old Scotswoman, who seems to resent my presence in the house. She used to be the boys' nanny, however, and Alec wouldn't think of getting rid of her. She has a wing all to herself, the east wing, which Andrew claims has been water damaged by holes in the roof which he hopes to eventually patch. That is how matters stood until last week."

Holmes cleared his throat. I had at least a dozen questions, and I was sure his must approach the century mark at least. However, he had made a promise. He gestured for her to continue.

"Monday morning I arose early, intending to look over the kitchen accounts before Mrs. Petrie arrived. I found

Andrew dead at the foot of the stairs. The staircase is old and worm-eaten, and some of the boards are loose. I have tripped on them myself, and had taken Andrew to task for not tending to them. Obviously he had come down in the middle of the night too quickly, and fallen. I woke everyone with my cry. Mrs. Petrie made some rather rude remarks in her grief. She claimed she knew my presence in the old house would bring tragedy.

"Alec was beside himself with grief. He ran into the hall in his dressing gown and held his brother's stiff body until the police and an inspector arrived. Of course, I cannot say what it must be like to lose a twin brother, but my husband was more broken up than I have ever seen him.

"Since then he has been very polite, but distant. When I taxed him about it, he told me it was grief. He seems very distracted, and once or twice he has barked at Mrs. Petrie, which I've never seen him do before. It's obvious he has been under a great deal of strain. I suggested he take a few days off from his firm to grieve properly, but he dismissed the idea out of hand. Two nights ago, I awoke to find Alec standing in my bedchamber, glaring at me. I almost cried out, but he merely turned and left the chamber. It gave me a strange, unsettled feeling. I almost wished I had never come there. That's all, I'm afraid. Yesterday I called our solicitor and asked for the name of a good detective, and he gave me yours. I made the appointment and here I am."

"Good?" Holmes asked.

"Well, competent rather. He said you were the best in London."

Holmes gave a thin-lipped smile.

"That is a pretty little story. May I ask questions now?" She gripped the hand rails of the basket chair.

"Ask away, Mr. Holmes."

"Did you immediately suspect the man dead at the foot of the stairs was your husband, or did that come later?"

I suspect some women would have fallen apart at the

bluntness of the question, but she swallowed and answered.

"It wasn't immediate, no, but his manner was so different afterward that I began to think he might not be Alec at all."

"Did Andrew Urquhart give you any indication that he might be attracted to you?"

"I fear he did. He watched me all the time. Sometimes I found him standing in a doorway just watching me. At meals he was very loquacious, quite unlike Alec, and he tended to flirt, even in front of his own brother. Twice he told me he wished he had been the first to meet me at the garden party."

"I assume Alec is the heir."

"Yes, Mr. Holmes. Alec owns all the property, such as it is, but he is also responsible for it. He provides the sole income we all live upon."

"May I take it Andrew had no knowledge of stocks and bonds or brokerage?"

"Not a whit," Mary Urquhart said. "Or so I assume."

"The only physical difference between them was the moustache your husband wears? There was no birthmark or other feature which might help you determine which brother is now living with you?"

"None, I'm afraid. I wish it were that simple."

"Perhaps it is that simple. Why not simply ask him if he is Andrew?"

"I've wanted to for ages, but if I did, and he actually is Alec, it would crush him. He is having a difficult time enough dealing with his brother's death."

"And if he is Andrew?"

"Then he could simply lie. He was an actor, and never as honest in his speech as my husband."

For a moment she shook, and I was concerned, for Holmes abominates emotion during a case. However, she mastered herself, and bade him continue.

"Do you think you could recognize a false moustache?"

"I think so, but Andrew was very good at such things. He kept a make-up table for his creations."

"Kept or keeps, Mrs. Urquhart? In your heart of hearts, do you believe he is or isn't your husband?"

"I'm not saying I believe, Mr. Holmes, but I very much suspect he is not. If it is so, has he killed his own brother in order to possess everything, all of it, including me?"

"That is what Watson and I intend to find out. Did Andrew Urquhart seem in any way prone to violence?"

She considered the matter carefully, tapping at her lip in thought. "He was not normally as forceful as Alec in speech, but he was more guarded. Who really knew what he was like privately? I will say this, he was not without strength. Some of the repairs he made required lifting heavy wood and rock. Just because his interest was in theater did not mean he was physically weak."

"How did Andrew die, if, indeed, it was Andrew? What was the coroner's verdict?"

"It was ruled an accident. Misadventure was the term he used. He fell coming down the staircase and broke his neck."

Holmes turned to me and raised his eyebrows.

"Yes, a fall down stairs can frequently result in a broken neck. The head is thrown into all kinds of contortions by tumbling against hard surfaces," I told them.

Holmes turned back to our guest and tented his fingers in front of him.

"And when you say you woke to find your husband staring at you, how exactly was he staring? Did he seem menacing, or troubled, or did he appear angry? What was your impression?"

"It was really remarkable. First of all, his nightshirt and hair were rumpled from sleep. The look he gave me I can only describe as fierce. I almost feared for my life. I would have tried to soothe him, but he suddenly turned and left the room, as if in a dream."

"I see," Holmes responded. "Tell me, Mrs. Urquhart, since you first met your husband, up until your arrival here today, did you find the inhabitants of Urquhart Manse to be secretive? Are they, for example, cut off from all their neighbors? Did you suspect that they were colluding together to keep some fact or facts away from you?"

"Oh, very much so, Mr. Holmes. That is exactly how I felt, and feel even now."

"Then Mrs. Urquhart, I accept your case. How amenable is the man you live with to accepting visitors?"

"Not at all, sir. As Mrs. Petrie says, 'we keep ourselves to ourselves.' However, the Old Kent Road is often used by hikers. I believe there are guides for walking in the area."

"Capital! Do not be surprised if a pair of tired and footsore travellers suddenly appear at your door this evening."

"I shall look forward to it. What of your fee?"

"I shall send a billet afterward. Nothing calamitous, I assure you."

"Thank you, Mr. Holmes. Dr. Watson."

I showed her to the door. When I returned, Holmes already had the Baedecker in hand and was looking up the railway time tables to Tunbridge Wells.

"Have you anything pressing in your surgery this afternoon or tomorrow?" he asked.

"Would it matter if I did?"

"I'm sure it would to someone."

He rubbed his hands in anticipation of an interesting case. Then he stuffed shag tobacco into his old oily clay and lit it.

"Surely this fellow can't think he can kill his own brother in order to take his wife, pretty as she was," I told him.

"Did you find her pretty? I hadn't noticed. I'm sure there is far more to it than wife-stealing, Watson, but it is no good theorizing before the facts. Let us have a good lunch and then prepare for a journey to Kent."

After lunch we changed into clothes more fitting for the country, along with stout walking shoes. We loaded a pair of rucksacks with enough clothing for a few days, and I chose a stout blackthorn stick and my old service revolver, just in case. We were at Charing Cross Station near one, in order to catch the South Eastern Railway commuter train south. I had no scruples about abandoning the hot, torpid city for rural Kent on such a beautiful May afternoon.

Arriving in Tunbridge Wells, Holmes purchased an ordinance map and a copy of A WALKING GUIDE TO HISTORIC KENT. Holmes does not take exercise, but he had a nervous, energetic constitution that was stimulated by a walk of a few miles. As for myself, my war wound was always aided by a marathon walk in the country, and my lungs invigorated by the air of the south coast.

We took an omnibus out of the old royal town and alighted again in the country a couple of miles from Urquhart Manse. Rather than growing tired, we were both enervated by the walk, and the anticipation of what we would find when we got there. Finally, we spotted the house, set back from the road by a tall wrought-iron fence. Its yard had been let go to ruin. The building was a horseshoe shaped affair, with both wings facing the back, and a portico in the front. The bones of the old house were still strong, but the surface had been weathered by years of neglect. It nearly had the look of an old haunted house. I could see how a new bride brought to such a house would find it daunting.

"This I where you turn up lame, old fellow," Holmes said.

I gave a cry of pain and removed my left shoe. Holmes leant me a shoulder and helped me to the front door, where we knocked loudly. After a few minutes a small, sharp-faced woman answered, looking at us with suspicion.

"I say," Holmes began. "My friend has just turned an ankle in the rut in front of your house. I think he needs medical attention."

"Away wi' ye!" Mrs. Petrie cried. "We need nane of your kind here!"

"Who is it?" a voice I recognized as our client's asked.

"A pair of vagabonds by the look of 'em," the housekeeper replied. "My friend is hurt!" Holmes called out. "He needs a doctor!"

"Oh, dear," Mary Urquhart said, and a moment later appeared at the door behind the housekeeper. "What has happened?"

"He has turned an ankle, ma'am," Mrs. Petrie said. "He can walk back to town well enough. It's probably a scheme to bilk us for money."

"What is it?" a man asked, appearing behind both women. He was tall, with a head of red hair and blue eyes. He wore a moustache. It could only be Urquhart, though which one was still a matter of dispute.

"This poor man has fallen and injured himself. I think he must get off his ankle."

"We don't take visitors here," Urquhart replied.

"But he has injured himself, probably in one of the ruts in front of the house. You really must do something about them, Alec."

"No visitors," he repeated.

"Such nonsense!" Mrs. Urquhart said. "Come in, gentlemen, and rest yourselves. No doubt you have walked for miles. Mrs. Petrie, bring some tea."

"I doubt there is much call for that," the housekeeper said. "Mary," Urquhart warned.

"Alec," she implored. "They are guests in our home, our very first, in fact. I hope you will see that they are given proper hospitality. I would not want to be embarrassed in my own home."

Confronted by an obstinate wife and two strangers expecting him to do the right thing, he finally relented.

"Very well. Come in, gentlemen. Forgive my rude country manners. I'm Alec Urquhart."

"Sherlock Holmes," my friend said, pumping his hand. "John Watson."

I limped forward and fell into a stuffed chair.

"We were taking a Kentish tour, with the aid of a guidebook," Holmes said. "Watson and I are solicitors in

London. My friend just had to get out of the City, you know."

"Fresh air," I muttered, as I slowly raised my "injured" ankle to a hassock. "I don't think it is broken."

"Then you'd best be on your way!" the housekeeper called from the doorway.

"Tea, Mrs. Petrie!" Mary Urquhart insisted.

Grumbling, the woman complied. She was a dour looking older woman, thin and bony, but with a will of iron. Obviously she had been given the run of the house, and had no problem offering her opinions. Mrs. Urquhart was challenged to keep her in her place.

"I work in the City," Alec went on.

"Oh, really? Where?" Holmes asked.

"Carr and Threadgill, in the Commercial Road."

"A stockbroker!" Holmes said to me. "We must be careful with this one, Watson. A canny firm by its reputation."

"It is. How far did you hope to get today?" Urquhart asked.

"Wadhurst."

"As far as that? I'm afraid you wouldn't have reached it unless you walked all night."

"You disappoint me exceedingly. Is there an inn nearby?"

"Not within five miles, I'm afraid."

"Alec!" Mary Urquhart cried. "Invite them to spend the night! We have plenty of rooms."

"I don't think that would be appropriate, being in mourning for Andrew as we are."

"But Mr. Watson is injured! He cannot walk anywhere, and there is no way to hire a vehicle at this time of night."

Urquhart looked about to argue, but after staring into the eyes of our client for a few moments he finally relented.

"I shall have to inform Mrs. Petrie."

"I'll do it," Mrs. Urquhart said. With a twinkle in her eye she left the room.

"We regret imposing ourselves upon you, sir," Holmes stated, after she was gone. "Watson and I could pay –"

"I'm sure that will not be necessary," came the reply. Urquhart's pale features colored.

Mrs. Petrie showed us to our rooms with as little grace as she dared. Dinner consisted of overcooked beef and undercooked potatoes. Afterward, our host treated us to whisky-and-sodas.

"Have you lived here long, sir?" Holmes asked.

"For generations, Mr. Holmes. My ancestor came south among the Sassenach with James 1st. Our family has been here even since."

"These old houses require a good deal of repair. There is always something breaking or needing to be fixed."

"You have no idea. It seems at times that the house is falling down about our ears. My dear brother Andrew was doing his best to maintain the house, but alas, he is gone now. He met with an accident on the staircase."

"We are sorry to hear that," Holmes said.

"Yes, he is gone, right when we needed him most."

Urquhart seemed disinclined to discuss the matter further. We left him brooding and staring into the fire.

"What are your impressions, Watson?" Holmes asked, when we were in our room.

"If the man is a villain, he is a better actor than I would have credited. What did you think of the moustache?"

"It appears genuine, but a trifle sparse. He could have grown it in under a false one within a week."

Holmes raised his arms to the ceiling and formed fists in frustration. "How I wish I could have seen the brothers together, side by side. They say twins can be identical, but really, no two people are exactly alike. The smallest blemish, spot or mole can distinguish one from the other."

"That housekeeper is a bit of work," I said. "I wonder if she is naturally averse to strangers, or whether there a reason she wants us out of here."

"Let us not forget Mrs. Urquhart waking to find a man glaring at her, no matter which brother it was."

"You know, Holmes, I suspect it might be somnambulism. If so, I suspect her life is in danger. Such cases can lead to violence, particularly if disturbed. If his brother tried to wake him on the stair, for example, just such an outcome might occur. But what are we to do?"

"We must wait until the family settles for the night, then go exploring."

"The East Wing!" I cried, rubbing my hands together.

"Yes, Watson, I am particularly interested in the East Wing." Holmes and I were old hands at waiting for the stroke of midnight.

We slipped off our shoes and made our way slowly up the grand staircase to the first floor. Holmes went ahead, feeling for every creaking stair in our path, while I brought up the rear with my "twisted ankle". We were taking a risk of being caught, but I knew I had my trusty revolver with me, if worse came to worst.

The East Wing was a shambles, with falling plaster, peeling wallpaper, and moldy old carpets. All the rooms, which numbered four to a side in this wing, were dark, save for one at the far end. The floor was ancient and dusty, but I noticed several footmarks going back and forth. Holmes measured his foot against one.

"Size ten," he said. "Very near the size of the Brothers Urquhart. One of them must have come here recently, but for what purpose I cannot say."

We began to open the various doors in the wing. All were unlocked. Some were bedrooms untenanted, and smelling of damp and wood rot. A few were in need of repair, and one had tools and paint tins on the floor. Holmes stepped forward and ran his finger across a lid, it came away covered in dust.

"So far, Mrs. Urquhart's opinion of her brother-in-law's carpentry skills have been confirmed. But hush!"

We heard a voice coming from the one room in the wing with light gleaming from under the door. It was at the far end, the farthest from the staircase. Why would a housekeeper want to be so far from her kitchen, I asked myself. I could not mistake Mrs. Petrie's shrill and peevish tone coming from the room. To whom was she speaking? From what I could make out, she was giving someone her litany of complaints about the new visitors and the lady of the house. I strained my ear but could hear no response whatsoever. Was it herself she was speaking to, or a dog, or was someone else in the room? I began to imagine all sorts of things. Something was very wrong in this house that Mary Urquhart had come to. It was far from the ideal home a bride expects upon her marriage.

We were progressing down the hall, in order to press our ears against the wall of the housekeeper's room, when I accidentally trod upon a board that squeaked. Holmes nipped behind an old standing clock, while I jumped back into the dark recess of a door frame. We were just in time. Mrs. Petrie stepped out with a raised candle and looked about her. She had a shotgun broken open over her arm. Our seeming advantage evaporated.

"Who's there?" she cried. "No tricks, now!"

We dared not move. She looked about and raised her lamp higher, but did not come further into the hall. If it were a dog she was speaking to, she might unleash it, and if the rest of the house was any indication, it would not be a border collie. However, she closed the door and apparently did not give us a second thought. After a moment or two Holmes stepped from behind the clock and gestured for me to follow him.

"That was a close call," I said, when we were out of the wing again. "Quite," Holmes said. "The last thing I expected was that Mrs. Petrie would be so heavily armed."

"What do we do now? Go back to our room?"

"No. We'll be forced to leave in the morning, so we must use our time wisely. I wish to examine the stairs where Alec Urquhart's body was found."

So saying, he pulled a small dark lantern from his pocket and lit it with a pack of vestas. Then he carried it with him and led the way to the staircase.

"Don't you mean Andrew Urquhart?" I asked. "Do I? That remains to be seen.

Reaching the bottom of the stairway, Holmes immediately went down upon his hands and knees, examining the carpet with the aid of the candle. At one point he crawled down the steps like a tomcat, examining the decayed wood of the steps. When he reached the floor where the body came to rest after the fatal fall, he even went down upon his stomach, examining the floor with a pocket lens. Finally, he sniffed the carpet thoroughly.

"What is it?" I asked.

"Soap," He answered. "Scented with bay rum."

"Shaving soap!"

"Precisely. I think we can both conjecture how it got there."

"I'm surprised the local inspector didn't notice it."

"I'd have been surprised if he had," Holmes said.

"Where do we go from here?" I asked, as he stood and stretched his lean frame.

"To our beds. If you will play watchman for the first few hours, and listen for any movement in the house, I will stay awake until dawn. We must be ready when Mrs. Petrie comes down for breakfast."

"Ready to do what?" I asked.

"Oh, I have a small diversion planned, but in order for it to work, we must separate the housekeeper from her rifle."

My three hour watch was uneventful, and after I shook Holmes awake, I lay down upon my bed and dozed while fully dressed. I was awakened at dawn by a rooster somewhere nearby, reminding me how far we were from the cosmopolitan streets of London. When I sat up in bed, I found Holmes sitting in a chair with his knees drawn up, tobacco burning in his clay pipe.

"Are you ready?" he asked eagerly.

"Is Mrs. Petrie stirring?"

"She has just gone to the kitchen to light the stove. Shall we explore the East Wing without her presence?"

"By Jove, yes!"

We climbed the stairs again, I with my hand on my revolver and he armed with a set of skeleton keys. Holmes was a match for any burglar. We reached the housekeeper's door, and while he picked the lock, I put my ear to the door, listening for any sound within. There was no whining from a dog that I could hear, or any cry, human or animal. The room appeared to be deserted.

"That's got it," my friend said, but before I could respond the door flew open in our faces and we were knocked to the ground. Something sailed over my head. I had just enough time to turn my head and glare after it.

"What was it?" Holmes asked, for I had a better look at whoever had knocked us over than he.

"It was most definitely a man," I stated. "Did you recognize him?"

"How should I have recognized him?"

Just then there was a scream from the corridor. It sounded like Mrs. Urquhart. We leapt to our feet and ran down the hall as quickly as possible. In the hall we passed Mrs. Petrie, armed with nothing more dangerous than a spatula. She glared at us scornfully as I ran past on my injured ankle.

Mary Urquhart wailed again, and as we neared her door we could hear the sounds of furniture being upended. As we entered, we saw Alec Urquhart locked in a desperate struggle with another man. Both were ginger haired, and when the other fellow turned his head I saw he was his double in every way, down to the very moustache on his upper lip.

Sherlock Holmes did not hesitate, but jumped upon the back of the combatant who was dressed, Alec Urquhart still being in his nightshirt. I joined the fray as well, seizing the man's muscular arm and trying to keep him from strangling Urquhart. Was this Andrew returned from the grave, I wondered, or had Alec set up this up to trap his brother into revealing his jealousy?

Whoever we were wrestling with, he was uncommonly strong, and seemed to have little difficulty tossing all three of us about the room. Holmes had an arm wrapped about the fellow's throat, but he had little effect against his bull neck. This version of Urquhart seemed larger and stronger, with a deep chest and apelike arms. With one shake of his arm he set me flying against the wall. Mrs. Urquhart, cowering in a corner, shrieked again.

"Archie!" I heard Mrs. Petrie's voice behind me. "Put the man down immediately!"

In answer, he swept the air with one of his long arms and knocked the poor woman senseless. Then he tore Holmes from his shoulders and flipped him over onto his back with a jarring crash. Having done that, he closed his hands about the throat of the last of the Urquharts, and began to squeeze the life from him.

Alec Urquhart's face was already pale, but now it turned chalky white, and his lips looked blue. I tried to remove the fingers from his fragile throat, but they were like steel. The poor man could not take much more of this. As a medical man, I feared he was approaching death. "Archie!" Mary Urquhart barked. "What do you think you're doing? You put him down this instant!"

The muscular attacker suddenly looked up, his concentration broken. His face looked perplexed, and possibly even ashamed.

"Did you hear me?" she continued. "Am I going to have to repeat myself? Take your hands away now.'

The thick, ruddy fingers began to pull away from Urquhart's throat, leaving him coughing and gasping for air. The intruder looked down sheepishly.

"You know this man?" I asked.

"I believe he is the man I found staring at me that night. He looks very much like my late husband. He can only be another brother!

"Thank you, Archie," she continued, using the name the housekeeper had supplied. "I'm very proud of you. Now can you come over here and sit beside me? I shall let you hold my hand if you do."

A feint smile grew on the fellow's lips and he crossed the room to her. I saw an expression on his face which explained everything. This brother was mentally slow.

"So," I said. "The Urquharts weren't twins at all. They were triplets."

"Precisely," Holmes said. "Watson, would you be so good as to see to Mrs. Petrie?"

I crossed to the old woman. She was in her sixties and the blow had sent her sprawling. I helped her up and nothing appeared broken, but she there was a dark bruise upon her cheek.

"My god," our host finally choked out.

"Do I have the honor of addressing Mr. Andrew Urquhart?" Holmes asked.

All of us leaned forward for the answer. Mary Urquhart hand even squeezed the hand that had been choking our host a few minutes earlier.

"You do," he finally muttered.

The young bride burst into tears. I handed her my handkerchief, while the strange doppelganger patted her hand with mute concern on his face.

"You mustn't think I killed him, Mary," Urquhart went on. "I was genuinely happy for Alec, even if I admired you myself. The morning I found him dead at the foot of the stair was the worst of my life, but I could tell no one."

"You shaved your brother's corpse, fashioned a false moustache, and took his place," Holmes said.

"I did. I'm afraid I panicked. We had always been trained to keep the family secret, you see, and to never let anyone know about Archie."

"Did he kill your brother?"

"I wish I knew, Mr. Holmes. Archie has a temper, and afterward he doesn't remember things. The truth is he has been very curious about Mary since the wedding. I warned Alec that it was time to move Archie to a proper facility, where he could be looked after properly, but he wouldn't hear of it. We'd had several arguments both before and after the wedding about how Archie was handling all the changes that had occurred, but Alec took all my suggestions as an affront to his abilities. He was head of the Urquhart clan, you see, and he would make all the decisions."

"You understand these events put you in a bad light," Holmes said. "You are the chief suspect in a murder investigation."

"I begin to suspect, sir, that your being here is no accident. Just who are you, really?"

"Mr. Urquhart, I am a consulting detective hired by your sister-in-law to look into the matter of several curious events that have happened since she arrived at this house. I cannot keep the matter hidden, you understand. A man has been slain."

"I understand that, sir, and I am ready to take any punishment the courts find necessary. I loved my brother, and a day hasn't gone by that I haven't regretted his death. I've made several mistakes, but only to try to rectify the large one Alec made when he brought Mary here, yet refused to tell her about Archie."

"I understand there are loose boards upon the staircase. Have you formed a conclusion as to what happened?"

"No, sir, I haven't. I mean, he could have fallen in the middle of the night. The stair was loose and I intended to fix it. However, Archie was agitated the night when Alec fell, but then he is often agitated without causing trouble."

"Many men in your situation would have taken advantage of the situation. Why didn't you?"

"I'd like to think that Mary's arrival awoke in me new possibilities. I wanted to be a better man to please her, not a worse one."

"So, you became a stockbroker," my friend, a thin smile playing on his lips.

"Actually, I rather enjoyed that part. Alec always talked about his work, so I knew the names of his partners, and what he did there. I was terrified on my first day, but I found I enjoyed the work."

"And what was Mrs. Petrie's part in all this?" Holmes continued.

I looked over and saw that the woman had begun crying, the tears rolling down her withered cheeks.

"I was the children's governess before I became housekeeper," she said. "We knew within a few years that something was wrong with Archie. Mr. Urquhart put it about that he had died of diphtheria, then sought out the best medical care. All of them suggested Archie be put away, because of his violent tendencies, but the old master refused. 'A family must look after its own,' he said."

"You kept the secret to this day," Holmes said.

"Aye, and I warn't Mr. Alec he had no business bringing a bride home to this old manse. Nothing but tragedy would e'er come of it. I've naught against you, ma'am. You've a good soul, but I knew the secret would come out one way or the other, and not for good."

There was a silence in the room for a moment or two.

"So, what happens now, Mr. Holmes?" Andrew asked. "According to the courts, I am a dead man."

Holmes turned to me.

"Watson, what is your opinion of Mr. Urquhart's actions?"

I considered the matter. Sometimes Holmes would saddle me with the responsibility for an entire case, almost on a whim.

"It would have been better if he had revealed what had occurred immediately, rather than keep it to himself.

However, he did not take advantage of his circumstances by placing demands upon another man's wife. I believe he was merely trying to contain the mounting problems in order to keep a secret that was not his."

"I believe you are 'off the hook', sir," Holmes told Urquhart. "I cannot fault Watson's logic or judgment."

"Thank you, Mr. Holmes, but what do we do now? According to the law, I am a dead man."

"You want an opinion, sir? Very well, I shall give it. You must resign your position on some pretense and sell this tragic old building. Archie must go into a proper facility with doctors to watch over him. Mrs. Petrie should be given a proper severance, if she wishes to leave. I suggest you move away and change your name."

I thought it a harsh sentence, but the only one under the circumstances.

"And what of Mary?" Andrew Urquhart asked. "That is a decision she must make for herself."

"I shall go home to my parents' house for a while. I have some thinking to do."

"And what of Archie?" Andrew went on. "He might be innocent of the crime."

"Perhaps, but your brother must be put away in either case, whereas if you are found responsible, you will surely hang for it."

Holmes turned and regarded our client.

"Mrs. Urquhart, do you consider this matter concluded?"

"Yes, Mr. Holmes. Thank you."

"Watson and I must return to London, then. Our continued absence encourages mischief among the Underworld."

We gathered our few possessions and made our way back to the station. Holmes did not speak about the case again until we were on the platform.

"A family secret causes all sorts of mischief, Watson. It is a conspiracy as much as any governmental plot, and the one whom is hurt the most is often the most innocent."

Some cases end with a timely resolution, while others we don't hear about for months or even years later. One day during the holiday season a couple entered our consulting rooms in Baker Street unannounced. They were a fashionably dressed couple living in Paris, where intrigue was not unknown. They were a Mr. and Mrs. Anderson of the 18th Arrondissement. He was a stockbroker, with a shock of red hair and a nice looking imperial. His wife, "Marie", looked quite content. As a medical man, I suspected she was expecting a child. Perhaps there would be more Urquharts after all.

The Adventure of the Seventh Stain

by Daniel McGachey

Preface: The Identity of Cases

Such does his celebrity continue to grow that, despite his retirement to his bees and his studies in Sussex, many are the letters that still arrive daily for Sherlock Holmes, and in particular since my friend finally granted permission that I might share with an admiring world the details of his return from that watery grave in which my published accounts had left him a decade earlier. This, naturally, is a source of considerable pride to the humble narrator of Holmes's adventures; the satisfaction further bolstered by the fact that the post brings me almost as many letters, gifts and requests for a reply or souvenir as are received by my celebrated associate.

Rather, it is *usually* a source of pride. Yet there is little to crow over when a goodly proportion of the day's mail is devoted to messages proclaiming one a liar, a fraud, or a charlatan. There have admittedly been prior accusations that my works are not entirely truthful records, not least from Sherlock Holmes himself who was never shy of offering a detailed critique, whether one had been invited or not. Yet opening a ninth, then a tenth missive in succession to accuse me not simply of the "embellishments" that were the basis for Holmes's disapproval, but of outright deception against my loyal readers, is not a situation for which I was remotely prepared.

The source of this unheralded epidemic of disapprobation lies with the latest edition of *The Strand Magazine*, in which I fulfilled what I considered a long-standing obligation in presenting the adventure I had dubbed "The Second Stain". This title had prompted its own flow of missives requesting further details, since I first made passing mention of it in certain earlier accounts. And it is these fleeting allusions that now cause such ire, for the details I had previously let slip and the particulars in my recently published tale bearing that designation do not tally. So, far from rewarding the curiosity excited by those teasing hints, I have succeeded only in provoking the wrath of those in whom curiosity has turned to frustration.

Revisiting those earlier references to a "Second Stain", I see that in one instance I have it listed as an episode in which Holmes failed to conclude his case satisfactorily, while in the other I have referred to an incident involving some of the most powerful houses in the land. And while, as in my now published statement, the household of the Right Honourable Trelawney Hope may surely be regarded as noble and powerful, certain of the international players initially mentioned are missing from the scene, and Holmes's return of the document that threatened not only his client's political career but also the fate of nations could in no way be regarded a failure. Thus, the public cry of "substitution" or "fake" is not so readily dismissed. So I readily admit that this case is neither of those to which I so recklessly alluded in the past. Yet nor is it a fiction to obscure the true events. It is without question the story of "The Second Stain". However it is not the *only* adventure of Sherlock Holmes to bear this title!

In truth, amongst my notes there exist details of no fewer than *seven* separate cases to which the appellation has been applied; though on delving into those files, closer examination of my occasionally unintelligible handwriting reveals one of these actually to be labelled *"The Second*

Strain", dealing as it does with the misappropriation of a brace of bacillus cultures, each harmless unless brought into contact with the other. It was only due to the rapid action of Sherlock Holmes that half of London narrowly avoided catching a fatal bout of cold. Thus we reduce the total to six, and the affair of the Trelawney Hope document diminishes the number yet further.

Of the others, the case previously referred to as unresolved falls into that category in which Holmes was unable, as in his customary maxim, to entirely eliminate the impossible, herein with relation to a chamber in which a supposed "phantom bloodstain" refused, after more than two centuries, to dry. Holmes was swift in finding the cause of a second, more recent bloodstain and, in turn, the murderess who sought to mask her crime with an ancient curse. But my friend's determination to dispel the far older mystery of the original, livid splash was to remain frustrated, and my report of the venture lies sealed with those other apparently impossible cases that may one day find their solutions in science, yet which, for now, remain within the province of superstition and the supernatural.

Two further sets of notes refer to acts of vandalism which were easily resolved and offer little to excite the reader's interest, while the sixth I find listed involved a celebrated Renaissance painting in a prominent gallery whose discoloured layers of three-hundred year old varnish artfully disguised its far more recent genesis on the easel of an illiterate flower-seller in the cellar of a Soho gin-house.

Which leaves us with one outstanding case, and this, indeed, is that which my readers have been clamouring for. But they must clamour in vain, for it remains one which discretion still stays my hand from signing over to the public gaze. But record it I will, for an undefined future reader, which is a nobler reason than – by documenting the events they are so curious about in papers which must still remain sealed away from their gaze – to spite all those who have taken time to put pen to paper and stamp to envelope to libel my name. Petty? Even if so, by the time other eyes peruse these pages, my pettiness will be long forgotten and posterity will have benefited, whatever my motive.

I. Three Callers at 221B

I had been married little under half-a-year and, as the bright summer days lengthened, my time was divided between the domestic comforts of the marital home and my efforts to establish my new practice. I had not forgotten my good friend, of course, nor would my dear Mary have allowed me to do so, and I endeavoured to make myself known at my former lodgings as often as my schedule permitted. The last such visit had seen our reminiscences cut short by the sudden arrival, and yet more sudden collapse, of Captain Gideon Blackhall of the *S.S. Genevieve*, and a leisurely few hours stretched dramatically into those several tense days in which we strove to uncover the reason behind the captain's sudden lapses into prolonged stretches of fearful, nightmare-haunted sleep. Now, having just received a much revived Blackhall in my surgery, I was able to confirm that the opiates he had been surreptitiously fed, so that his first mate and crew might tend to the practicalities of their thriving smuggling trade undisturbed, would soon be out of his system. So it was with the intention of relaying this good news to Holmes that I ascended the well-worn stairs to my old sitting room.

"Please, calm yourself," said Sherlock Holmes soothingly to the young woman who started from her seat as I bounded into the room. "You have no cause for alarm with Dr. Watson. He may have forgotten his manners as regards knocking on doors in houses where he no longer resides, but in other regards he is quite the gentleman."

"My apologies, Holmes," I stammered. "I shall call again at a more convenient time. I'm deeply sorry if I startled you,

Miss...."

"Miss Lodge had just begun telling me her most interesting story, Watson. I'm sure you won't mind my friend sitting in while we conclude our meeting, Miss Lodge. Besides being a gentleman, as I said, there is no man better to have at one's side in a time of crisis."

As grateful as I was for Holmes's endorsement, I was still more gratified to see the panicked expression on the young woman's face relax into a somewhat bashful smile. "I'm pleased to meet you, Doctor." She offered me her gloved hand, but as I bent to take it she froze indecisively, as if caught in mid-curtsey and, both rather flustered, we straightened up and parted.

Before I could return any pleasantry, Holmes cut in, declaring, "Seat yourself and stop distracting my client from the statement of her case, if you would, Watson." The face of mock chastisement I pulled at this command saw the lady put a handkerchief to her mouth to stifle a laugh, and even Holmes permitted himself a thin smile. "Well, as we all seem to be comfortable in one another's presence, let us continue. Miss Lodge, if you would briefly summarise what you have already told me for my friend's benefit?"

She turned to me, still too self-conscious to look me fully in the eye, and thereby allowing me the opportunity to inspect her more closely. She could have been no more than seventeen, neatly but plainly attired, though both the heaviness of her clothing and the thickness of her gloves were vastly unsuited to the summer's warmth. Her face was scrubbed and pink, her eyes bright, but with a puffiness around them that spoke of recent tears. "My name is Florence Lodge, sir, and my problem is my whole family's problem, for it is our poor older sister who has been taken from us." My eyes must have darted upwards, as if to the Heavens, for she shook her head firmly. "Taken by the law!" She paused, addressing the sudden rise in her voice, her tone as she resumed remaining studiedly polite. "Your pardon, but she has been taken from us by the police, Dr. Watson. She is a good, decent woman who would break neither the law of God nor man! And she would never betray one as has been so good in offering her a generous paying situation, and who has been the very soul of kindness itself to her those years she's been there! But still, she has lost that situation, and lost her liberty, and we don't know what is to be done to help her. For the police say there is proof against her, and she will not tell even us who she loves one word about what has brought her to such a pitiful plight. But I've read enough about you both, sir, to know that if anyone can see through false proofs to find the truth, then surely these are the men I speak to now."

"Oh, surely," agreed Holmes with a quick smile, waving the young lady to continue.

"I can offer you five pounds if you will help free my unfortunate sister. I would gladly give more, but those are all I have set aside. Though if poor Mathilda isn't cleared and allowed her position back, that fiver isn't going to go far in keeping us lot – my mother and little brothers – off the streets. Mathilda's been our chief support since Dad went, and though I try to chip in when I'm earning, someone has to help with the little ones, so it's not as often as I'd like. I'll be able to go to ten, fifteen even, if you can wait a little for the balance."

I was moved by the composure with which Miss Lodge set out her circumstances, with humility but no hint of pleading, and I was further touched by Holmes's simple reply of, "You need not trouble yourself over my fee."

His prospective client, on the other hand, appeared markedly less touched than I by the gesture, replying sharply, "We don't expect anyone's charity."

"Nor do I offer it. If an injustice has been done, my reward will be in seeing it righted. And I have little else to occupy my time at the moment." This latter was said with an edge of asperity, and I scarcely needed to follow Holmes's glance to confirm that it fell upon the pile of newspapers threatening to spill off the table, and the topmost headline – matching that which nestled discreetly in my bag and which was being yelled by every paper vendor in London – proclaiming, "Continent's Foremost Specialists Consulted in Marleigh Towers Tragedy". I could not have declared which was the most likely basis of Holmes's annoyance; that he himself had not been consulted in that matter which had gripped the city for days, or that there were others regarded as closer to the forefront of criminal investigation than he.

What then followed is one of those coincidences that would appear on the page as fanciful and farfetched if it were not absolute fact. My eye had no sooner lit upon that newspaper report than my attention was diverted by the rattle of carriage wheels drawing to a halt below. Having followed one of Holmes's manoeuvres in sitting with my back to the window in order to view his visitor's every change of expression while leaving my own features and the direction of my gaze partially obscured in shadow, it required a mere turn of my head to see that the carriage bore a coat of arms made instantly recognisable by its repeated presence in those news reports. Hurriedly gathering up the overflowing newspapers, I hissed, "Holmes, Lord Sternfleet of Marleigh Towers is on your doorstep."

I had expected these words to galvanise the languid detective, but before even he could spring, alert and energised, from his seat, his young guest was on her feet and at the sitting room door. "I must go! I cannot meet...No, I will not meet...." The chiming of the doorbell cut across her words, and she threw the door wide and rushed from the room.

"I have your address, Miss Lodge," called Holmes. "I shall call on you there to hear the remainder of your account, and so establish how best I may assist you."

The young lady paused at the head of the stairs, snapping heatedly in response, "You shan't find me there, for I'll be waiting vigil outside that place they're keeping her. I can see I wasted my time coming here, and that my sister's troubles and her story are much too petty for you, Mr. Holmes! You'd do us both a kindness in forgetting I ever was here."

"I cannot forget, nor would I wish to!" But my friend was left addressing an empty landing, as the rapid din of her receding footsteps on the stairs was followed by a deep, masculine voice letting fly an exclamation of startled annoyance, and Mrs. Hudson's concerned call after the hastily departing visitor, just as the front door slammed with some finality.

"Such an extraordinary change of demeanour," I shrugged. "Was she perhaps too embarrassed to meet such a distinguished figure?"

"Because she is merely a scullery maid or char and he a peer of the realm? No, there is more to it than that."

But before I could establish what Holmes meant, or how he had known the girl's mode of employment, his landlady hastily entered wearing a flustered look – one which turned rapidly to a grimace of mortification on sighting the cluttered mess of her upstairs front room – and announced severely, "A distinguished gentleman to see you, Mr. Holmes."

"Thank you, Mrs. Hudson, that will be all. My, my; a third caller since the clock chimed the hour? It is as well I am without ego, or such unforeseen popularity might turn my head! Lord Sternfleet, do come in."

"You know me, sir?" demanded the tall, stylishly garbed but grim faced gentleman who strode impatiently into the centre of the room, his dark eyes peering suspiciously from behind a swirling wreath of smoke from the cigar clamped in his gritted teeth; then, glancing at the newspapers I still held in my hands, gruffly adding, "Of course you know me, Mr. Sherlock Holmes. How foolish a question."

"Of course, your Lordship," replied Holmes, with the merest hint of a sly smile in my direction. "Alas, Watson, gone so soon are the days when our noble guests arrived masked and aliased, allowing us a scant few seconds' intrigue at least."

"There can be no intrigue over my visit, I trust," glowered our eminent caller, "as my unhappy circumstances are the most talked about scandal of the summer."

"A prominent foreign gentleman found in his bed with his throat cut while a guest under the roof of one of the nation's most highly esteemed diplomats, and another guest so traumatised by the discovery that she has taken to her own bed, while her renowned husband is torn between his official duties abroad and his husbandly duties toward his stricken wife." "You encapsulate in a few words what the press has devoted yard upon yard of column inches to in these past dreadful days," muttered Lord Sternfleet darkly, seating himself stiff and alert on the sofa toward which Holmes gestured, before he too sat, drawing deeply upon his pipe so that the combined smog from it and his guest's cigar threatened to fill the room.

"Already you have the pre-eminent experts of both affected countries en route to forage the ancestral grounds for traces of an assassin. I am sure your judgement in awarding these specialists *carte blanche* will eventually prove sound. They say that Herr von Waldbaum has the tenacity and stamina to turn entire households on their head in pursuit of his prey, while Monsieur Dubuque is more inclined to probe within the actual heads of those inhabiting the households." If it were possible for the nobleman's expression to darken any further, these words provided just cause. "I would have been most interested in studying these gentlemen at work, but as you observed from my now disrupted previous appointment, I am already engaged on a case."

Lord Sternfleet's eyes bulged in their sockets. "That unruly child who practically dashed me over on your doorstep?"

"My client," said Holmes blandly. "Yes."

"But you surely realise the enormity of my situation,

Holmes! My family's long-established name lies in hazard. My cousins are the Earls of Shardsmere. My own sister is married to a Duke! What affects my reputation also overshadows some of the noblest houses in Britain! And as this ghastly business has taken place on British soil, a British agency must take charge of these enquiries."

"And on whose advice do you approach me? Not on the say-so of Scotland Yard, for the official charged with taking the case over from your local constabulary – Inspector Godfrey Highford? Thank you, Watson – is not one that has consulted me in the past."

"Nor did he wish you consulted here, for what his approval matters. Yet your suitability and availability for this commission were vouched for by an utterly reliable source within those circles my position makes my own, Mr. Holmes. From any other, I would have suspected favouritism in the recommendation, but knowing my advisor's precise and logical nature, such a factor would, I believe, be absolutely incidental."

Hindsight now leaves it clear to me that this nameless advisor could only be Mycroft Holmes, yet at this time I had encountered Holmes's remarkable older brother but once, and the scant information I held on him gave no indication of the supreme levels of authority or trust he held within the government, nor, of course, of his influence in murkier, shadowed areas of power. And as such things were yet unknown to me, so too was the reason this reply appeared to nettle Holmes, who coolly responded, "Your advisor's cast-iron reputation for reliability must suffer a unique dent, for I remain otherwise engaged."

"Then, Holmes, you must disengage yourself! Before God, I promise five hundred guineas to the one who untangles this frightful affair. No? A thousand! More, if you would but name your price! And what can that wretched girl offer?"

"Your Lordship could lose the sums he speaks of a

hundredfold and only notice the loss if it meant switching to a less exclusive brand of cigar. That 'wretched girl' offered to the very limit of what she can give – beyond even that – and only the direst need would inspire such a sacrifice. Therefore her needs are more urgent, and my services are hers."

Fearing that my friend's pique had prompted him to act rashly, I spoke urgently. "Miss Lodge's case is no doubt important, but the matter at Marleigh Towers is the only crime being spoken of anywhere."

His Lordship turned an appraising eye on me, as if noticing my presence for the first time. "Lodge, do you say?"

"The name has some meaning for you, Lord Sternfleet?"

"A triviality, Mr. Holmes. A damn servant girl my wife imprudently trusted was caught taking advantage of these appalling events to cover her own petty thievery. She is rotting miserably in a cell now, but if only that cell held the malefactor who brutally did to death a guest to this nation as well as to my home! There are international implications here, sir. My guests were in this country for more than a mere holiday. Not that this is known save by those under orders of the strictest confidence."

"Then, as you have clearly decided to take me into your confidence, I had better hear the full particulars," said Holmes, mildly.

Lord Sternfleet rose to his full, considerable height, the steely look returning to his eyes. "Then it would be better for you to hear the account at the site of these grim events, if you would be good enough to accompany me."

"Well, Watson, will your good lady wife miss you dreadfully if you were gone a few hours? You have no objection if my friend, Dr. Watson, joins me, your Lordship? He is an invaluable ally and frequently highlights angles to a situation that I may have failed to consider."

Whether either my wife or Lord Sternfleet objected or not, Holmes did not wait to learn, as, throwing his dressing gown aside in favour of a light jacket, he led our procession downstairs and into the waiting carriage, although he did recall his manners long enough to permit Lord Sternfleet the task of instructing the driver to convey us to Marleigh Towers.

II. Guests of His Lordship

What was recounted during the drive to that stricken house was in keeping with the news reports. Lord Herbert and Lady Verity Sternfleet – herself the daughter of an illustrious house, whose elderly patriarch was said to be gravely affected by the possible scandal – had opened their home to a gathering consisting of Monsieur Francois Lefalque, the French industrialist and magnate, and his near neighbours on the far side of the much disputed Franco-German border, the Graf and Grafin Rupert and Natascha von Schellsberg. "This was a reunion of longstanding friends, you understand, who have often played host to one another, be it in manor house, chateau or schloss. Yet in recent years there had been a cooling in our kinship, and my dear Verity urged me to allow her to extend an invitation before we good companions had drifted irretrievably into the status of mere former acquaintances. To our great elation, the invitations were enthusiastically accepted, and the dining hall of Marleigh Towers rang with happy laughter, while the jovial discussion of old times led freely into plans for further reunions and a strengthening of bonds grown fragile due to neglect. The happy group that parted long after midnight was one fully expecting to reconvene over breakfast in a similarly joyful frame of mind. Yet all joy was dashed aside by the terrible discovery of that morning.

"We had, I suppose, dined and drank rather too well. Consequently none of us was notably early in rising, or else Francois Lefalque's brutal fate would have been detected far sooner. And when those horrified screams rang out and set bedroom doors crashing and footsteps hurtling along corridors, I had to forego dressing, throw on my dressing gown, and race from my room to discover the outcry's source. I almost collided with Verity, looking so pale and anguished as she grasped my hand for courage, and we both rushed to find the maid – Tanner is the name my wife cried out – standing shuddering and whimpering in the open doorway of Lefalque's bedroom, while Rupert von Schellsberg's swift arrival and efforts to discover the cause of the snivelling girl's alarm were hampered by the fact that, in his rudely awoken perplexity, he addressed her in his native German.

"At our approach, Tanner nearly threw herself into my wife's arms, such is the devotion and esteem in which the staff holds Lady Verity.

'Your Ladyship, the gentleman asked me to wake him, but the door wasn't locked nor even closed properly, because it opened at my knock, and I saw...Oh, it's too horrible, your Ladyship! You mustn't look!'

"The Graf, already left looking green and drawn by his consumption of claret the previous night, had now glimpsed what Tanner had seen, and he echoed her words. 'Your wife should not see this, Sternfleet. Nor any woman. My God, if Natascha had witnessed such a thing!' And he lurched to his wife's bedchamber, his hurry partly fuelled by his wish not to be seen looking so shaken as servants began swarming into the upper corridor, drawn by those cries. My wife instructed her lady's maid – that despicable girl I spoke of earlier, Lodge or Hodge – to give the gravely shaken Tanner something warming for the shock, and she wrapped a coat around her and took her down to the kitchens. Then, ignoring all warnings and my own attempts to prevent her, Lady Verity strode past me and into that bloody chamber."

So gripped was I by the account, I was startled back into the reality of our carriage by the raising of Holmes's hand. "Sir, you are lapsing into melodrama, and such is best left the province of the good doctor. My understanding is that what blood was visible was confined to the victim, his bedding and night attire, not slathering the walls of some gore-streaked horror chamber. I appreciate that emotions have run wild, but as it has been left too deplorably late for me to witness the scene for myself, I must ask that you are as accurate as possible in your report so that I may reconstruct the setting in my mind."

Plainly unused to being interrupted in anything, Lord Sternfleet even so acknowledged the reasoning behind Holmes's rebuke, nodding tersely before continuing. "I feel I have told this story a thousand times over, to a veritable parade of policemen of all ranks, and to my superiors and advisors within Parliament. I will attempt to be as precise with you as I was with them. But when I cast my mind back, the room and its contents recede, and all I clearly see is the glassy-eyed glare of my old friend and a monstrous quantity of blood! Francois was propped up in the bed, pillows at his back, and his nightshirt and sheets were soaked through. It can only have been a cowardly sneak attack as he had slept, for he had the strength of a bear. Once, as a younger man, I saw him tackle and best two men far larger than he, purely because he overheard them make some remark about a lady in our company. But here he had no time to fight back, and his throat was cut clean across."

"So, even if he had attempted to cry out," I mused, "he would have been unable to raise more than a choking gurgle."

"Thank you for that medical viewpoint, Watson," murmured Holmes. "I wish you had been allowed to extend your skills to an examination of the wound while fresh, but a coroner's report will have to suffice. Pray continue, Lord Sternfleet."

"I instructed one of the servants lurking in the corridor to assemble the male staff in the entrance hall. One was to ride out to summon the police, the others to secure the house and patrol every inch of the park."

The groan this elicited from Holmes was no doubt

in response to the idea of a troop of butlers, footmen and stable-boys trampling across the grounds and efficiently obliterating any valuable trails underfoot. However, rather than voicing a complaint I had heard him level at many a police inspector over similarly unthinking carelessness, he prompted, "You believed it was murder from the first instant?"

"If it had been suicide, then where was his instrument of self-destruction? His hands were free of any blade or shard. My wife refused to consider that a murderer may have stalked within our home as we slept, insisting some terrible act of despair must have caused our friend to end whatever woes may have beset him. I had actually to restrain her from dropping to her knees in search of a weapon that might have fallen under the bed. It was only the return of the Graf that brought her to herself, his shock now equally matched by concerns for the Grafin, who had practically fainted in her bed at the news and entered that state of profound shock in which she remains. Rupert was naturally inclined to take her immediately back to Germany but, even had Inspector Highford been of a mind to let him leave the country, Natascha's condition forbids it. Not that any suspicion falls on such a noble visitor, of course, and his continued presence is a mere courtesy. But it is for this reason he has summoned the specialist from Dantzig to hasten the progress of the enquiry."

"If you incline toward notions of an intruder or assassin, your Lordship, you must feel that Monsieur Lefalque was a man whose death would benefit some other agency. Was anything stolen, from his room or his belongings? No documents of a private and confidential nature?"

Lord Sternfleet released a long plume of smoke as he slowly exhaled, before shaking his head. "I do not understand, Mr. Holmes, what you may be insinuating."

"Come now, we have no time for game playing. The death of a minor visiting dignitary with no connection to government – or should I stress no *visible* connection? – is embarrassing, indeed painful, but unlikely to cause the international crisis you protest of. But if it has set so busy a man as Fritz von Waldbaum scurrying through the facts of the man's life, and has also caught the lofty attention of your – ha! – advisor, there is more to it than is being said. Plainly put, was Lefalque carrying any clandestine document that others may wish to either obtain or suppress?"

"There you go wildly astray, Mr. Holmes. Francois was no spy, nor would I use my own home for such sordid goings on as you imply. It is where I live, sir! It is where my wife and family should feel safe."

"Well, as family has been invoked, what of Madame Lefalque? It is she who summoned the feted Dubuque to take charge of discovering how she comes to be a widow, I believe? Was she not invited to this friendly jamboree?"

"Claudine Lefalque prefers to summer in the South of France, and has invariably done so for many years."

"But the marriage was still a viable one, with no estrangement? No? And Madame's relations with the rest of the party? Your wife, for example?"

"Amicable. Agreeable! Friendly! We were all of us friends, Mr. Holmes!"

Holmes nodded in silent acknowledgement of Lord Sternfleet's grim insistence, and that silence persisted as the bustling, cramped streets thinned around us to the outlying tranquillity that abides beyond the city's overflowing heart, with even these charming byways becoming less crowded with their pleasant terraced houses and gardens. I viewed as much of this as I could through yet another fog of tobacco fumes, eventually giving in and, at risk of ending up as cooked and wrinkled as one of Mrs. Hudson's breakfast kippers, I produced my own pipe and puffed merrily away until the gates displaying that same coat of arms that adorned our transport came into view, and beyond it the great wooded parkland that held Marleigh Towers in green seclusion. On spying our approach, from slouching as wilted as the rapidly drying out flowers in those suburban gardens, a constable stationed at the gates became as stiffly formal as any Palace guardsman, marching swiftly to open the way, before no doubt slumping once more the instant our carriage was out of sight along the tree-lined driveway whose verdant abundance shielded from the outside world that house whose unwelcomed notoriety had made it a beacon for the morbidly inquisitive.

III. Inside the Murder Room

Marleigh Towers' renown had not, of course, commenced with this recent outrage. Its stables have at various times housed several champions – including a particular thoroughbred whose best remembered victory had, in my bachelor days, brought me winnings enough to finance a holiday in Margate that was itself memorable for several happy reasons that shall not be divulged here – while I had long nurtured a wish to view the great clock whose hands famously remained frozen at the hour and minute its tower was struck by lightning in 1827, at the precise instant General Sir Hartford Sternfleet fell drunkenly under a carriage outside his club and was trampled to death. It was from high atop this tower that, on hearing the grave news, his young wife threw herself in her urgent desire to be reunited in eternity with the general. Perhaps unfortunately for her, she survived the plunge and lived to a greatly advanced age, though with injuries so awful to behold they eventually earned her the cruelly whispered title of "The Red Widow"; thus she remained confined both to her wheelchair and to a house that had become a constant reminder of all she had lost, and which she chose to spend her remaining years filling with her bitter, impotent rage, which some say has never quite fully dispersed. The disappointing truth, however, was that this infamous landmark looked like any other stopped clock, while the enduring grandeur of the house itself was something I observed but fleetingly, as Lord Sternfleet set a brisk pace in marching Holmes and me indoors through a pillared portico, past deferential servants and constables alike, and straight up the magnificent main staircase.

"You are taking us directly to the murder room?" enquired Sherlock Holmes, keeping step easily with his Lordship's long strides.

"I was given to expect that this is where you would prefer to begin. Now, you there, Constable Whoever-you-are, is Inspector Highford still skulking somewhere?"

The uniformed officer seated outside the bedroom door scrambled to his feet, apologetically replying, "He's down our local station, your Lordship. Said he reckoned that maid wasn't telling all she knew."

"Damn fool! She can wait," grunted our host. "The stupid child has nothing to do with this."

"Of course the poor girl has nothing to do with it!" The imposing voice that chimed down the corridor was followed by my first equally imposing sight of the striking and elegant Lady Verity Sternfleet. She strode with a gliding step to her husband's side and, as he discreetly extinguished his cigar, she slipped a fond arm comfortably round him, insisting, "We are allowing our own horror and suspicion over poor Francois to make us vengeful. You must instruct that inspector to stop hectoring her and let the poor, bewildered creature go free."

"My sweetest Verity, you are altogether too soft-hearted. The girl took advantage of this, was too brazen or foolish to not get caught, and must pay the cost of her own greed and stupidity. Now, now, do not upset yourself. No, do not argue, for I felt you shiver. Shall I have Tanner make you up another fire?"

"A fire? In this summer heat, would that not be rather excessive?" remarked Holmes.

"Exactly so, Mr. Holmes," agreed Lady Verity. "Indeed,

such a fuss, but my husband found me shivering before a freshly-lit fire in my bedroom on that awful morning, and since then he has been trying to bundle me in blankets and shawls, as if I might shudder myself into pieces."

"Shock can have profound and pronounced effects," I warned, delicately. "If you would like me to perhaps prescribe something for your nerves...."

"My nerves are perfectly all right, Doctor, merely jangled."

"But you are recovered enough to go out, I perceive."

As Lady Verity looked down at her own fashionable if sober dress, her pearls, and her long silken gloves, a pained look crossed her gentle features, and her poise momentarily deserted her as she wrung her hands together. But her natural grace asserted itself swiftly, as she tightly smiled. "Oh, Mr. Holmes, this costume is not for going out. I cannot go out, but instead I must face a daily procession of strangers in my home, and even now – particularly now, with so many eyes upon us – one cannot allow appearances to slip. If I am to be peered at and queried, I shall ensure it is on my own terms."

"Not the attire to go crawling about the floor searching for weapons," Holmes murmured sardonically, but if his words had been meant solely for my ears, they also reached Lady Verity's, and her genteel tone sharpened in response.

"If it helped discover who had done this terrible thing, I would crawl through the undergrowth clad in a ballgown and diamond tiara! I admit that I was not thinking clearly when first we found Francois. But perhaps I was clearer in my thoughts than it appeared, for the blade I sought was later found."

Holmes turned keenly, his eyes flashing at this fresh data. "I had not read of this."

"We have managed to keep some secrets back from the press. Here, I will show you the very spot. No, Herbert, I am not a weakling, and keeping me out of the room will not erase what I have already seen. Follow me, if you will, gentlemen."

The bedroom was spacious and comfortable, with expansive windows letting golden light flood in. A wardrobe lay open, its contents on display, the cut of a wealthy man's suits unmistakeable even here. A jug and bowl sat on the sideboard, pen and paper on the bureau, and all seemed so normal it would have appeared that the occupant had stepped out mere moments before, had it not been for the stark memorial the bed made to the violence that had been committed here. Stripped of its bedding, and with the stains already dried to a darkening brown, the mattress looked better suited to an abattoir than a bedroom; wings of blood apparently stretching out around the corpse my mind's eye placed in the bed. That blood had dripped and dried in rivulets down the side close by the door and an awkwardly placed bedside cabinet that nestled between door and bed, leaving powdery burgundy puddles on the polished floorboards, and a deep crimson crusting to the tufts on the rug.

"Inspector Highford claims the discovery of it, yet in a way I helped. No, not crawling on the floor. That officious little fellow had asked my description of that morning's events. Rather than repeating what I had already told his colleagues, I felt it easier to show him. But I fear I overestimated my own courage, for no sooner had I entered than I felt terribly faint. I reached wildly for support, forgetting this bedside cabinet was on casters. It slid easily across the floor and almost brought me sliding down with it. The inspector, in an attempt at gallantry I suppose, moved to assist me. But just as he had steadied me he very nearly knocked me aside again, crying, 'What's this I spy here?' And from the floor he scooped up Francois' razor, with its blade and ivory handle still red and wet from his blood."

"You knew it was Lefalque's own razor?"

"At that moment? No, of course. But I assumed it to be so – whoever else's razor would I expect? – and an inspection of Francois' shaving kit showed this to be true."

"And was there any indication of how it found its way underneath the cabinet?" asked Holmes, crouching smartly to run his slender fingers in the gap between the base and the floorboards, before narrowly examining the floor around both cabinet and bedside.

"We believed that Francois must, in his death throes, have dropped or thrown it."

"But the angle at which he would have had to release or propel it counts against that, otherwise why should I be summoned?" As he spoke, Holmes paced the room, his grey eyes prowling over every surface, fingers prising lightly at the window locks, knuckles rapping softly on wood panelled walls as if some secret means of access might be revealed, before his attention turned once more to the floor, prompting a tut-tut of disapproval. "This morass of foot-scuffs are evidence of nothing more than the British bobby at work. But since the floor was recently scrubbed, as you would expect before a visitor's arrival, and there has been no recent rain, no trail in the dust nor muddied footstep could be expected in any case. Yet if murder had been the intent, why would the culprit have required the victim's own razor? Surely any killer worth the label carries their own weaponry?"

"Unless the murderer wished the crime to look like suicide," I exclaimed.

"Without placing the instrument of death in Lefalque's hand to strengthen the illusion?"

"A burglar, then? An opportunist, taken unawares, who grabbed the first item that came to hand? Then, in their panic at the horror they had perpetrated, they threw down the razor wildly, before fleeing without whatever spoils they had come for?"

My hypothesis prompted only a noncommittal grunt from Sherlock Holmes, but I had expected no more, knowing well his preference to leave any clear statement of events until he had gathered and analysed all data available to him.

His eyes and attention now seemed transfixed by that fearful stain, practically as if it drew him to it. So closely did he lean in to inspect the grisly markings, angling his neck so that he alternately peered down at the ruined mattress and then up at the wall above the head of the bed, while stretching out his long frame and lightly describing arcs in the air with his thin fingers, that for a mortifying instant I believed he might lay at the centre of those bloody angel wings in an attempt to view the scene as if through the eyes of the murdered man. "If I may call on your expertise again, Watson; a cut throat would not produce a steady flow of blood?"

"Not necessarily," I advised, glancing apologetically at Lord and Lady Sternfleet before responding to Holmes's impatient gesture to elaborate. "If the carotid artery were severed, as I believe was the case here, then it would spray outwards...in gouts."

"I should desist from occasionally chiding your mastery of words, Watson. 'Gouts'! Exactly!" He sprung upwards, like an impatient jack-in-the-box. "Where are these gouts? We see the leakage of the life force, but where is the stain of that initial spray? Unless something obstructed its projection before it could spatter."

"You imagine that the killer, who would necessarily be close to him to strike, was that obstruction? Good God, Holmes, they would be coated all over in his blood!"

"And a fleeing, blood drenched murderer would leave a trail in their wake. Yet there is no red footmark nor handprint, and not even the tiniest crimson droplet to be found anywhere else in this room, or in the halls beyond."

"If you must continue with this barbarous talk, Holmes," barked Lord Sternfleet, "can we not at least get out of this charnel room?"

Sherlock Holmes, as if deaf to these protests, laid a finger absently against the lip of the water jug on the cabinet, murmuring, "With nothing removed apart from the corpse and bedding, who emptied the water jug? Ah, but he had drank heavily, so would have been thirsty." His distracted air dispersing with an abrupt clap of his hands, he continued, "Without the late occupant's presence, there is little more to be learned here. Besides, I must carry out my next interview in less distressing surroundings."

"If you would wish to interview me, Herr Holmes, it makes no difference if you do so here or anywhere else," announced the man who stood stiffly in the doorway. Here was a rugged fellow, made all the more so for the darkening growth of stubble on a strong, determined chin, which stood at odds to his smart suit, across whose jacket breast I could picture a row of medals, and yet smarter bearing and intonation. "My wife, however, if you wish to speak with her, must to be given time to prepare herself, and cannot be pressed on these dark matters."

"It has clearly been a strain, Graf von Schellsberg," said I, noting the shadows around his eyes, "for both of you."

"The Grafin is most upset, Herr Doctor," he replied, a polite nod acknowledging my concern. "She it was who introduced me to Francois Lefalque some twenty years ago, while I was merely a student, and he seemed so worldly. I learned from him how to live life and celebrate the living of it." A far-off look stole across his features, a shadow of a smile raising the tips of his moustaches. "Ha! Live? He could have been the death of us both. I remember now, to impress a woman he claimed to be wooing in secret, he stole some gaudy trinket from a hotel we had found ourselves supping in, then paraded his prize until the gendarmerie threw us both in a cell for the night to sober us up. Yet when he was told the next morning to expect a fine, he produced twenty times what the bauble would have cost. 'I could have paid for it, of course, but this experience with you, friend Rupert, I could never have bought.' Where he led the way, I followed, but when I was wed to my glorious Natascha and put such wildness behind me, it was he who quickly followed me, marrying Claudine but months later. We had become, you might say, respectable. If I may be glad of anything from these past days, it is to have a final memory of how he assisted me to my room, both of us staggering and laughing, as if we were become for an instant those youthful, drunken rogues once more.

"Yes, there had been some strain in the friendship. But purely in matters of business. Francois inherited many factories and dealings in his province, which you must know runs side by side with my own region. Between us there is the border, marked by the great river, across which our friendship has built bridges to match those tangible bridges of stone and timber. One signifier of this alliance was always the free flowing of workers from my region into his factories, and of rural labourers from his territory into the farmlands of my own. Of late, however, more and more of my people were informed they were no longer required, while his tenants were discouraged from taking up work in our fields. Francois was more business-like about it than I had ever seen. 'The factories become automated, Rupert, and it is but correct that my own people be first to learn these new technologies.' But if you think this a reason for vengeance, I would bear a very bloody hand if I took such revenge against all who inconvenienced me in affairs of business."

"I thank you for your statement, my Lord Graf," said Holmes with a slight bow, "which I would undoubtedly have sought. But if we may remove ourselves to the downstairs area, I wish to speak to the unfortunate servant who raised the alarm."

IV. A Rival of Sherlock Holmes

Though Lord Sternfleet objected to Holmes interviewing a lowly member of his staff before his guests, with his wife's calming influence brought to bear he bit down on his objections, as he also did when my friend requested that he might speak to Miss Tanner alone. So we were soon seated at the table in the large, white-tiled kitchen, with a healthily plump, tousle-headed girl of some twenty years, uncomfortable in an ill-fitting lady's maid's uniform, seated apprehensively on the very edge of a kitchen chair opposite us. "Will this take long, sir? Only with everything that's happened and us being short, and all, I can't neglect my new duties. Thank you, sir. But you won't make me describe it again, will you, sir?"

"We have already heard all about that, and you have been very brave," said Holmes with one of those placid smiles he would conjure up when dealing with excessively nervous witnesses. "But you said that the late gentleman asked you to waken him early."

"Most particularly early, sir. 'You will knock at five of the clock, and if I do not answer you are not to hesitate a moment, but to come in and waken me.' Only the master's party stayed up so late that by the time we'd cleared after them it was after two, and I near overslept myself and forgot until breakfast was nigh served up. You...you don't think, sir, that if I had been on time, the gentleman might still be alive? Or," and here her hand flew to her throat, "Or might I have opened the door on the killer swooping over the bed with the bloodied blade still at work? Oh, sir! Now I'm moved up there, next door to her ladyship, I don't sleep hardly any, knowing what happened just a few doors along."

I was quick in reassuring her that she had no call for guilt over failing to waken Lefalque on time, or to fear that she had narrowly escaped his fate. She displayed clear relief at this, and also that Holmes steered his questioning to events prior to her appalling find. "Any other requests from the gentleman, sir? Only, before dinner, for ink and paper. No, he sent no letter that I know of, sir, as it would have been me or one of the footmen sent out to post it."

"I saw both ink and paper on the bureau, but nothing written," mused Holmes.

"He might have put off writing whatever it was to the morning," I suggested. "Indeed, that may have been why he wished to rise so early."

"Or perhaps what he wrote never left the house. But surely, Miss Tanner, it's not a lady's maid's task to deliver mail. Oh, but you have been recently promoted, I gather, in place of that shameful rogue, Hodge...."

The maid's rosy cheeks reddened further and the quaver fled from her voice. "Lodge is her name, sir, and Matty isn't no rogue, sir, and whatever she done must have been because her family needed the money, or someone forced her to it, but not for her own self! She weren't like that."

"I thank you, Miss Tanner, as I am certain your friend would for your spirited defence and your loyalty."

"If any was loyal, it was she to me, and to the mistress, sir. If she done the thing she's accused of, she must have had reasons."

"Greed is as good a reason for theft as any wretched excuse I've heard over the years," snapped the diminutive, grimacing, fellow whose gingerish beard failed to conceal his weak chin, and who strode into the kitchen on the balls of his feet as if hoping to gain height, circling around us with all the purpose of a bull in fervent pursuit of a china shop. "We haven't met, Mr. Sherlock Holmes, but I've heard a very great deal of you from my colleagues, and how you have a knack of getting wound up in those cases of theirs that might attract public notice for your vaunted methods."

"Inspector Highford, I presume. Forgive me; I have heard nothing of you from your fellow officers. And I can assure you that gaining notice for my methods will not be the case here."

"No, sir, it is I who offer you that assurance! But as you have been called in by his Lordship, I will let you proceed, even if you do not have the same courtesy to wait until the regulars are present to begin your inquisition." Then, making abundantly clear his intention to monitor whatever may follow, he scraped a chair noisily across the tiles and sat, fixing Holmes with his pale and narrow gaze.

"Matty was proper shaken," the maid, after a nervous glance at the scowling policeman, continued. "Though she was more concerned about Lady Verity than her own self, I'd swear. A real kind gentlewoman the mistress is. She gave me as many days off to get over the sight of that poor gent's throat as I may need; only I've no family near nor anywhere to go, so I stayed here where there was folks about. And Matty, who had been so good and looked after me in my fright, she let go for the day to see her people."

"Which was more kind than sensible, as we had not had time to question everyone," opined Highford. "But she can't have expected me to still be here in my vigilance. These local boys aren't much, and it took a proper professional turning up before we even had the weapon, but with our Mathilda acting suspicious by the shrubs near the path, even this lot had to notice. And with her wrestling with a bag she tried to drop as soon as she saw the constable's approach, I had her. Yes, I can show you what the bag contained, for it is still here." And with an impatient cry he summoned a constable, before sending the man rushing off again to fetch the confiscated item. "We've had no time to take it to the local station, as I've more important matters to attend to here. But you be sure that when they're settled, I'll be taking Miss Mathilda Lodge and her bag of spoils back with me to the Yard and teaching her how those who abuse the trust of their betters are dealt with there. Come on, let's have them here, lad." The garments Highford wafted out across the kitchen table, as if laying a delicately embroidered table cloth, were a pair of women's nightdresses, the one of them plain but of the finest cotton, the other more feathered and lacily decorated than anything one might see in any but the most stylish and exclusive clothing shop.

"In all things feminine and fashionable I bow to your considerable knowledge and experience, my old friend, yet your blush tells me that this is not a common garment." I protested that, as a recently married man, I should keep my own counsel in such matters, provoking a barked laugh from Holmes. "But it is at least as uncommon in London as a maker's label declaring its origin in a deluxe continental boutique would make it."

"And worth a penny every bit as pretty as these ribbons and laces. Though not worth nearly as much as this," gloated Highford, tossing a large and sparkling ruby brooch onto the topmost nightdress, where it redly glistened like a fresh bullet wound to the heart of the garment's unseen wearer. "Lord Sternfleet confirms it as property of his wife, and the girl has no good explanation for why she would be in possession of it. For cleaning and polishing, she claimed, yet she could give the name of no jeweller to whom such a task had been assigned. No, there was nothing noticed as missing previously, but that simply tells me that after some petty pilfering the likes of these fine garments, she'd grown bold, and thought nobody would pay any heed to a missing jewel when there was murder on every mind."

"Matty isn't like that, I've told you already!"

"Mind your place and hold your tongue, Miss Tanner! If she's so innocent, how is it that when we took ourselves round to her old mum's address, we found towels enough to fit some nice gaps in the linen closet here, all fresh from the copper and hung out to dry in her back yard? Ha! Just as they've hung her out to dry? The mother doesn't even know what day it is, chasing after those nippers of hers, and I doubt she'd ever seen anything so clean and white hung there since her wedding day. If then! I would still have brought her in and got something out of her. Leastways suggesting that such an action might just be my next step, with the mum in the next cell and the little ones to the poorhouse, got Miss Mathilda talking, and she's admitted, finally, that she took them. And that the murder was the cause!"

"Did she, indeed?" responded Holmes, an eyebrow

sharply rising. "How so?"

"Folks, as I've long-since learned, are ghoulish. They were lining up outside the gates here the instant word was out someone had died nasty inside. Or maybe the mob just smelled the blood! Fine fabrics and the like will fetch a price anyway, as you'd know if you'd to deal with every dipper who'd hooked himself a pocketful of silk hankies. But as souvenirs of the murder house, she saw they'd double or treble in price. And this is the girl whose innocence everyone pleads? The depths to which some will sink to make money from misery. Unbelievable!"

"The exact word," replied Holmes. "And so you have left this frightened girl to fret and stew, and await her punishment as a common thief, while you scrabble to locate the clues to a killer you have not the slightest trace of, before your field of enquiry is invaded by private investigators from all across the continent."

As the inspector rose abruptly, glaring down at Holmes, I was put instantly in mind of one of those awful, spoiled lapdogs one sometimes sees snapping and growling defiantly round the heels of a much larger hound, oblivious to the fact that one single flash of teeth and snap of a jaw from the mightier beast would quickly silence its yapping. "And fretting and stewing has finally produced results, for her confession will be all I need when her time in the dock comes round."

Holmes leapt smartly to his feet, and I did likewise, if less nimbly, and followed as he strode towards the kitchen door. "Then you merely prolong her agony as you do your own. And we waste valuable time here."

Highford's unconvincing mien of superiority could not survive his awkward stumbling trot as he came clattering up the stairs and barging through the green baize door into the marbled hall in our wake. "What do you mean by that? If you know something, you'll tell me, Mr. Holmes!" These squawked demands brought a halt to the urgent conversation taking place by the foot of that great staircase we had earlier ascended, as Lord and Lady Sternfleet and the Graf von Schellsberg turned their combined scrutiny upon us.

"I cannot know, only suspect, while one who gains nothing from withholding what she does know is not being asked the proper questions, since, in your eagerness to arrest someone for anything, you treat her as a mere pilferer instead of a vital witness who may know exactly why Lefalque died and who it was that applied the killing blade." The instant these words passed Holmes's lips, Highford snapped his instructions for a constable to ride to the station and fetch the prisoner. Sherlock Holmes, lighting a cigarette, raised a concerned eyebrow. "You are surely not leaving such a valuable witness to the care of a fresh-faced constable?"

"The Dickens I will," cried Highford, storming toward the door, while Holmes drew the constable momentarily aside, murmuring a few quick words to him and eliciting a nod of assent before the policeman hurried off in pursuit of the inspector.

The echo of the constable's footsteps had barely been replaced by the rattle of the police wagon's wheels when a door slammed directly above. I looked to the top of the stairs to see a swaying apparition, hair awry around a pale and staring face, a clawed hand tugging her dressing gown around her while she grasped the railing with the other, as if dragging herself forward with every step. "You know. You know! No use now in hiding it," she shrilled, her words halting the Graf's ascent toward her, before he addressed her in urgent German. The distressed woman, so clearly his wife, replied in that same tongue. The language was lost on me, yet still the shifting expression on the Graf's face spoke eloquently of his shock, anger and finally utter sadness, while his refusal to accept his wife's proffered hand as she passed him was answered by a glance of such sorrow and regret that my heart was moved to both of them.

"Thank you for saving me the trouble of summoning you, Grafin von Schellsberg. The inspector will be back as if the devil himself was on his tail, so keen is he to have the experts repelled at the ports. Therefore, we have little time to piece this story together."

"Natascha, you are not well, and do not know what you are saying," pleaded Lady Verity, gripping her friend by the shoulders as if trying to calm a hysteric. But the Grafin had become calmness itself, brushing back her unkempt hair from her weary but striking face, and summoning up every inch of poise in her reserves.

"I know exactly what I am saying, Verity," she said, her English faultless and clear. "I should have said it all from the beginning, and saved all of you these dreadful days."

"And will you leave your friend to speak alone, your Ladyship?" asked Holmes. "Or would you have me speak for your part in the tragedy?"

"You impertinent swine," roared Lord Sternfleet, his eyes savage with uncomprehending fury.

"Mr. Holmes is correct. I must speak along with Natascha," said her Ladyship. "No, please, Herbert, do not look at me like that, as if I were a stranger. Just listen, and try to find it in your heart, if not to forgive, then to understand that we did only what we thought was for the best." Lady Sternfleet then placed her hand in Grafin's, and the women faced their dumbstruck husbands with an air of desolate nobility, before politely requesting that we move elsewhere so that they might relate their sad tale.

V. The Statement of the Crime

The clear blue day seemed to dim and the shadows lengthen, while the clouds beyond the windows of the vast drawing room in which we now gathered converged and loomed, darkening thc heavens and betokening storms as if in sympathy with the events taking place inside that room.

"You knew of my part in this from the outset, Mr. Holmes," said Lady Verity, "but may I know how?"

"I should also like to know this," snapped Lord Sternfleet, his temper as hot as the glowing tip of blazing cigar, "and also why you kept these monstrous accusations to yourself while sending the inspector off after trifling matters."

My voice echoed loudly in that vast room, as I snapped, "A defenceless woman's liberty is not a trifle!"

"Well said, Watson! I knew because, while the inspector and I both regularly encounter the worst and most depraved examples of humanity, I have also learned to listen when innocence is protested and where loyalty is invoked; for what purpose does it serve to pursue justice if we cannot believe there exists good in this world, despite its vices, temptations and ills?"

"You evidently mean the innocence and loyalty protested by Miss Lodge's sister," I surmised, finally slotting the pieces of that incomplete statement I had heard on my arrival in Baker Street into place within the larger puzzle of the day.

"Lord Sternfleet's brusque arrival interrupted a resourceful young visitor in the telling of her story, yet the dramatic reaction his imminent presence provoked was to provide me with two of the most vital missing parts of that tale. I now knew the household involved, and also that the 'good' and 'kind' employer spoken of could not be a reference to his Lordship; a supposition his very clear attitude to anyone not his social equal rapidly proved. This is why I did not instantly expose her Ladyship's involvement, for to earn the loyalty she has been shown, she must be a formidable woman, and my subsequent discoveries of the day have only confirmed that deduction. Why else would an innocent, facing imprisonment, remain silent for another's sake? To whom was she loyal, if not the mistress whose kindness and honour she has praised, not only within this household where deference would be expected, but beyond and with those she most trusts? And with that honour so highly spoken of, I could reasonably conclude that you, Lady Verity, had not been the late Lefalque's mistress.

"It is not prurience that causes such an allegation, so put aside your outraged sensibilities, your Lordship! That this soiree was arranged to coincide with Madame Lefalque's traditional absence was suggestive, and there have been too many coincidences along the way to allow the strange wanderings of nightdresses to be counted as such. We then have the possibility of notes being written that do not pass outside this house, and, as your Lordship assures me Lefalque was carrying no secret papers, what other kind of incriminating item might more easily require a fire to hasten its disposal than some indiscreet communication? Ah, talk of secret papers surprises some of you? But there has been little innocence to this gathering, and while your Ladyship was fostering intrigues and affairs of the heart, affairs of an equally delicate nature were the ultimate goal of other parties."

"Rupert, this is nothing but speculation and exaggeration," protested Lord Sternfleet.

But if the Graf even heard him, it was impossible to tell, for his focus remained on his wife, who quailed on seeing the pleading in his eyes. Even so, she shunned the chair I offered her. "I shall stand, if you please. I have been nesting in that bed upstairs for days, afraid to come out. I now stand before you all, and I admit that, yes, I once was the paramour of Francois Lefalque. Before you and I ever met, my dearest Graf, when I was but a reckless, imprudent girl, and he a wildly charming fellow. But the charm masked spite and jealousy, and when I met a decent man, an honourable man, I recognised that what I had thought of as love with Francois was as shallow an approximation of that sensation as his charm was an approximation of goodness. This was again the mask he wore when he vowed we could remain friends, even if no longer lovers. And, it tears at my heart to admit, it was the charm he used those shameful times when I forgot my own goodness – until he reminded me by his lack of warmth what it was I risked losing. He persisted, playfully, slyly, but I was strong, and finally he saw that his patience was never to be rewarded. I see this only now, after what I heard and saw when last I was alone with him. But before, I had not known that his passions burned so cold, and in this coldness was born that distancing between us as friends."

"Natascha had confided, long ago, of the excitement and danger of her affair," offered Lady Verity. "Two overgrown schoolgirls giggling in the dark over forbidden confidences. When Herbert spoke of the growing distance between us, I was reminded of this thrilling affair. I realised that a dash of spice might be added to entice Francois from his chateau, and perhaps a rekindling of old flames may have been what was necessary to thaw our cooled friendship. So I used my letter of invitation to suggest to Francois how keenly our mutual friend anticipated his affirmative response."

"You used my wife as bait?" hissed Graf von Schellsberg coldly. "Rupert, I knew nothing of this insinuation," insisted the Grafin. "I believed Francois to have forgotten our past. We were the friends we all once were. You drank and sang together, and then, when you tired, he helped you to your room, and I was delighted to see the young friends of happy memory still peering out from within those more careworn, mature faces. Yet it was not until I was in my own room and dressing to retire that I saw the message someone had pushed beneath my door. The opening lines puzzled and then chilled me, for they were words I had written, so long ago, in a private letter. I shall not tell you what these innocent words were, or how they read when removed from their setting, but beneath these were written, 'I have kept the originals all this time, and they are even now close to my heart. We will discuss these long departed sentiments – and establish whether they truly are departed? If you do not call on me in my room, I shall know you await me in yours, and you will hear my knock before the clock strikes the next hour.' The scheming devil had left me little choice but to face him and find out for myself what mischief he meant.

"Almost as I closed the door to his room, the sly, smiling welcome was gone from his face and he was upon me, grabbing at my shoulders, at my wrists, tearing my dressing gown from me and dragging me to him, an all the while pleading, 'Why did you ignore me so over dinner? Since when were your glances only for your husband? Is it a game to you, to hold my heart in your hand like one of the trinkets I won for you? Do you feel it pound for you?' His strong grip pressing my hand to his chest. His face red and looming over mine, the alcohol fumes of his breath filling my own breathing! 'This heart beats for you, the blood it pumps is for you, and if you have no use for my heart, what use have I of my blood?' And then the blade was in his hand, weaving so close to my face I still feel the chill of its passing on my skin. I beseeched him to think of his own Claudine, but he used such words to describe her, how little she truly meant to him, and how it should have been us who had made our match! I told him that my husband was a hundred times the man he was. 'Then, as his is the knife within my heart, let his blade be the one to still it, and let my blood forever stain what is his.' And when I saw the razor's handle and Rupert's crest emblazoned there, I understood that the purpose of his supposed kindness in helping Rupert to his chamber had been to steal this deadly thing. He meant to ruin us both, for who would believe the husband innocent when his wife is found covered in his rival's blood, and his razor is in that rival's throat?"

"I would have wielded it myself, had I known the kind of man he was," swore the Graf, moving rigidly to his wife and placing an uncertain arm around her.

The rush of anger instilled by this dreadful testimony giving way to a surge of protectiveness that made me wish only to be by my own beloved wife's side, and I grimly admitted, "There are many who would feel you justified!"

"No, you should not wish this," cried his wife, pulling him tighter to her. "You saw him dead, but I saw the life leave his eyes as they grew as wide as his mouth and his throat grew wider yet. Then I was only aware of such heat soaking through me, and the warmth on my face. As his grip loosened and I saw the blood upon me, I thought it was I who had been killed! Then he fell, and I cannot now remember what was in my mind as, even while he lay in that spreading darkness on the floor, I propped his head on pillows lest he choke on his own blood, and tore sheets and blankets from the bed to wrap round him and bring warmth back to his cooling body. But to no avail! Those white sheets so quickly bloomed dark and red. Perhaps his strength and madness had poured into me, for I dragged and heaved him across the room in his scarlet shroud and onto that bed, as if hoping to make comfortable what no longer had any sensations. I sat for long minutes, turning over and over what might have been had I just surrendered to his demands. His game won, he would have bored of his quarry easily in his satisfaction. None but I would have been the wiser, and I would have crept back to my own room to deal with my own guilt, so my beloved Rupert would never have been hurt by the knowledge of what I was."

"You must not consider that any alternative, Grafin. Not ever! Nor should you torture yourself with any possibility you may have spared your husband pain," I insisted, finally grasping Lefalque's instruction that the maid, Tanner, was to simply walk in to rouse him at so early an hour and what scene he had wished witnessed. "He intended your private shame to be discovered and shared, no matter what."

"You sat traumatised, only gradually comprehending that he was dead," said Holmes gently. "But the floor was awash with his blood while he sat up in bed. Even in your dazed condition you understood this was no natural scene. Whose notion was it to mop up the blood on the floorboards to ensure it looked like he had ended his life where he lay?"

"When I was wakened by a figure sobbing quietly at my bedside, white-eyed and scarlet from head to foot, I genuinely believed in that moment that the legends of the Red Widow of the Sternfleets were true after all. How I wish now that it had been that malicious old ghost!" declared Lady Verity. "Natascha confided all that you have just heard, and it was plain that neither the Grafin's reputation and marriage, nor whatever standing our late companion had once enjoyed, even undeservedly, would be served by deeper investigation of these matters." "Thus the empty water jug, as I'm sure the jugs and basins from your rooms saved traipsing up and downstairs with pails. Also the ransacked linen closet, for towels to scrub those floors as clean as you hoped your consciences might appear."

"My own maid, dearest sweet Mathilda, was roused from her sleep in the antechamber next to my room. On seeing Natascha's pitiable state she fetched one of her own shifts to replace that ghastly sullied nightdress. As I helped my poor friend wash away the traces of that man, the precious girl did the same on the floorboards, even having the vigilance to wipe clean those spatters that had followed Natascha along the hall to my door. I would have burned the towels and the nightdress, and my own which now bore his blood. But none of us are calculating criminals with any notion of what might betray us, and it was clever Mathilda who realised that the loss of the towels might be noticed and queried, while the disappearance of so singular a nightdress might alert the Graf to some irregularity. Any tiny thing might be our downfall. The towels might go unnoticed for days, but if we were to turn Natascha's very genuine shock to serve us, she need only stay bundled up in bed for a day or so while Mathilda stole the items away to wash and then quietly return them. I would not send a girl scurrying into the night with a sack of blood-soaked garments, but it was her notion and her insistence. I was so grateful I pressed my dearest treasure – the ruby brooch Herbert had given me when first we were engaged to marry – on her. I wanted her to know how grateful I was for her loyalty, and though she tried to refuse it and to wave it away, it was this token, truly meant, that damned her when she sought to return it."

"Yet it may well provide her salvation," said Holmes. "I watched you plead your devoted servant's case, and I have no doubt your winning ways would have inspired your husband eventually to relent in his judgement. But ponder on this, your Ladyship. Such a case as this could be the making of a man like Highford, and well he knows it. But what only we know is that he will never find his murderer. So when there is none to be found, he may look closer at the bird already in his cage, and if he looks closely enough, he might just find that one speck of blood on those towels that her hands failed to wring out, and then he will have found as good a murderer as any. The thieving maid, caught red handed stealing from her betters, who strikes back at her wealthy, noble captor and murder is done? What use would it then be for her to plead her convoluted case?"

"If it had come to that, I would have spoken for her."

"And brought the Grafin the infamy she had sought to escape? An old friend, or a loyal servant? I wonder if the choice would have been so easily made."

With a chastened look settling across her fine features, her Ladyship sighed, "You do not think much of us, Mr. Holmes."

"On the contrary, you have created a situation I never had encountered before, and one which may be unique – a suicide which has all the appearance of a murder which is attempting to disguise itself as a suicide. Now, looking out I perceive the approach of the police carriage in the drive, so little time remains. I will summarise what I believe to have then occurred, and you must correct any deviation from the truth.

"The maid smuggled the stained garments home, soaking and scrubbing them and leaving them to dry, before creeping back just as the horror was exposed. If your late night revels had not caused Miss Tanner to sleep on, the alarm may have found a missing lady's maid, but she slipped back in the confusion and it was only her kindness in offering her coat that might have betrayed her nocturnal departure and return. You two, meanwhile, having transformed the room to how you imagined a suicide scene should look, removed the last items which might incriminate you, such as the razor bearing the von Schellsberg coat of arms."

The nobleman raised a trembling hand to his stubble-flecked throat. "No wonder you clung to me, Natascha, calling me back when I attempted to leave you to make myself presentable! If it were not that my hand shook so much at the thought of putting a blade to my skin, I would have caressed my own neck with the very steel that pierced his!"

"As to the letters Lefalque had brought with him that spoke so charmingly of this past entanglement, your Ladyship concealed them in her own chamber. But when it dawned on you that there may yet be a search, you chose to burn them, hence the unseasonal fire in your grate. I have missed nothing so far, I think, but even in your thoroughness it was you that missed something."

Lady Sternfleet nodded solemnly. "I had Lefalque's own razor, but had not summoned the courage to put it in his hand. After settling Natascha, I found myself poised at the door of her room, my hand on the handle, my nerves steeled, when that scream went up. I ran out, hoping to reach that room before anyone else, but it was too late! My husband never saw that the chamber I had come from was not my own, but it was also he who prevented my placing the concealed razor into the blood beneath the bed, where it may plausibly have fallen. I had to bide my time, hoping my pounding heart would not burst as I awaited my chance to slip into the room and hide the bloodied blade somewhere it could then be found, for I could not simply leave it in plain view where it had not been before."

"And the blood that was on the blade when it finally was found?" I asked.

"Her own. A few drops, easily spilled. Watson, I recall your puzzled glance as I identified my earlier visitor as a char. It was her gloves that made it a likelihood. While she had scrubbed her face and donned the most respectable clothing she owned in order that she not be found lacking in our company, the gloves in such weather were too much. Thus she was concealing her hands, and the reddened, raw ravages of the hard work they were put to. And while her ladyship may also strive to maintain a respectable mode of dress, the gloves too are misplaced. You wince now as you wring your hands, Lady Verity." Removing her left glove in silent reply, she revealed the bandage wrapped inexpertly around the heel of her hand. With her nodded assent, I quickly examined the cut, confirming that it had not become infected, before reapplying the dressing. "You concealed the razor as close to the bed as you could, then arranged to stumble and bring about its revelation. But it was clear that this was not the only time that cabinet was moved, and it certainly was not to dust the floor, as there were several recent tracks from the casters in the dust still lying below it. This may also have occurred to even Highford in his murder hypothesis, and this too should be to our advantage."

"You hint repeatedly of salvation and advantage," protested Lord Sternfleet, "but what can you mean? Where is our advantage, and what salvation can we expect?"

"You alone, between yourselves, can decide how these events shall affect you, and if the deceptions and betrayals now brought to light are to be punished or absolved. But there is no good purpose served by staining your names as a consequence of an atrocious and selfish act by one who has deceived and betrayed you all in turn. However, this is not the only stain that must be lifted, and this one may not be as easily washed away as blood from a garment! While you may decline in your social standing, perhaps finding your official duties diminished, your places lost at a few dinner tables and functions, I talk of a deeper, darker stain which threatens absolute destruction of an innocent's future and a blight on the lives of those closest to her. Now, here is the inspector and his prisoner. Co-operate, and all will be as well as can be, but go against me and nothing is more certain than that which you most fear."

VI. The Adventure of the Second Statement

The anxious young lady escorted brusquely into the room by Inspector Highford was unmistakably kin to the girl who had fled from Baker Street scant hours before. There was the same clear complexion, the same sharp but pleasant features, and, alas, the same bright eyes rimmed red through the rubbing away of tears. As Holmes indicated that this Miss Lodge be seated, it struck me that even so simple an act as her sitting in this drawing room, surrounded by what society declared as her betters, was one that would be impossible under any other circumstance. It was evidently a prospect that caused her no little unease, although Holmes's generous smile and courteous tone swiftly eased most of her nerviness. "Now, Miss Lodge, you have no need to look so frightened, or to fear that we are going to bombard you with more questions than you have already endured, for all is known. No, you need not look to your mistress. She has told all. We know that you are guilty of no more than loyalty, and of putting this before the truth, and before your own best interests."

The girl was struck silent by incomprehension, yet the same could not be said of Inspector Godfrey Highford, who blazed around the room, issuing demands to know "what everyone else obviously damn well does!" His impatient outburst drew forth quiet, shuddering sobs from the utterly wretched maid, though these sobs subsided as my friend wove his chain of detail and event. I have on many occasions watched Holmes silence a room while he used every aspect of his innately theatrical soul to present the facts in a case with a clarity made startling by his dramatic emphasis on each salient point. Yet here was a performance beyond even those, for he delivered the steps toward his conclusions with so little artifice or guile that they took on the banal solidity of a grocer's list or railway timetable, rendering each detail mundanely realistic, even to the ear of one who already knew the truth.

There were, of course, truthful elements to this statement, as he spoke of Francois Lefalque's occasional streaks of violence and instability, and of a simmering, unfathomable resentment that he had nurtured for his erstwhile friends, weaving these facts seamlessly toward the moment when, to her horror, Lady Verity had discovered her trusted guest stealing from her home. Why would such a wealthy man do such a thing? That was for an expert on mental disorders to establish, but Holmes insisted that a perusal of the gendarmerie records from Lefalque's home province may show a history of similar acts. There had come a confrontation, with Lefalque declaring his intent to leave at the earliest opportunity in the morning. Yet, alone in the fastness of night, in all likelihood contemplating his loss of honour and the estrangement of his friends, he had opted to make a more drastic departure.

"But the razor, Mr. Holmes," insisted a smugly grinning Highford, "could not have been found below the cabinet if he had inflicted this upon himself. Surely that undermines your whole argument?"

"Place yourself in Lefalque's position. Your path is set, your anger and shame guiding you, and the mortal blade is in your grasp. But your drunkard's hand is shaking so badly you cannot hold the blade straight. No, neatness of the cut does not come into it. It is not an aesthetic qualm, but Dr. Watson may tell you of the results that are inflicted when a straight razor does not deliver the finishing stroke."

"Certainly," said I, gravely, and while I spared the most awful details in deference to those others present, what I briefly described left Highford looking as grey and crumpled as his suit waistcoat.

"He lays the razor down on the cabinet by his bed as he gulps down water to revive his senses. But that shaking hand drops the blade. To reach it, he merely has to slide the cabinet out on its casters. He sees no need to then reposition it against the wall as he commits his last hopeless act, and the killing blade falls once more to the floor. You will have observed, I've every confidence, those multiple marks of the casters in the dust. This is because the door, when her Ladyship burst into the bedroom that morning, struck the displaced cabinet and sent it rolling smoothly back into its usual position, inadvertently obscuring the razor and allowing a tragedy to appear an outrage."

"And the girl?" cried the inspector, gripping fast to the one thing he still held while the remainder of his case seemed to drift away quicker than the smoke from Holmes's cigarette.

"Mathilda Lodge acted out of loyalty to protect the reputation of one powerless to do so themselves. Petty though most of them were, had those stolen items come to light, what chance would Lefalque's posthumous honour have stood? In her overwhelming grief, Lady Verity asked her most trusted servant to remove them, but with the police trampling hither and yon, there was little prospect of returning the objects unseen, as was proven when she was so suddenly apprehended. But her sense of loyalty to her mistress would not allow her to plead her own innocence, while Lady Verity's horror of bringing dishonour to the name of her beloved friend stilled her from speaking up in her saviour's defence. Thus two well-intentioned acts of mercy resulted in an unfortunate stalemate."

I fought to suppress my grin as the Scotland Yarder

whined, "Can this be true?" It was evident that he wished to rail and shout at someone, but like many bullies I have seen, his tyranny of those unlucky enough to rank below him was matched only by his terror of offending those of a higher station.

"Indeed, it is so," replied Lady Verity. "And we are so deeply, desperately ashamed of our deceit, no matter how pure the motives."

"And Monsieur Dubuque and Herr von Waldbaum are coming all this way for a murder enquiry where no-one has been murdered?" A hard gleam of pleasure appeared in the miserable official's eye, and he became noxiously confidential. "If I may speak with them first, Mr. Holmes, sir? You have somehow spirited my entire murder case away defter than an Oriental conjuror at The Alhambra, so you could at least allow me that. I understand the Parisian has been searching out suspected mistresses on the say-so of Madame Lefalque, while the German has been investigating underhand political aspects. It would be good to tell them that while they've chased these side issues, we've used British common sense to lay the case to rest."

"I shall leave you to explain how we did so, Inspector. And I shall prepare my own full statement, should these visitors need any clarification on the points you will present. If, of course, that is what my client wishes."

"By all means, it is, Mr. Holmes, thank you," insisted Lord Sternfleet.

"Forgive me, Lord Sternfleet, but while I appreciate the courtesy you have shown in inviting me into your home and confidence, you, sir, are not my client."

Leaving the nobleman to choke on his cigar, my friend beckoned to the young constable who had returned with the inspector. "Yes, Mr. Holmes, the person was there, outside the jail where you said, and I delivered your instructions, and an honour it has been, sir, to assist. And here, now, is the wagon I ordered to bring her."

"As I informed your Lordship on numerous occasions this morning, I already have a client, and this is she." Just then, the young lady I had encountered briefly in my old sitting room walked in, looking warily around each face, as if suspecting her every footfall carried her further into a trap. Yet when her eyes fell on her sister she broke into the most dazzling grin and rushed to embrace her.

"When I saw them take you from the station I was set to follow, even if I had to run every mile of the way, but then the copper said Mr. Sherlock Holmes was waiting for us here and called on a wagon to bring me to you."

"I'm free, Florrie!" cried her sister, laughing and sobbing all at the same time. "I don't know how you managed it, but I'm free!"

"Without the valuable testimony of this young lady to her sister's circumstances, and her statement of the character of both your former servant and of your wife, I may not have found the thread needed to unravel this case, your Lordship. Yes, 'former servant', for I believe that while loyalty is said to be its own reward, you swore on oath a considerable sum – one thousand guineas? What a memory you have, Watson! – to any who would resolve this matter. That reward rightly belongs to my client. Minus, of course, the sum of five pounds, which I shall remit to cover my fee."

VII. A Brief Retrospection

I may be seen as sentimental, but as I look back on those closing moments in the drawing room, it is not the wary, uncertain glances and uncomfortable, unvoiced questions that hovered over the family and guests of that house which remain most vivid in my recall, but the simple joy and warmth of those two loyal sisters, celebrating their togetherness, and not yet even aware of the fortune that was soon to be theirs. And here the distance of time allows me to report that the money was invested well, and was only the seed that grew into a great family business and also benefited many a charity that seeks to improve the lot of the supposed lower orders. And if I suppress this other tale of a "Second Stain" – that being the insidious stain of suspicion, prejudice, and guilt – it is not for the sake of preserving any clandestine espionage route, nor to protect the confidences and tribulations behind the noble façade of those influential families whose affairs lay at the heart of it. It is, instead, out of loyalty to that faithful servant and her devoted sister, whose part in events beyond their control is best left unspoken until such times as the information can have no unhappy result for them.

I am confident that these past secrets are as secure as is the sisters' continuing bright future, but in that July of fifteen years past, there remained one last obligation before any who knew the truth in the case might consider security remotely possible. I was present the next morning when the famous European crime specialists called at Baker Street seeking, as Holmes had predicted, some clarification of whatever coup de théâtre had occurred to render their services redundant while they were still in transit, since the account presented to them by a preening Inspector Highford on their arrival in London had singularly failed to illuminate much beyond the Scotland Yarder's inexplicably high opinion of his own talents.

To this day I still retain the almost verbatim report I transcribed of that demonstration, and it is this transcript that has proved invaluable in allowing me now to recall and accurately record the tangle of truths, half-truths and outright fabrications that have long-since supplanted the true facts of the case. And as I watched those gentlemen as they, in turn, closely watched Sherlock Holmes faultlessly recreate that same sequence of betrayal, tragedy, and sheer chance that he had woven the previous day – Monsieur Dubuque, large eyes peering unblinkingly over the rims of his pince-nez like a peevish, professorial owl rather than a police officer; Herr von Waldbaum alternately tut-tutting and chuckling to himself as, with a tiny pencil clamped in his huge hand, he jotted the salient points in his little notebook, before drawing a line under them with some decisive finality – a growing reassurance dawned that, as far as the various authorities whose minds had been turned to it were concerned, the Leflaque problem could now be relegated to a dossier sealed and stamped as "Resolved with no further inquiry necessary".

If there was any ill feeling that their energies or journeys had been wasted, neither let it show, nor allowed it to sour a sense of mutual admiration amongst the best brains each respective country had to offer. It was, after all, Marcel Dubuque who would petition his own government to secure Holmes's assistance in prising apart the grip of fear in which Paris was held in the summer of 1894 by the notorious Boulevard Assassin, Huret; while my abiding memory of Fritz von Waldbaum shall forever be those few deadly seconds when he and I faced one another over the barrels of our revolvers until, with a timely warning cry from Holmes and a booming laugh of startled recognition from the German, each party realised that the other was skulking in that labyrinth of tunnels below the streets of Vienna on the self-same mission to prevent the ancient terms of a blasphemous covenant from being horribly fulfilled.

There is little more to relate with bearing to the Marleigh Towers incident, although you, my dear future reader, are no doubt asking the question that did not occur to me until I was seated with Holmes in a carriage bearing us back towards Baker Street. "In my sheer admiration at watching as you masked a suicide that had been mistaken for a murder that appeared to be disguised as suicide as an actual suicide after all, but one committed for completely different reasons – I believe I managed to get that right, but I cannot swear to it, or repeat it – I entirely forgot about these international implications that were the source of much talk whose ultimate meaning I quite failed to grasp."

"My boy, I had begun to wonder if you had lost interest," smiled Holmes from behind his pipe, "but you do not disappoint. Simply put, where an easy back and forth of workers and labourers exists across borders – and particularly borders as fractious and troubled as those in the very heart of the cauldron of nations across the narrow Channel – there lies an easy passage for all manner of others, whose work may be more enigmatic, and whose labours are decided in private rooms and silent chambers nearby. Yes, my dear fellow, a virtual open door with a 'welcome' mat on either side for certain covert agencies, for where man can travel freely, so too can what he holds in his pocket, his luggage, or simply in his mind. Well, I shall have our driver deposit me in the city, where I shall take my turn to play the reliable advisor in suggesting that a new route be found, be it over the Alps by elephant, or down the Rhine in a barrel. I rather think Lord Sternfleet may be delayed in relaying the news, as other, more delicate explanations must take precedence."

"That there should be such lack of trust and honesty between man and wife," I mused, sorrowfully, "and such betrayal and secrecy amongst friends."

"I shall not let it trouble me," said Holmes. "I have very few friends, and the best of them I trust implicitly, while I shall, of course, never marry, so need have no fear of the many dangers of that dubious arrangement. Ah, and here we are at Pall Mall, and I must leave you. And what shall you do now?"

I cast a stern eye in his direction and murmured, "Oh, I shall armour myself against those many dubious dangers, and go back home to my new wife."

"Ah, Watson, you forgive me, I'm sure? There, you try to hide a smile, so you do. But if I may paraphrase the recent utterances of an individual who holds you in the highest regard, and who is therefore a wise man indeed;

what purpose does it serve to pursue justice – and deserved happiness is most surely only a specific form of justice – if we cannot believe there exists good in this world? Goodbye, my dear fellow, until fate or fortune brings us together again."

The Two Umbrellas

by Martin Rosenstock

On a cloudy autumn evening, a young man in a Chesterfield coat crossed the courtyard of a Georgian-style office building and approached its gate onto Whitehall. In his right hand, he carried a satchel; an umbrella was tucked under his left arm.

"Have a good evening, Mr. Ferguson," called out the sentry in a wooden coop by the threshold.

"Thank you, Palmer. You too."

"Oh, and enjoy your holidays, Mr. Ferguson," the sentry remembered.

"I am sure I will."

Ferguson stepped onto the footpath. He passed a brass plaque affixed to the building's façade: *Admiralty House – British Royal Navy*. Taking his umbrella, he began to swing it, not quite in rhythm with his gait, as he headed down the street towards Charing Cross. The noise of cabs and coaches, delivering passengers to their supper destinations, filled the air; newspaper boys cried the evening editions. Men in suits and overcoats were moving determinedly away from their places of employ. Twice, Ferguson lifted his silk top hat in greeting and received an identical salutation in return. His features during these exchanges were controlled; the brown eyes behind a pince-nez widened briefly with practiced geniality. Once in a while though, when unobserved, a twitch passed over his face, and he would then press his lips together so as to reestablish an appearance of nonchalance.

Ferguson was slight of build. His shoulders did not fill his coat, and the legs of his trousers flapped loosely with each step. His face, at first glance, appeared nondescript, the face of a man who had gone, or perhaps rather had been propelled, through life without encountering major discomfitures, let alone obstacles. The features were fine and suggested schooling and cultivation. One could imagine him conversing on a Turner exhibition or the quality of a tenor's interpretation of a Verdi aria. Yet one would have been hard pressed to imagine him taking a paintbrush or stepping onto a stage. On closer inspection, though, this air of comfortable staidness appeared forced, yet perhaps not consciously so. A tightness sat around his jaws, as if his teeth were constantly on the verge of clenching in anticipation of pain. His head was fixed at a light upward angle, conveying a blend of fancy and ambition.

He pulled out his watch, looked at it, then increased his pace, now swinging the umbrella with more gusto. He did not hear the bicycle which, swerving between pedestrians, was approaching him from behind. At the last moment the rider shouted a warning, but too late. He hit Ferguson's shoulder at almost full speed. The umbrella slipped from his grasp, described an arc through the air, and landed clattering by the entrance of a whitewashed house that stood unimpressively next to Admiralty Arch. The satchel fell in front of him. As Ferguson's outstretched hands struck the footpath to either side of the satchel, it luckily prevented his face from hitting the pavement. His pince-nez detached itself, glanced off the satchel, and slithered two yards across the stones before coming to rest on the curb.

A middle-aged gentleman in a rumpled beige suit, who was emerging from the entrance in front of which the umbrella came to the ground, rushed to the victim.

"Are you all right, Sir?"

"Yes, yes. I...I think I am...." The middle-aged gentleman helped Ferguson to his feet, who, on rising, gripped his satchel.

He exhaled loudly, then surveyed the footpath in alarm. Some pedestrians slowed their steps, but as the crisis had already passed they continued on their way.

"Can you see my spectacles, by any chance?" "Oh dear. I'm afraid not...."

"I am rather dependent on them, unfortunately."

"These ruffians on their bicycles. They are a menace. The police need to do something about these newfangled things," muttered the man, gripping the edges of his suit and looking around. "There they are," he exclaimed and stepped up to the curb. He settled down on his haunches with a wheeze. "And you're lucky. They are not even broken." Having retrieved the pince-nez, he stood up. "A little scratched merely." He wiped the spectacles clean against the arm of his jacket.

Ferguson had remained immobile, staring into the distance. On now receiving his accoutrement, he hurriedly squeezed it onto his nose. "Thank you, Sir. Much obliged."

"You are most welcome. And the umbrella." The middle-aged gentleman picked it up from the footpath in front of the entrance. "I say, you were rather lucky, all things considered."

"I believe I was," agreed Ferguson, taking the umbrella and giving it an anxious glance. Apparently satisfied, he assumed his former expression, chin lifted, his features showing determined equanimity. "Thank you again, Sir. You have been most kind." He looked ahead to the corner where the bicycle must have disappeared and shook his head in anger. "Well, what can one say...? I must be on my way. I am in a bit of a hurry...." He pointed to a line of hansom cabs that stood waiting at Charing Cross, then raised his hand in good-bye and resumed his walk.

The crowd absorbed Ferguson's figure. The man in the rumpled suit remained behind, a few waxy blotches forming on his jowly face. Finally, he stepped back through the door out of which he had emerged. It had only been leaned to. Inside the foyer was another man. He had a cigar in his mouth and stood bent over a walnut table on which lay an umbrella whose handle had been detached as well as a few sheets of tracing paper. These the man held pressed down on the edges. The top sheet showed what appeared to be a construction plan of a warship.

"Looks as if everything were here, Mycroft," said the man around his cigar. "As you had expected."

The middle-aged gentleman approached the table. "Well," he said with stern contentment, "now things are back where they belong. And Ferguson is our deliveryman."

"Are you certain he will not mention his accident to his friends?

They might form a suspicion."

"Rest assured, he will not. He was able to brush himself off. Vanity will seal his lips."

"Look at these!" The man turned to another page, and the ash shook precariously at the tip of his cigar. "As good as the originals! I'd love to wring his thin neck! The cab will follow him?"

"Don't worry, it's waiting at Charing Cross," smiled the man called Mycroft. "If we're lucky, he will board it. If he takes another one, ours will follow the one he takes. All is going according to plan."

The man with the cigar voiced another doubt: "What if Ferguson looks at the new version and realizes it's not his...?"

"That is conceivable, but not likely. They will be in a hurry. We had to take that risk."

"I see." The man exhaled a thoughtful puff of smoke. "No more news about this character behind all this?"

"Not really. As I told you the other day, he only appeared a few months ago as if out of nowhere. One thing, he seems to be a mathematician by profession, of all things...."

"I never liked math." The man chuckled. "Bane of my school days. Let us make sure his career is short-lived. We should get underway, I suppose. If you are sure Ferguson is heading to the East End."

"I'm sure about the East End. Where in the East End I don't know, unfortunately. But I've seen to it that we'll have word once he reaches his destination."

The man with the cigar rolled up the papers. "Very good. I'll follow your lead, Mycroft; this is your operation."

Unbeknownst to the two men now leaning over the documents from the umbrella, the little drama on the sidewalk had had an observer. After Ferguson emerged from the office building, a stout man with a gray walrus moustache appeared from the inside of a black coach that stood idle on the opposite side of the street as if waiting for an important personage. The man wore the thick, double-breasted dark jacket of coachmen during the cold season. He now clambered onto the box, apparently having concluded a nap inside his vehicle, and began readying himself for a resumption of his duties. While Ferguson walked down Whitehall with measured steps, swinging his umbrella, the coachman nestled with the reins. His head jerked briefly to the side as a young man with a cap pressed down upon his forehead suddenly appeared on a bicycle, heading in the same direction as Ferguson. The coachman's head remained lowered, but his fingers became motionless. From a distance of almost a hundred yards, he watched the collision between the bicycle rider and Ferguson and the appearance of the middle-aged gentleman from the house door. The coachman waited until Ferguson took leave of his helper and resumed his walk towards Charing Cross, then maneuvered the coach into the street with a smack of the whip.

The coach maintained a slow pace, and the man with the walrus moustache watched Ferguson approaching the line of hansom cabs. One cab driver accosted the young man and tried to steer him towards a vehicle, but Ferguson ignored the imprecations and selected another cab. The coachman increased his speed as the cab with Ferguson inside pulled into the busy traffic of Charing Cross. Immediately, the cab whose driver had failed to receive the young man's business followed. The two cabs, the coach behind them, now made a half tour of the circle, passing under Nelson's Column, which pierced the gray sky like a barren mast, and headed down Northumberland Avenue towards the river. On reaching the Thames, they turned west along the Embankment, before finally crossing Westminster Bridge. The water lay dark in the evening light, emitting an odour of seaweed and dead fish. From down the river came the braying of a steamship's horn; the paraffin lamps of the cabs and coaches bobbed yellow in the dusk.

The man with the walrus moustache allowed other vehicles to insert themselves between his coach and the two cabs, but never lost sight of his quarry; the second cab followed the same practice with regard to the first one. A keen northwest wind blew towards the Channel, but could not dispel the pall of clouds and smoke over London. The cold air brought a flush to the coachman's heavy round features, crisscrossed on the cheeks by a spider's web of capillaries. The three vehicles passed through Lambeth into the Borough and crossed the river again on Southwark Bridge. They then turned east on Thames Street and made their way through the City towards Whitechapel. The buildings on either side began to take on a derelict aspect; some passers-by moved furtively, as if reluctant to be seen.

As the two cabs and the coach turned into the thoroughfare of Fenchurch Road, the coachman let his horse's croup feel the whip. The animal broke into a faster trot and passed the cabs. He did not look left. Another touch of the whip, and he had soon left the two vehicles far behind. He reached a three-storey redbrick building with Old Forge Hotel painted over the entrance in peeling verdigris letters. Turning into an alleyway, he followed it for fifty yards, turned into a lane, then into another one, and after thirty yards gingerly steered his coach into a walled courtyard. He jumped from the box with an agility surprising for a man of his bulk and walked back out of the courtyard, pulling a heavy gate closed behind him. Having secured it with a padlock, he retraced his way to the hotel and entered the building through a side door that led into a hallway. Down it ran a carpet of indeterminate colour. A man who looked like a prize fighter stood, arms before his chest, in front of a door. He now moved hastily aside and knocked, three raps followed by a pause and another single rap.

A rustling sound could be heard, then a bolt slid back. The door swung open and revealed a woman. She was tall and dressed in a mauve silk Caraco jacket whose top buttons were open. It set off her décolletage and slim waist advantageously. The frosted lustre of a string of pearls circled her slender neck. A flush was just receding from her cheeks, leaving her skin with a lightly rouged porcelain complexion. The room behind her lay in half light; thick curtains sealed the windows. The flame of a single gaslight on the wall imparted a copper glow to her wavy auburn hair. She had a thin nose that sloped upward towards the point. A hard clarity lay in her eyes and belied the expression of girlish ingenuousness on her features. At least two decades and a half had been hers on this earth, and some of those years had been rich in experiences. She now opened her lips to reveal a line of white teeth and was about to speak, when a voice from the shadows cut her off:

"Moran, come in. What is the news?" The voice was low and almost without inflexion, yet commanding. "Beatrice, shut the door."

The woman did so, after Moran had stepped inside.

"As you had expected, Professor," said Moran, a grin under his moustache. "They staged the accident while Ferguson was walking towards the cabs."

"Mycroft Holmes had to strike. This was his last chance.

Are they following Ferguson?"

"Yes, there's a cab behind his." "When will he be here?"

"In three, four minutes."

The man who elicited these quick replies sat reclining in an easy chair. His right calf dangled comfortably over his left knee.

"Pour yourself a drink, Moran." The Professor rose and gestured towards a decanter and some glasses on a sideboard. His hands were large, with long fingers, pianist's hands. A signet ring with a dark blue spinel gleamed on his left hand.

He took a glass of gin that stood on a side table and crossed the room with long steps. He was over six feet tall, yet appeared of only a little above average height. His back was slightly bent, as if he had spent too much time hunched over a desk. Yet a closer look revealed that in fact his entire frame was coiled in wiry expectancy. He was middle-aged in an ill-defined manner. He had thin, metal gray hair, combed back straight from his forehead. His features were taught and unlined. The shadow of a beard covered sallow cheeks and a bony chin. The only feature that bespoke the body's fleshly substance was his lips. They lay full and sensuous on his face as if painted on, displaying a prominent Cupid's bow.

He took up station by the window and with index and middle finger pushed the curtain an inch aside. Every once in a while, he took a sip from his glass, rolled the liquid in his mouth, and then swallowed with an expressionless face.

"Professor Moriarty." The woman's voice had the modulation that comes with years of training. Yet now she spoke a little unsteadily, and a hint of a Yorkshire accent flattened her vowels, while her fingers played with the antimacassar on the chair behind which she was standing. "I've asked you this before, but what will happen when... things don't go as he hopes?"

"And as before, my dear, I tell you he will be heartbroken."

"That is all?"

"You will never hear from him again. There are two types of men, Beatrice, those who are capable of revenge and those who are not." She seemed to be considering this when Moriarty turned. "But you *must* leave with him tonight."

She looked into the Professor's strangely unblinking gray eyes.

"I never renege on a bargain."

"Good." He passed an appreciative glance down her figure, as if beholding a fine piece of artisanship he had created. Then he turned back to the window.

"Here they are...." he announced after a minute.

"Shall I go into the lobby?" asked Moran, who had settled down with his drink on a sofa next to a cold fireplace.

"No, someone is already there."

The familiar knocking signal came after half-a-minute. Her dress rustling, Beatrice crossed the carpet to the door. Ferguson entered with all the aplomb of a schoolboy tiptoeing into the classroom after the bell has rung. Yet in the presence of the woman his appearance changed rapidly. He straightened up, and his chest appeared to broaden. His pupils expanded behind the pince-nez, lending him an air of determination and focus. A ruddy colour crept into his cheeks, and a smile that betokened a belief in assured well-being spread over his thin face.

He leant forward awkwardly. Both his hands were full; in his right he held his satchel and top hat, in his left the umbrella. "Miss, Miss...J-Jones." He recovered himself and brushed her cheek with his lips. "Sorry I'm a little late –"

"I was becoming worried for you, Henry." Her voice had acquired a playful lilt and had risen by half an octave.

"Nothing to worry about," he assured her. "All went well...."

She pushed the door closed, then slipped his hat from his fingers and hung it on a hook in the wall. Turning, she gestured towards the man who had crossed the room behind her.

"As the Professor told you it would. He is rather good at anticipating events."

Ferguson switched his satchel into his left hand, and Moriarty took the young man's right. There was a grasping quality to the Professor's motion, as if he were laying claim to a coveted object.

"Good evening, Mr. Ferguson."

"Good evening, Sir."

"No surprises. I am glad."

"It happened almost exactly as you had expected. A cyclist hit me."

Moriarty lifted both hands, palms up, to indicate his invariable correctness in such matters. "These are the clumsy ways our friends in the government mount their efforts."

"We took quite a risk," Beatrice observed. "I am relieved."

Ferguson shrugged. "It was nothing, really. And I did put on a good show, even if I say so myself."

Moriarty gave a short, rasping laugh. "I am sure you did. Now to our business," he added, steering Ferguson by the elbow to a desk in the corner.

Moran and Beatrice joined as the young man placed his satchel on the desk and took the umbrella in both hands.

"First, the wages of my accident," he said with an emphatically wry smile, unscrewing the wooden handle.

Moriarty bent forward to inspect the umbrella. "They produced a nice duplicate, I have to say."

"I left mine in the office occasionally, so they would have enough time." Ferguson pulled a role of tracing papers from the shank and held it out to the Professor.

"So," said Moriarty, his long fingers closing around them, "this is what Mycroft Holmes would have me pass on to my clients." He unrolled the papers and eyed the top one, head tilting left to right and back. Then he repeated the procedure with the remaining sheets. A lopsided grin formed on his full lips. "Not bad at all. Every number, angle, curve is wrong, but believably wrong. One must appreciate dedicated work." He laid the papers on the desk and pointed at the satchel. "That contains the genuine plans."

"It does. Hidden in plain sight, so to speak. As you suggested."

"Oh, not my idea." The Professor raised a modest hand, the spinel shining dully. "Some years ago, I read a story about a detective in search of a stolen letter. I forget the title, but the story was rather good. The idea was that the most obvious places are never searched."

"It appears Henry has kept his side of the bargain," Beatrice interjected now.

"Indeed he has," agreed Moriarty. His left hand closed on the satchel's grip, while his right pulled an envelope from his jacket. "And I never renege on one, Miss Jones." The envelope passed into Ferguson's sheepishly outstretched hand. "The sum we agreed upon in government bonds. You are a wealthy man now, Mr. Ferguson."

The young man held the envelope mutely between thumb and index finger.

"Please, do have a look inside." The Professor gestured invitingly.

Ferguson fingered open the envelope, Beatrice by his side. Her lips parted as her lover's thumb grazed the edge of the bills. Then her large blue eyes quickly rose to meet his glance, and with a smile he slipped the envelope into his coat. His left arm passed around the small of her back and pulled her against him.

"Wouldn't you like to have a look at the genuine plans?" He pointed at the satchel.

Moriarty shook his head. "That will not be necessary. I trust you, Mr. Ferguson. And now we must see to it that you have a chance to enjoy your newfound wealth. Mycroft Holmes appears to bear...enterprising government employees somewhat of an animus. Even the ones he believes to have been useful. A pity, isn't it? This hotel has more exits than are readily visible, Mr. Ferguson," he continued. "If you were to leave by the front door, you would be pursued, I am afraid, and would not see the end of it...until the end. Happily though, I've been preparing for such eventualities."

He gave Moran a nod, who set to work moving the chairs and table to the edge of the room. The others watched, as he bent down and rolled up the carpet until a trap door became visible in the wooden floor. A handle was set into the door's boards in such a manner that the surface was flush. Very carefully, Moran took the handle between thumb and forefinger of his left hand and lifted the metal half moon into an upright position. In the handle's centre the nub of what looked like a screw became visible. A penknife appeared in Moran's right hand and with a click a stiletto blade sprang out of the handle. He proceeded to push the blade's tip under the metal nub. Once he had dislodged it, he laid aside the knife and pulled a thin splint from the centre of the handle. The splint was just long enough to traverse the body of the handle to the inside. The splint's tip would inevitably puncture the skin of anyone who gripped the handle without being aware of this hidden danger. Moran rose from his knees, walked over to the side table, and placed the splint in the table's centre. Then he returned and with one swift movement yanked open the trap door.

Moriarty approached the gaping black hole. A few steps of a ladder where visible before darkness closed in.

"You see, Mr. Ferguson. Everything is prepared. This passage leads to a house some distance away. My associate here, Colonel Moran, will take you. You can trust him implicitly; he has worked aside me for many years. From this house, you will all three travel by coach to a spot somewhat east of the docks. A boat will be waiting. I understand you have given some valuables for transport to your charming lady here. You will find them stowed in your cabin. You will be in Calais by tomorrow morning, Mr. Ferguson. There, Colonel Moran will take his leave from you. Our customer does not reside in your place of destination. I'm afraid the crossing might not be comfortable tonight, but such is the lot of us who travel light."

Moran had lit an oil lantern and now descended the ladder. The hole was not as deep as it had initially appeared, somewhat over eight feet. The entrance to a side passage became visible; the passage was a little under six feet in height and a foot and a half in width. A wooden beam, the first in a long line one might conjecture, supported the entrance. Having reached the bottom, Moran stood in the centre of a dirty three-by-three foot square and held up the lantern.

"Please," said Moriarty, looking at the pair. "Don't worry. I assure you, it's quite safe."

Beatrice nodded, but first went over to the hook in the wall and took Ferguson's hat. She placed it in his hand as if to say that he would forget his own head if it were not attached. Then she pulled up the hem of her dress, turned her back to the hole, and placed a dainty shoe on the first rung. In a few seconds she was below, Moran gallantly raising a hand to assist her with the final steps.

"Our ways part here, Mr. Ferguson," said Moriarty. "I wish you good fortune. Remember, you must never again set foot in this country, no matter how homesick you become. And beware of Her Majesty's many agents; the reach of their arm is long."

Ferguson paled at these words, yet nodded as if to intimate that he had considered his choices long and carefully. Moriarty did not extend his hand. In his left he held the papers, in his right the satchel. Ferguson turned and slowly descended the steps.

"We're ready," Moran's voice called from below after a few seconds.

"Don't forget the merchandise." The Professor lowered himself on one knee and extended his arm holding the satchel downward. A careful observer might have seen that one of the satchel's two straps, both of which had been closed, now hung half open and dangled outside the loop.

"Thank you," came Moran's voice from the hole, and the Professor retracted his arm, hand empty, and rose.

Without further ceremony, he closed the trapdoor.

Beside him on the floor lay a manila folder of exactly the size that fitted snugly into the satchel. Moriarty took the folder and laid it on the side table. He picked up the splint Moran had placed there. Holding it between his fingertips, the Professor retraced his steps. He kneeled down and fitted the splint into the hole in the handle, before carefully settling the handle into place. Then he went over to the sideboard and poured himself a gin. Thoughtfully, he emptied the glass. He finally set it down and returned to the trapdoor. Unlike Moran, he used a fingernail to dislodge the splint before pulling it out. He held it up towards the gaslight. On the tip, an oily sheen was visible. Moriarty pulled out a handkerchief and wiped the splint clean with a few vigorous motions. He looked at it critically, then nodded. A sting, yes, for sure, but no longer a deadly one. He replaced the splint in the handle, stood up, rolled back the carpet, and moved the pieces of furniture to where they had stood before. His work complete, he crossed the room and opened a wardrobe.

Inside hung a tattered black pea coat, a pair of patched trousers, and a collarless shirt. A shelf held a false gray beard and some other items that might be found in an actor's dressing room. On the wardrobe's inside door was a mirror. He took off his dark lounge coat, while pulling a silver comb from its inside pocket. He threw the coat over the wardrobe's door and then proceeded to smooth back his hair. Smiling approvingly at his image, he unbuttoned his satin waistcoat. He would walk out the front door. An old salt on shore leave could afford this place. Maybe he would be swaying a little; old salts on shore leave generally did.

Mycroft Holmes was walking along the gas lit streets of Billingsgate towards London Bridge. He had thrown on a brown Newmarket coat over his rumpled suit, but had neglected to close either. A woolen scarf hung uselessly around his neck. His hands were rammed into his trouser pockets. The large man carried his head bent; wisps of hair hung into his high forehead. His steps had a discontented, stomping quality. A few times, he almost bumped into another pedestrian, who invariably was the one to swerve so as to avoid the collision.

A thin rain began, whipped into sheets by the wind, and Holmes raised his collar and quickened his steps. He passed a pub, halted, walked back, and entered the premises. He blew his nose on a well-worn handkerchief, then approached the bar and settled down on a stool at the corner of the short side. Closing time was less than an hour away. The pub was half empty. Its regular patrons were the merchants of the City, and on a Friday night many of those gentlemen had more fashionable or disreputable venues to attend. A group of men sat chatting by a fireside; some of them held instruments on their knees, but only one occasionally scratched at a violin. A few tipplers lined the bar. Tobacco smoke hung under the ceiling, immobile and as if it had always been there and always would be.

Holmes ordered a stout, and sat with it, hands circling the glass. Every once in a while, his eyebrows would crease or he would press his teeth against his upper lip as if in response to a thought that had come to an end. Then he would take a sip of beer.

He did not notice the figure slipping onto the stool perpendicular to his own. The next time Holmes emerged from his thoughts, he saw a bearded man across the edge of the bar. He was wearing a tattered black pea coat and a cap from under which protruded a mass of gray hair – an old salt on shore leave. He seemed familiar to Holmes in a vague way, one of the thousands of faces he had encountered, none of which he ever forgot. The man's left hand was closed around a glass of gin; his right hand lay invisible below the bar.

"Yer looked like yer were woolgatherin' there, guv'nor," said the old salt and gave a good-natured, hoarse laugh.

"It has been an interesting day." "Mine too, mine too."

Holmes lifted a tired eyebrow.

The sailor took a gulp of gin, then said, "I got me 'ands on sumthing, guv'nor, sumthing I been after for a while."

"A nice coincidence..." mumbled Holmes.

"'Ow so, Sir?"

"I lost sight of someone today, someone I've been after for a while."

"That's a rum thing, guv'nor." The sailor's eyes twinkled with cold merriment underneath heavy brows. Then his voice changed, losing any trace of Cockney and acquiring a mocking, imperious tone.

"But there are no coincidences, only excuses of a lazy mind."

The two men looked at each other. Slowly, Holmes began to rise. "Sit down, Mr. Holmes. A gun is pointed at your stomach. And you never carry a weapon yourself, I know."

Holmes settled back on his stool, his hand closing tightly around his glass. "What do you want, Moriarty?"

"To meet, at last," smiled the Professor. "After all these months of circling each other like two backyard tomcats. Have you discovered the tunnel from the Forge Hotel yet, Mr. Holmes?"

"We have. I'm sure your hands were calloused after all the digging."

"Please, Mr. Holmes. Why so acerbic? We both know, some do the digging, some think for the diggers. Our two institutions are much alike in this regard. And anyway, what could you have done? Arrest Ferguson? Would that not have suggested he was under observation?"

"We would have waited a while."

"Even then, would an arrest not have cast doubts on the genuine nature of Ferguson's documents? I might have become suspicious, thought you might have exchanged them for false ones at some point. Who knows, even my clients might have developed second thoughts –"

Holmes's lips thinned.

"Speechless, Mr. Holmes? Did you really think I'd fall for your fakes? I'm rather hurt, I must say."

Holmes's mouth opened, but Moriarty waived him to be silent. "Please, Mr. Holmes. Who cares about boring details?"

"We will find him. He will stand trial for high treason."

"Maybe you will, maybe you won't. Maybe he will, maybe he won't," Moriarty said flatly and sipped from his gin. He glanced at the bandaged middle finger of Holmes's right hand. The Professor's face appeared perfectly expressionless, but Holmes could not be certain. An urge to rip away Moriarty's false beard welled up inside Holmes, yet at the same time he feared that he would behold a triumphant grin, perhaps worse, a pitying smile.

"Is he together with that tart you placed in his way?" he asked.

"An ugly word, Mr. Holmes! Miss Beatrice is a thespian, an artist! And yes, I believe he is sharing her company, blissful as a child at Christmas."

Holmes snorted. "You know what will happen, Moriarty. One morning, he will wake up, and your thespian will have danced out of his life, with the money."

"My good Holmes, Ferguson is a young man. These are the mistakes young men make. He will learn. Yet for now he is happy because he acted upon his desires. Thus it should be. I merely gave him the opportunity for happiness." After a pause, he leaned conspiratorially over the bar. "Really, my enterprise is to make people happy, Mr. Holmes."

At the other man's raillery, the colour rose in Holmes's cheeks. His fingertips turned white around the glass. Moriarty had been watching closely. He lifted a hand as if to suggest one last moment of reprieve before the inevitable fight. The spinel still gleamed on his ring finger, out of keeping with his modest attire.

"You may not believe this, Mr. Holmes, but even your happiness has been on my mind." He slipped his hand into his jacket's side pocket, brought out a folded sheet of tracing paper, and pushed it across the bar. Holmes did not take his eyes off the other man's face. Finally, he reached for the sheet and unfolded it. He studied it for close to half-a-minute, his skin turning ashen.

"This is from the genuine document..." he whispered.

"It is," confirmed the Professor. "But don't you worry. I sent Moran on his way with the false version you provided us."

Holmes swallowed.

"How did...?" His voice deteriorated into a croak, and he cleared his throat. "How did you get this?"

"Immaterial, Holmes. Immaterial. But there are things I like to keep for myself. I am a bit of a collector. Who knows, perhaps I am even a patriot. And my clients will be satisfied. Your version is compelling enough. They will not notice the difference. You may keep that," he said, pointing to the paper. "A memento, if you will." Moriarty slipped from his stool. He placed some coins on the bar. "Allow me, your drink is on me. I had ever such a pleasant conversation this evening. I will also leave you this." He hung an umbrella by its handle on the bar's edge next to Holmes. "You should be more careful, Mr. Holmes; otherwise you'll catch a cold."

With that, the old salt turned, crossed the room with long, silent steps, and disappeared into the night. Holmes eyed the umbrella that was swinging lightly. He recognized its somewhat widened shank. The urge to break the blasted thing rose from his stomach like acid. He looked at his bandaged middle finger. The wound stung, but the pain was not physical. An odd chill seemed to emanate from the empty place across from him, as if a void had been left there. He had played the game too loosely, but they would meet again, many times, he had a sense. The next round would find him better prepared, much better prepared.

Holmes's eyes fell upon the gin glass Moriarty had left standing upon the bar. Holmes stared at the glass for a while as if trying to impose order on a string of inchoate thoughts. After a while he reached over and carefully picked the glass up by its rim. He turned and held the glass in the direction of the fireplace. Moriarty's fingerprints were clearly visible. Raising his eyebrows, Holmes turned back to the bar and set down the glass. He looked at it, occasionally rubbing his chin. It was time to come up with some new ideas. Slowly, he finished his pint.

Beatrice let her head fall back against the rear of the coach and closed her eyes. The sound of the horse's hooves and of the wheels on the cobble stones was soothing. She felt tired, but her heart beat rapidly. Everything had worked as planned. They were already outside Calais. A few hours to Amiens and tomorrow on to Paris! She would see Paris, finally! She would do more than see it; she would make it her own!

She opened her eyes and brushed a strand of her auburn locks behind her ear. Henry Ferguson lay slunk into the corner, his mouth half open, producing chortling noises. His complexion was still greenish. Moriarty had been right about the Channel crossing. She reached over and pulled two envelopes from the inside pocket of Ferguson's coat. Placing them on her lap, she passed her fingers over the top one. She could feel Moriarty's government notes inside. Laying it on the upholstery, she took the other. The envelope bulged slightly. She unsealed it and pulled out a folded set of tracing papers. They made a low crackling sound as she smoothed them out on her knees. She inspected them for close to a minute. For all she could tell, they showed boats and their parts. Men were such fools! All this intrigue for some drawings, of which one could tell one's lover to make as many copies as one pleased! Oh well, if this was what they considered worth spending money on, who was she to tell them otherwise? She folded the papers and replaced them in the envelope. Then she slipped both envelopes back into Ferguson's coat. She had an idea who might be interested in this set of copies.

Her eyes rested on Ferguson. Despite his complexion, his sleep appeared happy. Oddly, she had found of late that she rather liked him. His presence was comforting. He would never leave her, never make demands. What to do with him? Time would tell. She turned to look at the green hills of the French countryside. The storm had blown itself out over night, and now the drops on the yellow leaves of the beech trees sparkled in the late morning sun. A pink hue lay on her chest. She felt like laughing, but she preferred her lover to remain asleep, and so she only smiled.

The Adventure of the Fateful Malady

by Martin Rosenstock

A quick reference to my journals confirms that the year 1889 was a very busy one for Mr. Sherlock Holmes. Notwithstanding the fact that marriage had precipitated my departure from the flat at 221b Baker Street, I called upon Holmes regularly, and he was kind enough to include me in several of his more peculiar adventures. I have already set down for public consumption such strange tales as that of the false beggar,[1] and the woman's wit that foiled both a king and a genius.[2] But other problems, such as the mystery of Mr. Philip King, the famous inventor, who boarded the Flying Scotsman at King's Cross Station and was never seen again,[3] cannot be told until the principals of the matter have passed beyond the ken of human existence. These cases must be safely locked away until a new day has dawned, and the terrible events depicted in the following narrative are just such an example.

It was during one of my visits to Baker Street that autumn when Holmes found himself engaged by a client of no small renown. We were sitting in front of the afternoon fire where I had reclaimed my former arm-chair, while Holmes was animatedly describing to me, in minute detail, my movements of the day. Despite having repeatedly been on the receiving end of Holmes's series of logical deductions, it nonetheless amazed me when he inquired whether my trip to Hatton Garden had been a successful one.

"I fail to see, Holmes, how you could possibly know precisely which street I visited today?"

"It was simplicity itself, Watson. The first observation is the faint sparkle of gold coming from the distal right sleeve of your coat."

I reflexively glanced downwards and verified his inspection. "What of it?"

"Why, Watson, how many methods exist for a man to obtain gold dust upon his sleeve? Surely very few, especially when that fellow is a practicing physician and not an artisan? When you add to the chain of logic the facts that this man was married almost a year ago, but at the time was rather deficient in his pocket-book, it suggests that he was engaged upon the errand of buying a gift for his wife. And where else in London does a man go to purchase jewelry other than Hatton Garden?"[4]

I laughed appreciatively. "Guilty as charged, Holmes."

He smiled back. "I think in this case, you are literally wearing your heart upon your sleeve,[5] Watson." He paused and listened for a moment. "Ah, if I am not mistaken, the sound of a brougham stopping outside our door suggests that we are about to be visited by a client." He rose and peered out of the bow-window towards the street below.

I had little time to be pleased that Holmes had automatically involved me in the case, for the door was swiftly opened. An austere man entered, his springy steps communicating a great energy. His iron grey hair placed him at a shade over fifty years of age, though his cleanly-shaven face was unlined. His nose and chin were angular, and his features as grave as a sphinx, though his eyes shone with vitality and shrewdness. As to his dress, his double-breasted woolen frock coat and cashmere-striped trousers were of the highest cut and quality. He removed his top hat and perched stiffly in the basket chair that Holmes had indicated.

"My name is Sir James Saunders,"[6] began our visitor, but

he was forestalled by Holmes.

"If I may, sir? You recognized, of course, Watson, that Sir James is a fellow medico. However, rather than a general practitioner, he specializes in dermatology. You are engaged at the highest levels of a hospital, and it is upon their business that you come."

"You are correct, Mr. Holmes. For the last six years I have had the honor of being the Director of the Charing Cross Hospital.[7] But you must know these facts already, to be so familiar with my history."

"Not at all, Sir James. The simple method to distinguish a dermatologist from other medical men is to compare their hands and face, one rough from constant washing, the other smoother than is typical for their age. Your career has been successful, for how else would you afford such a fine brougham? But it is plain from your horses, which are hardly fresh and glossy, that your practice is not located in the vicinity of the nearby Cavendish Square, where the most eminent physicians hang their lamps.[8] Therefore, I reasoned that you are most likely the head of a hospital, and so it proves to be."

Sir James nodded. "That is excellent, Mr. Holmes. This is precisely why I have consulted you." He paused and studied Holmes for a moment. "I have been informed that you are a man whose discretion can be trusted absolutely."

"I am glad that it is so said," replied Holmes mildly.

"It is of critical importance that no word of this matter spreads to the public. If Fleet Street[9] hears of this, the reputation of the Hospital will suffer a mortal blow, from which it could never hope to recover."

"Perhaps if you told me of your problem, Sir James?"

The man sighed. "Very well. I am afraid, Mr. Holmes, that the Black Death is once more upon us."[10]

"Indeed," said Holmes, his lids drooping over his eyes.

Sir James appeared dismayed that his dramatic words had such little effect upon the demeanor of my friend. "I am not certain that you understand the gravity of the situation, Mr. Holmes," said he, urgently. "The Great Plague of London may have been two hundred years ago,[11] but nothing that caused such a massive upheaval is ever truly forgotten. As the harbinger of a terrible comet appeared in the sky,[12] a hundred thousand died in London alone.[13] Of course, that was small fry compared to the Black Death pandemic itself.[14] Over a million souls dead, Mr. Holmes, up to a third of the entire population of England! Imagine if such a horror was to return?"

"Surely this is a matter for the authorities, Sir James?" I interjected. "How have you succeeded in keeping this quiet?"

"This was not a decision that I came to on my own, Dr. Watson. The Board of Health has been notified. The Necropolis Railway[15] has refused to take the bodies, for fear of spreading the contagion, and it was the Board that secretly approved the extraordinary measures of permitting us to cremate them *in situ*.[16] Mr. Holmes, I assure you that the matter is dire."

"I recognize, sir, that you believe that a great pestilence has descended upon your hospital. However, I fail to perceive of what service I could be to you? Your particular problem seems to be more along the lines of Dr. Watson here than that of a consulting detective. I am no physician." He sank back into his arm-chair, his interest clearly waning.

"I don't require for you to help the patients, Mr. Holmes. A team of skilled doctors, ably assisted by caring nurses, is laboring night and day to accomplish that herculean task. What I ask of you is to determine from where the plague is originating. We have isolated every patient, and yet new cases continue to occur, almost every day."[17]

Holmes frowned. "It was my understanding that such miasmas have been mainly eliminated in no small part due to the sewers engineered by Sir Joseph Bazalgette?"[18]

"But, Holmes, the plague is mainly spread via rats,"[19]

I interjected. "That is indeed the accepted hypothesis, Dr. Watson," replied Sir James. "It is believed that the Black Death first descended upon Europe via grain ships originating from China, which unwittingly harbored the infected rats."

"Surely you must have a mechanism in place to safeguard against such an infestation?" asked Holmes.

"Indeed we do, Mr. Holmes. Like many hospitals, we kept a clowder[20] of Manx mousers, descended from a cat that legendarily sailed about the *HMS Ajax* at Trafalgar.[21] However, three weeks ago all of our Manx were suddenly found dead."

Holmes sat up again. "That is most remarkable."

Sir James shrugged. "Is it? I thought it a coincidence, perhaps one that initiated the infestations. So we have taken pains to rectify the situation. We brought in a famous rat-catcher from Shadwell, by the name of Dick Whyte."[22]

"But the results have not been satisfactory?"

"Mr. Whyte continues to catch large numbers of rats, Mr. Holmes, but it has made no impact upon the spread of the contagion."

"Then what is your theory?"

"I came to seek a theory, Mr. Holmes, not to suggest one. However, Dr. Edward Purcell, who we brought in this summer to help us combat London's outbreak of cholera, suspects that it might have been introduced to the hospital by a coolie from Wapping or Rotherhithe."[23]

Holmes glanced at his pocket watch. "The hour is getting late," he noted, "but hospitals never sleep and rat-catchers are nocturnal beings. Let us waste no more time here, but rather see what we can ascertain tonight."

Sir James insisted on driving us to the hospital in his brougham. On the way, I mentioned how odd it was to find a disease typically associated with the history books now stalking the streets of London.

"Not really, Dr. Watson," said our new employer. "As

you well know, the plague has never entirely vanished. The Ottomans battled it until a few decades ago, and China continues to experience outbreaks.[24] As our means of transportation grow ever more rapid and our world shrinks, diseases long thought past, or even those yet to be discovered, will spread ever so much faster."

"So this outbreak is affecting all of London?" inquired Holmes.

"No, Mr. Holmes, the Board of Health tells me that Charing Cross Hospital is the only one seeing cases so far. They are monitoring it closely, to ensure that it does not spread beyond our walls."

"Most singular! When exactly did the outbreak begin?"

"It was roughly two weeks ago. Dr. Purcell was the first to note the symptoms. The patients all developed high fevers, flushing, blackened tongues, tarry excreta, and finally fits[25] before they died. In the beginning, only those who were already ill seemed to catch it. The first several victims had severe cases of cholera. Dr. Purcell thought that perhaps it was some never-before-seen variant of that great scourge. But as this year's cholera outbreak waned, our plague persisted. It struck down a man with consumption,[26] another with an inoperable tumor on his liver, and a woman with severe dropsy.[27] And then the most tragic thing of all happened. It struck down one of our physicians."

"An elderly practitioner?"

"Quite the opposite. Dr. Alfred Taylor was but a few years out from his degree at the University of London.[28] He was in the prime of health. A great loss, for his career was considered to be very promising. He was researching the pathology of chorea,[29] and was due to win the Golding prize."

"Ah, and will someone else be awarded the prize in his stead?" asked Holmes, mildly.

Sir James shook his head sadly. "Certainly not! It will be awarded posthumously. Still, we have been fortunate, really, given the history of the medieval plague doctors. Most of them survived little longer than their patients. Every member of the hospital staff has been exemplary in their bravery, for none have deserted their posts."

I thought about the costume of the plague doctors, with its heavy waxed overcoat, brimmed hat, glass-eyed mask, and cone-shaped beak, and shook my head at the terror that might be unleashed were such signs of imminent death to make a return to the streets of London. These grim ponderings were cut short by our arrival at the hospital.

Although it had once been situated near the similarly-named railway station, the building now lay just off the Strand on Agar Street. The ionic capitals flanking the front door and gleaming white façade inspired confidence, and gave little hint of the terrible pestilence that currently ravaged the inhabitants. As we were about to mount the front steps, Holmes placed a hand on my shoulder. "Watson, there is no need for you to go any further. I will gladly report back to you what I discover."

I frowned. "Whatever are you talking about, Holmes?"

"Death might stalk these halls, Watson. There is no need for you to expose yourself."

"Do not be ridiculous, Holmes. I have faced greater dangers than this, and I still have the Jezail lead in my shoulder to prove it."

He shook his head. "But you had no other to think of when you braved those perils. Now you do."

I nodded in sudden comprehension. "Ah, I see, Holmes. But Mary understands who it is she married. The Reaper may walk in the door of my consulting room at any moment. Should I bar it as well?"

Holmes smiled. "Capital! Well, I must admit that I am glad to have you at my side, Watson. I am somewhat out of my element, but we are very much in yours." He turned to his client. "Now, Sir James, if you will be so kind as to point us in the direction of Mr. Dick Whyte, we will begin our investigation with him. We will look for you in your office when we are finished."

The hospital director reminded us that Mr. Whyte had not been entrusted with the true reason for his sudden employment. He then indicated that the rat-catcher's wagon could be found parked by the side entrance off William IV Street, named in honor of our great Queen's father. Holmes nodded and turned his steps in that direction. The four-wheeler proved to be easy to identify, for it was a ramshackle affair whose weathered boards looked as if they were on the verge of utter collapse. A sorry nag, far past the time when it should have been put out to pasture, was harnessed to the front, slowly grazing from a feed bag. The conveyance was deserted when we arrived, though we could hear rustling and squeaking sounds coming from within the locked compartment, which suggested that the man's outings had thus far been successful.

We had not long to wait before the owner made his appearance. Mr. Whyte was a middle-aged man with huge black whiskers, and his mouth was only visible from where his beard parted to permit the blackened stem of a pipe. He wore an eccentric scarlet topcoat, waistcoat, and breeches, with a huge leather belt from which hung a series of small cast-iron cages. The rodent occupants of these cages were clearly terrified by a small black and tan terrier that nipped at them constantly. As the man drew nearer, he seemed alarmed to find us inspecting his wagon.

"What gives, Guv'nor?" he cried, briefly removing the pipe from between his lips.

"You are Mr. Dick Whyte, I presume?"

"I give my name only in return for another, Mister Questioner."

"My name is Sherlock Holmes, and this is my associate, Dr. Watson."

He shrugged. "What of it?" he asked in a surly tone.

"I have been retained by Sir James Saunders to inspect

the hospital for potential sources of contagion. You have a very dangerous profession, Mr. Whyte."

"No more than some. I've a mate who lost his leg working the rails, and another who drowned off Gravesend. But my beauties rarely bite, Mr. Holmes." The pipe rapidly returned to his mouth between sentences, such that I doubted that he ever took a breath directly from the air.

"Are you not concerned about disease?" inquired Holmes.

His face twisted in disdain. "Nah, I am well protected from that."

"Really?" said Holmes, his eyebrows rising. "How so?"

The man stared at Holmes for a moment, and then shrugged again. "I guess there is little harm in letting you onto my little secret. Do you know, Mr. Holmes, the occupation of the only people to uniformly survive the greatest malady of them all, the Black Death, which some have blamed on my beauties?"

"No, I am afraid not."

"It is said that none who kept a tobacconist shop died, Mr. Holmes. Thus, the finest Virginia leaf is my charm," said he smugly, emitting a great cloud of blue smoke.

Holmes burst into a hearty laugh. "Then I too must have little to fear, Mr. Whyte, for Dr. Watson here has often accused me of poisoning myself with a surfeit of tobacco.[30] Now then, perhaps you might deign to show me your catch for the evening?"

Whyte's brusque manner appeared to have vanished after the discovery of this shared habit, and he proudly displayed for us his rats. From a distance, I gazed at the pack with some revulsion, but Holmes bent close and stared at them with his singular intentness. Finally, he straightened up, a gleam in his eyes which suggested that he had seized upon some irregularity.

He turned to the rat-catcher and glanced at his terrier. "That is a fine dog you have there, Mr. Whyte. It is a fortunate thing that you brought a canine to assist you, given the sudden deaths of all of the cats that once lived on site."

Whyte grinned broadly. "Tommie here is a grandson of the famous Jacko himself.[31] There has never been a finer ratter, Mister. A far sight better than some mangy cats!"

Holmes nodded. "You may have noted, Watson, during the period when we shared our lodgings, that there were some nights when I would never return home?"

I was surprised by this sudden *non sequitur*, but managed to stammer a response. "I have so remarked, upon occasion."

His face lit up with a whimsical smile. "I have several small retreats scattered about London, most of which can be found in less than salubrious locales.[32] It may surprise you to learn that one such refuge lies over a boxing den in Cambridge Circus which, in its former life, served as a rat-baiting pit. The denizens of that spot are still to be found in great numbers."

"I fail to comprehend your point, Holmes."

He shook his head. "That is because you see, but do not fully observe." He turned to the rat-catcher. "Tell me, Mr. Whyte, these are old English rats, are they not?"

The man's expression turned wary. "That's right."

Holmes smiled. "Also known as the black rat, or ship's rat? Where exactly did you find them, Mr. Whyte?"

"In the hospital, of course."

"Indeed? For black rats are nigh impossible to find in urban London now that they have been replaced by the Norwegian, or brown, rat."[33]

Whyte suddenly turned a ghastly color and looked from one to the other of us like a hunted creature. "I don't know what you mean," he stammered.

"I submit," said Holmes in his sternest tone, "Mr. Whyte, that you poisoned the clowder of Manx that once lived in this hospital so that the Director would be forced to hire you to take over the business of keeping it free of rats. And that you introduced a pack of ship's rats, collected by you on the wharfs, to this building, thereby introducing a terrible contagion. I am afraid that you will procure a charge of manslaughter, at the very least."

Whyte was shaking his head violently. "No, Mister, I swear it's not true. I never killed no cats! You are right about the black rats, but they were never set free in the hospital. I just bring them along for show, pretending that I caught them here, since they pay me by the rat. Truth be told, this place has no rat problem. It's as clean as a whistle. If I didn't pad my catch, I wouldn't make a shilling in this gig."

Holmes stared at the man intently for a moment, and then laughed sharply. "I believe you, Mr. Whyte. I suggest that you terminate your employment forthwith and return to your former haunts of Shadwell. I shall inform Sir James of your departure."

"Whatever you say, Mister!" the rat-catcher exclaimed. Within moments, he and his terrier were planted upon the wagon's seat and his nag was being whipped into motion.

Holmes watched them go for a moment and then turned to me with a chuckle. "I have been pursuing a red herring, Watson. Given the veritable den of thieves that constitutes greater London, it is perhaps of little surprise that there should be two villains in this case, a small one in the form of our Mr. Whyte, and somewhere else a much more important one. William of Ockham would be much displeased.[34] Still, we have learned a few facts of note from Mr. Whyte."

"We have?"

"Oh, yes, Watson. We shall docket those for the time being and see what additional matters will bear upon it. What steps would you propose to take now, Watson?"

"I would inspect the medical files of the victims in an attempt to find some common link."

"Excellent, Watson! The same thought had occurred to me. Let us rejoin Sir James and have him grant the necessary access."

In the office of the Director, Holmes quickly recounted

what had transpired with the rat-catcher. Sir James absorbed this news with little expression other than a small frown, and then agreed to show Holmes the records of the stricken patients. "They are all in Dr. Purcell's office. If you will follow me, gentlemen?"

The place in question proved to be a good-sized chamber, half of which was lined with bookcases, while the other portion was set up as a chemical laboratory. In the former sat a heavy oaken desk upon which lay several theatre playbills and a stack of manila folders filled with handwritten papers. The broad, low tables of the laboratory side were littered with curved retorts, test-tubes, measures, litmus-paper, glass pipettes, and a formidable array of bottles filled with all manners of solutions and dry materials.

Holmes surveyed the place quietly. "What exactly is Dr. Purcell working on in here, Sir James?" he asked, waving his hand towards the chemical apparatus.

"Ah, yes, well, the man is a veritable genius. When he is not directly attending to patients, Dr. Purcell is always experimenting on new compounds which might help alleviate the suffering of our patients. When he first arrived, he was working on developing anti-cholera agents, but he has since shifted his aims towards trying to find some vaccine against the plague. His work is being supported by our great patron, Miss Vivian Crawford, heiress to the Crawford paper fortune."

"Is such a thing really possible?" I inquired.[35]

"Dr. Purcell believes so. He has taken for his inspiration the fabled 'Four Thieves Vinegar.'"

I shook my head. "I am not familiar with that particular medicinal." "It was the secret recipe of a medieval gang of burglars from Marseille who used it to protect themselves from the plague while they plundered the homes of the sick and the dead."

"Dr. Purcell clearly believes that it is composed of vinegar, wormwood, marjoram, sage, cloves, rosemary, camphor, and several other herbs which I do not immediately recognize,"[36] said Holmes as he inspected the contents of the tables. He turned back to the Director. "Well, Sir James, Watson and I will now spend some time perusing these charts in order to determine if we can find some common thread that binds these victims together."

With that dismissal, Sir James left us to this work, which proved to be exceedingly dull. Hours of attempting to decipher the nigh illegible scrawl of a hurried physician strained my eyes mightily, and at one point I closed them for a minute of rest. The next thing I knew, Holmes was shaking me awake.

"My dear Watson," said he, smiling. "Let's return you to your home. There is nothing more to be learned here tonight."

"I am very sorry, Holmes," I replied, stretching. "Did you learn anything of note?"

"No, but the hour is early, metaphorically-speaking. I have hopes that tomorrow will bring some progress."

The following morn, my wife and I were breaking our fast when the clang of the bell announced the arrival of an early visitor. At this hour, I presumed it to be a patient and put on my coat so as to be ready to receive them. To my surprise, it was Sherlock Holmes who stood upon my step.

"Good morning, Watson. How long is your docket of patients this morning? Do you think Jackson or Anstruther would handle them for you?"

"Yes, certainly. Have you solved it, then?"

He shook his head ruefully. "Not yet, Watson, not yet. But I think it possible that Dr. Purcell might have something interesting to tell us, and I knew that, having begun upon a case, you would be loath to not see it through to the end."

"Of course. I would be happy to accompany you."

"Very good. He lives not far from here, in Harley Street, but in the interest of time, I have engaged a hansom."

The residence of Dr. Purcell proved to be one of the

somber, flat-faced, ochre-colored brick townhouses wherein the great specialists of the age practiced their arts. The door was answered by Dr. Purcell's valet who, at the presentation of our cards, admitted us into the well-appointed sitting room. There we were soon joined by a middle-aged woman. Even in the long-past bloom of youth she could not have been considered handsome, for she had a thin pointy nose, protuberant eyes, obstinate chin, and the deep lines of her cheeks suggested that the frown that lay upon her face was perpetual. The cut of her gloomy black dress harkened from many seasons ago, and from her neck dangled a pair of silver pince-nez upon a brown silken cord.

"How do you do, gentlemen?" she began, her tone cold. "I am afraid that my husband is resting after a long night. He is engaged upon a medical matter of the utmost urgency."

"Indeed, Mrs. Purcell, it is upon this same matter that we come. We were brought into the case by Sir James Saunders."

"Oh, I see." She raised the pince-nez to her eyes and peered again at our cards. "But only one of you is a doctor. You, Mr. Holmes, are a detective?"

"That is correct, Mrs. Purcell. I hope to determine how this plague is entering Charing Cross Hospital."

"Ah, then my husband will be most interested in talking with you."

Holmes smiled. "Thank you, Mrs. Purcell. By the way, you must be a great enthusiast of music to share the name of England's greatest composer.[37] I once heard Foley singing his *Dido and Aeneas* at the Royal Opera House. It was exquisite."[38]

Mrs. Purcell shrugged. "I care little for frills such as music. If you excuse me, Mr. Holmes, I will rouse my husband now."

Once she left, Holmes smiled and nodded slightly, as if she had confirmed some theory of his, though I could little see how a three-hundred-year-old Baroque opera had anything to do with the pestilence stalking Charing Cross Hospital.

He turned to me and raised his eyebrows suggestively. "Do you have any views upon the case, Watson?"

I shook my head. "I am baffled, Holmes. I read through the same charts as you last night, but failed to see any clue as to the origin of this plague."

Holmes raised his finger as if to elaborate upon some point, but paused as we were joined by our host. I knew him to be closer to fifty than forty, but the slight flecks of grey at his black temples lent him a distinguished appearance rather than an aged one. His face was square, with a firm jaw and heavy eyebrows, from which penetrating brown eyes studied us. His finely cut suit was of the newest fashion, which indicated to me that his practice was remuneratively successful.

After introductions were made, Dr. Purcell waved us to the settee, as he sank into one of the armchairs. "So Sir James has asked you to help me find the source of the plague?" said he, with some measure of haughtiness in his voice.

"Just so, Dr. Purcell," replied Holmes, agreeably. "I expect that Sir James felt you might be near the point of exhaustion, and could benefit from a fresh set of eyes."

"Yes, of course. You have heard, gentlemen, that we lost another man, Mr. Garrett the emphysemic diamond-cutter, to it just last night? It shows no sign of relenting. At the moment my hypothesis is that it was brought in by some fool who was mingling with one of those damnable Lascars down by the docks.[39] But I am having the devil of a time determining how exactly it continues to spread from patient to patient."

"Have you identified the index case?"

"No, I have been too busy trying to find some ward or vaccine against the plague itself. I don't have time to be traipsing around town interviewing relatives of the deceased. But, now that you are here, Mr. Holmes, that might be just the job for you?"

If Holmes was offended to have some tedious task foisted

upon him, his face did not show it. "Indeed. My thoughts were proceeding along the same lines as yours, Dr. Purcell. Tell me, the plague miasma is typically a summer malady, is it not? Do you find it unusual that it continues to linger into the autumn?"

Dr. Purcell shook his head. "Not at all. It has been unseasonably warm, don't you think?"

"Certainly. By the way, what do you think happened to your colleague, Dr. Taylor?"

"What do you mean?" Purcell asked, sharply.

"Just that the plague had, for the most part, struck down only those already enfeebled by some other illness. Dr. Taylor was the only strong man to fall."

The doctor shrugged. "I cannot say for certain, Mr. Holmes. No autopsy was performed in our haste to minimize spread of the contagion. Perhaps Taylor had some hereditary weakness of his heart?"

"Ah, yes, I had not considered that possibility," said Holmes, mildly. "Well, I shall waste no more of your time, Dr. Purcell. Watson and I will begin by investigating the antecedents of the victims."

Once we had departed the house and walked some distance in the direction of Baker Street, Holmes emitted a sharp laugh.

"What is it Holmes? I heard nothing out of the ordinary."

"Again, Watson, that is because you heard, but did not listen. But do not concern yourself, for in this failing you are joined by nearly every other person in London, and the world, for that matter."

I shook my head at the extent of Holmes's pride, but recalled that his powers of observation were extraordinary. I had not forgotten how Holmes had once solved the shocking affair of the Chadwick murder simply by noting that her afternoon tea was a full ten degrees cooler than it should have been.[40]

"So, are we now going to interview the relatives of the

deceased?" "Not at all," Holmes snorted with amusement. "I have another tactic

in mind. I think that for now, Watson, you can safely return to your patients. I have a few experiments planned, and the smells may be particularly malodorous. If you would be so good as to call upon me in the morning, I expect to have all of the answers that I require."

I arrived at Baker Street as the sun was rising, and was therefore much surprised to find the Director already present. Sir James's composure seemed much shaken. "I am afraid that we have no choice now, we must close the hospital completely," said he, a hint of despair in his voice. "We cannot continue to put lives in danger."

"What has happened?" I asked.

"I received this telegram from Dr. Purcell this morning. He has identified what he believes to be the source of the contagion."

"Indeed?" said Holmes, mildly. "And what was it?"

"Dr. Purcell believes the index case was a patient, Arthur Bryant Collier, who was treated by Dr. Taylor on the ninth of August. Mr. Collier was an explorer for the Royal Geographic Society, known for his travels amongst the Berbers of the Atlas Mountains. Collier died of apoplexy two days later, but having re-reviewed his charts, Dr. Purcell noted that there were some of the same features found in the other victims. Purcell's note speculates that Collier's clothing accidentally carried a mutated form of microbe back from Africa. Likely via the unhatched eggs of a sand fly, and it is now being transmitted via the bite of those now emerged flies.[41] That must be how it has spread so readily around the hospital!"

"Dear me!" said Holmes, his shining eyes and lively tone suggesting that he was much amused by this development. "Then you have no further use for me, I presume?"

"I am sorry for wasting your time, Mr. Holmes. I assure you that you shall nevertheless receive your full fee."

Holmes held up a hand. "If you would refrain from

closing the hospital for another few hours, Sir James, I think that I may still be of some assistance. In fact, I highly doubt that you shall see any more cases after today."

Sir James appeared little mollified by this. "You have yet to hear the worst of it, Mr. Holmes. This morning, Dr. Purcell himself was struck down."

"Indeed," said Holmes, mildly. "This plague strikes quickly. Why just last night, Dr. Purcell and I both happened to attend the premier of Grieg's latest violin sonata,[42] and he looked to be in the prime of health."

"I fail to see...."

"I assure you, Sir James, that I can explain in more detail later today. But time is of the essence if we are to ensure that this scourge ends with Dr. Purcell."

"Very well," agreed Sir James, with obvious reluctance.

Holmes and I were soon seated in a cab, whose driver was given orders to proceed to Harley Street with all haste. Holmes appeared both merry and concerned at the same time. I could certainly understand the latter, as we rolled towards a house which contained a pestilence that could prove to mean our deaths, but the source of the former emotion was an enigma.

"I cannot fathom your attitude, Holmes. You seem most happy that Dr. Purcell has contracted this terrible disease. The man is likely to die!"

Holmes chuckled. "Well, I cannot help but take some enjoyment over this development, Watson. It has transpired almost precisely as I predicted it."

"What?" I exclaimed. "You knew that Dr. Purcell would fall ill?" "I thought it highly probable."

"And the records of Mr. Collier? How did we miss those the other night?"

He smiled broadly. "We did not. In fact, I looked quite carefully through the notes on the last days of poor Mr. Collier."

"So you already knew that he was the index case?"

"Not at all, Watson," said he, shaking his head. "I am afraid that Dr. Purcell has made a grievous error, for no such symptoms were recorded in Mr. Collier's chart two nights ago."

With a confused brain I considered this new information. When we arrived at Harley Street, it was a morose Mrs. Purcell herself who eventually opened the door. "I am very sorry for the delay, gentlemen. You see, the staff has all deserted us. They learned that the Doctor had fallen ill, and did not wish to risk contracting it."

"And yet you remain, madam?" asked Holmes.

She shrugged indifferently. "Someone needs to watch over him until he gets better."

"What makes you so confident that he will pull through?"

"He told me that he perfected his anti-plague vaccine last night. He assured me that it will reverse his symptoms. He also gave me a dose to protect me."

"Have you taken it?" asked Holmes suddenly, his tone sharp.

"Oh, yes. Just now. The taste is far from pleasant, so I followed it with some tea."

Holmes dug into his coat-pocket and extracted a small phial. "If you value your life, Mrs. Purcell, I entreat you to take this immediately," said he, gravely.

"What is it?" she exclaimed, her eyes widening.

"It is the syrup of ipecac.[43] It will cause you to violently expel the contents of your stomach. I am afraid, Mrs. Purcell, that there was an error with your husband's formulation."

"Oh," she said, looking stunned. "But what of the Doctor? He too has taken it."

"My colleague, Dr. Watson, here, will attend to him at once. Please, Mrs. Purcell, look to yourself."

"Very well," she agreed, clearly persuaded by Holmes's commanding manner. She swiftly departed into the water-closet.

"Come, Watson, it is past time for us to have a little

discussion with the Doctor," said Holmes, gravely.

It was a pitiable sight that awaited us in the room at the top of the stair. Despite the fine autumn day, the drawn grey curtains of the sick-room cast a melancholy atmosphere. A rubicund, feverish face peered at us from beneath a thick quilt. His mouth hung slightly open, and his parched tongue was as black as coal. From a distance I had little doubt that the man was close to death. But he stirred as we entered.

"Ah, Mr. Holmes, Dr. Watson, I would stand back if I were you. I do not wish for you to fall ill as well," said he, feebly.

"That is most kind, Dr. Purcell," said Holmes. "But I do not think we are in much danger. In fact, I think you may rally soon." He took one of the seats at the side table, while I maintained my place by the door.

"What do you mean?" the doctor croaked.

"It is a strange plague that you have contracted, Doctor. For one, the tarry stools. In your experience, Watson, what does such a thing indicate?"

"Why, bleeding in the intestines, of course," I answered.

Holmes turned to me. "Do you recall, Watson, when Stamford first introduced us at the laboratory of St. Bart's? I had at the time just perfected my chemical re-agent which is precipitated only by the presence of hemoglobin.[44] And yet, when I tested a sample of effluvium taken from the unfortunate Dr. Taylor, it was strangely negative for blood."

Dr. Purcell pushed himself up in the bed, and wearily swung his bare legs over the side. "Perhaps the sample had degraded?" he postulated.

"Yes, that is an interesting suggestion, Doctor," said Holmes agreeably. "And, pray tell, what is your explanation for this?" He opened his left hand and revealed a shiny bit of metal slag.

The man sighed heavily and shuffled over to the table. He picked up the curious metal and rolled it between his fingers. "I really cannot say, Mr. Holmes," Purcell replied, sinking into the other chair.

"Ah, but I can. It took me several hours yesterday afternoon, but I finally isolated the key ingredient in your medicine to be the subsalicylate of bismuth.[45] This agent can have extraordinary benefits at treating the flux.[46] I suspect you learned as much during your research into methods to fight cholera?"

"I have long sought an adequate remedy for that terrible disease," Purcell replied, mildly.

"Bismuth is the only known medicine to leave behind a metal slag after being heated by a Bunsen burner."

"Is that so?"

"But that is not the only remarkable property of bismuth, Dr. Purcell. It also is very toxic to felines." "Truly?"

"And when given repetitively to humans, it has one very unusual side-effect. It turns the tongue and excreta black."

Dr. Purcell sat silently, staring at Holmes. "What of it?"

"Do you not think it strange that these are two of the key features of the plague that has descended upon Charing Cross Hospital?"

The doctor shrugged. "It is an interesting coincidence, Mr. Holmes, to be certain. But if you are implying that my medicines are causing the plague, then you are clearly mistaken. For bismuth is not associated with either fevers or fits."

"No, you are absolutely correct, Dr. Purcell. To produce such an effect you would need to mix it with something else. Say the leaf of the belladonna which, as you may be aware, contains high levels of the alkaloid known as atropine?"[47] Holmes pulled from his coat pocket one of the bottles that I had seen in the doctor's office and set it upon the table.

A fire flared in the man's eyes. "What are you implying, Mr. Holmes? That I have poisoned myself?" cried he, motioning to his feverish countenance. "That would be mad!"

"Not if you had carefully worked out the precise dose

that falls below the fatal range. Perhaps by poisoning a series of already terminal patients?"

"And why would I want to do that? What would I have to gain?"

"From killing the patients? Nothing. But by removing your hated rival, Dr. Taylor, you now have the attentions of Miss Vivian Crawford all to yourself."

"Who?" he stammered.

"Come now, Dr. Purcell. It will do you no good to deny it. I was not the only one to see the two of you in the box at St. James's Hall last night.[48] Many witnesses could be found should you care to continue with your protestation of innocence."

"You were there?" he croaked. "I did not see you."

"That is what you might expect when I am watching you. I had little concern that you would penetrate that particular disguise." Holmes turned to me. "You must have noted, Watson, that Dr. Purcell is a great aficionado of classical music and opera. Hence the playbills upon his desk at work. His dour wife does not share his enthusiasms, and he eventually decided to eliminate her in favor of a younger replacement who, it should be noted, also commands a considerable fortune. And what better way to ensure that no questions are raised than if the ill-fated Mrs. Purcell died from the very same plague that struck down so many others? I imagine she would have been the last victim, is that not so, Dr. Purcell? You would then dose everyone with your harmless compound of 'Four Thieves Vinegar' and declare the plague cured."

The man sneered. "You have no proof."

Holmes smiled. "Yes, your clever plague scare ensured that the bodies were rapidly cremated. I suspect that you first noted that your cholera treatment had the unusual side-effect of a blacked tongue. But your great inspiration occurred at the symphony, did it not? A quick perusal of the past performances at St. James's Hall demonstrates that on the twenty-first of August they performed the *Danse Macabre* of *Saint-Saëns*.[49] It was during that medieval allegory on death that the full formulation of your plan came together."

Dr. Purcell shook his head defiantly. "No, you are terribly mistaken, Mr. Holmes. Perhaps you yourself are manifesting the initial symptoms? Delirium is quite common. I forgive you for these accusations."

"And will your wife forgive you, Dr. Purcell?" "What do you mean?" he asked, sharply.

"I assure you that Mrs. Purcell will be quite fine. While she had indeed just taken the dose that you gave her, my ipecac will prevent it from proving fatal. She will not go the way of your poor patients."

As his shoulders collapsed, the fight seemed to drain from his body. "They were dying anyway."

"Not Dr. Taylor." Holmes shook his head. "There are scarlet threads of life running through the bright tapestry of the universe, Dr. Purcell. What gives you the right to cut a man's thread?" asked Holmes, severely. Dr. Purcell stared blankly at the tabletop. "It was a mercy," he whispered, clearly still thinking upon the innocents who fell during his care.

Holmes stared at him silently for a moment and then pushed the bottle towards the Doctor. "So is this."

Holmes rapidly turned and strode out of the room. I followed him silently, my thoughts morose. When we reached the sitting room, he turned and studied my face. "Do you disagree with my methods, Watson?"

I considered this for a moment. "I am not certain," I finally replied. "Well, I for one cannot say that it is likely to weigh very heavily

upon my conscience. Dr. Purcell literally took upon himself the role of Atropos."[50]

"Atropos?" I asked.

"I learned of her when reading about the effects of atropine in the first volume of the *Encyclopedia Britannica*.[51] She is the eldest of the Three Fates. It is her abhorred shears that ends the lives of us mortals."

"And have we overstepped our roles, Holmes? Are we not acting as judge, jury, and executioner?"[52]

"Not at all, Watson. We merely offered him the choice. It is up to him whether he meets his destiny in his own bed, or at the end of a hangman's noose."

After a moment, I nodded. "Then let us hope he chooses wisely."

"Indeed. Do you have any other thoughts upon the matter, Watson?"

"You know, Holmes. I never really thought it was the plague."

"And why is that?" he asked, clearly puzzled that he may have missed some clue.

"Because there was no comet to herald its coming."

Holmes smiled grimly and shook his head. "Good old Watson. Come, we have waited long enough. Let us learn the decision of Dr. Purcell."

It was a singular scene which met our eyes when we re-entered the bedroom. On the table lay the bottle, its cap off and the contents emptied. Beside the table, upon the wooden chair, sat Dr. Edward Purcell, his cravat loosened. His chin was slumped upon his breast, and his eyes were fixed with a horrible vacant stare at the floor. His tongue protruded slightly from his mouth, and it was still stained that deep black color. He made neither sound nor motion, and had surely passed beyond the veil to the bourn of that undiscovered country.[53]

Such are the true particulars of the death of Dr. Edward Purcell of Charing Cross Hospital. It is not necessary to prolong this narrative in order to tell of how Holmes broke the news to Sir James Saunders. Suffice it to say that Holmes spared Mrs. Purcell the public ignominy of having been wed to a murderer, and Sir James thanked Holmes warmly for his professional service. The official verdict, as carefully directed by my friend, came to show that the Doctor had met his doom at the hands of a brief but terrible outbreak of the Black Plague, which fortuitously burned itself out after the death of that once-renowned specialist.

When we had finally settled back at Baker Street, my friend sighed heavily and shook his head while gazing at the fire. "As I have said before, when a doctor goes wrong, he is the first of criminals. The ways of destiny are difficult to comprehend, Watson. Is the world nothing more than some ugly beast against which we must wage eternal battle?"

"Perhaps the madness exists so that you have something to combat?"

Holmes glanced at me and laughed. "I never get your limits, Watson. Very well then, I suppose that we shall embrace the madness. By the way, Watson, I have a small gift for you." He reached into his coat pocket and extracted a small book, which he proceeded to hand over to me.

I was greatly surprised by this unexpected act from a man whose paucity of expressed sentiment led so many to regard him as a little more than a cerebral automaton.[54] "I believe this is a first, Holmes." I studied the volume, which proved to be a compact edition Boccaccio's *Decameron*. Flipping it open, I found the name of Joseph Stangerson upon the fly-leaf, and smiled broadly at the recollection of our initial adventure together.[55]

"Have you read it?" he inquired.

"When I was a school-boy. It's been over twenty years."

"And do you still remember the premise?"

"A group of young aristocrats of Florence tell a hundred ribald stories, if memory serves. A sort of Italianate *Canterbury Tales*, is it not?"[56]

"Ah, but there were not in Florence, were they, Watson? They had fled to a villa in the hills in order to escape the Black Death. I found Boccaccio's description of it quite illuminating: *'The form of the malady...black spots or livid making their appearance in many cases on the arm or the thigh or elsewhere, now few and large, now minute and numerous.'* If

I recall correctly, Watson, you on one occasion, in the very early days of our association, demarcated the limits of my knowledge in a detailed list."

"Your memory is precise, as usual, Holmes," said I, chuckling.

"At the very top of that list you rated my knowledge of literature as 'nil.'"

"Well, until you quoted Boccaccio at me just now, I would have sworn that was still the case."

"Indeed, for during my training I could see no purpose to cluttering my little brain attic with words written centuries ago, save only when they were a description of crimes, of course. But you see, Watson, if I had but read Boccaccio earlier, I would have realized much sooner that

Dr. Purcell's supposed plague was a fraud. The blackness was all wrong. His patients' tongues may have been black, but they had no spots upon their skin, for he could find no method to simulate them. If I had not limited myself, Mr. Garrett might still be alive, and Mrs. Purcell would not have come within minutes of her death, saved only by our fortuitous arrival," he concluded, solemnly.

"You cannot blame yourself, Holmes. You are but a man. You cannot know everything."

"But why not, Watson?" he shook his head, grimly. "That is my profession after all. To know things. There is no reason I should not add to my mental resources, for who can tell when some rare smidgen of knowledge might mean the difference between life and death. It is possible, Watson, that I have made a mistake. But it is perhaps better to learn wisdom late, than to never learn it at all. I therefore promise you that this is a deficiency which I plan to rectify straightaway."[57]

It was then that I understood that the pocket-edition of Boccaccio was not Holmes's gift. The gift was, in fact, a brief glimpse into the all-too-human soul which lurked, carefully hidden, behind the façade of that cool reasoning machine.

NOTES

1. This is clearly a reference to the events recorded in "The Man with the Twisted Lip".
2. Certainly, this denotes Irene Adler and "A Scandal in Bohemia".
3. This problem sounds similar to the cases of both James Phillimore ("The Problem of Thor Bridge"), but also Louis Le Prince, a French motion picture pioneer who boarded the Dion-Paris Express on 16 September 1890, and mysteriously vanished. His case is still unsolved.
4. Hatton Garden is a street in the Holborn district of London which has been London's jewelry quarter since medieval times.
5. The famous line of Iago, from Shakespeare's *Othello* (Act 1, Scene 1).
6. Many years later it is Holmes who enlists the aid of Sir James Saunders in "The Adventure of the Blanched Soldier".
7. Charing Cross Hospital is where Dr. James Mortimer trained (*The Hound of the Baskervilles*, Chapter 2) and is where Holmes is taken after he is beaten by thugs in the employ of Baron Gruner ("The Adventure of the Illustrious Client").
8. Cavendish Square is the historic home of London's medical specialists, where Dr. Percy Trevelyan hoped to one day have his practice ("The Adventure of the Resident Patient"), while a red lamp is the usual sign of the general practitioner, such as Dr. Barnicot ("The Adventure of the Six Napoleons").
9. Fleet Street was the traditional home of the British national newspapers until the 1980's, and as such it is a metonym for the British press.
10. In 1889, the exact cause of the plague was not yet known. Five years later, Alexandre Yersin of France was credited as the primary discoverer of the bacterium that eventually became known as *Yersinia pestis*.
11. The Great Plague of London (1665-1666) and was the last major plague epidemic in England. It has been hypothesized that the coincidental Great Fire of London (1666) was responsible for putting an end to the epidemic, as the rebuilding of London did away with many of the previous conditions that fostered the spread of the plague.
12. Comets have long been considered heralds of doom and omens of world-altering change.
13. This was fifteen percent of the population of London.
14. The Black Death pandemic hit southern England in 1349.
15. The London Necropolis Railway opened in 1854 to transport cadavers and mourners between the Necropolis Railway Station in London (near *Waterloo* Station; this was destroyed in an air raid during World War II) and Brookwood Cemetery (built to replace central London's squalid and overcrowded historic cemeteries).
16. Cremation was not legal in Great Britain until 1885, but the practice took a long

time to catch on. In all of 1888, only 28 cremations took place in the UK, though the number increased greatly after this method was chosen in 1905 by the famous Shakespearean actor Sir Henry Irving, whose company manager was Bram Stoker, and who staged the play Waterloo in 1894 for Arthur Conan Doyle.

17. The incubation period of bubonic plague is two to five days, with the septicemic form being even shorter.

18. Sir Joseph Bazalgette (1819-1891) was the chief engineer of London's Metropolitan Board of Works who, in response to the Great Stink of 1858, set out to create the sewer network that resulted in the cleansing of the Thames and relief from recurrent cholera epidemics.

19. The connection of rats to the plague has long been recognized, for whenever large numbers of rats were found dead, an outbreak was sure to follow. However, the link to the rat's fleas was a more modern discovery. Of note, only one other unrecorded story details Holmes and Watson dealing with rodents: The giant rat of Sumatra ("The Adventure of the Sussex Vampire").

20. A clowder is one of the accepted terms for a group of cats.

21. The tail-less Manx cats from the Isle of Man are prized as hunters, and a strong preference for them as ship's cats is thought to be responsible for the world-wide spread of what originated as a very insular breed.

22. Classic rat-catchers were still active into the early 1900's in many parts of the world. The most famous was an eccentric character named Jack Black, appointed Her Majesty's Ratcatcher.

23. A "coolie" was a cheap and unskilled laborer from Asia. They congregated in the London docklands, where they were feared to be spreading disease. Holmes blamed them for his fictitious Sumatran fever ("The Adventure of the Dying Detective").

24. The Black Death ravaged much of the Islamic world until at least 1850. The Third plague pandemic (1855 – 1859) started in China, and eventually spreading to all inhabited continents. It killed 10 million people in India alone. Even in "civilized" North America, the plague struck San Francisco in 1900-1904, followed by another outbreak in 1907-1908.

25. Americans would call these "seizures".

26. Also known as tuberculosis.

27. Dropsy is an archaic term for edema, principally of the feet, and most often caused by congestive heart failure.

28. Where Watson also got his degree (*A Study in Scarlet*, Chapter 1).

29. Sydenham's Chorea (historically known as St. Vitus' dance) was a disorder characterized by rapid jerking movements of the face and hands, and was a common sequelae of Streptococcal infections in the pre-penicillin era.

30. Watson condemned Holmes's excessive tobacco consumption in both "The Adventure of the Five Orange Pips" and "The Devil's Foot".

31. Jacko was a black and tan Bull Terrier that set the world record in 1862 for the

time it took him to kill a pack of sixty rats. The sport of ratting was not formally banned in England until 1912.

32. Watson also noted the presence of these refuges in "The Adventure of Black Peter".

33. This is true, but clearly unknown to Holmes or Watson was that only black rats are potential carriers of the plague, another possible reason why it has largely died out over time.

34. William (c.1287-1347) of Ockham (or Occam) was an English medieval philosopher whose maxim on the law of parsimony states that "entities should not be multiplied unnecessarily." This "Razor" competes for fame with the maxim of a later Englishman: "When you eliminate the impossible, whatever remains, however improbable, must be the truth."

35. Indeed it was soon to be. Waldemar Haffkine, a doctor working in Bombay, India, was the first to invent and test a vaccine against the plague in 1897.

36. Four Thieves Vinegar was a legendary ward against the Black Death. One recipe from Marseille states: "Take three pints of strong white wine vinegar, add a handful of each of wormwood, meadowsweet, wild marjoram and sage, fifty cloves, two ounces of campanula roots, two ounces of angelic, rosemary and horehound and three large measures of camphor. Place the mixture in a container for fifteen days, strain and express, then bottle. Use by rubbing it on the hands, ears and temples from time to time when approaching a plague victim."

37. Henry Purcell (1659-1695) was considered the premier English-born composer until the late 1800's, when he was supplanted by Edward Elgar (1857-1934), and later Ralph Vaughan Williams (1872-1958).

38. Holmes was not feigning his interest in the opera. In the Canon he can be seen attending it at the end of both "The Adventure of the Red Circle" and *The Hound of the Baskervilles* (Chapter 15).

39. "Lascar" is a now archaic term indicating non-white (typically Indian) sailors aboard British ships. The most famous Lascar was the confederate of the beggar Hugh Boone ("The Man with the Twisted Lip").

40. Unfortunately, a more complete account of the Chadwick murder, and how exactly the temperature of her tea played a role, has yet to be discovered.

41. It was not until 1896 that the rat flea, *Xenopsylla cheopis*, was identified as the vector of *Yersinia pestis* from rats to humans, so at the time, Dr. Purcell's theory would not be implausible. In fact, the North African sand fly is capable of transmitting a terrible disease, *leishmaniasis*, also known as *kala-azar* or *dum-dum fever*, which remained a major problem until the advent of the antibiotic era in the 1950's.

42. Edvard Grieg (1843-1907) was the greatest Norwegian composer. His Sonata No.3 was written in 1887. Holmes's familiarity with it may have influenced his later choice to adopt the guise of the Norwegian explorer Sigerson ("The Adventure of the Empty House").

43. Known to Western medicine since the root was brought back from Brazil in the

1600's, but no longer on the market, for many decades it was recommended that ipecac be kept in every house in case of accidental poisoning.

44. As noted in *A Study in Scarlet* (Chapter 1).

45. Bismuth salts have been used as an antidiarrheal agent since the 1700's, but were not sold directly to consumers until 1901. The black-colored salts can have the unintended side-effect of turning the tongue and stool black.

46. The flux is an archaic term for dysentery, itself a catch-all term for various severe intestinal infections caused by bacteria, parasites, or viruses. Dysentery was historically a great killer, taking the lives of such famous individuals as King John Lackland (1216), King Henry V (1422), and Sir Francis Drake (1596).

47. Holmes himself was familiar with the use of belladonna, which he used to dilate his pupils in "The Adventure of the Dying Detective". Atropine was isolated in 1831, but knowledge of the effects of the various plants from which it may be derived is ancient. In addition to *Atropa belladonna,* mandrake and henbane can also produce the typical symptoms, which may be remembered as "hot as a hare (or Hades), dry as a bone, red as a beet, mad as a hatter."

48. The Royal Philharmonic Society moved to St. James's Hall on Great Portland Street in 1869, where it remained until 1894, when they moved to the Queen's Hall. The Hall was a neo-Gothic masterpiece, whose cavernous interior imitated the Moorish palace of the Alhambra. Holmes also heard both Norman-Neruda (*A Study in Scarlet*, Chapter 4) and Sarasate ("The Red-Headed League") play there. Dickens gave his last public reading there shortly before his death in 1870. In 1902, St. James's Hall was bought by the owner of a rival concert hall, who had it demolished in 1905.

49. Camille Saint-Saëns (1835-1921) was a great favorite of English audiences of the 1880's, where he was considered the greatest living French composer. In 1874, he wrote his *Danse Macabre,* his take on the medieval allegory on the universality of death, which originally arose out of the terrible horrors of the Black Death.

50. Atropos one of the three *Moirai*, or Fates. She was known as the inevitable, for she cut the thread (woven by Clotho and measured by Lachesis) with her abhorred shears.

51. The first volume of the Encyclopedia also played a significant role in the false employment of Mr. Jabez Wilson ("The Red-Headed League").

52. Holmes often took matters into his own hands when he thought he could serve the spirit of justice more readily than a British jury. Some of the most famous examples include his pardoning of James Ryder ("The Adventure of the Blue Carbuncle"), Captain Croker ("The Adventure of the Abbey Grange"), and Dr. Sterndale ("The Adventure of the Devil's Foot").

53. From Hamlet's great soliloquy in Act III, Scene 1: "Who would these Fardels bear, / To grunt and sweat under a weary life, / But that the dread of something after death, / The undiscovered Country, from whose bourn / No Traveller returns, Puzzles the will, / And makes us rather bear those ills we have, / Than fly to others that we know not of."

54. Watson compares Holmes to a machine in several other places in the Canon, most notably in "A Scandal in Bohemia": "He was...the most perfect reasoning

and observing machine that the world has seen;" and "The Adventure of the Crooked Man": "[the] composure which had made so many regard him as a machine rather than a man."

55. Holmes must have acquired this from Gregson after the successful conclusion of the events of *A Study in Scarlet*.

56. This is a typical example of an English-centric world view of the Victorian era. The *Decameron* of Boccaccio (1313-1375) was completed in 1353, while *The Canterbury Tales* of Geoffrey Chaucer (1343 – 1400) was not published until 1483, and was almost certainly inspired by the earlier work.

57. Holmes certainly did so, for soon after this adventure he could be found reading a "pocket Petrarch" (one of the great Italian Renaissance poets) upon the train to Ross ("The Boscombe Valley Mystery").

About the Contributors

The following contributors appear in this volume
The MX Book of New Sherlock Holmes Stories
Part I – 1881-1889

C.H. Dye first discovered Sherlock Holmes when she was eleven, in a collection that ended at Reichenbach Falls. It was another six months before she discovered The Hound of the Baskervilles, and two weeks after that before a librarian handed her The Return. She has loved the stories ever since. She has written fanfiction, but this is her first published pastiche.

John Heywood (not the author's real name) was born in Gloucestershire in 1951, and educated at Katharine Lady Berkeley's Grammar School and Jesus College, Cambridge. After graduating, he supported himself in many different ways, including teaching, decorating, house-sitting, laboring, and mowing graveyards, while at the same time making paintings, prints and drawings. He continues to make art, and his work is now in collections in Europe and America, and is regularly exhibited. He currently lives in Brixton, South London, and works as a painter and as a teacher of art and English in adult education. In 2014, his first book, The Investigations of Sherlock Holmes, was published by MX Publishing. It was enthusiastically received by the critics, and has recently been issued in India.

In the year 1998 **Craig Janacek** took his degree of Doctor of Medicine at Vanderbilt University, and proceeded to Stanford to go through the training prescribed for pediatricians in practice. Having completed his studies there, he was duly attached to the University of California, San Francisco as Associate Professor. The author of over seventy medical monographs upon a variety of obscure lesions, his travel-worn and battered tin dispatch-box is crammed with papers, nearly all of which are records of his fictional works. To date, these have been published solely in electronic format, including two non-Holmes novels (The Oxford Deception and The Anger of Achilles Peterson), the trio of holiday adventures collected as The Midwinter Mysteries of Sherlock Holmes, and a Watsonian novel entitled The Isle of Devils. His next project is the short trilogy The Assassination of Sherlock

Holmes. Craig Janacek is a nom de plume.

Sir Arthur Conan Doyle (1859-1930) Holmes Chronicler Emeritus. If not for him, this anthology would not exist. Author, physician, patriot, sportsman, spiritualist, husband and father, and advocate for the oppressed. He is remembered and honored for the purposes of this collection by being the man who introduced Sherlock Holmes to the world. Through fifty-six Holmes short stories, four novels, and additional Apocryphal entries, Doyle revolutionized mystery stories and also greatly influenced and improved police forensic methods and techniques for the betterment of all. Steel True Blade Straight

Steve Emecz's main field is technology, in which he has been working for about twenty years. Following multiple senior roles at Xerox, where he grew their European eCommerce from $6m to $200m, Steve joined platform provider Venda, and moved across to Powa Technologies in 2010. Steve is a regular trade show speaker on the subject of mobile commerce, and his time at Powa has taken him to more than forty countries – so he's no stranger to planes and airports. He wrote two novels (one bestseller) in the 1990's and a screenplay in 2001. Shortly after he set up MX Publishing, specialising in NLP books. In 2008, MX published its first Sherlock Holmes book, and MX has gone on to become the largest specialist Holmes publisher in the world, with around one hundred authors and over two hundred books. Profits from MX go towards his second passion – a children's rescue project in Nairobi, Kenya, where he and his wife, Sharon, spend every Christmas at the rescue centre in Kasarani. In 2014, they wrote a short book about the project, The Happy Life Story.

Daniel McGachey Outside of his day job – which, over the past quarter century has seen him write extensively for comics, newspapers, magazines, digital media, and animation – Scottish writer Daniel McGachey's stories first appeared in several volumes of The BHF Book of Horror Stories and Black Book of Horror anthology series, and Filthy Creations magazine. In 2009, Dark Regions Press published his first ghost story collection, They That Dwell in Dark Places, dedicated in part to M.R. James, whose works inspired the creation of the collected stories. Since 2005, he has reviewed television and radio adaptations of James's stories for The Ghosts and Scholars M.R. James Newsletter, while his sequels to several of James's original tales appeared as the Haunted Library publication Ex Libris: Lufford in 2012. Moving from M.R. James to his other lifelong literary hero, his 2010 Dark Regions Press collection pitted Sir Arthur Conan Doyle's rational detective against the irrational forces of the supernatural in Sherlock Holmes: The Impossible Cases. His radio plays have been broadcast since 2005 as part of the mystery and suspense series Imagination Theater, including entries in its long-running strand of new Holmesian mysteries, The Further Adventures of Sherlock Holmes. He is working on a new "impossible case" for Sherlock Holmes and Dr. Watson in the novel, The Devil's Crown.

Steve Mountain is a "born and bred" native of Portsmouth in the UK. Married with two grown-up children, he works for a local Council as a civil engineer, trying to retro-fit cycle riding facilities into roads not originally built for the purpose. This is usually, but not always, successful. Seeing his name in print is nothing new, although to date this has been mostly in articles in the local newspaper complaining about the effect of said cycle facilities on other road users. Having helped his daughter solve a problem with one of her Holmes pastiches, he caught the fiction writing bug himself. He has self-published one of his early stories with Lulu.

Mark Mower is a crime writer and historian and a member of the Crime Writers' Association. His books include Bloody British History: Norwich (The History Press, 2014) and Suffolk Murders (The History Press, 2011). His first book, Suffolk Tales of Mystery & Murder (Countryside Books, 2006), contained a potent blend of tales from the seamier side of country life – described by the East Anglian Daily Times Suffolk magazine as ". . . a good serving of grisliness, a strong flavour of the unusual, a seasoning of ghoulishness and just a hint of the unexpected...." Alongside his writing, Mark lectures on crime history and runs a murder mystery business.

Sidney Paget (1860-1908), a few of whose illustrations are used within this anthology, was born in London, and like his two older brothers, became a famed illustrator and painter. He completed over three-hundred-and-fifty drawings for the Sherlock Holmes stories first published in The Strand magazine, defining Holmes's image forever after in the public mind.

Derrick Belanger is an author and educator most noted for his books and lectures on Sherlock Holmes and Sir Arthur Conan Doyle, as well as his writing for the blog I Hear of Sherlock Everywhere. Both volumes of his two-volume anthology, A Study in Terror: Sir Arthur Conan Doyle's Revolutionary Stories of Fear and the Supernatural were #1 best sellers on the Amazon.com UK Sherlock Holmes book list, and his MacDougall Twins with Sherlock Holmes chapter book, Attack of the Violet Vampire! was also a #1 bestselling new release in the UK. His novella, Sherlock Holmes and the Adventure of the Peculiar Provenance, is forthcoming from Endeavour Press. Mr. Belanger's academic work has been published in The Colorado Reading Journal and Gifted Child Today. Find him at www.belangerbooks.com.

Martin Rosenstock studied English, American, and German literature. In 2008, he received a Ph.D. from the University of California, Santa Barbara for looking into what happens when things go badly – as they do from time to time – for detectives in German-language literature. After job hopping around the colder latitudes of the U.S. for three years, he decided to return to warmer climes. In 2011, he took a job at Gulf University for Science and Technology in Kuwait, where he currently teaches. When not brooding over plot twists, he spends too much time and money traveling the Indian Ocean littoral. There is a novel somewhere there, he feels sure.

Will Thomas is the author of seven books in the Barker and Llewelyn Victorian mystery series, including Some Danger Involved, Fatal Enquiry, and Anatomy of Evil. He was nominated for a Barry and a Shamus, and is a two time winner of the Oklahoma Book Award. He lives in Broken Arrow, Oklahoma, where he studies Victorian martial arts and models British railways.

Daniel D. Victor, a Ph.D. in American literature, is a retired high school English teacher who taught in the Los Angeles Unified School District for forty-six years. His doctoral dissertation on little-known American author, David Graham Phillips, led to the creation of Victor's first Sherlock Holmes pastiche, The Seventh Bullet, in which Holmes investigates Phillips' actual murder. Victor's second novel, A Study in Synchronicity, is a two-stranded murder mystery, which features a Sherlock Holmes-like private eye. He is currently completing a trilogy called Sherlock Holmes and the American Literati. Each novel introduces Holmes to a different American author who actually passed through London at the turn of the century. In The Final Page of Baker Street, Holmes meets Raymond Chandler; in The Baron of Brede Place, Stephen Crane; in Seventeen Minutes to Baker Street, Mark Twain. Victor, who is also writing a novel about his early years as a teacher, lives with his wife in Los Angeles, California. They have two adult sons.

Stephen Wade has a special interest in crime history, having published widely on regional crime. His book, The Girl who Lived on Air (Seren) was a Welsh Book of the Month for Waterstones last year. He was formerly a lecturer in English, and also worked as a writer in prisons for six years. His latest book is a short story collection, Uncle Albert (Priory Press). The current fiction project is a collection of crime stories featuring Lestrade.

David Marcum first discovered Sherlock Holmes in 1975, at the age of ten, when he received an abridged version of The Adventures during a trade. Since that time, David has collected literally thousands of traditional Holmes pastiches in the form of novels, short stories, radio and television episodes, movies and scripts, comics, fan-fiction, and unpublished manuscripts. He is the author of The Papers of Sherlock Holmes Vol.'s I and II (2011, 2013), Sherlock Holmes and A Quantity of Debt (2013) and Sherlock Holmes – Tangled Skeins (2015). Additionally, he is the editor of the three-volume set Sherlock Holmes in Montague Street (2014, recasting Arthur Morrison's

Martin Hewitt stories as early Holmes adventures,) and most recently this current collection, The MX Book of New Sherlock Holmes Stories (2015). He has contributed essays to the Baker Street Journal and The Gazette, the journal of the Nero Wolfe Wolfe Pack. He began his adult work life as a Federal Investigator for an obscure U.S. Government agency, before the organization was eliminated. He returned to school for a second degree, and is now a licensed Civil Engineer, living in Tennessee with his wife and son. He is a member of The Sherlock Holmes Society of London, The John H. Watson Society ("Marker"), The Praed Street Irregulars ("The Obrisset Snuff Box"), The Solar Pons Society of London, and The Diogenes Club West (East Tennessee Annex), a curious and unofficial Scion of one. Since the age of nineteen, he has worn a deerstalker as his regular-and-only hat from autumn to spring. In 2013, he and his deerstalker were finally able make a trip-of-a-lifetime Holmes Pilgrimage to England, where you may have spotted him. If you ever run into him and his deerstalker out and about, feel free to say hello!

JAICO PUBLISHING HOUSE

Elevate Your Life. Transform Your World.

ESTABLISHED IN 1946, Jaico Publishing House is home to world-transforming authors such as Sri Sri Paramahansa Yogananda, Osho, the Dalai Lama, Sri Sri Ravi Shankar, Sadhguru, Robin Sharma, Deepak Chopra, Jack Canfield, Eknath Easwaran, Devdutt Pattanaik, Khushwant Singh, John Maxwell, Brian Tracy, and Stephen Hawking.

Our late founder Mr. Jaman Shah first established Jaico as a book distribution company. Sensing that independence was around the corner, he aptly named his company Jaico ('Jai' means victory in Hindi). In order to service the significant demand for affordable books in a developing nation, Mr. Shah initiated Jaico's own publications. Jaico was India's first publisher of paperback books in the English language.

While self-help, religion and philosophy, mind/body/spirit, and business titles form the cornerstone of our non-fiction list, we publish an exciting range of travel, current affairs, biography, and popular science books as well. Our renewed focus on popular fiction is evident in our new titles by a host of fresh young talent from India and abroad. Jaico's recently established translations division translates selected English content into nine regional languages.

Jaico distributes its own titles. With its headquarters in Mumbai, Jaico has branches in Ahmedabad, Bangalore, Chennai, Delhi, Hyderabad, and Kolkata.

SINCE 1946